UNDER
HIS WINGS

To Bonnie,

May you continue
under His wings all
the days of your life.
Ps. 91

Love,
Maxine
3/23/14

UNDER
HIS WINGS

MAXINE JOHNSON

TATE PUBLISHING
AND ENTERPRISES, LLC

Published by Tate Publishing & Enterprises, LLC
127 E. Trade Center Terrace | Mustang, Oklahoma 73064 USA
1.888.361.9473 | www.tatepublishing.com

Tate Publishing is committed to excellence in the publishing industry. The company reflects the philosophy established by the founders, based on Psalm 68:11,
"The Lord gave the word and great was the company of those who published it."

Book design copyright © 2014 by Tate Publishing, LLC. All rights reserved.
Cover design by Gian Philipp Rufin
Interior design by Jomar Ouano

Published in the United States of America

ISBN: 978-1-63063-213-7
1. Fiction / Christian / Historical
2. Fiction / Christian / Romance
14.02.5

DEDICATION

I would like to thank our Creator God who has bestowed, on us all, his image. He is the one who gave me the story. I also want to dedicate this "first fruit" to him.

Acknowledgments

I want to thank my wonderful husband, Bob, without whom this work of love would never have happened. He has been my encourager and as patient as Job with my peaks and valleys. I love you!

In addition to him and his support, our three children have provided their fair share of encouragement. I especially want to thank my daughter, Lorien Smith, for her much-needed editorial skills and delightful insights, and Eowyn Lasecki for her "tech support." There have been so many who have helped over the years, literally, to bring this book to publication: Helen McDowell, the first to read and proof it; Connie Crews, my friend and prayer partner; my Texas cousins, Kathy, Linda, and Joy who helped with providing research opportunities and proofreading skills, you were invaluable. To Julius and Marvin Neunhoffer who shared their ranching knowledge and some wonderful family tales of their own, I'll be back, guys! A huge thanks to Linda Simcox who was my supervising teacher when I did my student teaching. She has remained a dear friend and was the one who gave me some really great suggestions for some changes and encouraged me that it was a book worth reading. I had begun to have self-doubt, one of Satan's favorite tools, and she really encouraged me. Thanks to all of you for your love, encouragement, and prayers. Here's "our" baby!

Texas Hill Country, 1880

CHAPTER 1

She could taste the blackness of the night as it engulfed her. The tom-tom rhythm kept her company through the tips of her fingers as her hand lay there on her chest. The rock of loneliness sat in her stomach every time she lay down. It became a boulder that rolled onto her shoulders when she stood up. Every beat of her heart day in and day out lamented, "Lone-ly, lone-ly." She never thought it would be like this. *It was never supposed to be like this! Things were supposed to be better coming west! Why? Why? Why did the Almighty One do things like this? Why was I left all alone?*

"This will be our great adventure, you'll see," Pa encouraged them as they loaded yet another treasure onto the covered wagon. "There's a pot of gold at the end of this trail for us, you'll see."

Katie poked Abigail with her elbow and whispered, "The only pot of gold I'm interested in better come wearing a pair of pants. I'm tired of moving so much. I'm ready to settle down."

"Me too. I just hope there are enough nice men out there for both of us."

"How many do you want? You only need one. I only need one. Let me see, one and one equals two, if I remember my ciphering. I'm sure

there are two men in Texas looking for eligible young women who can cook, clean, and be wonderful wives and mothers."

"I'm not so sure I'm ready to be a mother. I don't mind the cooking and cleaning part."

Their laughter echoed in the almost-empty room they once called their own.

"Girls, c'mon down here! We have to get these things loaded. The wagon train leaves in an hour. Have you seen Benjamin?" Ma called impatiently.

"No, ma'am." They looked at each other and frowned. "He is never doing what he is supposed to be doing," Abigail whispered. "Katie, why doesn't he ever get into trouble?"

"He is 'Benjamin, son of my right hand.' The baby of the family, father's pride and joy. Do you think he will get into trouble?"

"Oh, and we are just girls, right?"

"Right."

"Girls! Come! Now!"

"Coming, Ma," they chorused together, then laughed as they skipped down the stairs. The skirts of their dresses bouncing with each step reflected how their stomachs felt in the anticipation of their adventure.

Excitement filled them. The hairs on their arms tingled. Their feet would not stay still. Pa helped them into the wagon clearly as excited as they were. He told them about the house for the "hundredth" time.

"The house is two stories with a porch that wraps all around it. The view of the hills out the back will take your breath away, Katie girl. There are horses, goats, chickens, and cattle. I told the Randolphs to sell the pigs. We don't want to keep those. They said they would do that. Benjamin, you will love learning to work with all the animals, especially roping cattle and working out on the range. Yes, I think we will call this move our last one."

Yes, the wagon had been stuffed full with all the precious cargo they just couldn't leave behind. Now, all Katie had left were their things. None of it qualified as really precious. Was it just four years ago?

———————

"What drudgery!"

"I sure hope that pot of gold Pa keeps talking about is still at the end of the road 'cause all we've had so far is a pot of dust and a trail of mud."

There had been plenty of wagon trains going south and west so that the "roads" were very passable. Accommodations, trading posts, and even towns along the way were plentiful for a while.

"Better get it now. Things get scarce down the road," became the refrain everywhere they stopped for supplies.

People kept telling them to be prepared, that later on the roads would get worse and supplies would grow thin. Sure sounded like jealousy or just hard sales talk to Katie, but Papa's eyes told her maybe they weren't being so outrageous in their descriptions. Would things get scarce? Would there be hard times ahead?

"If we could just have a little rain," Katie thought out loud.

"You better be careful what you wish for, Miss Katie, you just might get it," Mama reminded her.

Oh, truer words were never spoken. Not a week later when they were in some very flat lowland in Louisiana, the sky turned black as night and lightning began dancing from cloud to cloud then from cloud to ground as if it was competing in some wild fandango contest. It was a display worthy of an artist's painting, recording it for future generations. Katie and Abigail huddled together, holding each other tighter with every streak of fire and roar of thunder ringing in their ears.

"Is that what the Almighty sounds like when he is angry?" Abigail asked.

"It has to be him. Nothing else is that big."

They shivered and cried most of the night; tears creating trails down their cheeks any wagon train could follow. Ben slept. He had silently watched the sky until he just melted into the blanket in the corner of the wagon closest to the back and drifted into the arms of sweet sleep.

"How can he sleep like that?"

"Oh, I just hate this. It's like we are being attacked by the Almighty for some sin we don't know we have committed."

"Now, girls, it is only thunder and lightning. There is nothing to fear."

"We know, Ma, but it is just so scary. You have Pa to protect you."

Abigail nudged Katie and nodded toward Ma and Pa.

"Look how Pa keeps his arms around her. He keeps whispering in her ear. She's scared too."

"Look how the little wisps of hair hanging down next to her cheek flutter every time he says something. They look like they are truly excited about what he is saying. I wish I had someone who would talk to me that way and comfort me in the storms of life. Oh, Abigail, let's get to Texas and find husbands. I'm ready to get married and have my own home."

The girls did not sleep until the storm passed beyond their hearing, and even then they slept fitfully.

As bad as the storm was, the next day was worse. Papa and Ben worked and worked to get the wagon moved further on down the trail. They finally moved, but it took them all day, well, eighteen hours!

Katie wrote in her diary.

Papa and Ben managed to get the oxen to pull the wagon a whole 800 yards through the thick glue-like mud which covered everything for miles! I'm sure someone could sell this horrid muck as chinking between logs and people would never ever have to rechink! They call this El Camino Real! King's Highway! I don't think any king would want to take this road! What a mess!

And that was the beginning of sorrows. She could not let her mind remember any more for now. If she did, she would die.

Angry? Of course she was angry! She had every right to be angry. What was she going to do? She had barely made it through the winter, and that was only because Papa had been alive long enough to have some meat put up in the smokehouse and Mama had not died until after they had put up all the vegetables from the garden.

"I know how to milk the cow..."

"I can do some of the chores..."

"But now it's time to plow the field and plant the hay. How will I do that? How do I find the cattle and brand the new ones, if they even survived the winter?"

She stared at the picture of Ma. She lovingly picked it up and ran a finger down the image of her ma's face.

"Oh, Ma. Who can I trust? I haven't seen anyone all winter. Not a soul called or checked on us all winter. No one even knows you and Pa died. The only person who came by was that drifter who stopped here a week ago. Oh, Ma, how he frightened me. He made my skin crawl. I wish you could have seen how he looked at me. I felt like some kind of sweet treat he had not had in a very long time, and he was the kid in the candy store with the right to take what he wanted. His dirty red hair hung around his blue eyes. His eyes held nothing but bitterness, hate, and something that Pa would have called lust. Ma, you know I have not had any experience with men, but he made me feel very uncomfortable and dirty. When he asked where my folks were, I couldn't help but tell a 'little white lie'."

Tears started leaking their way out of the corners of her eyes; her hands began to shake so much she quickly put the picture back down. She turned her back and crossed her arms hugging herself and closing her eyes, remembering what she had told him.

———

"'They're out in the field, just out back. Not far. You want me to go get them?' The way he squinted his eyes and spat scared me more than the near-fire I had in the house when the log rolled out of the fireplace in January. How could I have been so careless? I had sworn I would be very careful from then on about everything! Even things like this. I wondered if he could see the knife I was holding in my hand? I had it hidden in the folds of my skirt. Maybe. Whatever made him nod and move toward his horse, I did not care; I was just so thankful he was leaving. He mounted his emaciated animal. The poor creature's rump looked like the cypress knees we saw sticking out of the black swamp water as we crossed Louisiana. I remembered what Pa had said about being able to tell the quality of a man by the look of his horse. The drifter slowly turned toward the road, and then he leaned forward and spit again, the slime of it dripping from his beard and onto his horse's mane. He briefly glanced toward the field out back. That's when I decided to deliberately walk that way and holler, 'Ma! We've got company!' Oh Ma, that's when he rode a little harder toward the road. Will God forgive me for lying?"

"Tears were running down my cheeks as I rounded the corner of the house. I slowed my pace, and walked toward the field out back. I slowly walked to the corner of the field closest to the house, dropped to my knees, and looked at the two markers—simple flat stones indicating

the final resting places of the two people I loved most in my life: Caleb and Rachel Kurtz, Pa and Ma."

Katie turned and picked up the picture once again.

"Ma, remember how we had to bury Pa in the field because the dirt was softer here and easier to dig? We had to do it by ourselves with the closest neighbors miles and miles away and cold weather already moving in from the Rockies. Then just a week after we had finished canning, Ma, you just dropped dead washing up after the last of the jelly making. My heart stopped that day, too, but it didn't know it; it just kept beating that tom-tom beat chanting, 'Lone-ly, lone-ly.' I yelled at it, 'Shut up!' But it wouldn't listen!"

Katie didn't even know what day of the week it was, but the sunrise caused those hills she had loved so much when they first moved to the hill country to glow with a pink light. Now she hated them. Now she hated everything! She just hated living!

"What will I do today? Live? Again?" she said to no one.

Her routine included getting up, getting dressed, fixing breakfast, milking the cow, doing something like yell at the Almighty and asking him to explain to her why, and then asking if he wanted her to live, to send someone to show her how to do what needed to be done.

"Like how to plow, plant, do what it takes to take care of the animals, fix the barn, chop wood, help me find the money Pa hid so I can buy what I need. I feel so helpless. Why do you hate me so, Almighty? Do you not love me even a little?"

What was she supposed to do with the animals? She had done the best she could with them. She had helped some with them, but Ma was the one who had done that after Pa had died. She had been the one to take over doing the household duties, and Ma said she had helped Pa and knew what needed to be done outside. They had chopped wood together. To tell the truth, it had taken both of them to do it. She hoped they had cattle left. She had just let them roam the hills all winter. She just couldn't deal with all of it. Yet, this was home, and Ma and Pa were here.

"I would rather just die....I wonder who would bury me? I haven't seen a neighbor more than once a year since we moved here. Guess we were not on the "social list," since we did not go to church. I really don't care."

She could not bear the thought of not being put in the ground next to her parents. Her skin shivered at the thought of the alternative, as if ghosts of the past were dancing up her arms. Quickly crossing the room to the front of the house, she opened the door to let the fresh air in. She walked blindly back over to the stove, bumping into the table as she went, then gripped the edge of the stove. Katie tried to will herself to actually start a fire and fix something to eat, a biscuit or pancake or something, maybe just coffee, anything to get her mind off of her loneliness.

"'Katie, you must eat.' I can just hear you, Ma. 'You must do something!'"

As hard as she tried, she could not talk herself into doing anything. She really didn't feel like eating anything; it had just become a habit. She was so busy feeling sorry for herself and trying to talk herself into doing the simplest task, with her hands gripping the stove and her knuckles becoming white against the black of the stove handle, she did not hear the sounds on the steps or across the front porch. The room became a little darker, but that didn't even bother her. She thought it was her mood. The voice caused her to jump and turn so quickly the blood nearly spun right out of her head. Stars sparkled before her eyes. She blinked several times trying to clear her vision, yet all she could see was the silhouette of what seemed to be a very large man. The sun was directly behind him. There was no way she could see his face. What could she use for a weapon? Where was the gun?

What use was that? Was it even loaded? Why was she so stupid? The knife was over by the dry sink. Could she move that way without drawing attention? Hardly!

"I'm sorry I startled you, ma'am. Would it be all right if I got some water from your well for my horse and me?"

The voice of the man floated around her ears and wrapped itself around her shoulders as if a warm blanket had just been given to a small child to snuggle into on a very cold winter night.

"Ma'am?"

"I'm...I'm sorry. You startled me so. I was so deep in thought, I didn't hear you and just was, well, so startled...uh, what was it you wanted?"

"Just some water. Oh, for me and my horse. I can draw it from the well and drink out of the bucket. We won't be any trouble."

"Help yourself."

She managed to loosen her fist and wave a hand in the direction of the well out front.

"Thank ya, Ma'am."

"You're welcome," she said as her arm fell back against her body.

He tipped his hat in her direction and turned to go. When he turned, the sun streamed past his back, looking like wings, giving his silhouette the image of an angel.

For the first time in nearly six months, Katie smiled.

CHAPTER 2

"here are your manners, Miss Katie Kurtz?" His presence, although it startled her, did not really scare her. All she felt was comfort and peace. "All he wants is a drink of water, and you are going to let him drink out of the bucket? Take him a tin cup, at least! Ma would be appalled at your behavior! You must make her proud," Katie continued the conversation with herself she seemed to have constantly. Most of the time she didn't even realize she was talking out loud.

The whole time she talked to herself, she pinned her hair up and looked for a cup. Finding one, she put on an apron and walked out the door. There he was fixing a feed bag and watering the most beautiful chestnut horse she had ever seen in her life. He appeared to be a gentle horse, but looks could be deceiving. She needed to remember that. Yes, she needed to remember that, now!

"I'm sorry; I should have offered you a cup from which to drink, Mr...?"

"Michael."

"Mr. Michael?"

"No, just Michael. Thank you. I really don't want to bother you any. I know you must be busy with your fields needing to be plowed and planted. Your hands haven't gotten here yet, or are they out working already?"

Her eyes flashed with a light of fear or worry, he wasn't sure which. Better to err on the side of caution.

"I'm sorry, it really is none of my business, but I would like to talk with the foreman. You see, I am looking for work and am hoping to maybe sign on if he needs someone to help out."

She looked into his hazel eyes so warm and honest. His hair was a little shaggy but clean, a deep warm brown with little streaks of fire flashing through it in the sunlight. She wondered if that meant he would be mean or protective. He was basically clean shaven, even though he needed a shave this morning. She felt he would welcome the opportunity to shave if given it. His build sure spoke volumes of hard work and the ability to do more. This man was definitely a man who could hold his own no matter what needed to be done. He cared tenderly for his horse who showed signs of being very well cared for, so no doubt about it, he was a caring person; nothing like that red-haired man who abused his animal. Pa had said you could tell a man's character by how he treated his horse. Maybe, just maybe, he could help her. She smiled as she pictured this man pushing the plow and yelling "Yee ha!" while driving the mule.

"What?" he asked.

She sure lit up when she let a smile cross her face. It transformed her from the terrified woman he first saw into a carefree child. He had wondered why the Lord prompted him to turn into the lane that brought him to this ranch house. He wasn't even sure anyone lived here. It truly looked deserted from the road. Everything looked in need of repair. It did not look like it had been touched in months.

"What do you mean, 'what'?" Katie asked.

"You were smiling. I was wondering what I had said that brought such a response. Would your foreman not like me?"

"He's not here." Katie waved her hand dismissively then let it drop to her side. "Have you had anything to eat? Would you care to come in and have some breakfast? I was just going to fix some, and we can wait together. We can talk inside where it is a little warmer out of the wind. If you want to put your horse in the barn, you can do that too." Her eyes wandered around the ranch, then she stared at the hills in the distance as she bit her lower lip.

She could not believe those words came out of her mouth! What had she said? She was going to be careful! Well, too late now. And smiling? She had smiled twice this morning already when she hadn't smiled in months. What did this man have in him, or about him, that would cause her to forget even temporarily her sorrow and experience a speck of joy?

"Thank you. I would love to have a hot breakfast. And I truly appreciate what you are doing for my horse. He's my best friend."

"Good, then I'll go on in and get things started in the house. Come on in when you get things settled in the barn, uh… Michael."

"Thank you, Mrs…?"

"It's Miss, Miss Katie Kurtz."

"Thank you, Miss Kurtz."

You are welcome, Mr., oh…Michael. I'm sorry, but that seems so awkward. I'm sure you have a last name. Can't you let me call you by your last name?"

"I just get ribbed about it so much that I quit using it. So, if you don't mind, I would rather you just call me Michael."

"Okay, but it still feels so awkward! Just come in when you are ready. I can't promise it will be anything to hoot and holler about, but it will be breakfast."

What are you doing, Katie Kurtz? Have you lost your mind? It is like you are out of control of your words and actions. I hope this does not get you in trouble, Miss Katie! she thought to herself as she rounded the corner of the house, marched up the stairs, and stomped the dirt off her feet at the back door.

For the first time since the day her mother died, Katie didn't hear the tom-tom beat "Lone-ly, lone-ly" and the boulder on her shoulders was just a tiny bit lighter.

"Maybe I could 'hire' him if he would take payment after the crop came in and the cattle were sold, if there are any cattle. Maybe I can find where Pa hid the money. I wonder how much he hid. 'That is one of those things that is not for women to know.' Pa, you were so wrong! Look what a mess you have left me in."

Inside the barn, Michael began to understand as he looked around. "Lord, I know you led me here. Now that I see this barn and these pitiful animals, I know one of the reasons. I came just in time. I'll start right now. This will give her plenty of time to get breakfast going. This could take a while. Man, I don't know who has been doing the work, but I'm beginning to think, nobody! Am I right, Lord?"

Yes, Michael Israel, you are here to save this woman in more than one way. Be prepared for the unexpected.

"With you, Lord, there is always something unexpected!"

CHAPTER 3

"here is he? I didn't think it would take that long to get his horse settled into the barn. Maybe something has happened to them out there. Maybe they are hurt. Maybe he found Pa's money and has ridden off without saying anything. Maybe he has just ridden off. Maybe he…Oh, maybe, maybe, maybe!"

The boulder was growing again. She could feel it.

Just march yourself out there and find out, Miss Katie! Her conscience yelled at her.

Could she do it? Should she take the knife? The coffee was ready. The table was set. The biscuits were ready and in the warming oven, butter and jelly all set on the table.

"Let's see, anything else? Eggs? Do we have any eggs? Do we have any chickens in the barn?"

She could use that for an excuse. There, that would be as good as anything to use as a reason to go out there. It would be perfectly logical if he should still be out there.

She steeled her nerves, smoothed down her apron, and started toward the door just as the sun disappeared from view. Her head jerked up. There he was, basket in hand, piled high with—eggs!

"I was just headed out to see if I could find some eggs!"

"Then I am just in time. I saved you the trouble! I'm sorry I took so long. I decided to take care of the other animals while I was out there. They kind of needed it."

"Oh, I uh, I..."

"I don't know who your foreman is, but he is not doing what he is supposed to be doing. I know that your parents should be aware of it and have a serious talk with him. The condition of those animals is quite serious. The animals are the heart of the ranch."

Her eyes began to sting and then she could not hold back the tears. She sat down hard onto the chair at the table, her hands shaking uncontrollably.

He quickly moved a chair beside her, put the eggs down, sat, and took her hands in his. Michael noticed that her hands were lost inside his. She was small and vulnerable. She needed to be protected from so many things, things she didn't even know about yet. She couldn't be more than five feet two inches tall. Her hair, about the same color as his horse's, was a beautiful chestnut brown with golden highlights. Her eyes were brown with golden specks of light which sparkled like flecks of mica in a streambed when the sunlight caught them. Sometimes, her eyes looked dark, like thunderclouds ready to burst, and at other times, like now, they turned a bright green. It was as if God had hidden a treasure deep in them. Her eyes were deep caverns yearning to be explored, but dangerous as well. He would call her eyes mysterious, just like she was.

He bowed his head and prayed.

"Lord, I don't know what is wrong or what is going on. I need your help if I am going to help Miss Kurtz. Thank you in advance for your wisdom. Please calm her heart and show her your love."

"Why did you do that?" She sniffed and looked at him questioningly.

"What?"

"That. I've never heard anyone talk to the Almighty like that before. In fact, when I talk to him, I usually yell at him." She wiped at her tears on her cheeks.

"I didn't realize I had prayed out loud. Did it bother you? I apologize if it did."

"No." She sniffed and coughed trying to clear her throat.

"Why are you yelling at God?"

"I don't know if I should tell you."

"Do your parents know?"

Her tears started again. This time she sobbed with them. He began to realize he had not seen her parents or any evidence of any other human beings around yet. Maybe there was no one else here. Should he say anything or wait for her to feel safe enough to admit she was alone? This time he silently prayed, *Lord, help me. Give me wisdom.* Suddenly she became very quiet.

"I want you to meet my parents."

That surprised him. But then the Lord always surprised him. "Okay. Where are they?"

"Out in the field, behind the house. It's not far. C'mon."

She got up and took her hands out of his, leaving a void he was not sure he understood. He had not had that kind of feeling before, and his hands felt suddenly very cold. How could hands that small create such warmth and depth of feeling? He wanted to grab them and fill his again, but she was hurrying out the door and heading around the back of the house.

His eyes scanned the field, but he could see no one. He looked further out and still could see no one standing out there even in the trees lining the field. He almost ran into her as she stopped in front of him. Maybe she was mistaken and they had gone to some other field or pasture and she was looking for them too. No, she was looking down. He looked at her again and then looked down to see what she was seeing. Then he understood. He understood so much. His prayer was answered and God gave him wisdom.

"Miss Kurtz, you are not safe. You cannot stay here alone. You don't have a foreman. Do you?"

"No. But I can't leave. I can't! I can't!"

"Then I will stay."

Her head jerked up, her hair coming loose and flying in all directions. That was not what she was expecting. Her eyes, wild with wonder, joy, suspicion, fear, caution, and all of them twirling around and around, not settling on any one emotion, came to rest on his, begging him to mean what he said. She had *never* trusted anyone instantly like she had trusted Michael. She could not explain why, she just did. There was a *peace* about him she needed. There was a *light* about him that drove away her darkness. Oh, how desperately she needed that! She had only known him a couple of hours at most, and already she would do anything he asked her to do. She could not begin to explain why. Perhaps she was reacting out of sheer desperation! She hoped not. She hoped she had more sense than that. She had shown some sense when the other man rode into the yard. Michael was *not* the same. He had proven himself to be quite the opposite.

"You need help. You have no one. The animals need help. They have no one. I am here. I want to help. Is there a problem?"

"I don't have any money to pay you?"

"Did I ask you to pay me? If we can make the ranch make a profit, then I will accept some pay. But for now, let me do this for you."

"Why? Why are you doing this?"

"Miss Kurtz…May I call you Katie?

"I call you Michael. I have poured out my sorrows to you. I can't see why not. So, yes, yes, of course you can.

Katie, God led me here. He has something for me to do here. I'm sure you need it. So, let's just go from here and see where he leads us. We need to eat breakfast. I need to look over the ranch and see what needs to get done first. Do you have cattle?"

"Yes, I think so. I couldn't deal with them, so I just left them out in the range all winter and let them roam. They are branded."

"We need to hire some hands. You don't have any money?"

"Well, Pa has money. I don't know where it is. He hid it somewhere. He said women didn't need to know where the money was kept. I tried to honor my parents, but sometimes men can be so bullheaded! Sorry, Michael, but it is true. Why couldn't he tell Ma? He was so sick. He could have told her. All I ever heard him say was that it was a lie."

"What did he mean by that?"

"I don't know. He was out of his head with fever. He just kept repeating, 'Money, lie, money, lie.' Ma didn't know what he meant by it either. She just told him to sleep and rest, to get well, but he didn't. He died keeping the secret in him."

"God knows where it is. He can reveal that secret to us. We need to ask and listen to his voice. Anything you remember, please tell me, it may be important."

"I will, but I don't think I heard anything that meant anything."

"You never know what you may have heard. Sometimes we hear things and just don't know we are hearing them."

"I think our breakfast is cold! I probably need to start over! At least the eggs will be fresh. I'm sorry for all the crying. I haven't cried in months. I thought I had dried up, but I guess not. Forgive me?"

"There is nothing to forgive. 'My tears have been my meat day and night, while they continually say unto me, Where is thy God?' Psalm 42:3. There is nothing to forgive."

"Who are you?"

"Let's eat."

As they walked back into the house, the aromas of coffee and biscuits filled the house and took her thoughts to brighter places than they had been in a very long time. The coffee was strong even by Texas standards. The biscuits had gotten a bit hard in the warming oven while she quickly scrambled some eggs, but it was the best meal she had eaten since before Pa had died. The boulder on her shoulders had gotten much lighter and that tom-tom noise pretending to be her theme song, "Lone-ly, lone-ly", could hardly be heard. She couldn't even remember what he had said at breakfast, but she laughed—out loud!

That was when he said, "'A merry heart doeth good like a medicine: but a broken spirit drieth the bones.' Proverbs 17:22. Get well, Katie. I must get to work now. So must you. I'll see you about noontime."

Get well? She wondered. "Am I sick?"

But he was gone and almost to the barn before the words came out of her mouth. She looked around the house. It was dark, dirty, and disgusting. Why hadn't she seen it before? How could she have been living like this? She had so much cleaning to do.

"Best be getting started," she said as she tied her apron a little tighter.

She needed water boiling and soap scraped. She needed the place aired out since the day promised to be warm. How much of the morning did she have left before she had to have the noon meal ready?

"I'd better get some bread started before I do anything else, and then start cleaning. What do I have in the larder? Mercy, he's such a big man, he could eat a whole steer."

With skirts flying in all directions Katie twirled around, and then stopped. She collected her wits and took one thing at a time, finally deciding on making a list since her mother wasn't there to tell her what to do next or remind her of what needed to be done. By noon she was prodigiously proud of herself and of all she had accomplished. The front room with dining and kitchen area glowed. The sunshine pouring through the clean windows brightened the house. The still-to-be-re-hung clean curtains on the line flapped in the sun soaking up the fresh smell of God-kissed Texas breeze. She had cooked that Texas favorite, chicken fried steak, with baked potatoes, gravy, green beans, bread, and some blackberry pie from the berries she and Ma had put up last summer. She was amazed at how much food she had found in the pantry, larder, smokehouse, and root cellar. They could eat for a long time. She had nearly starved this past winter simply because she could not force herself to go into the kitchen. She turned and looked toward the table.

———

There was a groan and the sound of a thump on the floor. She turned to see her ma crumpled in a heap just beside the table with the dish towel in her hand. Katie's hand flew to her mouth as she gasped, then cried, "Ma!" and fairly flew across the room. Her ma looked like she was just taking a nap there on the floor, eyes closed, mouth shut, but not one breath coming in or going out of her lungs. Katie fell down beside her and put her ear to her mother's chest. There was not one sound.

"Ma!"

There was no response. She listened again, still no sound. She lifted her mother's eyelids, but there was no light in the eyes. They were dark and lifeless, and Katie knew she was truly alone.

"Nooooooo! God, why?"

It would not be the last time Katie would yell at God. She lifted her mother's head and shoulders and hugged her to her heart, rocking back and forth on that kitchen floor until the next morning, having cried a river of tears. Now, she had not a tear left. Her mother's body was stiff, and Katie knew she needed to get her buried soon.

"I can't leave you. I just can't. Please don't leave me. Mama, please come back."

It was so hard to walk away and leave her. She knew she must, and she had to do it now. The ground was still soft out next to Pa. They had not had their first frost yet and it had rained the night before last. She could do this! She was angry enough to do this!

Katie left her ma on the kitchen floor after putting a pillow under her head and covering her with a blanket.

"I don't want you to get cold. I'll be back soon," she said as she closed the door.

"Who am I trying to fool? Ma's cold as a stone already. Besides that, she can't hear her Katie girl and doesn't care when I'll be back; she's already gone!"

Katie reached the tool shed, slung the door open with a bang, and brought out the shovel and pick. She hoped she wouldn't need the pick, but she didn't want to have to go back for it. As she walked back behind the house where they had buried Pa, the tears began making tracks down her cheeks again. So many deaths, too few burials.

The shovel cut into the dirt as Katie said, "Ben was the first to die. Crossing the Sabine River…the rain had caused it to be higher than normal but the ferryman said it would be fine."

She lifted another shovel full and let it fly. "We strapped down the wagon and then tied ourselves to the wagon. We were all situated as we started to cross. Ben was to be at the back of the wagon tied to the tailgate while keeping an eye on the oxen as they swam across behind the ferry. None of us knew what happened. He probably didn't strap himself to the wagon like he was told. We just heard a yell, turned, and saw Ben fall into the water. He thrashed about and then got snagged on a tree floating down the river in the current. It rolled, and we never saw him again. Some men on the bank rode along the shore for miles but never found him. The red clay mud of that river makes it so hard to find anything. We might as well say it is his grave, might as well."

Another shovel full of dirt went flying out of the hole. The ground next to Pa gave way with welcoming ease. Katie had the hole for her mother's last resting place sufficiently dug within a short time with sweat and tears rolling down her face. The task of carrying her mother out there proved to be harder. She tenderly wrapped her in the blanket and tried to lift her. By now it was too difficult. With tears streaming down her face and onto her sweat-soaked dress, Katie managed to get her mother's body across the wheelbarrow and tried to wheel her over to the grave. The balance was not right and she kept falling. Katie sobbed, wailed, and yelled angrily at God. Finally, she dragged her mother over and rolled her into the grave accomplishing the task. It was the darkest day of her life.

"I'm sorry, Mama!"

"I'm sorry, Mama!"

"I'm sorry, Mama!"

Katie didn't eat for days after that. She didn't get out of bed. Then she didn't go to bed. She just wandered around the house looking and looking and looking for Ma, Pa, humanity, a mouse, a cricket, an ant, anything. That was when the loneliness had really set in and the tom-tom had begun its death beat.

She was standing there staring where the sunbeam had danced across the kitchen floor, whispering to herself, "I'm sorry, Mama." The shadow had taken the sunbeam away. In its place was a dark pit, black as the darkest night ever to envelop man, drawing her in. Further and further and further in it pulled her. She fell to her knees, her arms reaching out, her hands clutching at nothing, her voice screaming, "I'm sorry, Mama!"

"Sorry for what?"

She jerked back from the pit, back from the blackness, back from despair. The sun was shining, but why?

She scrubbed at her eyes trying to see clearly. Blinking she looked away toward the voice.

"Oh, Michael, it was so awful!" she said through her tears and her fear.

He knelt beside her still-kneeling, shivering form.

"What was?"

"Ma died right here and I had no one to help me. I couldn't believe she was gone. I sat there holding her and rocking her in my lap all night. By morning she was stiff. I dug her grave, but I couldn't get her out there. I tried everything, even the wheelbarrow, but she kept falling out because I couldn't balance it. Finally, I had to drag her out there and just roll her in the hole. I hated the indignity of treating her like that! She deserved better than that! I loved her and couldn't give her the respect she deserved in our final moments together."

Again tears were making their all-too-familiar pathway down those too-thin cheeks.

"Katie, let me help you to the table." Michael eased his arm around her waist and used his other hand to lift her under her elbow. She was light despite her inability to help much. She felt like a corpse herself, just dead weight. If she had not been breathing, he would have questioned if there was life in her. Her skin felt cold to his touch and pale, where this morning she had begun to look better after they had talked. Did he dare leave her alone?

She sat down heavily, resting her elbows on the table and cradling her head in her hands.

She thought, *Michael is here now, he could bury me. Why couldn't I just die now? Then I could go to be with the rest of my family and leave this miserable, loveless world.*

"Katie, when God sent the children of Israel into the promised land, he told Joshua he would never leave him nor forsake him. He also told him to be strong and courageous. That is what you need to remember right now. The children of Israel wandered in the wilderness forty years and then died there. The next generation went in and took the land. I'm not saying this is exactly the same, but it is similar. You are the next generation. Your parents left this promised land to you. They want you to be strong and courageous and to take the land and do something with it. God is with you. He will never leave you nor forsake you."

"Where was he when Pa was so sick? Where was he when Ma just dropped dead?" she yelled. "Where was he when I needed him so much I could taste it? I have been so lonely, Michael, all I wanted to do was die. I've just been too afraid to die. Who would bury me?"

The haunted look returned to her eyes, dark and dreadful, lost in the cavern of despair. Michael knew he needed to draw her out. She needed to be able to see the sunlight and to know the Son, but how to reveal him to her? Her heart, at this point, was closed tight and trapped in darkness.

Lord, show me the way, he silently prayed. "What smells so good? I'm starved!" He questioned trying to move her mind from death, which seemed to be her constant companion.

"What? Oh, I'm sorry. I'm so sorry. I fixed chicken fried steak. Everything is ready. Just get washed up, and I'll get it on the table."

He started to protest and say he would help, but she read his mind in his eyes and put her hand on his lips.

"*No! I need* to do this. I'll be fine. Please, wash up. I'll be fine."

He went out the door planning to go around to the well to wash but noticed she had put out a wash basin with soap and towels on the back porch. That would be so much better. Smiling at such hospitality and thoughtfulness, he just knew there was hope in this project. He knew there was more than darkness in her heart.

When he came back in, the table was all set, and the aromas fairly danced into his nostrils. He could not wait to taste the banquet before him. He had really worked up an appetite out in the barn. That place looked a wreck, but he had made good headway with it. Things always looked worse before they could get straightened out.

"Katie, do you mind if I thank the Lord for this food?"

"No, go ahead."

"Dear Lord, how we thank you for the bounty that is before us and for the hands that prepared it. Bless this food to the nourishment of our bodies and our bodies to your service, amen."

"Thank you, Michael. Pa never prayed like that. He sounded more demanding and harsh. Why do you pray like that?"

"I pray from my heart, and that is what is in my heart."

"What is in your heart? Well, that's a new idea to me. I'll have to think about that some. I wonder what is in my heart. Darkness, I think."

Michael, thinking to himself, *Don't dwell on the darkness, Katie*, looked at her as he took his second bite and said, "This is the best food I've ever had! I don't think I've ever eaten chicken fried streak. I know I wouldn't have forgotten it if I had. This is great!"

"I don't make it like most people. I use oil and flour instead of eggs and milk with the flour. It's a little different. It still puts a crust on it."

"You are really a great cook, Katie. Have you cooked for many people before?"

"No, not more than eight, that's not many. Why?"

"I was thinking. If I can hire some men to help round up the cattle, brand the new ones and take them to market, I wouldn't have to hire a cook, too, if you could do the cooking?" He winked at her and smiled.

"Well, are you talking about on the trail?"

Michael paused and looked at her for a moment before replying. "Hmm, that may not be safe, although staying here alone is not really safe either, especially now that winter's over and drifters are on the move again. For now, let's just think about you cooking while we are working the hills around the ranch. Do you have a bunkhouse?"

"Yes, there is a small bunkhouse back of the pasture west of the barn. It is not too far away, but far enough. It sleeps six."

"I fixed me a place in the barn. I'd like to be a little closer to the house in case you need me. So, if I can find six men to help, with you and me that's eight. You can handle cooking for that many without too much worry, right?"

"I can handle that."

"Good." Michael shyly looked at her with half a grin. "Uh, could I have another piece of that steak, another potato, and some beans?"

She laughed, the light was back in her eyes, and the sun was shining again.

"Save room for the blackberry pie!" Katie scolded him.

His eyes bulged out of his head. He rubbed his hands together and dug into his third helping. "I'll have room," he said around mouthfuls. "I have to keep up my strength, you know. Blackberry pie, my favorite!"

Later, completely satisfied, Michael pushed back from the table, stretched, and smiled.

"Now, that's what I call good eatin'. You are going to completely spoil me! I won't be able to work if I keep eating like this. Stew will have to do out on the trail, or beans and biscuits!"

"We will see," she said smiling.

"Well, I need to get back to work. Do you ride?"

"Well, yes, I can ride tolerably well. Actually, I have had much practice and I can keep up with most riders. When we first moved here, I rode all over these hills. I just love it here. I can't imagine being anywhere else."

"Good. I want you to plan to go for a ride later this afternoon. You can show me around the ranch so I can get my bearings. I think I will be pretty much done in the barn by later this afternoon and can have the animals well settled in by then. They will be much better off than they have been. No offense intended,

Miss Katie. I will see you when I finish. I plan to go to town tomorrow and see about hiring some help."

"But, how will we pay them?"

"Let me and the Lord worry about that. I'm sure he has a plan. By the way, the house really looks good, Katie. You've worked hard in here today. You have gotten so much done and cooked a big meal too! I'm proud of you. You have plenty of strength and courage, Katie; keep exercising it. You will get through this, especially with God's help."

Katie felt the warmth of color rise to her neck and cheeks with his compliment. How long had it been since she had heard words of encouragement? She could not even remember when. Her ma had been very stingy with her compliments. *Ma, why did you feel that whatever a woman did was what a woman was supposed to do, no matter how well she did it?* She would not explore those thoughts now—she could not. They would take her places she did not want to go. Katie was free of the darkness for now and did not want to go back there.

The sun shining through the windows reminded her of the curtains hanging on the line, certainly dry by now.

"Okay, wash the dishes, clean up the kitchen, hang the curtains, then start on the next room. Oh, I need to plan the garden. When Michael goes into town, he can buy the seeds I need. I'll need to get the ground ready to plant. Spring always brings so much preparation for so much reward later. Ma, you always said, 'Work now, reap later.' How true." Her words echoed off the now-empty house. What a difference another human being made.

CHAPTER 4

She had finished hanging the curtains and was airing out the mattress from her parents' room when she saw Michael leading two horses toward the house from the barn.

"Is it that late already? I need to change clothes!"

She quickly ran upstairs and pulled out the soft leather riding skirt they had bought from the Caddo Indian woman at the trading post in San Augustine as soon as they had gotten into Texas. She had wanted to get right back on a horse and ride back to the Sabine River and look for Ben. She swore she would, but Pa wouldn't let her. They bought her the riding skirt anyway. She had made good use of it on the ranch, and now she would use it again. The leather felt soft and comfortable against her as she walked down the steps, grabbing her hat as she passed the hat tree next to the door.

"You're ready." He made more of a statement than asked a question. She squinted at him a moment then smiled.

"Well, almost. Wait just a minute."

She scooted back into the house. He hit his leg with his hat watching the dust rise and drift away on the breeze. She had surprised him. He had not expected her to be ready or as willing to go. He had been hesitant to leave her alone all afternoon.

Her depression seemed to grip her whenever she found herself alone, surrounded by memories. He hoped this ride would be good medicine.

She seemed to pop out of the door, letting it slam behind her. "Now, I'm ready."

"What do you have there?"

"Oh, nothing much by your standards anyway, just a little snack. I thought you might need something to tide you over until supper tonight. I fixed a couple of cheese sandwiches, put in some hardboiled eggs, apples, and some blackberry pie. Think you can handle that?"

He studied the basket she carried, looked up at her, and then looked back at the basket. He reached over and took it from her hand. "Well, this will be just fine, but what are you going to eat?"

They both burst out laughing and continued to do so as he gave her a boost up onto her horse, Nellie, then he mounted Solomon.

"Which way, my lady?"

She led Nellie toward the back side of the ranch, down the lane that runs beside the bunkhouse. "Southwest, toward Big Arroyo. I named everything when we first arrived. That will be the best place to begin the 'big' tour!" She smiled and waved her hand in an arch to indicate the scope of the ranch. "We will probably see most of the cattle there as well. That is the farthest part of our property. We own a little beyond that but it isn't worth much, mostly rocks, limestone; there are some caves up in the hills that way." She pointed southwest. "Pa always said to stay away, so I did. I don't like caves and closed-in places, especially if there's no light. He said there are hundreds of bats in there. Uck! That alone was enough to keep me away. Big Arroyo has a nice stream flowing through it; it has fish! The cattle like it down there, so I'm not too worried about them if they stayed there all winter. It gets cold here, but it doesn't stay cold like it did up north. I like the weather here much better."

"Yes, the weather here is much better. They're still getting snow up north now. We may still get some cold snaps, but the bluebonnets and Indian paintbrushes are already beginning to bloom. I believe spring has decided to arrive."

"Yes, I believe you're right. I hadn't noticed them. When did that happen? If we head north from the big arroyo, thus the name "Big Arroyo", we cross My Hills; that's what I call them. I love them. I can see them from the window in my room, and I love to watch the sunset from there. The colors thrill my heart. I haven't watched the sunset now in months. I've missed so much just grieving. I think I'm getting over it now, Michael, thanks to you. I believe you came just in time. I don't know what I would have done. Are you really going to stay?"

"I'll stay as long as I'm needed. Only God knows how long that is. We will have to listen to his voice and obey him."

Katie didn't like the sound of that. She looked away from him and looked at her hills. She remembered that Psalm that starts, "I will lift up mine eyes unto the hills, from whence cometh my strength." Was it a question or a statement? What if God wanted Michael to leave tomorrow? She was not ready for that. She wanted him to stay for, well, she did not know for how long. He gave her comfort, and she knew she needed that now more than anything. She needed help. She felt like this day had been a year. Much had happened, and she had changed so much.

Did the hills give her strength? From where did her strength come? Not from the hills. If she had not learned anything else from the past few months, she certainly had learned that. It didn't matter how many times she had stared out at those hills, they had not helped her one bit. She had not felt any strength until Michael came, and he said the Lord had sent him. If that were so, then her strength, in essence Michael, came from the Lord. Had God really heard her cry? Did he and does he do anything for Israel other than punish? When the right time came, she would ask Michael. She was not that brave…not yet.

"Look at that!" called Michael.

Katie looked up just as an eagle swooped down and grabbed a rabbit they had frightened out of its hiding place.

"Oh no!" Katie gasped as she watched the eagle fly away with the rabbit clutched in its talons.

"Don't be sad, Katie. God designed the animals that way. They must eat to survive. Eagles help control how many rabbits there are on the earth. If they didn't eat them, we would be overrun with rabbits! You wouldn't get upset if I came back from hunting with a rabbit or two, and we could have rabbit stew. Would you?"

"No, I guess you're right. I hadn't thought of it that way. We sure would be overrun with rabbits! They are everywhere and reproduce like lightning!"

"Think about it, Katie. Their fur is so soft and so nice to make hats, gloves, slippers, muffs, and all kinds of nice warm articles of clothing. We don't waste them. It's not like we are just killing to be killing. We're killing out of need. God designed it that way."

"So you said. I feel like I'm in school. You make a good teacher, Michael. Look there. See that rise just to the left of that outcropping of rocks?"

"Yes, I see that."

"That's the beginning of Big Arroyo. C'mon, let's ride."

"Now, wait just a minute, little lady. I have this basket of nice food here that I don't want to turn to mush. I'd rather wait to 'ride' after we've eaten it. Then we don't have to worry about the hard-boiled eggs becoming scrambled up with the blackberry pie, if you get my meaning?"

"Oh, sorry. I forgot about your stomach! Okay, we will just saunter on up this way then. Maybe by the time we get to the arroyo, it will be time to eat, again!"

"Maybe."

They enjoyed yet another laugh together and took a gentle ride on up to the arroyo. They were not surprised to find a nice herd of cattle enjoying the shade provided by the walls of the arroyo and the crystal clear water in the stream at the bottom. There seemed to be plenty of feed. Michael could see there were quite a few new calves that would have to be rounded up and branded. Yes, God had been taking care of Miss Katie even though she did not know it. She had been taught what punishments were. Now, she needed to be taught what blessings were. She needed to be saved from despair.

"Katie, what a blessing God has poured out on you! Do you see all the calves?"

"Calves? Well, I hadn't noticed them. I'm thankful that the cattle are all right and mostly, it seems, here. But, yes, now that you mention it, there seems to be quite a few new little ones."

"There are probably more cattle up the arroyo. It keeps going and gets wider further in. There is plenty of water, at least there always has been and seems to be now. The little arroyo isn't this nice, but it still is protected and has water most of the time. The three buttes have two canyons between them. Those canyons are pretty wild. I can't imagine any cattle going there to winter when they can have this. But just like people, I guess, some of them are stupid! I don't like going to the north side of the ranch. Those buttes give me the chills. I don't know what it is about them; I just don't like them. They are high and hard climbed. I guess it's the danger involved, and then the canyons make me feel trapped. Most of the time they're dry, and there are many snakes in that part, rattlers mostly. Oh, I just get chills thinking about it!

"The wind moans when it blows through those canyons like someone's in there sick or dying. That's just too vivid for me. I want to yell and say, 'Who are you?'...Michael, do you want to ride all the way over there?"

"No, Katie, that's all right. I can probably find those buttes on my own. I would like to see the little arroyo, but let's eat our snack first, and then we can *ride!*"

"Now, you're talking."

Hopping off his horse and helping her off hers, he grabbed the blanket from behind his saddle. Michael let her put it where she thought would be best. Michael put the basket on the blanket. The whole time he surveyed the surrounding area. He could not shrug off the feeling of being watched. He could not see anyone. It was just a feeling, but his feelings had not yet been wrong and he trusted them. He didn't feel they were in danger, just being watched.

The watcher could be anywhere, behind the mesquite trees or rocks, or in gullies. There were all kinds of good hiding places, especially with the variety of colors painting the landscape with bluebonnets, red Indian paintbrushes, greens of new growth, whites and yellows of the sandstone, and red rock standing out. No doubt about it, God had done a beautiful job decorating this part of the world.

"Michael, didn't you hear me? I asked if you are going to sit down, or just keep standing there looking around?" Katie laughingly interrupted Michael's thoughts.

"There is so much to see. The beauty here is breathtaking. I can truly say I've never seen anything like it. I can't seem to take it all in."

Katie smiled at him. "I do love it. New York doesn't come close."

"Is that where you came from?" Michael asked as he sat down on the blanket.

"Well, we have relatives there, and that is where we started from. Daddy always had the wanderlust. He never stayed anywhere very long. I thought this would be it, and it was. My grandparents came from Germany. They moved to England and Ireland. My daddy and his sister, Katherine, were born there. I'm named for her. She died of a fever on the boat to New York. My parents met in New York and married. We moved from New York to Philadelphia. That didn't last long. Then he had to go west. So, we went to Nashville. That lasted until he read about Texas and found an AD for this ranch. He came out, talked to the people, and bought it. He came back to Nashville; we packed up and moved out. Everything went fine as long as we were on the Natchez Trace. It was a well-established road and well-traveled. We had good times and bad, but nothing like what was to come. That El Camino Real was the beginning of sorrows as far as I'm concerned. I can't go there now, Michael. I just can't. I want to stay in the sun. It's too dark in those memories. I need to stay away from them for a while."

"I'm sorry. Let's pray. Lord, thank you for this beautiful day and for this food we are about to eat. Thank you for the hands that have prepared it and for providing it for us. Your blessings are new every morning. Thank you, dear Father. Amen."

Michael ate quickly, for that feeling of being watched did not go away. In fact, it became more menacing by the minute. He noticed Katie had not taken a bite for several minutes either.

"Are you finished? I'm finished if you are."

"Yes. Suddenly, I'm not hungry at all."

She wasn't sure why she felt that way. She had been very hungry when they had stopped and was really glad they had. Now, she could hardly eat. She felt the urge to get back on her horse and ride like the wind. She just wanted to ride and ride as fast as she could.

"I just want a drink and then I'm ready." She took the canteen and swallowed the surprisingly cool water, got up, and began collecting what was left of what Michael had not already gathered together. She had never met any man who would help out with the clean-up before. Her pa had always told her that's woman's work. She had believed him, until now. Michael seemed so comfortable with it. He didn't seem to think it was beneath him or even like he was doing her a huge favor by doing it.

He grabbed up the blanket and shook it out, making a popping sound that almost sounded like a gunshot. She jumped at the sound, making her realize her nerves had gotten on edge. *Why?* she wondered.

He quickly glanced her way and asked, "Would you make sure I put everything in the basket? I wouldn't want to leave any of that great food behind. I might need it for later."

She hurriedly walked over and looked into the basket. It was perfect, just like him. When she picked it up, it felt much lighter. She didn't think they had eaten that much; maybe they had. The blackberry pie was completely gone. She carried the basket back to where he was. He helped her mount Nellie, tied the blanket behind his saddle, mounted Solomon, took the basket from her and, smiling, said, "Let's ride!"

They took off like the wind was at their back and they were sails on a schooner racing across the Atlantic. What a ride! She didn't know Nellie had it in her. She wasn't that old; Katie just had never tested her speed.

"Michael, I wonder why popping that blanket scared me. I felt a heaviness back on the rocks like that odd feeling one gets when they think they are about to be scared. I remember one time Ben jumped out of a dark corner and yelled, 'Boo!' I thought he had been asleep for an hour or so. My heart jumped to my throat and nearly choked me. I wanted to choke him! I'd give anything if he could still do that to me; I would hug him!"

"Ben?"

"My little brother. He drowned on the trip out here. We never found his body. He was spoiled, and I always felt he should have been punished more. Now, I just wish he was here. I just love him. I was jealous of how much Pa would let him get away with when I couldn't get away with anything. Pa would have told Ben where the money is. We may never find it. What will become of the ranch? What will happen to me? What happens to women alone out west, Michael?"

"Katie, God is not going to let you lose the ranch. He sent me here to take care of you. He has a plan. Now, all you have to do is stop worrying. 'It is of the Lord's mercies that we are not consumed, because His compassions fail not. They are new every morning: great is Thy faithfulness.' Lamentations 3:22–23. Remember those words, Katie, cling to them. God loves you with an everlasting love. He will take care of you."

The wind in her face brought her back to her hills. These hills with their gullies and stands of mesquite charmed her like nothing else had. Her heart beat in rhythm with the hooves of the horses as they crossed the hills headed to Little Arroyo. Rabbits scampered here and there, confused by the sudden onslaught of the horses. They seemed not to know where to go, whether to run or to hide. How many times had she felt that way in the past few months? She had chosen to hide. She had hidden in the dark cave of her home and her heart; the dark memories drawing her ever deeper and deeper into the place she would never dare go in the world. She would never dare go to the cave beyond Big Arroyo where the bats live and the guano lies waist deep on the cave floor, ready to swallow up and drown any poor unsuspecting soul who might wander into that terrible place. People enticed by the promised beauties of the stalactites and stalagmites, the crystals and clear pools, of hidden treasure to be found, forgotten by conquistadors of long ago. These have become the main characters of the ghost stories told by campfires and hearths at home on a stormy night. No, she would never go there in this world, but in her mind she allows herself to travel there and very nearly drown in the same kind of "guano" of the mind. She shuddered as she thought, *I must get over it. I must, or forever live in darkness.*

"Is that the arroyo?"

She looked up to see where Michael was pointing. Shading her eyes with her gloved hand, she could see the telltale features of the land which clearly marked out the arroyo. If no other landmarks could be seen, the windswept spruce which looked so much like an anvil-shaped cloud marked the mouth of the arroyo.

She continued to look at the tree, nodded, and replied, "Yes, I can always tell by that tree if nothing else. I call him 'Ole Thunderhead.'"

"I can understand why. Shall we? I'll lead the way if you don't mind. I want to look at the tracks and see what I can see before we mess them up with our own."

"Fine with me. I didn't know you were a scout, Michael. Were you with the army?"

"No....I do know how to read signs though. I just thought it would be good to know what went in before us since we are not on top this time. We could ride on up if you would rather."

"No, I don't think I want to do that. I think I would rather go in. If there is water, the horses need it, especially after that run."

"That's just what I was thinking. Let's go in single file, not side by side. I want to be able to see both sides of me."

"That's good. Maybe I'll look on both sides and see if I see what you see. Maybe I'll even see something you don't. We can be a team. Mostly, I'll be looking for snakes! Oh, how I hate snakes!" Katie shuddered.

"With it warming up like this, they will be coming out. That's not a bad idea. Nellie will probably help with that as well. Better be ready to hold on tight if she sees the snake first."

"Not funny, Michael!"

"Sorry! Let's head in."

Michael scanned ahead looking not only for cattle prints but for recent horse prints. He just had a feeling they were not alone out here. *Who would care what they were doing on the Kurtz land? No snakes. No cattle prints. No horse prints. There were some pretty dry cattle droppings, so cattle have been here. They could still be here just further on up the draw,"* he thought.

Solomon shied a bit and as he did, Michael noticed the low scrub on the right had a broken branch. He was looking for a snake. He didn't see the rattler kind, but the human kind might be up ahead. This branch had been broken recently. How did this person know where they were headed? How did he get there before them? They had ridden like the wind of a storm. Maybe he would be dealing with more than one person. They could have signaled using mirrors. He had seen that done before. Maybe there is a better trail across the hills to this arroyo than the way they came. He would have to ask Katie later or investigate it for himself if he didn't get the answers he wanted from what he found here.

Katie interrupted his thoughts. "Michael, do you hear that?"

He was so focused on looking and thinking he wasn't listening. He stopped to listen to see if he could hear what she was talking about.

"What *is* that noise?" Katie asked.

Michael tilted his head as if he could hear it better that way. "I'm not sure. It sounds like cattle and thunder. It sounds more like a stampede to me; but if there are cattle in there, what would have spooked them?"

"I don't like this. I feel trapped." Katie looked all around her, up and down and to both sides.

"Katie, I don't see any high ground. It would be better for us to turn and ride out. We could go up above. I think you are right about feeling trapped. That sound is getting louder. Turn around, Katie, and ride like you did getting here."

They both turned their horses and galloped out of the arroyo, still not seeing anything coming toward them. When they made it back out, they turned sharply and rode up the face of the rise to the top of the hill.

The wind felt fresh and clean on their faces. The sun kissed the shadows from their eyes and they felt they could suddenly see clearly. They rode along the edge at the top of the arroyo looking down to see if they could see the stampede. There was nothing. They arrived at the point they had heard the noise and nothing was happening. Looking at each other quizzically, they shrugged and moved on along the rim of the arroyo. They reached the bend they had been approaching; and as they crossed to the other side of the bend, Katie's eye caught a flash of red in the sunlight just behind a boulder on the other side of the stream. There were a few cattle just up the stream, but not enough to be considered a stampede if they had begun to run.

Not speaking a word, Katie nudged Michael and pointed to the boulder. Michael leaned forward. As he did, the red became a man whose face turned toward the stream and the cattle. He didn't look their way but he could be seen clearly. Katie gasped and put her hand over her mouth. Her eyes closed, hoping to make herself invisible or to make the man go away by doing so. She felt her horse move, forcing her to open her eyes. Michael was leading her away from the rim and out of view of the man.

"I don't know who he is, but he has been following us today."

"Oh, Michael, two or three weeks ago, maybe more, maybe less, I don't know, he came by the house. I was so scared. He made me feel so dirty the way he looked at me. He smelled bad and he was so filthy. His horse was just pitiful; I felt so sorry for it. He asked for some water. I told him to help himself. Then he asked if my parents were around. I lied and told him they were in the back field and that I would go and get them. I turned, started walking toward the back, and hollered for Ma. He spit and got on his horse. I kept walking and hollered again telling Ma that we had company. He rode out then. I was so afraid. I had a knife hidden in the folds of my skirt. If he had come after me, I don't know if I could have used the knife. He probably would have used it on me instead. What is he doing here?"

"I don't know. We need to find out, but not out here. It is good that we know about him though. If he knew our plans to come out here today, then he has been listening to our conversations. He knows about your parents, Katie. You won't be able to fool him again with that story. If he hasn't heard you tell me about them, he certainly has seen their graves. He has probably been prowling around the ranch looking for anything of value."

"Well, the only things I know of are Ma's silver candlestick and Pa's money, and nobody knows where he hid that. Why couldn't Pa trust us?"

"He thought he was doing what was best. He felt God had put him in charge of the family and he was not to put anything on the shoulders of the women that would mean more responsibility for them than they needed. Man was created first to be the provider and protector of all God put him in charge of. Woman was created to be his helper. Your father evidently didn't feel a need to have "help" with the money. He provided for and protected his family. He believed he was doing what God had directed him to do."

"Yes, but he died! He was sick and he knew he was very weak and could be dying. All he could say was, 'Money, lie'. That was a really big help!"

CHAPTER 5

The ranch buildings were coming into view. Michael lifted up in the saddle and turned and looked behind them. They had not been going in any hurry, and he did not see anyone following them. The feeling of being watched had left him when they had ridden off the hills and toward the ranch. For all he knew, the red-haired man was still in the arroyo waiting to ambush on them. Funny about the sound of that stampede. Then it came to him. "David!"

"Who?"

"I was just remembering about King David when he went out to fight against the Philistines. He asked God how he wanted him to attack. The first time, God said to attack straight on, so they did. The second time, God told David to go to the side in the trees and wait until he heard the sound of marching in the balsam trees then move out to battle because that would mean God had gone out in front of him to strike the Philistine army. He would win the battle. I am thinking God did a similar thing for us today, only in reverse. We were riding into an ambush. I saw a freshly broken branch on a bush so I knew something had passed that way recently. Then I saw a horseshoe mark in the mud by the stream. I was just going to remark on it when you said something about the noise. I think God was scaring us away from the danger around the corner. The man with the red hair did not hear us or the stampede. He was still sitting there waiting for us. He did not see us above him. The cattle near him were making enough noise that he did not hear us on the other side of the bend. He may still be sitting there waiting. I need to check out the bunkhouse. Katie, do you want to go in with me, or do you want to go back to the house?"

"I want to stay with you. I don't feel like going to the house alone. What if he left the arroyo and rode back to the house a different or faster way. We did take our time. We stopped by that creek to give the horses water and to rest a bit ourselves. He could have avoided us and found another place to ambush us."

"I don't feel the same uneasiness I felt out on the hills. I think we are safe. I do need to check the bunkhouse and see what condition the bunks are in and what needs to be done to them. I want to hire some men and be able to offer them some kind of assurance that they have a comfortable place to stay. I still plan to go into town tomorrow. We need to get those calves rounded up and branded as soon as we can. We need to sell some cattle to get some money to get this ranch back on its feet or else find your father's hiding place."

"We could risk God's ire and call on the witch at Endor, see if she could call my father back up from the dead, and then we could ask him."

"Don't even joke about that, Katie. God would not be pleased at all for us to entertain any kind of conversation with Satan. I'm sure your father left you and your mother clues, you just did not recognize them. If you just think about what he said or did before he would get money to go to town or pay his workers, something might come to mind as being the same every time. Say to yourself, 'Every time Pa would need money he would always say or do…,' and then fill in the rest. Maybe you will remember something that was a habit to him that he did only at that time and at no other."

"All right, I'll try. Maybe tomorrow while you are in town, I'll have some time to do that. I can finish cleaning up the house. I really let it get run down just like everything else, I guess. I will probably have a big mess out here in the bunkhouse. Here it is. Let's see what we have. Probably mice! Uck! They are almost as bad as snakes, in my mind, just not as dangerous."

As they got down off their horses, something didn't look right to Katie. She stopped and looked around, her hands going to her hips. She turned to one side and then to the other, a puzzled look on her face. Michael studied her then asked, "What's wrong?"

"Nothing really. I could have sworn we had a rocker on the porch and a wash bucket hanging on the wall out here. I don't remember anything being done with them when the last group moved out. I came out to check things. That's when Pa had gotten so sick and Ma was busy with him, so I came out. I didn't move them and didn't know if they were supposed to be moved, so I just left them. I don't think Ma ever had the chance to come out and check or even wanted to after Pa died. We were so busy. She was taking care of the barn animals, though, so maybe she did."

"Well, Miss Katie, let's go in and see what the inside looks like."

Eerily, the door didn't make a sound as they opened it.

"Uck! We need some light in here. Michael, get the shutters off the windows and light the lamp. Open the windows, we need fresh air. What is that smell any way? Oh, I think I'm going to be sick. I can't stand that. Quick, let some light in. Michael, where are you? What are you doing? What is taking you so long?"

Thunk!

"What was that noise?"

"I think I just ran into the rocker that was supposed to be on the front porch. Don't worry, though, nothing's broken."

"Oh, it's solid oak."

"Thanks for your concern."

"Huh?"

"I said, 'thanks for your concern'?"

"Oh, you were talking about nothing was broken on you? Michael, have you looked in the mirror lately? You could walk into a mountain and split it in two. How could a rocker hurt you?"

"Well, I just thought maybe you might be a little worried about my little toe. There, the window is open, and there is some light in the room. Now to find something to light the lamp with and have a look around."

"This is not good, Michael. Pa never allowed alcohol on the ranch. Look at all these bottles. Light the lamp quickly, we must see this place. This is not the way I left it. Someone has been staying here."

"Katie, I believe I know who it is, at least one of the "someones." Your redheaded stranger has probably made himself at home. He cannot be seen from the house here. With that stand of trees lining the pasture, he can keep watch on what is going on and even come in close and eavesdrop on our conversations from outside the house, especially when the doors or windows are open. We have had no need to think anyone was around, so we have not taken any steps to make sure we were not overheard."

"Ouch!"

Michael spun around with the lamp in his hand. Katie looked down at her foot holding her riding skirt in one hand and holding her leg with the other.

"What's wrong? Are you all right?"

Holding the lamp closely so they could see, Katie gasped as she saw a trickle of blood ooze between her fingers.

"Sit down, Katie. Let me see that. What happened?"

"I was just trying to look around when my foot ran into something on the floor. I felt a sharp pain. You know the rest. I should have waited for you to come over with the lamp. Ma kept telling me I was always a bit ahead of my head. She wanted me to think before acting. I'll be all right once we get this bandaged."

"I'll see about that. What did you run into, I wonder?"

Michael shined the light over where Katie had been standing while she discreetly tore some fabric from her under things for a bandage. She didn't think they could find anything clean in the bunkhouse.

"That's odd. Why would someone tear up the floor like that?"

"What?"

"See, the floorboards are pried up. You ran into a jagged broken board sticking up just out from under that bed. You couldn't have seen it in the dim light.

"I don't want him to know we are on to him," Michael added. "Now that we know where he is staying, it will be easier to watch him and know what he is doing. If he knows we are on to him, he'll just find somewhere else to hide, and our job will be that much harder. We need to get out of here and put things back the way they were."

"Even the rocker?"

"I don't think he'll notice that. But he will notice the windows and shutters. I'd better put the lamp back. How's your leg?"

"I have it all bandaged. Thanks. It's just a little scratch, really. I would like to get home, though, and get it washed. Besides, this place just makes my skin crawl. Maybe there are spiders and bugs all over everything, and my skin *is* crawling. Oh, Michael, why did I say that? Let's get out of here!"

Michael got her situated on Nellie then made sure things in the cabin were back to what had been normal when they rode up. He carefully brushed their prints from in front of the bunkhouse and made it look like they had ridden right by the place back to the house.

"I hope he doesn't see anything I might have missed. Let's ask God to send a wind to blow any sign of us away and mice to clean up any trace we left in the bunkhouse."

"Are you serious about that?"

"Of course. God is much better at taking care of details than I am. And he really cares about both of us."

"You amaze me."

"God amazes me."

"I wish I could see him in the same way you do. He has always been 'the punisher' to me. It seems as if he has given nothing but bad things to my family ever since I can remember."

"If that is so, how could your father afford to buy the ranch and move out here and still have his 'pot of gold' he kept hidden."

"It's not a pot of gold. He had his money hidden. He just told us the ranch would be a pot of gold. He was always saying things like that. There was always something better beyond the next hill, around the next corner. We probably would not have stayed here either. He would have heard about some other place that promised something better, and he would have sold the ranch and run after that 'pot of gold' next. Pa was a wanderer, a Hebrew. That's what that means, you know, 'landless one.'"

"Well, it looks to me like he was sure trying to put down some roots for you and your ma. He sure has some pretty land here for being a 'landless one.' I think your pa may have changed, Katie, and you just didn't know it."

"Maybe. If he had, he sure was subtle about it."

"I'll put the horses up and rub them down and feed them and the other animals. You take care of that leg. Do you need anything out of the smokehouse before I do all of that? I'll bring it in for you so you don't have to do any unnecessary walking on that leg."

"Well, I was thinking about killing a chicken, but maybe we'll just have some more chicken fried steak. What do you think about that?"

"Well, now, Miss Kurtz, you know I might just have to force myself to eat chicken fried steak again. I'd hate to make you have to go out of your way to make something else. So, whatever you think is best, I'll just force myself to eat."

"Oh, I know how hard it will be for you to have to force yourself to eat! Well, I have what I need in the house, so you just take care of the horses, Mr. Michael Mysteriouslastname, sir."

The sound of his laughter reminded Katie of the bells she had heard at Christmas in New York ringing and ringing on Christmas Eve. She had always loved that sound and had always wondered why they sounded so joyful. Michael laughed all the way to the barn and then she could even hear his laugh echoing inside the barn. Shaking her head, she limped her way into the house smiling from ear to ear. Oh how good it felt to smile again. She hoped she would never stop.

"Ma, I do miss you, but I am not crying as much. My heart doesn't sound as if it is going to drive me crazy with its constant lament. I wish you could be here to see what God is doing. He isn't all mean. Maybe you knew that. You just never told me."

She put down the picture and slowly began unwinding the bandage around her leg.

"Ooo, that hurts! I should have wet it down first. Ma, I just don't remember all your tricks. Now it's going to bleed again. Well…that doesn't look too bad."

She cleaned the cut and put some salve on it, then wrapped it with a clean cloth.

"Now, I can start to feed Michael's tapeworm. I don't want to have the same thing with the steak. Let's see what I have in the pantry."

As he rubbed the horses, Michael prayed. "Lord, what is going on? Give me knowledge and wisdom so I can discern what I need to see and to know. Help me protect your child. Thank you for sending us a warning as to the man waiting to ambush us. You are Mighty God! Keep his eyes blinded to our presence in the bunkhouse. Keep him ignorant as to our knowledge of his presence here. Help us to see what he is up to and to catch him before he causes any more trouble. Thank you, Lord. Amen."

"Now, Solomon how does that feel? I'm sorry you had to wait, but you know, ladies first, so Nellie was ahead of you. She really appreciates your gentlemanliness, too. She promised she wouldn't eat all the oats and hay. I'm going to let you both out in the pasture for a while tonight. I need an excuse to come out there. You don't mind, do you? I'll be out sometime after supper to put you back in the barn."

Michael put his fork down, stretched and tried to muffle a burp, "Oh, excuse me. That was great! Katie, I believe you are the best cook I've ever met."

"Why, thank you. I can't believe all you have gotten done in the barn. It looks like a new place. I don't think it looked that good when we moved here. How do you get that much done by yourself?"

"I just keep at it, I guess. Why don't we go out on the porch and sit. I think it will be cooler out there and we can enjoy the view."

With Michael's nod toward the back and his wink and look at her leg, Katie understood they could be overheard, and also understood he wanted to scare off anyone who might be listening to them.

"Oh, I would love to sit out there. I might even feel up to a little stroll. I am so full, I really could use a short walk, maybe out toward the road or back toward the bunkhouse, either way there is a nice view."

"Great, let's go out and see what looks good to us."

"I think our friend was scared away," Michael whispered. "I wasn't even sure he was here, but I heard a noise like someone running as we got up."

"Me too. I never would have noticed if we had not seen all that we saw today. I wonder how long he has been spying on me," she whispered back. "Oh, Michael, I am so glad you came when you did."

"It's hard to believe it was just this morning."

"No, it couldn't be just this morning? I can't believe how much has happened. I've changed so much. At least, I hope I've changed. Michael, I don't want to go back to that dark place where I have been. It was so awful. Will I ever go back there?"

"I don't know, Katie. Only God knows his plan for you. We do need to trust him and his plan. We know it is good. Remember what Jeremiah wrote? 'For I know the thoughts that I think toward you, saith the Lord, thoughts of peace and not of evil, to give you an expected end. Then shall ye call upon me, and ye shall go and pray unto me, and I will harken unto you. And you shall seek me and find me, when ye shall search for me with all your heart.'" He paused and looked up at the orange-and-red-streaked sky, a vision of God's fingers stretching out to touch them. Turning toward Katie, he smiled and said, "Let's walk toward the road. I think our visitor will be looking for us to walk toward the bunkhouse and will be listening."

"That sounds logical since I have said I love those hills and the sunsets. Let's do something entirely out of the ordinary. He will really have to run to catch up with us if we walk toward the road. Then he will risk being heard."

"If he tries to cut across the pasture, the horses are in there, and they will whinny and let us know. He won't risk that either. I think this will be safe. After you, Miss Katie."

"I just can't get over the fact that you arrived here just this morning. Can that much happen in so few hours? Can someone change in so short a time?"

"Yes, and yes."

"That's all you have to say?"

"Yes."

"Why?"

"I have to tell you some other things while we are alone. I am going into town tomorrow to see if I can hire some help. Yes, I have gotten what appears to be much done in the barn, and yes, it is a great deal better than it was. I believe you exaggerate about the condition when you arrived. However, in order to round up the cattle, brand the new ones, take the ones we want to sell to market and take care of all the rest of the ranch work, I am going to need help. In order to get that help, I am going to have to go looking for it because it doesn't just appear; it's not going to come looking for us. My concern is your safety while I am gone."

"Do you think he will know you are gone?"

"If he doesn't see me ride out, he will know within an hour or so when he doesn't see me working. He will be sneaking around looking in on you for sure, Katie. You will have to keep the doors locked. Don't go out to the privy. Use the inside slop jar and empty it after I get back. Get everything you need from the outbuildings this evening for whatever you are planning to do tomorrow. Don't do any work out of doors. Just stay locked in the house. Is that clear?"

"Yes, Michael. What if the house catches on fire?"

"Don't start playing 'what if' games in your head. The house won't catch on fire. Even if it does, don't you know by now that God is watching over you? He has you under his wings."

"I like that thought. He's just like the mama chicken keeping her chicks under her wings to hide them and keep them safe. I'll be just fine. I stayed in the house all winter with not a soul to talk to, except Ma of course. I talk to her picture and pretend I'm talking to her. Sometimes I can hear her talking to Abigail and me when we were little and telling us how to do things, or to behave, or giving us advice. It helped. Lately, I couldn't hear her voice anymore. All I could hear was my heart beating. I think I was going mad. I just wanted to die like everyone else. Why did I have to live?"

"God has something for you to do, and you haven't done it yet. It may be years from now that you will be faced with that task. Maybe he has more than one thing for you to do. It could be that what he has for you to do, you are doing, and it will take years to complete. Just know this; you will not die until it is completed. God never leaves a job undone or unfinished."

Katie let out a deep sigh and kicked a stone quite a distance down the lane. She shrugged her shoulders, looked at the sky, then over at Michael.

"Let's get on with it then. I'm tired of just sitting and waiting. It has been a long winter of loneliness. Michael, I've been wondering, how are we going to pay our hands if you can hire some?"

"Hands don't get paid right away. That will give us time to look for your pa's money while we continue to clean up. Hey, maybe that's why the floor was torn up in the bunkhouse. Red must be looking for the money.

"Red?"

"Yes, I just decided to call him that because of his red hair."

"That makes sense. Good choice."

"He must have heard you telling me about it this morning. While he was waiting for us to go out for our ride this afternoon, he decided to do a little searching on his own. So, I think we can rule out the bunkhouse. If he had found it, he wouldn't still be here. I think he went out first to see what he could hear. He wanted to find out if we had found the money or remembered where it was. If we hadn't, he would ambush us and then have free reign of the ranch and hunt all he wanted without any interruption from anyone. I'm beginning to get a better picture of what is going on in his head. I'm more worried about leaving you tomorrow, though. Maybe you should come with me to town."

"No, I don't think so, Michael. I feel like I should keep cleaning the house and get the dirt out of it and out of my head at the same time. I have so many things to deal with here. Besides, I'm not sure I'm ready to deal with the rejection I feel from the people in town. They don't like me very much. I don't understand why. I've never done anything to them. I don't really know them."

"All right, I'll go. You stay here. You promise to stay in the house no matter what?"

"Yes, I promise."

"Good. Let's get back to the house. Look at that sky, Katie. I love it when it gets all purple like that just after the sun goes down. Look at the stars. The moon is not very big so we will see hundreds of them tonight. Why don't we sit a while on the porch and enjoy the outside while we can? Red's probably doing some more hunting since he couldn't listen in on our conversation."

"I need to get the supper things put away and cleaned up, but I'll join you as soon as I can."

"I'll help you, then we can both enjoy it longer. I don't mind doing the dishes. I've had to do them plenty before."

"I really am amazed, Michael. I have never met anyone like you."

"I'd say I'd race you back to the house, but that would not be fair with your hurt leg, so we'll save that for some other time."

"Like it will be a fair race then. Just how long are your legs?"

"Same length as everybody else's. They reach from my hips to the ground."

With that they both laughed and walked back to the house. Michael kept his eyes on the trees lining the pasture by the bunkhouse. He was sure he could see a light shining through the trees every time the wind blew the branches a certain way.

Either the shutters weren't closed tight or "Red" was outside with a lantern doing something, digging perhaps? Michael thought to himself.

He would have to do some more investigating out there. He wanted to make sure Katie was safe inside the house first.

"Michael, do you want some coffee before you get back to work? I know you have more to do out in the barn. I looked at all you had gotten done earlier and could not believe the difference. You are right though, there is more to do. Do you need any bedding for tonight? Sheets, blankets, pillows?"

"Not tonight, Katie. Thanks. I have a nice little spot all fixed for my bedroll. I'll get a room fixed up later. But for now, I want to make sure all the animals are in their proper places. I have all the chickens back in the henhouse, I hope. I don't need any bird settin' on my head. We might still find some wandering around, though. If we do, we'll just get them put in with the others. The goats have gotten settled in the pen out back. The milk cow was good where she was. I guess you had been keeping up with her. I have a little more to do with the horses. I think it will take a while to get the mules taken care of, but I do have some plans for them. They look better than I thought they did—a little bit better. They aren't beyond repair. We will be able to use them when we round up the cattle. They can pull the chuck wagon."

"Well, if they aren't, I can just stay here, and your men will just have to come back to the house to eat."

"Right!"

They laughed together as they walked up the porch steps and entered the house. They washed up the dishes and then walked out on the porch. The night had deepened and cooled down. The stars were brilliant, and fireflies blinked in the trees lining the pastures and fields.

"I'll pass on the coffee. I really do need to get busy. You sure you want to stay here alone tomorrow?"

"I'm sure. How soon do you want to leave?"

"I'll head out right after breakfast and the chores are done. Katie, let me know what all you need to have done—wood brought in, water, anything like that. Remember, I don't want you to go out at all."

"Yes, I remember. I'll even use the slop jar. That reminds me of when Pa would always go to town. He would, without fail, use the outhouse. He would never use one in town for fear of having people pull a mean trick on him."

"That's not nice no matter where you live."

"No, it's not. Let's see, what do I need from outside? I have plenty of wood, but I know I will need water. I won't even be tempted to go out. Would it be all right for me to make a list of things I need from town? I would really like to get some seeds to plant so I can start the kitchen garden."

"Oh, of course. Does your father have an account at the general store?"

"I don't know. I think he always paid cash."

"That may be a problem. I'll see what I can do. I know the Lord will go before us and prepare the way. He went before the children of Israel as a cloud by day and a pillar of fire by night. He will do the same for us. Don't worry, he will take care of it. If there's anything else you need from there, just add it to the list and I'll get that from you in the morning. I'll go ahead and bring in some water, then lock up when I leave. I probably will work late and won't see you again tonight. Sleep well. God bless you, Katie."

"And you, Michael. Thank you, again."

"You are welcome."

CHAPTER 6

The pink light of morning kissed the golden hills, promising a beautiful day. The rooster lifted his voice, praising the glory of the morning and waking the rest of the world at the same time. Katie stretched and sighed, realizing her fingers didn't feel that old familiar tom-tom beat. Michael laughed and sang his own song of praise, Psalm 100.

The only sour note that could be heard on the whole ranch was heard by no one except a little gray mouse who scampered across the floor of the bunkhouse trying to hide from the evil that swore and just missed stepping on her as he arose from the bed he had pushed against the wall beneath the window facing the pasture. "Good, I don't see no movement yet. I'm up 'fore they is." He smiled and mentally gave himself a pat on the back. "Today is my lucky day. I just feel it!" he laughed.

Katie yawned and stretched again. "Gracious, I haven't slept like that in years. Ma would say, 'Not since you were a baby.' I don't think it has been that long. I could use a few more nights like that, though. Well, I need to get going and get breakfast started. I sure am glad I got that list made last night. My head feels like it is full of cobwebs this morning. I need coffee!"

Scurrying around taking care of all her needs before going downstairs, Katie looked like a squirrel chasing an acorn down a hill. She nearly flew down the stairs and came to an abrupt halt when she saw the stove was already hot with the coffee perking.

"Michael? Are you in here?"

"Yes, I came in the front door. I guess we forgot to lock it last night."

"I thought I did. Maybe I didn't. I'll be sure to put the bar over it today just to be sure. Thank you for the coffee. I need it this morning. My head feels really funny. How did you sleep?"

"Wonderful. I love the smell of hay. The animals make me feel so comfortable and give the air a very homey scent."

"Have you always lived in a barn?"

"I can't explain what I mean except that I love animals and have always been around them. They are very special to me," Michael replied.

"Don't misunderstand me, Michael, I like animals. I just don't want to sleep with them. They smell like, well let me see, they smell like animals. They smell like dirt and grass and whatever they eat and step in, if you get what I am talking about. They smell like mud and rotten things, like dead leaves and smashed mushrooms. I'd much rather smell clean sheets that smell like sunshine and the west wind that brings the fresh scent of spring on each breath it blows on the wash drying on the line. I like the smell of lilac and roses in a vase sweetening the fragrance in the room that chases away any moldy odor lurking in the corners or other dark places. I want to be where things smell bright and full of light; where I don't have to be afraid of the darkness hiding in my soul."

"I don't think you would have to be afraid of that if you were sleeping with the animals. There is no darkness there. Maybe to you there are unpleasant smells which make you think of unpleasant things or wrinkle your nose, but darkness? No, I don't sense any darkness, at least not the evil kind there."

"Well, I will sleep in my room for as long as I can. When it is time to 'hit the trail,' I will sleep where you think it is best, but I hope it is in the wagon and not on the ground."

"I'll keep that fact in mind. I brought another bucket of water in with me this morning. That should give you plenty. Do you have your list made? I need to get on the road soon before 'Red' gets wind of what's going on, if he hasn't already."

"Yes, here it is. These are the things I need from town in the order I need them. So, if you can't get all of it, just start at the top and stop when you can't get any more. I'll be happy with just the seeds. I really need to get that garden in. We, or I, need to get the soil ready. Ma and I used to do it. This is when I miss my sister and brother. We would have so much fun planting the garden. If you can find me a little brother and sister I'd really appreciate it."

"I'll see what I can do," smiling at her, he winked.

"I'll start breakfast. Thanks Michael, again, just for being here. I hadn't realized how lonely I had gotten. I don't think I would have made it through yesterday if you had not come. Thank you, too, for helping so much."

"You're welcome, Katie. It is truly a blessing to help you. I trust one day you will believe that."

She stared after him as the door bounced closed behind him. The room always seemed so empty once he left it. She felt it was not so much because of his size, however. He filled everywhere he went with more than his physical presence. She just didn't know what to call it.

"I better fix eggs today. I certainly have enough of them with what he gathered yesterday, and he will bring in more today. I'll make a pie today with meringue on top, a custard one. That will use some more eggs. Oh, maybe he can take some in and sell them at the general store. I'll ask him. That would give us some money. Oh, goody! Ma, that's a great idea, don't you think? You would have thought of that. Now, let's get busy."

She actually started singing as she worked. Michael was humming as he worked, too, but the man watching was scowling.

"Where did that giant come from and why don't he ride out? What business is it of his to be here? I need t'find out more 'bout him. I know 'bout her, but 'til I know 'bout him, I cain't do nothin' with her. I bet he's after th' money too. Well, he ain't gonna get it. It's mine. I'll find it or make her tell me where it is."

"Great breakfast, Katie. I'd like to stay and help you clean up, but I'd best be getting to town."

"I fixed a basket of eggs to take to the general store to see if Mr. Breland would buy them to sell. That way we could have a little 'egg money.' We really have more eggs than we can use. I tested all of these and they are good. What do you think?"

"I can take them and see."

"Good. Then I'll lock up and even bar the door after you are gone."

"Do the back door now. I have Solomon at the front door waiting. I brought him around this morning before I came in. I pray 'Red' didn't see him."

"Oh, all right. I thought he was still in the barn."

"Now, Katie. I'm not getting on Solomon until I hear the door lock and hear the bar go over the door. I want to know you are locked in."

"All right, all right. I'm locking."

She closed the door and barred it. Satisfied, Michael mounted Solomon and headed out to the road, holding the basket of eggs in one hand as he rode.

Michael moved slowly up the lane careful not to make much noise. He did not want to attract any attention should "Red" be up and listening. Maybe he would be hiding in the back and not see him go. It was worth a try to get away and let Katie be safe for an hour or so any way.

Katie moved to the kitchen area and began the clean up. It did not take long. Satisfied, she decided to go upstairs while it was cool and work up there cleaning the rooms.

"Red" stayed hidden behind the smokehouse waiting for someone to come out the back door. He was hoping it would be the "big guy" so he could keep an eye on him and know where he was. When he saw his chance, he could sneak in the house and get "Miss Katie" to tell him where the money is hidden. He was getting tired of hiding. He was still sore from crouching behind that boulder yesterday for hours waiting for them to come. He still couldn't figure out what had happened to them. "I heard 'em say sumthin' 'bout her leg las' night. Maybe she got herself hurt on they's way over ta that other arroyo and came on back instead. Yeah, that mus' be hit," he said to himself.

Michael made it out to the road and still had a feeling of peace. Solomon clomped along for about a quarter of a mile and suddenly picked up the pace without any indication from Michael.

"Okay, boy, let's ride, but don't break any of these eggs. Katie won't like that. God has provided them. Let's try not to destroy what the Lord provides, right?"

They made it into town more quickly than he thought they could. People were milling about and the general store was open. Michael's first stop was going to be there so he could sell the eggs before anything happened to them. If the general store didn't want them, maybe the hotel restaurant would. In his heart he felt he should leave the basket on the saddle horn. He lifted an eyebrow and did as he felt prompted. He casually walked into the Crystal Springs General Store and immediately heard a voice he did not like.

"Tad, I told you yesterday, the mail doesn't come in until the afternoon! Now quit botherin' me 'bout it. Come back just before supper time." The voice sounded irritated and much too loud for someone who caters to the public.

Michael couldn't hear the soft reply. He did see the young boy, about ten years old, standing in front of the counter looking up at the heavyset man glowering down at him.

Michael walked up to the counter, smiled and said, "Excuse me, do you buy eggs?"

"My, ain't you a big'un?"

Tad just stood with his feet planted in front of the counter, his mouth gaping.

"Yes sir, I've been told that. Now, about the eggs?"

"Well, I…"

"I bet my ma would buy them. She and my pa own the restaurant at the hotel."

Tad's bright eyes shone with an eagerness to help anyone and everyone he could. Michael knew he probably brought home every stray cat and dog he found.

"Now, Tad, your ma may not need eggs. She probably has all she can use."

"No sir, Ma was just saying she hoped she had enough for the crowd this morning. So, mister, if you want to come with me, I'm sure Ma will buy your eggs."

"Well, I will buy your eggs right now and pay you top dollar for them."

"How much would that be, Mr. Breland?"

"I'll pay you $.15 a dozen."

Tad's head fell forward and his shoulders slumped. He knew his mother could not pay that much for the eggs.

"Well, Mr. Breland, it seems you have made a sale. I have four dozen eggs I will sell to you. May I start an account for Miss

Katie Kurtz with $.45 of that money? I will take the other $.15 to her for her 'pen' money."

"Miss Katie Kurtz? Why? Her pa does all her shopping for her."

"I'm the foreman and I was told to start an account for her with her egg money. The rest is her business. Now, if you will excuse me, I'll go out and get the eggs. Tad, will you help me?"

"Sure, mister."

Michael and Tad walked out the front door as two ladies came in. Michael tipped his hat and nodded. He and Tad walked over to Solomon. Michael lifted down the basket of eggs.

"Hold out your shirt, Tad, so I can put the eggs in there."

"Why not just carry them in the basket?"

"Because I have five dozen eggs, not four and I want to give your ma a dozen eggs compliments of Mr. Breland. He paid more than they are worth just so your ma couldn't have them. The least I could do was to make sure your ma had a dozen she didn't have to pay for. He'll charge her more for the ones she does have to pay for. So, take these to her now. She's probably needing them. I'll take the rest in to Mr. Breland."

"But you told him you had four dozen when you had five dozen."

"Yes, I told him I had four dozen I would *sell to him*. I didn't tell him I brought in five dozen and would give the other dozen to your ma. Now take those to her before they hatch right there in your shirt." Michael almost laughed as Tad started to run then slowly walked across the street and down to the hotel.

Tad turned his head while he walked and yelled, "Thanks!"

"Be careful. Don't break any," Michael hollered back.

Tad then slowed down even more when Michael called after him. Michael laughed to see him.

As he came back in the store with the eggs, he heard Mr. Breland telling the two ladies the prices of seeds and thread.

"Hmm. Those are the top two items on Katie's list," he thought. He moved to the side aisle and looked at the thread and picked up what she needed and then to the back of the store to get the packages of seeds she wanted. When he came to the counter, the two ladies were just finishing with their purchases. Mr. Breland was all smiles and bid them a good day.

"Here are the eggs, sir, and here are some items Miss Kurtz needed."

"Well, let's see here. I'm not sure you will have enough credit to buy these items."

"What do you mean? The seeds are $.01 a package and the thread is $.02. There is plenty of money in the account and money left over. Unless you want me to call on the sheriff, Mr. Breland, I suggest you check your accounting practices. We made a deal. I don't take kindly to people who overcharge customers just because they feel like they have made a mistake in a bargain. It better not happen again to me or to Miss Kurtz if she comes in here. I'm beginning to understand why she didn't want to come. I want to see you mark this in your books, Mr. Breland, in ink. I also want you to date it and initial it, and so will I."

"That is highly irregular, sir. I don't allow customers to tell me how to run my business."

"This is Miss Kurtz's money you are holding, not your money. You will certify that you have been honest with it, or you will give me the cash and I will put it in the bank for her where it will gain some interest. I could just take it to her and then bring it back each time she needs something. Then you would not have it to invest and make money from in the meantime. It is to your advantage, Mr. Breland, for your customers to have accounts. Is it not?"

"Well, I see what you are saying. If you put it that way, then I guess we have an understanding, Mr., uh, I didn't get your name."

"I didn't give it."

"Oh, I see."

"The books, Mr. Breland."

"Here, $.45 minus $.12 leaves $.33. H.B. Now it is your turn to sign."

"MI"

"MI? It could be anything. Couldn't it?"

"Yes, Hector Breland, it could."

Michael turned and walked out the door leaving H.B. stunned. He had never told anyone in Crystal Springs his first name. How had this man known it? He had always been "Mr. Breland" or "H.B." No one knew what the "H" stood for. He would have to be careful around this man.

"Who is he?" Hector wondered.

———————

"Hey, mister, Ma wants you to come over to the restaurant to see her, please."

Tad was all smiles still. He was like a ray of sunshine on a gray and dismal day. That gave Michael an idea.

"Sure, I'd love to meet your ma."

They walked into the hotel, which was not grand by any means, but adequate and comfortable. The restaurant was off to the left, the desk straight ahead, and the stairs to the right of the desk. The red velvet chairs and settee were arranged around the lobby to give anyone arriving the feeling of coming into a homey living room.

Tad pulled on Michael's arm and led him over to the restaurant entry. The aromas wafting through the opening almost lifted Michael off his feet and carried him through.

"Wow, this is heavenly!"

"Ma is over there. C'mon." Tad grabbed Michael's hand and pulled him along.

"What do I smell?"

"Breakfast, I reckon. Ma, this is the 'mister.'" Tad poked his thumb back toward Michael who stood there with a big grin on his face.

"My name is Michael. I didn't get the opportunity to tell Tad that when we were discussing 'business' out on the street."

"Hello, I'm Esther Schmitt. I want to thank you for your gift this morning. It was such a surprise and a much-needed one as well. It came just as I cracked the last egg and wondered where I would get more. Mr. Breland always charges outrageous prices. I just can't afford him."

"Ma, can I go in the kitchen and see Miss Rose?"

"May I? Yes, you may. Don't get in her way, Tad, don't stay long. If you can help, fine, but if not, come right back out."

"Yes, ma'am."

Esther turned to Michael, "Rose is our cook. She has helped me out so much. After Tad was born, I couldn't do the cooking by myself anymore. I thank God for her, every day!" Esther looked toward the kitchen as if she had just wandered down a well-used yet very familiar trail. Suddenly, she shook herself. "I'm sorry. What were you saying, sir?"

"If you will allow me to help, I work at the Kurtz ranch, Mrs. Schmitt. Miss Kurtz has so many hens she is overrun with eggs. She would love to sell them to whoever needs them. If you would like to buy them, she is willing to sell them for whatever you can pay. What do you think is a fair price?"

"Well, I could pay $.10 a dozen. I know she got so much more from Mr. Breland, so I understand if she would rather sell to him."

"Mrs. Schmitt, Mr. Breland was doing that this morning just to make your son feel bad. He will not offer that price again. And believe me, I won't sell to him again, either. There is something else I would like to ask you. Do you need Tad here every day? Is he in school?"

"No, right now we don't have a school teacher. They are talking about getting another one. The last one married and got in the family way right away so they wouldn't let her teach any more. It wouldn't be decent for kids to see that, they say. Most kids see that at home every other year anyway, so what difference does it make I say, but nobody asked me. Tad just hangs around here or runs around town. He's a good boy so he doesn't get into trouble."

"Would you allow him to come and help out at the ranch? Miss Kurtz wondered if I could find someone younger who could help her plant the kitchen garden. I didn't think much of it at the time, but now, I think Tad would be perfect. We could pay him in eggs or milk that might be a better price than the money we mentioned."

"I'll say. I think he would enjoy having something to do that is productive as well."

"I'll bring in some eggs in the morning and pick him up, then bring him back later in the day. We will feed him. Don't worry about packing a lunch or anything. If he can help with some chores, too, that would be good. Maybe, Miss Kurtz can help him with his schooling during breaks. This could work out very well for all of us."

"Praise the Lord! I was beginning to worry about Tad. I don't want him to get behind in his schooling. His brother, Joshua will be home soon, any day really, and I was hoping he could help out with Tad. I don't know what Joshua will want to do though. I know working in the restaurant is not his cup of tea. He has been in the cavalry out west. He said he has had enough of that and wants to settle down."

"Would he be interested in ranching? I came in today to see about hiring some hands to help out with rounding up the cattle and branding the calves. We need to take them to San Antonio to sell."

"That sounds more like what he would like. He has been riding and living out of doors. He is an excellent shot and knows how to handle a horse. I'll send him out your way as soon as he arrives and have him talk with you. I'm surprised Mr. Kurtz isn't here doing this. He never sent his foreman in to hire before."

"Well, I'm taking care of it this year. Do you know of any others who need work? Maybe some of the older boys who aren't in school and don't have any work but could use some?"

"You might try the Tucker twins. They drive their ma crazy. I don't know if you would want them. Their parents live here in town. She sews and he is the blacksmith. The boys are about sixteen, I think, and they are really glad there is no school, but those boys need it. They should be finished but haven't gotten too far along yet. I think some cattle work would be good discipline for them. They can ride really well and are good around animals. They have helped their pa out some. If you want to put a sign up here by the door advertising, I'll sure let you do that."

"That's a great idea."

"I have some paper I wrap sandwiches in here behind the counter. You can use some of that. Here is a pen and ink. When you are finished, we'll hang it up on the other side where people coming into the hotel can see it too. There's a nail on that side that sticks out a little. I've been wanting Adam, he's my husband, to get his hammer and fix it, but maybe it's a good thing he hasn't done it yet. I've been afraid someone was going to catch a sleeve or something on it and tear a perfectly good shirt. In the meantime, we'll put that nail to good use.

"I can't tell you how thankful I am for all your help, Mrs. Schmitt."

"You are welcome, Mr....? I'm sorry. I don't remember your name."

"I don't think I told you. I apologize. My name is Michael."

"Thank you, Michael. Thank you for the eggs and for taking an interest in our son."

"He is a wonderful boy. You should be very proud of him."

"We are. He…"

"Ma! Guess what?" Tad ran in and broke into the conversation excitedly.

"Tad, you should never interrupt people when they are talking. You say 'excuse me' this instant, and say you are sorry."

"Excuse me, I'm sorry. Now, Ma, guess what."

"What?"

"Hi, mom," a voice behind her said.

"Joshua?"

"I was trying to tell you, Ma!" Tad exclaimed.

Joshua's arms were around his mother and hers were bound around him as if she had no intention of ever letting go. Tears of joy ran down her cheeks. She just barely managed to turn her head toward Tad.

"Go find your Pa. He's out back."

Michael caught her eye, nodded his head, and walked away. He was not about to interrupt this family reunion. He slipped the note on the nail and left. He would go and try to find the Tucker twins. They sounded like a good possibility to him as well.

Esther pulled back from her son and chuckled. "Josh, you are covered in dust. What did you do, ride all night?" Then she hugged him again.

"Yes, Ma, I did. I think Ranger wanted to get here as badly as I did." Josh spoke into her hair. "I have been telling him all about home and how much he would like it compared to the fort. He hasn't known anything else. I think he wants a change. He didn't mind me riding all night. It sure was cooler. The sky was so beautiful, and God seemed so near. I had a really good time talking with him, and he assured me he has something very special for me to do here, so I couldn't wait to get here to see what that was. So, what is it? Do I scramble eggs or boil them?"

Esther finally loosened her arms and looked him in the eye.

"Neither one, I think. I believe God wants you to do a little ranching, if you are willing."

"Ma, are you serious?"

"Yes, why?"

"Oh, you don't know how long I have dreamed of owning my own ranch. I have always wanted to be a rancher; I just didn't have the heart to tell you and Pa that the restaurant business is just not in my blood. I don't think less of you for loving it and making it your life's work. I just can't do it."

"How long have you wanted to be a rancher?"

"Ever since I was little."

The sound of footsteps caused them to look at the doorway as Josh's dad walked through with Tad right behind pushing.

"Hello, son!"

"Pa!"

Quickly walking over to his oldest son, Adam gave him a hardy one-armed hug and a firm handshake. Not letting Josh out of his grasp, Adam turned to Esther and smiled. "Let's move this 'party' upstairs sweetheart; I think we are getting in the way of our customers."

"That's an excellent idea."

Adam put his arm around Josh's shoulders and led the way. Tad jumped for joy as Esther talked with Liz, who was manning the register, to let her know what was going on. As they left, the room seemed to return to its normal routine. Michael's note hung on the nail. He had asked for anyone interested in ranch work to please inquire at the Kurtz ranch.

While the Schmitt's were getting reacquainted, Michael made his way over to the blacksmith shop to see if he could find Mr. Tucker. The sound of hammer clanging against metal on the anvil rang through the street as he approached the doors of the shop. He could just see the form of a large man lifting the hammer for another blow to the anvil. His arms were as large as some men's thighs.

I better stay on his good side. I don't want this man for an enemy. Michael thought to himself.

As he walked through the door, the smell of sulfur, sweat, and hot metal overwhelmed Michael's senses. He had to blink to keep his eyes from stinging and watering. The heat was nearly unbearable.

"Mr. Tucker?" Michael asked loudly so he could be heard over the noise.

"Yes sir, that would be me. What can I do for you?" Tucker turned and faced Michael. Resting his hands on his hips, he still clinched the hammer.

"My name is Michael. I was told that you have two boys who just might be needing some work. I'm looking for some help with rounding up cattle and branding the calves. I will probably need some help taking the cattle down to San Antonio to sell at the stockyards. I was wondering if your boys would be available to work."

Tucker took a minute to answer. He appeared to be thinking out loud, looking down at his feet. "Well, now. They don't have much 'sperience with ranching. They do ride well. They can rope some." He looked Michael in the eye and said, "They think they can rope well. But they think more highly of themselves than they should. They's climbin' fool's hill right now, and they's driving their ma to distraction. I try to keep 'em busy 'round here. To tell the truth, there ain't much here they can do. It's too dangerous for them. Quite honestly, that might be a real good idea for them, if you don't mind having to discipline 'em. Don't 'spect 'em to be men, 'cause they ain't. They's 'dentical twins and think it's real funny to play pranks on people about which one is which. Sometimes, even I have a hard time telling 'em apart."

"Well, Mr. Tucker, I think I can handle them, if they want to work. I don't want them if they don't want to work, so don't force them. Are they around? Can we talk with them?"

"Last I saw of 'em they's down by the river. They said they's goin' to go fishing. If you want to talk with 'em alone, that's fine with me. You might get a better response from 'em if I'm not there."

"With your permission then, I'll go find them. I guess I'll know who they are all right, since they look alike."

Michael shook Mr. Tucker's hand and left to get Solomon. Mr. Tucker looked after him for a minute, turned shaking his head, and went back to work.

After riding along the river for a short distance, he spotted one boy under a tree with his back leaning against the trunk. Two poles stuck in the ground and anchored with rocks angled toward the water. Suddenly, the line of one tightened, and the pole began to bend. A hand shot out from the side of the tree away from Michael, grabbed the pole, and then began to work the line so as not to lose the fish.

A real fisherman, Michael thought. He looked at Solomon, "Jesus would be proud. Now, I wonder if he will be as good with cattle? Let's go find out, shall we, Solomon?"

Michael rode quietly up to within a short distance of the tree, dismounted, and walked up. The boys were having a great time pulling in the fish, who was not coming in willingly. What fun to watch them play with the line and to see them try to keep the fish from breaking it. All too soon, the fight was over, and they had him on the bank, admiring him. They had won.

"Looks like you boys will eat well tonight," said Michael. "You did real well pulling that big boy in."

"Golly mister, you scared the pants offa us! Ya coulda let us know'd you was ther'."

"Sorry, I didn't realize you hadn't seen me watching you wrestle him to shore. He gave you a good fight. I'm proud of the way you handled that pole and line. It looks like you boys are real fishermen. Are you the Tucker twins?"

"Yeah, I mean, yes, sir. I'm Wade and this is Cade."

"Your pa said I'd probably find you down here. I asked him if he knew of any *men* who might be looking for work doing some cattle ranching. He said the two of you might be interested."

The two boys elbowed each other at the word "men" and puffed out their chests a little bit more than they had been. They looked at each other then back at Michael.

"Have you had any experience rounding up cattle and branding calves?"

"Not so much as ta say it's real experience. We've ridden horses and have gone out after a steer or two. I don't think we've ever branded anything. I haven't. Have you, Cade?"

"Nope."

Wade punched him in the ribs with his elbow, hard this time. Cade looked at him.

"I mean, no, sir, I haven't." He looked at Wade and scowled at him. The look spoke volumes—*Just wait; I'll get you later.*

"Well, it seems you are honest. Are you willing to learn and work hard?"

"Sure. Would we live at t'a ranch or live at home and ride back 'n forth?"

"You would live at the ranch. We have a bunkhouse and you will eat there as well."

Their elbows evidently were their main means of communication between the two as they made contact again with their ribs.

"We'd like ta give 'r a try, sir. We'll even fish ev'ry now and then if'n the misses would like some fresh fish for supper. We jest love ta fish!"

"I'm sure that will be fine. Miss Katie Kurtz will be doing the cooking. I'm sure she will be pleased with any contributions."

"Who's Katie Kurtz?"

"You will meet her when you come out to the ranch. I'd like for you to come out tomorrow morning first thing. Head north out of town about five miles, there is a large canyon to the east and then a valley. Just after you enter the valley, there is a lane on the west side of the road. Turn in there."

"The Randolph's ranch?"

"It may have been. It's the Kurtz's ranch now."

"Okay. We'll be there."

Michael turned to leave, and then turned back around.

"You didn't ask about pay."

"Oh, whatever is fine. We're jest gettin' away from home! Ya-hoo!"

Michael turned quickly away so they wouldn't see his smile. He waited until he was far enough away before he burst out laughing at the boys, or maybe he was laughing with them; he wasn't sure which.

"Lord, you are amazing. Three hands and it isn't even noon. That may be enough to start with tomorrow. I feel like I need to get back and see about getting something done about Red. The bunkhouse has to be cleaned up. We have guests coming tomorrow."

CHAPTER 7

"Red" glared at the house. His fists clinched. The muscle in his jaw tightened. "He sure is spendin' gobs a time in the house this mornin'. Maybe I could sneak out to the barn and look through his thangs so's I could get an idea of who he is."

"Red" snuck his way around the field and behind the stand of trees, then back of the bunkhouse. Keeping the trees and barn between him and the house, he made his way across the pasture to the barn, where he entered by the back door.

"I'd best keep low, so's he don't see me if he comes in. I hate gettin' in these places where I feel trapped. Wonder where he keeps his thangs."

The smell of sweet hay contrasted with the pungent odor of the sweat and dirt clinging to "Red's" body and clothing. He squinted after being out in the sun, and his eyes adjusted to the darkness of the inside. He didn't see anything that looked like a room.

"Ma'be his stayin' in the house. Na' I could'a swore he's sleepin' out cher'. I'll find it."

He reached the end of the row of stalls and finally saw what he was looking for. The last stall looked like a cozy campsite rather than an animal stall. Nothing was there of a personal nature, just blankets, a pillow, and a lantern which was placed up on a small barrel.

"Where's his saddlebags? For that matter, where's his horse?"

"Red" looked out in the pasture where the other horses were. He had been so busy sneaking to the barn earlier, he had not even looked at the horses. Now, he did look and did not see the big chestnut.

"Saddle isn't here either. Where is he then?"

He looked out the crack between the front doors of the barn but didn't see any horse in front of the house. He moved to the back of the barn again and headed left moving around the goat pen to get a good look at the back of the house. The horse still wasn't there.

"When the devil did he leave and where'd he go? I bet I could march right into that house and get little missy to tell me in no time. I could get 'er to tell me more 'an 'at."

Feeling braver than ever, "Red" decided now was the time to act.

Katie had cleaned everything up from breakfast and had barred the doors. She had promised and had followed through with that promise.

Katie lovingly picked up the picture of her mother, stroked the sepia cheek and smiled. "What should I clean first today, Ma? I should clean my room, I guess, but I really don't want to do it yet. I think I'd like to do the two extra bedrooms upstairs. They aren't as personal, and maybe I won't feel any of those dark feelings I get when I'm alone and start thinking about the past. I'll just be cleaning."

With that settled in her mind, Katie took what she needed upstairs and opened the doors to the rooms across the hall from hers. The musty smell caused her to cough, and the dust made her sneeze.

"I think I'd better crack a window. It will be okay up here. I won't open them wide and nobody will see them. I can do the same with my window and create a cross breeze to help air this mess out. My, I don't know if I can breathe up here. I may have to go downstairs and bake something while it airs out a bit."

Having decided that was the only thing to do, Katie started the airing out process then headed downstairs to the kitchen. She started a batch of cookies. Those were always good to have on hand. They were quick and easy to make and would fill the house with a wonderful welcoming aroma for when Michael returned. She could picture him eating almost all of them at one time.

By the time she was finished, she was humming a tune.

"What fun! I haven't done this in so long, Ma; I had forgotten how much fun it was to bake cookies. Mmm, they are so good! I need to get away from them or Michael won't have any to eat."

Again, she tenderly ran her finger down her mother's cheek as she passed the picture, then gathered her skirts in her hand and began to climb the stairs.

She paused a moment with her foot poised just above the top step, her left hand gripping the rail. Her heart began to pound against her ribs. Panic seized her. There was no mistake. She heard footsteps in the room to her left. She turned and ran down the stairs, almost falling as her foot caught on the hem of her skirt. She caught herself with her hand on the rail and the other on the wall.

"I'll get you!" he yelled. She heard the hard clomp of boots on the stairs behind her. She knew it was "Red."

Katie grabbed the bar off the door in the kitchen and swung around with it, hitting him beside the head. He staggered back, holding his head, giving her time to unlock the door and run outside.

She reached the yard and had turned toward the barn when a hand grabbed her hair, yanking her head back, and another hand tightened around her neck.

Am I going to die now that I don't want to? she wondered. *God, please don't let him hurt me*, she prayed.

"Red" let go of her hair, gripped her around her waist, and dragged her over to the barn. He slammed her against the side of the barn, causing her vision to darken and sparkling lights similar to fireflies to dance in front of her. She thought she would faint. With his hand still around her throat pressing her tightly against the rough wood, "Red" moved his face inches from hers. She feared he would kiss her. His breath reeked as badly as his body.

Save me dear Eternal One, God of Abraham, Isaac, and Jacob, she prayed over and over.

"Where's it?" he uttered menacingly.

"Where is what?" she asked breathlessly, hardly able to speak.

His hand tightened around her throat.

"You know what I'm talkin' 'bout, the money! Quit playin' games, or I'll kill ya. Then I'll have tha run o'th place."

He took out his knife and moved it toward her neck.

"I don't know." She barely got out before she fainted, sliding down the rough surface of the barn wall to the ground.

Cursing, he swung around to go back to the house just as a fist connected with his jaw.

CHAPTER 8

"Katie, Katie. Come on, Katie, wake up."

Michael wrung out the wet cloth and placed it on her forehead again. He walked over to the window to check on "Red." He was still tied to the tree by the smokehouse with Solomon tied near him. Solomon would let Michael know if something out of the ordinary happened. His horse was good about that. He walked back over to Katie.

Lord, the bruises on her neck look worse by the minute. Maybe I should take her to the doctor in town. What if he cracked her skull? I don't know what all he did to her. What should I do, Lord? I know what I want to do. I want to go out there and beat the living daylights out of him. I need to get him to the sheriff. Help me know what to do first.

Michael dropped his head into his hands, and then with a deep sigh lifted his eyes to her face.

"Katie, I'm going to take you to town. I have to get you to the doctor and 'Red' to the sheriff so the law can take care of him. I don't even know if you can hear me, but I'm going to go out to the barn and hitch up the wagon and fix you a bed in the back, so the trip will be more comfortable. I'll hog-tie him and keep him far away from you. You won't have anything to fear, I promise. I'll be back real soon."

Michael moved quickly out of the house and over to the barn. He gave a glance over his shoulder at "Red," who was still unconscious and tied to the tree.

"Maybe I shouldn't have hit him so hard. Yes, I should have. Maybe I didn't hit him hard enough!" he muttered as he walked away.

Michael made his way out to the barn, kicking up dirt as he went. He quickly hitched the horses to the wagon, stacked some sweet hay right behind the seat, and rigged an awning of sorts under which to lay Katie to keep her out of the sun as they traveled into town. "Red" could just burn in the back.

Inside the house again, he spoke to the still-sleeping woman as he picked her up and started carrying her to the wagon. "C'mon Katie, I'm going to get you situated in the back of the wagon behind me. There's sweet hay to sleep on and a cover to keep the sun off. Please wake up. You really have me careworn." He gently lowered her onto the hay. "I know the Lord has a plan; he just hasn't told me what it is yet."

Michael left her for half a minute to go and get "Red." He didn't treat him nearly as gently. He just hefted him up over his shoulder and dumped him in the back of the wagon. He tied his hands and feet to the sides and made sure he was secure, including his mouth. He didn't want "Red" saying anything that Katie might hear.

He decided to tie Solomon to the back of the wagon and take him with him to town. That way if he needed to leave the wagon over night, he could ride back to the ranch quickly to take care of the stock. Maybe he could ask Joshua to come out and help him. Together they could get the bunkhouse repaired, cleaned up, or whatever it needed done to be ready for when the others came tomorrow.

"I'll have to wait and see what the doc has to say. I'll take "Red" to the sheriff first and get him off my hands, then take

Katie to the doc. I'll see how long he thinks he will take, and then I can go see about Joshua." Michael kept up this running dialogue with himself. It helped him keep his plans in order when he heard his own voice. Then, he changed the direction of his conversation.

"Lord, help me to have wisdom. I just can't seem to keep my mind straight. I thank you for bringing me back sooner than I had intended to come. I marvel at your mighty ways and your excellent greatness. Keep your healing hand on Katie, dear Father. She does not know you yet. She understands the Eternal God, but not Abba Father. Oh, how I long for her to know you in that way. Open her heart to you, dear Lord. Take the darkness from her soul and mind and give her the light of your son. In Jesus' name, amen."

Michael began singing a psalm of praise as he drove into town—his favorite Psalm 148:

> Praise ye the Lord. Praise ye the Lord from the heavens:
> Praise him in the heights.
> Praise ye him, all his angels: Praise ye him, all his hosts.
> Praise ye him, sun and moon: Praise him, all ye stars of light.
> Praise him, ye heavens of heavens, and ye waters that be above the heavens.
> Let them praise the name of the Lord: For he commanded, and they were created.
> He hath also 'stablished them for ever and ever: He hath made a decree which shall not pass.
> Praise the Lord from the earth, ye dragons, and all deeps:
> Fire, and Hail; snow, and vapours; stormy wind fulfilling his word:
> Mountains, and all hills; fruitful trees, and all cedars:
> Beasts, and all cattle; creeping things, and flying fowl:
> Kings of the earth, and all people; princes, and all judges of the earth:

Both young men, and maidens; old men, and children:
Let them praise the name of the Lord: for his name alone
is excellent; his glory is above the earth and heaven.
He also exalteth the horn of his people, the praise of all
his saints; even of the children of Israel, a people near
unto him; Praise ye the Lord.

CHAPTER 9

he blackness covered Katie. She couldn't see anything. She was in a void. Was she floating, standing, sitting? She couldn't tell.

"Mama, where am I? Mama, are you here?" she whispered.

There was no reply. Her throat hurt. Her head hurt. All she could remember was "Red" and the fear of his hand around her throat cutting off her air. She did not want to die. If this had happened the day before yesterday, she would have welcomed it. Yesterday changed everything. Michael changed everything. She had changed.

"Ma, this blackness is different. It isn't full of horrors. It's nothing. What is it?" Her whispered voice could only be heard by the sweet hay next to her mouth.

"My child, you must find the light. Follow my voice, I am the Good Shepherd. My sheep know my voice."

"I know nothing of sheep."

"You will."

"How will I know?"

"Listen to Michael and those that I send."

"Michael is good. I like Michael. He helps me and is kind."

"Yes, he is. I sent him to you. Sleep now. You need the rest. You have a long and hard journey ahead."

"Where am I going?"

"Not far, but farther than you have ever been. Now sleep."

"Yes, yes, I will."

———

Michael slowed the wagon as he came into town, pleased to find Tad there as if he'd been sent to watch for them.

"Whoa!"

"Mr. Michael, what happened?"

"Tad, run, get your brother and your ma if she's free to come, please. Quickly!"

Dust and dirt flew from the back of Tad's heels as he raced to the hotel. His hat landed in the street behind him. Not stopping to pick it up, he ran straight up the steps and into the lobby, letting the doors slam behind him. Michael stopped the wagon in front of the sheriff's office and tied the horses to the hitching post.

Joshua was crossing the street by the time Michael finished tying the team. Tad was right on his heels, his hat now back on his head.

"Tad, can you run in and get the sheriff?"

Joshua looked at the big man beside him and at the man tied to the wagon, then at the woman under the canopy at the front of the wagon. She seemed to be resting comfortably, but something didn't appear quite right. She was young and beautiful. Why would she be sleeping like that in the middle of the day?

"What can I do to help you?"

"Thanks for coming right over. I really need your help in so many ways. First, I need to get..."

"Okay, what's going on here?" Brian Daniels asked as he came out the door with an excited Tad pulling on his arm.

Michael looked up and almost laughed, but decided that would not be the appropriate response. The sheriff was in his early thirties and needed to be treated with respect.

"Tad, quit pulling on the sheriff." Joshua said looking sternly at his little brother.

Tad dropped Sheriff Daniels' arm and meekly whispered, "Yes, Joshua."

"Sir, this man attacked Miss Katie Kurtz at her ranch around noon or just before. He was choking her as I rode back in from town. I saw him over by the barn but couldn't see her because he was between us. I was sneaking up on him just as I saw her fall to the ground.

"He has been causing all kinds of mischief out there and we just haven't been able to catch him. She was going to stay locked up safe in the house while I was gone to town this morning. He must have gotten in one of the upstairs windows. I saw the curtains blowing in the breeze as I rode up; that was what made me a little more cautious in my approach. Otherwise, he would have heard me. I think I hit him a little too hard, maybe."

Brian looked down at "Red" then back at Michael. "Maybe, maybe not. This is a wanted man. Did you know that?"

"No. We didn't know who he was. We've only seen him from a distance. We've been calling him 'Red' because of his red hair."

"Funny, that's what he goes by, Red Galliger. There's a reward. I'll wire the marshal and we'll get this taken care of. The country will be much safer with him locked up. You fellas want to help me get him in the jail?"

"Sure," Joshua and Michael chorused together. They looked at each other then smiled. They helped carry Red in while Tad stayed out with Katie.

"Well, that will take one burden off Katie's mind. Where's the doc's office? As soon as ole' Red's packed away in his cell, I want to get Katie over there and have him look her over. She just won't wake up. I hope he hasn't done something permanently damaging to her."

Joshua looked at Michael. "She may be in some sort of shock over what happened and just doesn't want to face what may be waiting for her if she opens her eyes."

"I hope that's all it is."

Michael untied the horses, and they began to lead them down the street toward Doc McConnell's office. Tad rode in the wagon holding Katie's hand. He whispered to her as they went.

"Have you seen much of that in the army?" Michael asked Joshua.

"More than I'd care to see. Not just settlers either. I can't say I'm very pleased with what I saw happening with what's being done to the Indians. God would not be pleased, in my opinion. I felt it was better to leave the army than end up in the brig. I can do more good here."

"Joshua, I came to ask you if you wanted to work on the ranch. I sure could use the help. I talked with your mother this morning. I know you just arrived back and probably don't want to leave your family again right away. You may not even want to work on a ranch, but I'd appreciate it if you would give it some prayer and thought."

"Michael, I told my folks almost immediately that I wanted to find work on a ranch. This is an answer to prayer. In fact, someday I want to own a ranch. It's been my dream since I was Tad's age. Ah, here we are. Looks like Doc's buggy is here. That's a good sign."

"I think that I'll get him first and see if he wants us to move her."

"Michael, I don't think he is going to want to examine her in the wagon. That's not very private. Look, you go get him and tell him what happened, and I'll get her out of the wagon. It will save time."

The look in Michael's eyes warned him to be careful.

"Don't worry; I'll be as gentle with her as Jesus with a baby lamb."

"See that you are."

With that, Michael turned and disappeared into the shadows of the doctor's office.

Tad scooted around in order to help his brother. Joshua very gently grabbed the edges of the blanket on which Katie lay. He pulled her slowly toward the back of the wagon while Tad pushed the sweet hay underneath along with her. As the sun hit her face, a slight smile crept across Katie's face.

"Wow, what a beautiful woman. I don't think I've ever seen anyone this beautiful before in my life," Joshua sighed to himself.

As Joshua lifted Katie, he felt a tingling sensation travel up his arm and straight to his heart. He carried her very carefully into the doctor's office where he was met by both Michael and Doc McConnell.

"Bring her in here, Josh. Just put her on this table here, and then you boys skedaddle. I'll be done in fifteen to twenty minutes. I may need your ma, Josh. Will you go and get her for me?"

"Sure, Doc."

"Thanks."

As the men left, Doc leaned over Katie and looked at the angry marks on her neck. The bruises were dark and were obviously made by a hand. The outline of the fingers could be seen. He turned her head to see the back of her neck and saw some scratches or scrapes that had bled. They weren't deep and had stopped some time ago. They looked like they had been made by wood.

"Looks like there might be a splinter in this one. I'll have to get my magnifying glass and look more closely at it."

He was so focused on Katie he didn't hear Esther come in.

"Talking to yourself again, Doc?"

"Esther, thanks for coming right over."

"Joshua told me Katie Kurtz had been attacked. I knew you'd need me."

"I hope it's not any more serious than this choking. That's bad enough. She is a pretty little thing, isn't she?" he glanced at Esther and looked back at Katie.

Esther looked lovingly down at her. "I don't think I've seen her in years. Not since they first moved here; it must be four years ago now. I wonder why? My fault, I guess. I just got busy and never went out to visit. Well, here, let me help get her dress loosened for you."

All Katie could feel was gentleness. She could hear soothing sounds and had a sense of caring all about her. She felt no fear, and she slept on. She didn't want to awaken.

"Praise God, he did not hurt her."

Tears were running down Esther's cheeks. For reasons she could not explain, she felt responsible for Katie. She loved her instantly as a mother would her own daughter and wanted to care for her in that way. She longed to lavish her with all the things mothers want to give daughters. The little girls she had lost as babies would be about Katie's age.

"I wonder where her mother is. Why did she not come with her?" Esther asked.

"I hadn't even stopped to think about that. It does seem odd though, doesn't it? They've always been loners, but it's not like folks not to come in with their child when she's hurt."

"I need to ask Michael about this."

"Wait, Esther, let me try to wake her with smelling salts while you're here. I'd rather have a woman present if she does wake up."

"All right, but hurry, I'm dying of curiosity."

"Now, settle down, Esther. All good things come to him who waits. You'll get your answers soon enough. Let's take care of this matter now. Isn't a human being more important than soothing your curiosity?"

"Yes, Doc. Thank you for your reproach. I need correction every now and then, but my curiosity is still eating me up. I'll exercise patience however hard that will be."

They laughed together as Doc retrieved the smelling salts from his cabinet and opened them under Katie's nose. She breathed in and instantly jerked her head away.

Yuck! she thought.

He did it again. This time her eyes fluttered and she opened them jerking her head to the side away from the smell again.

"Oooo, take that away," she whispered. Her voice was very weak.

"She's going to need some tea and some lemon if we can find any."

"The only lemons I can think of are in the form of lemon drops over at the general store. I could send Tad over for them, but I don't think we'll get all of them back."

"Well, it'd be worth the reward for him. He's been a big help today. He's a wonderful boy. You've done a great job with both your sons, Esther."

"I wish I had had more. God's will be done. He knows best. The other little ones are waiting for me in heaven. I'll see them there."

"I know you will. I'm sorry you had such a hard time. The two you have are fine jewels in your crown."

"Thank you, Doc."

"Where am I?" whispered Katie.

"Oh, I'm sorry. I'm Esther Schmitt, and this is Doc McConnell. Michael brought you in to town because you were hurt. The doctor was looking you over to see to your injuries, and I was helping him. How are you feeling?"

"Um, I'm not sure. My voice feels funny. I can't talk out loud."

"I put some salve on the scratches on the back of your head, neck, and back. There were some splinters in them and I removed those. The bruises around your neck will go away in time. You will need to drink plenty of hot liquids. Tea will be best with honey and ginger in it if you have any. You can also suck on some lemon drops since we don't have any lemons up here yet. They grow them down by the coast, but it is too early yet. We may get some in a month or two, but by then, we trust you will be all healed. I think you are going to be sore for a few days, maybe even a week. It looks like you hit the wall of the barn or house pretty hard."

Katie gasped. "Oh, I remember. "Red" was in the house. I ran to get away from him. I got outside, but he caught up to me and grabbed me by the hair, pulled my head back, and then started choking me. He pulled me over to the barn and pushed me against the wall. He asked me a question and I didn't know the answer, so he pushed harder against my throat...I fainted I guess, because I don't remember anything else."

Katie started shaking.

"It's all right now. He's in jail."

"He is?" Eyes wide, Katie looked from Doc to Esther.

"Yes, Michael brought him in when he brought you in. You don't have to worry about him anymore."

"I don't understand. Michael was in town. How did he know?"

Esther took her hand and soothingly rubbed the back of it. "He will have to explain all that to you. Right now, I think the best thing for you to do is to rest. I'm going over to the restaurant and get you some nice tea. I'll send Tad for some lemon drops. He is my littlest son. Josh is our oldest. I lost two girls as babies."

"Please, I can't, uh, I don't, uh..."

"I own the restaurant, Katie. Don't worry about paying for anything. I know you didn't bring your money with you. I wouldn't charge you for it even if you did. What kind of charity would that be? Jesus wouldn't want that from me. He would want me to love you, and that is all I feel toward you anyway. I love you, dear, with the love of Jesus. You are just as precious to me as any child of God in need."

As Esther hurriedly left Doc's office, she hoped she had not said too much. She tended to do that.

"Did I open my big mouth again, Lord? Why can't I keep silent until I check with you? Well, it's too late now. I told her I love her and that's that."

She lifted her skirts to avoid the hazards of walking across the roads, careful not to show too much ankle. She quickly climbed up the steps and into the restaurant. Adam met her.

"What's happening? Why did all of you leave in such a hurry without a word?"

"So much…Katie Kurtz was attacked by a man who tried to choke her. She should be fine in a few days, physically anyway. I need to take her some tea for her throat, and Tad needs to go get some lemon drops from the general store for her. Do you know where he is? I need to ask Michael a question too."

"Slow down, honey, you'll run over yourself. You get the tea. I'll take care of the lemon drops, that will be faster than finding Tad. I'll also tell Michael you need to see him as soon as you deliver the tea to Doc's. He may be over there by now anyway. I saw him go over to the sheriff's. I'll meet you at Doc's with the lemon drops. Okay?"

"You are a love! I thank God every day for you, Adam. Thank you."

"You can't mean it, sheriff." Michael shook his head and ran his fingers through his thick, dark hair. "He's wanted for murder? His name really is Red? We didn't know his name and just called him that because of his red hair. He first came by the ranch and scared Miss Kurtz a few weeks before I arrived. She bluffed him into thinking her parents were out back. They were actually out back, but that's because they're buried there. They both died this past fall within weeks of each other, and Katie has been all alone since then. When I arrived, she was on the brink of despair. I truly think she was about to die from loneliness. She was grieving and had seen no one for nearly six months, except for that one encounter with Red. I really do not know how she did it."

"She was all alone all that time?" The sheriff's voice took on an angry tone. "How did the town let this happen? I want to know. Have we gotten so callous and self-centered that we don't even notice when someone doesn't come to town in months? We didn't even think of them at Christmas?"

"Well, since they didn't attend church, I could see why people might not think of them at Christmas." Michael interrupted.

"Why not? They think of the poor who don't attend church. They take them food baskets and clothing and show the love of Christ to them, why not the Kurtzs?"

"How long have you been here, Sheriff?"

"Only a couple of years. I admit I didn't know the Kurtzs at all. I don't think I ever saw them. He might have come into town occasionally, but I don't think I noticed him, if I saw him. That's a sad commentary on my ability as a lawman. I should know everyone here and notice everyone. I'm going to have to do better."

"Don't be too hard on yourself. I get the impression from Katie that her pa wasn't the kind of man who would stand out and that he didn't want to be noticed. What he wanted was to be left alone. People usually ignored the Kurtzs or gave them a hard time. That's why the Mrs. and Katie didn't come into town much. Katie hated coming to town."

Just then a shadow darkened the sunlight coming through the doorway. "Excuse me, Sheriff, this wire came for you."

"Thanks, Horst."

"Afternoon, Sheriff. I got to get back to the telegraph."

"Afternoon, Horst …and thanks, again." He unfolded the telegram, read it, then looked up at Michael. "Well, this says, the marshal has wired the bank to release the reward money. So, I can go and collect it for you today. How does $100 sound to you about now?"

"One Hundred dollars? I never dreamed it would be that much! Wow! Now, Katie doesn't have to worry about finding her pa's money."

"What do you mean?"

"He hid his money somewhere on the ranch. I guess Red found out about it. Maybe eavesdropping on us, he heard her telling me about it. We'll have to ask him. Anyway, he's been looking for it, and I think that's why he attacked her. He wanted her to tell him where it is. Only thing is, she doesn't know. Her pa didn't tell anyone before he died. If he gave any clues, she doesn't recognize them for that. Maybe with Red out of the way and the reward money to help ease her mind, she can remember things he said or did. The Lord will tell us when it's time."

The sheriff nodded in agreement. "I'll go over to the bank. You want to come with me?"

"No, I want to go over to Doc's and see if he's finished with her yet and can tell me anything about her condition. I hope she wakes up soon."

"We'll add attempted murder to the charges Red already has against him. He won't get out of jail. In fact, assuming he's found guilty, which I'm pretty sure he will be, he'll probably hang for those murder charges."

"Where will his trial be?"

"Austin."

"You have to take him?"

"No, the marshal will send a couple of rangers to haul him up there."

"Good. That's a job I wouldn't want. I'll see you later, Sheriff."

"Hey, Michael, call me Brian when it's just you and me, okay?"

"You've got it!"

"See ya in a bit, as soon as I'm finished at the bank."

"I'll be at Doc's. Hey, Brian, don't say anything about Katie's folks to anyone yet, okay? She needs to be the one to make that decision. I only told you because it related to what happened. She's safer if there are hard feelings toward the family, and people think she has her parents still living out there."

"I see what you mean. I'll keep it under my hat."

CHAPTER 10

Michael crossed the distance to Doc's faster than a jackrabbit chasing a doe in heat. He knocked at the door and then walked into the waiting room. As his eyes adjusted to the darkness inside the room, he said a brief prayer.

Lord, help Katie to see your light and your glory in all things. Help her to feel your protection and your comfort. Help me and those around her to give her the love and support she needs. Surround her with your tender mercies. In your name I pray, amen.

The door to the examining room opened, and Doc McConnell stepped out.

"Well, you're here just in time. I was about to send out a search party." He laughed as he said it.

"There's a little lady in here who would very much like to see you."

A huge weight lifted off of Michael's shoulders. With those words, he knew Katie would be back to normal in no time. He quickly stepped through the door and saw her sitting in a chair over by a window. There was a chair next to her. She patted it with her hand and smiled.

"Come sit here." She barely spoke above a whisper. "I'm waiting on my tea."

"When will the servants be back?"

"Any time now." She held her chin up and gave a very regal look at him.

He laughed.

"You make a very good queen. How are you feeling, your highness?"

"My throat's very sore. The doctor says it's bruised. I need to rest it, drink plenty of tea, and suck on lemon drops. Sounds like really 'bad' medicine to me."

"I might have to have a sore throat, too, if I can have lemon drops."

Katie's expression became serious. "Michael," she asked, her brow furrowed, "Is Red really in jail?"

"Absolutely, Katie, you're safe from him. Oh, that reminds me. The doc may need to go and see him. Red's just starting to wake up from the hit I gave him. He'll probably have a pretty bad headache."

Katie scowled. "I hope he does. He should have worse. He tried to kill me! Oh, he scared me so much. I can't believe he came in upstairs! How did he get up there?"

"He used a ladder to climb up on the porch roof and from there it's not hard at all to climb in any of the windows upstairs, especially if they're not locked."

"Where did he get a ladder?"

"There was a ladder in the barn and another one in the shed. He could have gotten either of those. He put it up on the south side of the house away from the kitchen. If you were in there, you probably would not have heard him lean it up against the porch roof. Then it was just a matter of climbing up and opening up one of the windows that wasn't locked. He found one and climbed in. Fortunately, you heard him and made it outside before he caught you. Otherwise, I wouldn't have known he was there. When I rode into the lane, I saw curtains flying out the windows on the second floor of the house. I thought that was strange, so I slowed down and began looking around. Red was over by the barn, but I couldn't see you. I couldn't figure out what he was doing. He was very intent on it, though, and he didn't hear me. When I got up right behind him, I saw you fall. That was when you fainted, Katie. He turned, and I hit him, hard. I wanted to beat the pulp out of him, but since one punch knocked him out, I didn't."

Katie's eyes twinkled. "Hmm, I wonder how one of your punches could knock out someone? You are so small and weak. Michael, seriously, have you ever had to hit anyone more than once?"

"I reckon not." Michael looked at his hat, turned it in his hands, and studied it like it was a scientific experiment of great importance. He looked back at Katie, took a deep breath, then asked, "The sheriff, Brian Daniels, do you know him?"

"No."

"He didn't remember meeting you or any of your family either, Katie….I had to tell him your parents are dead so he'd know the background of Red and you, why he was there and all. I hope you don't mind, Katie. I told him not to tell anyone. Telling people needs to be your decision."

"I see." She sat in silence for a few moments thinking. "I don't know why I don't want people to know. I just feel funny about it. Almost like well, they didn't care while they were alive, if they were alive; why should they care if they are dead?"

Michael ached for her hurt. "It might mean something to some people but nothing to others. You can't keep it a secret for long. Joshua will be coming out to the ranch to work, and so will Tad. Tad's going to help you with the kitchen garden and any other chores you have for him. He also needs help with his schooling. There isn't a schoolmarm here now, so school has been closed. In exchange for his work, I bargained your teaching him and feeding him lunch."

"That will be such fun! I'll really enjoy having a youngster around. How old is he?" Katie asked in a very weak, gravely voice.

"He's ten. He is also full of energy. His parents own the hotel and restaurant. His mom was here earlier and helped the doc." Michael fought the urge to "help" Katie by clearing his voice when it wasn't even his that needed it.

"Oh, I thought she was an angel! What a sweet woman. I suppose it would be hard to keep Ma and Pa's deaths a secret from them with Tad working right there next to their graves. That would be kind of obvious, wouldn't it? If they asked him about my parents, I couldn't ask him to lie." Katie paused, thinking, and then continued. "I should tell them. I just don't want it to become the big gossip of the town. You know what I mean. 'Oh look, there's poor Katie Kurtz. Did you hear? Both her parents died and left her penniless. Poor child, she'll probably have to marry the first old codger who will have her. What else can she do that isn't immoral?'"

Michael smiled, "I don't think you need to worry about that. You do need to rest that voice. I can barely hear you. I don't want you to worry about money. Red did help us in that way. It seems he has a price on his head. So, we get a reward for his capture. I think I'll open a bank account for you, though, instead of keeping the money at the ranch."

"No, Pa didn't trust banks. He would not want me to keep the money in the bank. It can't be that much anyway."

Michael smiled bigger this time. "I'm glad you're sitting. It's $100."

"No! Michael, you can't be serious. They don't offer rewards like that for people unless they are really bad."

Michael sobered. "I know."

"Are you saying Red is really bad?"

"He's wanted for murder, I think more than one. They were probably committed while doing other things like bank robbery or holding up a train. Who knows? He is a bad one. The sheriff's over at the bank now getting the money that's been authorized by the marshal's office. I'd feel better if we weren't carrying it around with us. Are you sure you don't want to put some of it in the bank?"

"Oh, I don't know." Katie was wringing her hands and twisting the skirt of her dress. "I just don't have enough experience with all this. Why did Pa have to die? Why did all this have to happen? I want to go back to sleep. It was so nice and calm. I didn't have to face all this." Katie turned away to look out the window. The sound of footsteps from the waiting room brought her head back around as she looked to see who was coming. Tears were pooling on her bottom eyelid.

"Knock, knock, can I come in? I've brought some hot tea and some lemon drops."

Somewhat relieved at the interruption, Michael took a deep breath and answered, "Yes, Mrs. Schmitt. How kind of you. Just in time. I think Miss Kurtz's in need of a nice cup of tea."

"Is she? Well, we can fix that right now."

A tear leaked out of the corner of Katie's eye and slid down her cheek.

"There now, dear, a cup of tea is just what you need." Esther began to serve the tea with grace and confidence.

"None for me, thanks," Michael stood. "Katie, may I go and take care of things as I see best? Do you trust my judgment?"

Katie nodded as she wiped her cheek. "Please, I just can't think about it now. I do trust you."

Esther looked first at one then at the other. She raised one eyebrow, then handed Katie a cup of tea and sat down in the chair next to her. As Katie sipped the tea, Esther studied her face, especially her eyes. There was so much pain deep in those eyes.

"Katie…may I call you that?"

"Yes, of course."

"Katie, I don't want to upset you. I just can't quit wondering why your mother didn't come with you when Michael brought you in. Is she ill? Do I need to go and check on her? Did your father stay with her? Things must be desperate for neither one to come with you when you were attacked like that. I know it's none of my business, but if I can help, I certainly want to."

Tears were flowing freely now. Katie's hands were shaking and the cup was rattling in the saucer. Esther took the cup and saucer and set them on the table nearby. She gently took both Katie's hands in her own and then reached around her and held her close.

"There now, I know all this has been overwhelming. Just tell me all about it, and I will see what I can do to help out. You are too young to carry all this inside you. It will help to get it out. What is wrong?"

"My parents died a little over six months ago. I have no one. If it had not been for Michael, I probably would not be alive right now. I'm so scared and yet so happy at the same time. I can't explain it."

"Oh, Katie, I am so sorry, dear. You have suffered so. God forgive me for being so self-centered. Sometimes, or perhaps more often, people get so involved in their own lives we fail to notice what is going on around us. I am so ashamed that I did not even notice the absence of your father coming to town all winter. That was thoughtless of me. Can you forgive me?"

"Mrs. Schmitt, no one ever came out to visit us even the year before. Why would anyone bother this year? When people found out we didn't fit in with their idea of 'normal' or what should be, then they quit having anything to do with us. They even went so far as to being cruel to father when he came to town. I did not expect anyone to notice, and even if they did, I didn't expect anyone to come with any condolences."

"This is a sad commentary indeed on the state of our Christian behavior. I must speak to my husband about this and the pastor as well when he rides through again. This must stop. We cannot continue to live like this here in Crystal Springs."

"Please, I don't want people to think I'm complaining. It's just the way it was and probably will continue to be. I've never met anyone like you before. You call yourself a Christian, yet you treat me with love. I don't understand it. Why would you do that? Unless you don't know who or what I am, is that it?"

"It makes no difference to me who you are or what you are, Katie. You are a child of God, one of his creations. He loves you and so should I. I do. I am drawn to you and love you as much as I would love the daughters I lost. I can't tell you how my heart aches to take care of you. I know you are grown and can take care of yourself. You've proven that. Yet, I want to do things for you and love you as if you are my very own grownup daughter. I know that doesn't make sense to you and I guess it might even offend you. I pray it doesn't. I'll try not to smother you. Please at least let me be your friend."

"I can't remember ever having a friend. My sister, Abigail, was my best friend. My heart broke when she died. I couldn't believe she was gone. I had no one. That was the beginning of my loneliness. I still had Ma and Pa, but they were my parents, not my friends. After Pa died, Ma was more like a friend, but that was for only a few weeks, then I truly believe she died of a broken heart. I wasn't enough for her."

Tears were trailing down the fine china-like skin of Katie's cheeks once more. She covered her face; then the sobs came. Esther hugged Katie to her.

"Oh, my precious one, you need a good rest somewhere other than the doctor's office. I want you to come home with me. I'm going to go talk with the doctor. I think he'll let me take you home. I'll be the perfect nurse."

They sat for several minutes in complete quiet while Katie cried. Slowly the sobs began to subside and she began to sniffle, blow her nose, and yawn. Esther began to hum a hymn and rock her gently as she held Katie in her arms with her head still on her shoulder. She heard the door slowly open. The doc peeked in. Esther nodded and motioned with her head for him to come in.

"Doc, I want to take Katie home with me so she can get some rest in a proper bed. I'm going to send Joshua out to the ranch to help Michael get things set for the ranch hands and do whatever he needs there. He's been anxious to get to work on a ranch, and this really looks like the Lord's leading to us. Katie doesn't need to go back out there yet. I'll send some food out with the boys…so their supper will be taken care of. They can fix their own breakfast. We will just wait and see what tomorrow will bring."

"That sounds like a good plan to me, Esther. How about you, young lady? What do you think of that plan?"

Katie was having trouble keeping her eyes open. She glanced up at the doctor and then closed her eyes again, continuing to lean against Esther. "I just want to sleep right now. I'll do whatever you say, doctor."

"Good, then I prescribe a bed at Esther's and a hot meal to go along with it. Drink plenty of tea with honey and ginger. Don't forget to suck on the lemon drops, if Tad left you any."

"Adam got them, so they're all there," laughed Esther.

Her expression changed to concern. "Can you walk, Katie? Do I need to find Michael or Joshua to carry you?"

"No, no, I can walk, I'm sure."

"Good, then let's go on over to the hotel and get you settled. I'll bring you a hot cup of tea. A bowl of soup should go down easy too."

Relief washed over Katie. She would be safe and sound in no time. She felt better already.

Feeling a need to get back to the ranch, Michael opened the door to the sheriff's office, stuck his head in, and asked, "Brian, will you need Joshua or me anymore today?"

"No, Michael. You two do whatever you need to do."

"Thanks. I took care of an account for Katie at the bank. I still need to make repairs at the ranch, and Joshua's ma told him to come on out with me and start to work. Esther is keeping Katie with her at the hotel, so Esther can be her nurse. Katie told her about her parents, but doesn't want it to be generally known yet. She feels like people didn't care about them when they were alive; why should they care if they are dead. Pretty sad, I'd say."

"I have to agree with you. From her side of the coin that sure is how it looks. I can tell you I've casually mentioned them to a few people, and the reaction I've gotten makes me believe she might be right. I can't believe it. Then again, I would have to say I didn't know him, if someone asked me if I did. I feel rotten. How did I get so isolated from the people I'm supposed to be protecting? I should know everyone and know them well. I need to work on that part of my job."

"Well, you're welcome out at the ranch anytime. I'll even let you work some if you've a mind to. We might even feed you!"

"I might do that." Brian smiled broadly and rubbed his stomach.

"See ya, Brian."

"Bye now."

Michael rode over to the livery stable which was attached to the blacksmith's shop and found Joshua just getting the last of his things strapped on Ranger. He paid Mr. Tucker and mounted up.

Michael nodded at Mr. Tucker, "I'll see your boys in the morning out at the ranch, Mr. Tucker. Thanks."

Joshua, already on Ranger, looked over his shoulder at Michael. "Let's go. I can't wait to get out there. I can't tell you how long I've waited to do some ranching. I know it isn't all roping and branding. I just love the whole idea of ranching. I've always wanted to do it."

"I'm glad. There's plenty to do. The bunkhouse is a mess. Red really tore it up looking for hidden money he thought Mr. Kurtz had on the ranch. Katie doesn't think there is any there. If there is, she doesn't know where it is. That's why he attacked her. He wanted her to tell him where to find the money."

"Hidden treasure. The next thing you know, someone will be seeing ghosts too. We could have all kinds of stories going on about the 'Mysteries of the Kurtz Ranch.' We could sell tickets and have tours. Who needs cattle!"

They both laughed as they rode out of town and on toward the ranch.

CHAPTER 11

The man sat tall on his horse with his right leg hooked around the saddle horn. He tipped his hat back and looked around. "Man, this place looks deserted; lived in, but deserted at the same time. Almost like the people just picked up and left suddenly. Maybe there was an emergency, and they won't be back for a while. Would everyone leave? Where are the hands? What do you think, Star? Should we stay or leave?"

His horse snorted and stamped his hoof. "Yes, I think you're right. I think we should just wait. It could be the hands are out in the hills and the family went into town. Maybe someone will be back soon. Besides I believe you'd like some water, and that well looks mighty inviting."

Star snorted and stamped his hoof a second time. "Well, no one is here to tell us no. I'll assume it's a yes. I thought you'd agree. Here, I'll let you have the first drink."

The man dismounted, gave his horse a drink, and then drank some water himself. He sat on the steps of the porch and waited. He had almost decided to leave when the sound of a cow bawling caught his attention. He stood and looked around. He took tentative steps toward the barn, and then turned toward the back pasture, then back toward the barn.

"Sounds like the barn, Star. I'm going to have a look. I'll be back."

He disappeared into the darkness of the doorway, and within a few minutes the bawling stopped. Sometime later, the man emerged from the barn carrying a bucket of milk. He took it up on the porch and set it down. He appeared unaware of the two men watching his every movement from the trees in the lane leading up to the house. After setting down the milk, he walked back over to his horse, rubbed her neck, looked around, and then looked at the sky.

Patting his horse's neck, he whispered into his ear. "Let's give them thirty more minutes and then we'll move on. I like this place, Star. There's something about it that just feels right. What do you think?"

Star stamped one hoof.

"Good, I'm glad you think so too. I hope they ride on in then. We can't get acquainted until they do."

With that, he turned and sat back down on the steps, settled his hat over his jet black hair and vivid green eyes, and leaned back, thinking about taking a little nap, or just wanting it to appear that way so the two men by the trees would feel free to ride on in.

"Josh, what do you make of that?"

"I don't know. It looks like he milked your cow. Do you know him?"

"I've never seen him before in my life."

"Well, it looks like he's waiting for you. He certainly isn't lazy. He worked while he was waiting. I say we ride on in and see who he is and what he wants."

Michael nodded agreement. "Well, we certainly won't learn anything out here." He gave Solomon a nudge to move on.

Michael and Josh slowly approached the house. They didn't want to startle the man or make him nervous. Both men noticed he was wearing a gun belt. That was a little worrisome. If he had been on the trail it was understandable, but they didn't want to take any chances. As they pulled up, he cocked his hat up and stood up. He had shaved that morning and was neatly dressed in working clothes. His gun belt sat comfortably on his hips but was not tied down in gun-slinger fashion. Michael guessed he was in his late twenties, about the same age as Joshua, maybe a little older.

The man looked up at Michael and Josh, smiled, and said, "I was beginning to wonder when you two would decide to come on in." His voice sounded very natural and there was no hint of nervousness to it.

"We saw the horse before we saw you. Then you came out of the barn carrying the milk. We were kind of curious what you were going to do with it, so we waited. Then we wanted to see if you were going to get on your horse and ride out or what. This has been a day for unusual events. We thought we would just wait and see what this one would be before we rushed in."

The man looked around. "Yes, the place looked like something had happened. Like some kind of emergency happened and everybody just took off. The cow was bawling so I milked her. I fed the stock in the barn too. I didn't want to overstep any boundaries, but I hate to see animals suffer. I didn't see any harm in helping out some. Hope you don't mind."

"Not at all. My name is Michael and this is Joshua."

"I'm Riley." They shook hands. He had callused, honest, hardworking hands. Michael liked him. There was a connection with him that could not be ignored.

"What can I do for you, Riley? Since you've been waiting a while, I have to think you need something."

"You're right. I need a job. I sure would be proud if you could offer me one."

Thank you Lord, Michael thought as a smile lit his face. "Well, as a matter of fact, I can. Josh and I are just coming back from town to get things cleaned up in the bunkhouse for the new hands coming in tomorrow. If you'll lend us a hand, it could be ready to sleep in tonight. We have cattle to round up out in the hills. Most are in the arroyos so it shouldn't be too difficult to get them. We need to brand the calves and then drive the ones to sell down to San Antonio. We need to get the hay and corn planted. There's plenty to do. Still want the job?"

"Yes sir, I want the job. Show me the bunkhouse and I'll get busy. What needs to be done?"

"Okay, follow me, gentlemen."

They rode out to the bunkhouse. It was not in much worse condition than it was when he and Katie had seen it before. They opened the windows and door to get the place aired out.

"Who was the pig living in here?" asked Riley.

"Red Galliger was hiding in here. He's in jail now." Michael picked up the rocker and moved it outside.

"The Red Galliger?"

"Yes, that was our emergency today. He attacked Miss Katie Kurtz, the owner of the ranch. I'm her foreman. She's staying in town with Josh's parents, at least for tonight. We'll see how things go before we decide if she'll come home tomorrow. I think it would be very good for her to stay and rest a few days, but she is worried about her garden and getting things ready for the roundup and trail ride."

"Is she okay? He didn't, I mean, oh, never mind. She wouldn't be alive if he had. He's a vicious man. He's left more than one woman dead in his wake. It wasn't very pretty. The man is an animal."

"How do you know him?" Michael looked at Riley suspiciously.

"I don't know him. I just know about him. I've been in towns that he's been in, even attended the funerals of a couple of his victims, not because I knew them, but just because I wanted to show my support for the families."

Michael rubbed his hand through his hair trying to rid himself of the pain he felt for the victims. "Somehow, when I learned he was wanted, I pictured him wanted for bank robbery and the murder of other men. I never imagined women."

"Oh, he didn't limit himself to women. He did rob banks and trains. He did murder men. That was his line of work. His 'recreation' was women and young girls, very young girls. It's about time someone stopped him. You fellas deserve a medal."

"It wasn't me," Joshua corrected. "Michael did it."

"By yourself?" Riley asked incredulously.

Michael shook his head. "Not alone, God was with me. He did it. I was just his hand. Now, I wish I'd hit that varmint harder. There's no going back. It just makes me sick thinking about all that he has done to hurt others." Michael looked up as if remembering he needed to be a servant of God, not the judge. "Maybe he'll find the love of God before they hang him. I don't wish anyone to hell, but he certainly needs a complete change of heart or else that is where he is headed."

"That's where everyone is headed unless they have come to a saving knowledge of Jesus, whether their deeds are good or bad. Remember, 'none are righteous, no, not one,' and 'all have sinned and come short of the glory of God.' It's only through Jesus we are saved. We are all going to hell unless we accept the free gift of salvation."

"You are so right, Josh. By the way, I've been meaning to ask you, do you mind being called Josh? Sometimes I call you Joshua as your parents do and sometimes I call you Josh like I've heard others call you. What do you prefer?"

"Well, I'll tell you, I prefer not being called late for dinner! Just call me whatever comes to mind otherwise."

"Okay, I'll do just that."

Their laughter joined with the rhythm of the hammering as they repaired the torn-up flooring and other damage done by Red. They hung the mattresses over the fence to the pasture and beat them, getting most of the dust and dirt out of them. Then while the mattresses were airing, the men got out brooms, mops, and buckets to get the rest cleaned up.

When they were done it didn't look like the same place. Michael had moved the rocker and the wash tub back out on the bunkhouse porch, where he envisioned they had been by the description given by Katie.

"I hope that helps her forget what it looked like the last time we were in here."

"What now? I say we eat. I don't know about you, but I've worked up an appetite." Riley rubbed his hands together as in anticipation of a banquet.

"Well, Riley, I'd say we've earned a good meal. My mom sent out some food with us. I put it in the house after I put the milk in the spring house. I say let's go eat it. Want to take a vote?"

"You're the officer. I'd rather just salute and say, 'Yes, sir,' then ride. But the last one back to the house has to wash the dishes!" teased Michael.

With that, Michael leaped on Solomon and took off toward the house.

"What'd he say?" asked Riley.

Josh and Riley looked at each other, ran to their horses, and raced to the house.

"That was no fair," Josh said with mock ire.

"Hold on, you two," said Riley after reaching the house, putting both hands in the air, and looking very much like a referee. "In the interest of peace, and since I am the newest member of the clan Kurtz, I volunteer to wash the dishes. However, I take no responsibility for broken ones, and I will not dry or put away."

"That sounds reasonable. And since I have no idea where anything goes, I'll dry," added Josh.

"Oh, so I guess that leaves me with the 'put away' phase of the project."

"Yes." Riley looked around the kitchen and eating area. "I believe we are getting ahead of ourselves, gentlemen, since we haven't even begun to eat. Shall we cook or at least serve up what has been prepared? And since Michael knows where to put things when they have been dried, perhaps he knows from whence to retrieve them prior to their being used."

"Where did you learn to talk like that? Why don't you just talk?" Josh asked putting his fists on his hips and jutting his head forward.

"You mean just say, 'Michael, set the table'?"

"That's better." Josh relaxed, leaned back, and smiled.

"But such simple speech is so boring. I'll tell you my story sometime when the atmosphere is more appropriate. This just isn't the right setting. The tone and mood just aren't right. No, the Bard would agree with me on that. It will have to wait."

"Michael, do you think you might reconsider hiring this one?" Josh looked at Michael with a half smile on his face, trying to keep a serious expression, but not succeeding.

Michael laughed. "Very interesting. No, I think I'll wait for the 'right setting, tone and mood.' I want to hear his story. If I send him packing, we'll never know."

Laughter filled the kitchen which just a couple of days ago seemed so dark and full of death and despair.

CHAPTER 12

"Y ou have to eat, sweetheart, or you will never regain your strength." Esther cooed over Katie.

"I just don't feel up to it. I know you are a wonderful cook…"

"Oh, honey, I didn't cook this. Yes, I can cook, but Miss Rose cooks all the meals down in the restaurant. There's not a better cook in all of Texas! I might even say the West, but I haven't covered the West. I really haven't covered all of Texas, but the people who have eaten here keep telling me that, so I believe them."

"I know you are a good cook, though, or you never would have had to hire a cook to help you. Isn't that right?" Katie still whispered, though her throat felt a little better.

Esther smiled, pleased. "You are a very discerning young woman. Yes, that is right. When business became too much for me to handle by myself, Adam had to quit his job and help out; but he loved it anyway, that's what he had always done. It had been his idea from the start. We just needed regular income to get us started. By then we had Joshua. It got so I just couldn't keep up with waiting tables and cooking. So, he ran the front and I ran the back. But the men customers liked a pretty face coming to their table rather than a man, so Adam decided he would either find a good cook or a new waitress. Well, we found Miss Rose first, so I was replaced in the back, and she is a wonder. She is a much better cook than I, and it wasn't too long after that we found out we were going to have Tad, what a surprise! Well, then, we needed to find some help out front, and the rest is history. Now, I have more time to be a mother to both my boys. Of course, Joshua is way beyond needing to be mothered; he is more in need of a wife. He just doesn't know it. I don't know how to tell him."

"Maybe it will come to him all by itself when the time is right. That's what my mother used to tell me. Ma would say, 'Katie, quit moping around looking for your young man. When the time is right, he will show up.' I wish he had shown up before she had died. It would have been so much easier to share that burden."

"My sweet lamb, you have had such a hard time. I wish I had known your mother."

"She was a hard woman to get to know. I loved her and love her still. She was very special to me, and I understood her. But she did not take to strangers and was very much a hermit. When we first came, people would come to visit and bring food as gifts. Mother was very abrupt with them, never invited them in, and all in all very inhospitable, now that I look back on it. No wonder no one ever came out to see us again after they had been there the first time."

"Tell me, in the towns where you had lived before, had your mother or father been mistreated?" Esther asked curiously. "Had people done bad things to them, been mean to them?"

"Well, I do remember one time Pa came home very angry because he had been using the privy behind the blacksmith shop in town, and someone turned it over while he was in there. He was very embarrassed. He vowed never to use another public privy. He never did, as far as I know."

"Where was that?"

"Philadelphia, the city of brotherly love. I was young then, but I remember Ma crying and saying over and over, 'Not again, it can't be happening again.' It made a big impression on me, because I wondered how many times Pa had been tipped over in a privy. Later, I wondered if she meant something else by that. I don't remember ever having any trouble with any of my friends at school or in our neighborhood. I don't remember anyone calling us names or being mean. Maybe I was just being naive and blind to what was really going on. I don't know. Maybe that's why Pa moved so much."

"Now, don't go getting all worked up over it. I was just trying to figure out why I'd never met your mother." Esther shook her head. "I am so ashamed of myself."

Katie leaned toward Esther and tried to comfort her. "You have no reason to be ashamed. Why should you be? Is it your job to ride a circuit around and make sure everyone in the county is called on at least once a month or even once a year? I think not. I really do think you are too hard on yourself."

"But, dear, don't you see, the Lord told us to visit the widows and orphans and to provide for them. Your mother needed me, and so did you. Now, if I had been doing what you suggest, I would have known that. We need to be more aware of what's going on in our community."

Esther folded her arms across her middle then moved her hands to her hips. "Some sort of system needs to be worked out, not necessarily a circuit riding visitation committee, but something, even if it is just neighbors looking in on neighbors occasionally and letting others know. That is what should be happening. It needs to be for the right reasons, though, not for gossip. I hate gossip."

Katie was afraid the conversation would go to areas she was not ready to discuss, so she decided it would be better to eat than to talk. She picked up the spoon and began to eat the soup. To her surprise, her whole body began to warm, and her mind traveled back to a warm hearth, soft blankets, and good times with her sister on a cold winter night. She couldn't remember what the occasion was, but it was a good memory. The taste of vegetables and thick tomato/beef stock caused her to sink down in the bed and wish for a long, deep sleep. She felt love all around her and knew she was safe and protected. How could the taste of soup do so much for the soul? She peered into the steaming pot next to the bed to see what there was to drink, almost afraid of what she would find. To her relief, it was hot tea.

"Do you think Red will be taken away soon?" she asked.

"I know the marshal told the sheriff that he was sending some men to pick him up. He is wanted for various serious crimes. He won't be getting off. There is a price on his head. They don't do that unless there's plenty of evidence against someone. You won't have to worry about him anymore."

"Don't get me wrong, Esther, but until that man is in a hole in the ground, I won't feel safe. Anything can happen. He terrifies me, and I hope I never, ever see him again, dead or alive."

"I hope you don't ever see him again either, unless God changes his heart and his soul is saved and he is redeemed for eternity. He'll have to suffer the consequences for his sins here on earth, but God loves the entire world. He sent his son to die for those he has chosen to redeem. Red may seek forgiveness for his sins. If he does, God will not say no."

"How could God possibly forgive someone like Red?"

"Did he not forgive Nebuchadnezzar?"

"Oh."

"You rest now. I'm proud of the way you have eaten. You'll feel much better very soon, I'm sure."

"Excuse me, could you give me directions to this Kurtz ranch? I'm not from around here and I read this note about work on the restaurant doorway. I'd like to look into it."

Adam looked at the man, first noticing the patch over one eye, then the wild head of snow-white hair; his tan, leathery skin; and his obvious cowboy clothing. His odor wasn't offensive, just smelled of horse and a long day out in the sun. Adam smiled.

"Sure, I can tell you where it is. Our son is out there with the foreman tonight. They had a little trouble and had to go take care of some things after being in town most of the day. It's getting late now. Would you like a room so you can start out in the morning when you can see better, or would you rather camp on the road headed out of town?

"Do you have hot water?"

"Yes sir, we do."

"How much are the rooms?"

"I'll take you over and introduce you to the clerk so you can get all your questions answered, but before I do, let me draw a map to the Kurtz ranch. We start serving breakfast at 5 a.m. You won't find a better one."

"Thank you. You've been very kind. Most people aren't."

"Jesus said to love one another. I try to do that."

"I don't hold much stock in him. Christians, they're just a bunch of hypocrites!"

"Well, yes, many times we are. It's called sin. But you know what I've noticed? Those who aren't Christians are a bunch of hypocrites too."

"Well, you know what? You're right. I've never thought of it quite like that. Maybe I'd better be more careful about what I say because I've been a hypocrite myself, now that I think about it. Sorry."

"Apology accepted. We're all sinners, and that's why we need Christ. Just because we accept him as our savior doesn't mean we automatically stop sinning, we just try not to sin, and we get help from the Holy Spirit in that effort. The Holy Spirit also helps us to love others especially when we don't feel like doing so." Adam finished drawing and handed the paper to the newcomer. "Here's your map. I hope we see you in the morning. By the way, my name is Adam Schmitt. What's yours?"

"Mr. Schurtz, Wulfgang Schurtz."

"Well, Mr. Schurtz, welcome to Crystal Springs. I hope you find peace here and make this your home."

"That's not likely. Thanks anyway. Thank you for the map."

"Let's go over to the desk clerk and I'll introduce you."

Riley put down his fork and leaned back in his chair. "My, that was a fine breakfast. You boys are prodigiously fine cooks. I don't mind a bit washing up after such a nutritious repast. I could work for hours. So, what is on our agenda for today?"

"If you don't start talking plain English, no one'll know what the fat you're sayin', Riley."

"What part didn't you understand, Josh?"

"Let's see, there was something about a prodig-something and then some other thing in the past. What was it you were trying to say?"

"Now, that we have eaten a good breakfast and are ready to work, what are we going to do today? Is that plain enough for you, Josh?"

"Well, why didn't you say so? I'm not ignorant, but I don't have a degree in the King's...I guess now it's the Queen's English."

"Men, I think the first thing we need to do is find out what this fella wants."

Michael sipped the last of his coffee, continued looking out the front window, and watched a man ride in on a black horse. He couldn't see much of the man since the morning sun made a silhouette out of him. He could tell he sat a horse well. He could see that the horse looked well taken care of in that it rode in with no problems and held its head straight. It was a fine mount.

"A job, I hope. The more hands the easier the work," replied Riley.

"I sure hope he isn't here looking for trouble."

"I don't think so, Josh. He looks like he has come here with purpose, not sneaky or looking around warily. He is riding straight for the house." Michael turned and handed his coffee cup to Josh.

"Lord, give us discernment and wisdom in all things today." Joshua quickly prayed out loud.

"Thanks, Josh. We sure can use God's help in all things, especially in light of recent events." Michael turned and clapped him on the shoulder and moved to open the door.

The stranger stopped his horse in front of the house, tied him to the hitching post, and then walked up the stairs. As he reached the top step, Michael opened the front door and stepped out.

"Morning. My name is Michael. I'm the foreman here. Can I help you with anything today?"

"I believe you can. I saw a note at the hotel restaurant that said to see you about a job. I'm here to do just that."

"Well, you have good timing. We were just leaving to go out and round up some cattle. Let's have a seat out here and have a chat. Would you like some coffee?"

"No thanks, just some water is all I need to wash the trail dust down. I'll just drink out of the well right here. I'll give my horse some, too, if you don't mind."

"Go right ahead. I'll get you a cup."

"Don't bother. I'll drink right out of the bucket; makes no difference to me."

"Suit yourself then."

Michael eyed the stranger, noting he had not given him a name and had refused any kind of help. The scar slicing its way across his face, indicating a knife or maybe a sword had taken his eye from him, made him look fierce. Michael told himself not to stare at him but to focus on the man, not on the appearance of the man. Michael rocked slowly as he watched the man drink his fill from the bucket then give water to his horse. He seemed to be speaking lovingly to the animal and giving his neck gentle pats as he talked to him.

"That's a fine animal you have there."

"He is my best friend. He has risked his life to get me out of some very tough situations."

"I feel the same way about my horse. Have you done any ranching, cowpoking, anything like that?"

"I've done it all. I know how to work cattle, if that's what you want to know. I know how to follow orders, and I know how to give them. I know when to say yes and when to say no. There was a time when I didn't pay much attention to my gut feelings, but now I do."

"What's your name? I don't believe you said what it was when I gave you mine."

"No, I didn't. People usually don't talk to me long enough to want to know my name. Then, once they hear it, they move on. So, I've gotten in the habit of not giving it. Sorry."

"It must be a strong habit, you still didn't give it. If you want me to hire you, you're going to have to give me your name."

"Wulfgang Schurtz. People who stick around long enough to get to know me call me Wulf."

"Well, Wulf, I don't think I'm going anywhere, so are you sticking around long enough for me and the rest of the guys to get to know you?"

"Does this mean you're going to hire me?"

"Are you willing to work?"

"Yes, sir, I am. But only if the work is hard and I earn my pay."

"The work is hard, and believe me, you will earn your pay. This ranch needs much repair, and we have a cattle drive to get ready for. Oh, yes, you will earn your pay. The bunkhouse is just beyond that pasture on the other side of those trees."

Michael pointed in the direction of the bunkhouse as he walked Wulf around the corner of the house. He looked for the others as he did but saw no one around. He would introduce them later.

"Head on over and stow your things. We're heading up to the arroyos to round up the cattle; take what you need for that and leave the rest. There are a couple of other boys I'm waiting for. J. R. Riley and Josh Schmitt are already here. The twins should have been here. If I have to go get them, I'll have to tan their hides… unless maybe they didn't understand they were to be here this morning. I may have to ride into town. I'll see if I can find the other men and introduce you. Go ahead out to the bunkhouse. If you see a vacant bed, it's yours."

"Much obliged."

"My pleasure. Make yourself at home, Wulf."

With that, both men headed in opposite directions. Michael headed back into the house thinking he would find the other two nursing cups of coffee and waiting for a report on the stranger. He was surprised to find the house empty. The kitchen was clean and the coffeepot was cold. He turned around and headed out to the barn.

"Well, paint me yellow and call me an ear of corn. You fellas just decided to do something without being told?"

"Joshua, did you hear some *attempt* at communication coming from *el jefe?*"

"Yea, whatever you said, Riley, I agree with one hundred percent. He couldn't be more tempting if he was a steer ready to be branded, or something," mumbled Josh.

"You misinterpreted what I was trying to encode to you. I thought your superior ability to decipher complicated signs in the wild would at least give you an advantage over our fearless leader here in the way of understanding what is being said to you and the general audience."

"Josh, what is he saying?"

"Blamed, if I know, Michael. All I know is that he said while you were out there conducting an interview with the next employee, we should be making ourselves useful. The next thing I know, we're out here working, getting the cow milked and the stock fed. Does that help any?"

"Not with what he said, but with who has the most sense it does. Okay, we have a new hand. I sent him out to the bunkhouse to stow some of his gear and get settled in. His name is Wulfgang Schurtz, just call him Wulf. He's well experienced. Has a really bad scar across his face, took out his eye, I guess. He wears a patch over it. He takes good care of his horse. That alone says a a great deal about a man. I'd like to introduce you to him, but I need to get to town and see why the twins aren't here yet. They were supposed to be here for breakfast."

"Maybe they forgot, you know how kids are."

"No, Riley, I don't think these boys would forget. Something else is going on. I think I need to go in and see about it."

"We'll go on over to our humble abode and make ourselves known to our new comrade so he'll feel welcome, and then we'll show him around. Anything you have on your list that's high priority for having accomplished before Miss Kate comes home?"

Michael considered what was on his mental list. "Well, there are repairs that still need to be made to the barn. Also the tool shed needs to be put in order; it's a mess! We need to be able to find things when we need them. Just work on those things. We really need to get to those cattle up there in those hills."

"Is there a holding pen built out there, or are we going to bring them all the way back into the ranch each day?"

"I haven't seen a holding pen. With so few men, we need one. I hate to waste the time building it. I sure wish we had another man. Then we could have one or two stay with the herd branding the ones that need it as we gather the rest, and then bring them all in at once. After we get them all here, we will separate the ones we want to keep here and take the rest on the trail drive to San Antonio. I'll pray for another hand as I ride into town. You two pray as well. See ya."

From the bunkhouse, Wulf watched Michael ride out and the other two men walk from the barn, stow the milk in the root cellar, and head toward the bunkhouse. He used his one good eye to size up each man as he came down the drive toward where he stood. He was concealed in the shadows of the trees and leaned his lank muscular body against the side of the building.

Riley spoke without looking anywhere but his feet. "Ever get the feeling you're being watched?"

"Yes, like now," Josh replied, surveying the countryside.

"Do you see him?"

Josh looked back down at the lane then toward the bunkhouse. "No, that bothers me. Usually I can see people when I know they are there."

"Maybe he's looking out a window." Riley suggested.

"No, I don't believe Wulf would hide inside. I believe he would conceal himself in the shadows."

"Once again you have proved to be correct. I see him now. He's good. He's very good. I wonder if he is part Indian." Riley queried, not expecting Josh to comment. With his head down, Riley suggested, "Let's let him think he pulled one over on us. Let's just walk in and not even look in his direction."

"Fine by me, but what will that prove?"

"He will feel like the lead dog, the top dog, or however you want to put it. He'll feel like he is superior in our little pack. However, we know that we are allowing him to feel that way, which in turn gives us a better in with him in allowing him into our pack. We don't feel stupid, he feels superior. We all feel good."

"Do we ever tell him we knew where he was?" Josh questioned.

"That depends on what kind of a lead dog he turns out to be. If he gets all superior with us and flaunts his superiority we may have to bring him down a little with a little chat about the first time we saw him in the shadow of the trees leaning against the building. That should give him pause to think."

"I really wish you would just use fewer words." Josh groused.

"If I did, I might lose the others. I'd never want to do that." Riley said smiling.

"But you don't need all those words. Don't they ever get in your way? I mean, with people never knowing what you're saying? Then you have to explain all over again what you meant. It just seems to me to be a whole heap of trouble." Josh complained as they neared the bunkhouse.

"I look at it this way. I am probably helping to develop in someone, who is listening, a new sense of appreciation for the English language or at least some of their vocabulary. Just think, someone could be becoming more literate just because of the way I speak, my choice of words, the way I phrase my sentences. What a wonderful gift I may be giving to someone just because I'm using the vocabulary and communication skills I learned from Mrs. Helms. I do miss her. She was the kindest woman I have ever known. I hope she has found much love and happiness with her husband."

"Who is Mrs. Helms? You haven't told us about her."

"Well, now is probably not the right time. Michael isn't here and I know I told him I would tell him later about my story. So, I'll wait. We have time."

Wulf watched the two men walk into the bunkhouse without even looking his way. He smiled, and then his smiled faded. Was this a game they were playing? Surely Michael told them he was there. They weren't much good at range riding if they weren't even looking for him as they walked up to the bunkhouse. He turned and opened the door. The two men turned from their beds and looked at him. He smiled at them.

"How soon did you see me?"

"Well, now it did take us some time. You blended in pretty well with those shadows and the wood on the side of the building, but we were about halfway up the drive before we could see you." Josh confided.

"I'm really losing it if you could see me that soon."

"Were you really trying to hide?" Josh asked.

"Seems to me if you were really trying to stay out of sight you could have done so more effectively by taking yourself behind the corner of the building over at the other end there in the shadows where the other stand of trees is. We wouldn't have seen you from the drive, and you could have watched us until we passed the end of the building. Then you could have stealthily moved to the other corner and watched or looked in the window at the north end of bunkhouse." Riley surmised.

Wulf smiled. "Well now, I do understand what you were saying about using all those words. But I do agree with you as well, it is good to hear them put to use, and it does challenge me to use more myself."

"Oh no! I'm surrounded by them. Lord, help me increase my vocabulary so I can join them, or bring Michael back so I can have a sane person to talk to." Josh teased as he rolled his eyes. "I'm Josh," he said as he held out his hand.

"And I'm Riley." They all shook hands. "Josh, you could always go back into the cavalry. I hear they have very limited vocabulary. 'Forward ho, aroar har!'" Riley motioned with his arm as if leading imaginary followers.

"Aroar har? What is that?" confused, Josh asked.

"I don't know. I heard it once when a bunch of blue coats were riding out of town. I didn't know what it meant and I still don't. I was hoping you could shed some light on it for me."

Bewildered, Josh looked at Riley. "Never heard it before and wouldn't know what to do if I did."

Laughter rang throughout the bunkhouse. Wulf got settled in, and the men began to file out when Wulf quickly drew his gun and fired.

"What the…"

"Rattler."

The men looked around him and saw a six-foot diamondback on the ground just off the porch in front of the door.

"I hate snakes. Never met one that didn't mean me harm." Wulf's eye narrowed as he looked at the men.

"Are you talking about the kind that crawl on the ground or the two-legged kind?" Josh asked.

"Both. They need to be dealt with in the same fashion. I've been *bitten* before and I mean to not be *bitten* again."

Josh and Riley cast each other a look that spoke volumes. Neither man intended to "bite" Wulf and both hoped he knew it.

"You were pretty fast with that gun. I don't mind tellin' you. I hope if we are in a fight, you're on my side." Josh said, trying to make conversation.

"No reason not to be, yet."

"Well, Wulf, you have my gun anytime you need it."

"Thanks, Josh, I'll remember that."

Josh and Riley knew they would have to discuss this further sometime in privacy. They had an eerie feeling about Wulf. Maybe it was that eye patch and scar, but there was something foreboding about him. It made Riley just a bit itchy all over. They would have a talk with Michael when the opportunity arose.

They walked toward the tool shed with the intent of cleaning everything out, making repairs, and getting that place in order. Josh opened the door and surveyed the interior.

"Well men, prepare to get really dirty. This place is full of cobwebs, and it is a mess. It looks like someone just rummaged through it tossing things here and there. It could have been Red. Or maybe it was just Katie trying to find the things she needed to bury her folks. Doesn't matter, it all comes out, and we see what needs to be done, then we'll get it organized and put back."

"Yes, sir!" Riley smiled as he saluted.

"Let's get on with it," growled Wulf.

Josh reached in and pulled a few tools out and passed them off to the men and kept working his way in until there was room for two men inside. As they worked, the shed began to empty, but the out-of-doors looked like a pile of junk.

"We need to organize this into piles of the same things or tools that would be used together, like the wood-working tools together and the leather-working tools together. Big things like the ladder and hoe need to be set aside until we decide what to do with them."

"Who put him in charge?" Wulf asked, elbowing Riley.

"Well, he was the first hire, and Michael kind of gave us both instructions; but I don't know where everything goes yet, so I just go with the flow. Less hassle that way, you know? Besides, why not? He has that experience in the cavalry, so giving orders and organizing comes natural to him. Do you mind?"

"No, I'm just trying to find out whose orders I follow."

"Don't follow mine unless Michael or Josh tell you to, believe me. I'm probably the least experienced here. I'll be looking to you for help in some things, I know."

"Well, I'll be glad to share any of my experience with you if that's what you want."

"Thanks, Wulf, I appreciate that. You're a good man."

Wulf stopped and looked Riley in the eye. All he saw was sincerity and truth. There was no joking in that statement. He wasn't sure how to handle that. He hadn't experienced this kind of acceptance in many years.

"You a Christian?" Wulf asked as he eyed Riley as if taking his measure.

"Absolutely. I couldn't live without Christ. He is my salvation, my guide, and my all in all. He is everything to me. I truly don't know how people make it without him."

"What about Josh, he one too?"

"Why don't you ask him?"

"Just trying to get my bearings. I don't hold much with Christianity. All I have seen are people who don't live like what they say."

"I'm sorry to hear that. I try to live according to God's word. Sometimes I fail. It's called sin. When that happens, I ask God to forgive me and anyone I may have hurt by that sin. I know he will forgive me, and that's the end of it. Sometimes people aren't so gracious. My sin is really against the Lord, not so much the people. It was him I did my wrong against. He expects more out of me, and I try to live according to his will."

"I've never heard anyone talk like that before."

"I hope if I ever offend you, you'll let me know so I can make it right. Will you do that for me, Wulf?"

"Riley, you want me to tell you if you do something I don't like?"

"Yes, I don't want to hurt you in any way. If I'm sleeping in a bunk you would rather have, just let me know and I'll switch. If I say something and you are hurt by it, tell me. I certainly don't mean to intentionally hurt you. I don't know you well, so I could say something that is innocent and yet because of something you have gone through, you might take offense. Please allow me the opportunity to apologize when that happens."

"If all Christians were like you, this world would be a better place. Right now it's not worth a cow patty."

Riley paused, and then said in a quiet voice, "We must try to make it better then."

They were about done sorting the tools into piles when Josh came out with the last load. He was covered with cobwebs and dirt, loaded up with chains.

Riley started laughing.

"What's so funny?" Wulf asked, suspiciously feeling left out of the humor.

"Have you ever read *A Christmas Carol* by Charles Dickens? Well, there comes ole Marley. Now all we need is Scrooge."

"The way I've been living seems like I could qualify for someone named Scrooge. What was he like?"

"Well now, he didn't believe in Christmas. He was miserly and mean-spirited toward everyone. Be careful, Wulf, you don't want to be equated with that kind of character."

"If you knew me, you would see that I fit that description."

"But he doesn't stay that way. He changes. You can change too."

"I don't know about that. We'll just have to see. I don't know that I want to change. I've had some very bad experiences that have shaped who I am. I don't think I can change, even if I do want to—and I'm not sayin' I do."

"God can change anybody. Why don't we have Bible reading each night before we hit the hay and see just how God changed some of the lives of the people in the Bible?"

Josh had dumped the chains and was listening intently to this exchange. He had been so busy working he hadn't noticed the two had been talking while they worked. He had been trained to do his job and keep quiet.

"I like that idea. How about you, Wulf?" Josh asked as he walked over, dusting his hands off on the legs of his pants.

"Don't matter. I don't have a Bible, so don't expect me to read."

Riley spoke quickly, "That's fine. I have one and will be happy to share. Do you have one, Josh?"

"Absolutely, I kept it in my saddlebag so I could have it even when I was on patrol. I didn't stop keeping it there when I left the service. I want it close."

"Let's start tonight. How about we read about Saul and David?"

"That would be great. I like that account," Josh said smiling.

"Aren't those just stories?" asked Wulf.

"No, Wulf, they are accounts of the lives of men and women God used. They are true stories, if you want to call them stories."

"Well, lets get the repairs made now. If Michael comes back and we are still standing in the middle of all these tools, he won't be happy. I don't want him to fire me before I get a chance to see my second day on the job," Riley joked.

With that, Wulf picked up the chains, placed them in the appropriate pile, and walked over to the doorway of the tool shed to survey what needed to be done.

Josh and Riley looked at each other and shrugged.

"What do you think, Wulf? What needs to be done first?" Josh looked at Wulf's back and waited for a reply.

"Well, if you really want to know what I think, I think that big hole in the roof should be the first thing fixed."

"I agree. What do you think, Riley?"

"Just tell me what to do. I'll go along with what you men think best."

"He's a peacemaker. Is he always like that?" Wulf looked Josh in the eye as he asked the question.

"Pretty much. He is very accommodating." Josh looked over his shoulder to see Riley picking out some wood from the woodshed where he had found some boards. The hammer and a bucket of nails were sitting on the ground not ten feet away.

"Hey, Josh, is there another ladder? I only see one."

"I think it may still be on the other side of the house where Red put it when he climbed in the window."

"Who is that Red fella you keep talking about?"

"Oh, sorry Wulf, I forget you weren't here yesterday. He's a wanted outlaw who attacked Miss Katie yesterday. He would have killed her and worse if Michael hadn't come back from town early. He's in jail now waiting for the US Marshal's men or Texas Rangers to come pick him up."

Wulf spit and grunted. "I know who you're talking about. He didn't kill her? She's a lucky girl. He's done some pretty horrible things to some girls, pretty young ones too. I just don't understand men like that. If I had been here, he wouldn't be alive. Men like him don't deserve to live."

"All men deserve a chance to accept Jesus as their savior. Maybe he hasn't had that opportunity yet, and God is going to give him that chance. Of course, he can turn the offer of salvation down. Many men and women have done so. The Bible says that even the faith to believe is given by God. Maybe Red has heard, but God didn't give Red the faith to believe. I don't know, but I believe all of that is up to God. I'm just glad I don't have to choose who will go to heaven and who won't."

Wulf looked like he was going to say something when he caught sight of Riley struggling around the corner of the house with the ladder.

"I best go give that 'weakling' a hand," he said with laughter in his voice.

Josh thought he heard a chuckle as Wulf walked away from him. He took the ladder he had there and put it up against the side of the shed. Climbing up, he took in the view of the ranch. It was neatly laid out, and with some repairs and care it would be a beautiful place to live. *"Not unlike its owner, beautiful."*

The two men struggling across the yard with the ladder were comical. Josh decided he'd better not laugh, or he might fall off the ladder where he was. The roof looked in need of more than just repair. It was in desperate need of new boards and new shingles.

"Hey, Riley, were there any shakes in that woodshed?"

"Yes, bundles of them. It looks like someone may have been making plans to shingle a roof but didn't get to it."

"This one is going to need it. This roof is in really bad shape. I think this job may take all day, maybe more than that if we don't get to some serious work."

"When do we stop for lunch? What time is it anyway?" asked Riley.

Josh, Wulf, and Riley looked up to see where the sun was. It was almost directly overhead.

"Who's the cook?" Wulf looked from one man to the other.

"Well, Miss Katie is, but since she is still in town with my mother, we are going to have to make do on our own. I grew up helping in the restaurant, so I can cook. If you don't want a hot meal, we can get out some sandwich makings and see if there is any canned fruit or something. I saw cookies in there last night." Josh wiggled his eyebrows up and down. "What's your pleasure?"

Riley looked at Wulf and then back at Josh who had come down off the ladder. "I think we should keep it simple. We have so much to do out here and if you cook, that will take your hands away from out here. Then there is the cleanup. If we keep it to sandwiches and other simple foods, including cookies, we can get fed and back out here in a shorter period of time."

"Food is food to me. I don't care if it is sandwiches," Wulf added. "Cookies, I may need a reminder on how they taste."

"Great, let's go ahead and break for lunch before we get started on this project. The sky is clear and my shoulder is telling me it is going to stay that way." Josh said, rubbing his left shoulder.

"You have a weather-forecasting shoulder? Please enlighten us as to the acquisition of such a marvel." Riley put in.

"Let's eat and forget the shoulder!" Wulf said, adding his brand of humor.

Again laughter rang across the ranch as the three walked toward the back door of the house.

CHAPTER 13

Michael rode his way into town, being very careful of the basket of eggs he had hooked on the saddle horn. He also had remembered the milk. He would have to bring the wagon back with him if he was going to continue to carry the eggs and milk in. It would be much easier to do in the wagon.

His first stop would be the hotel. He wanted to check on Katie and give the eggs and milk to Esther. Then he would find the twins and find out what the problem was that they were not out at the ranch this morning.

He pulled up in front of the hotel and very carefully lifted down the eggs and the skins of milk he had slung over the back of Solomon. As he walked up the steps, he noticed an elderly man with white hair watching every movement. He looked over at him, nodded in his direction, and said, "Morning," then continued to walk into the hotel. He noticed the smile on the old man as he nodded his way.

Esther smiled, too, when she saw him walk in. "Oh Michael, you are a godsend. I had forgotten your deal with me about the eggs and milk. With so much happening yesterday, it just simply slipped my mind. Thank you so much. I'll get Tad, and he will be ready to go in no time."

"No hurry. I want to see Katie if she is up to it. I also have to try to find the Tucker twins. If the Lord wills, I need one more man to ride with us to round up the cattle. I could use him around the ranch too. So, if you see anyone, please send them my way."

"I did have someone ask me about the sign this morning. He was an older gentleman with snow-white hair. I told him where the ranch was and gave him a brief description of you."

"I saw someone like that outside. How brief was the description?"

"Oh, I said that you were big, really big."

"Maybe that was him. He was certainly looking at me. It looked like he was trying to decide whether or not to speak. He didn't. He just nodded when I said morning to him."

"You probably scared him."

"No, he smiled."

"Well, I'll take these to Rose; you run up to Katie's room, number 10, and see her. She will be glad to see you. See you in a few minutes. I'll bring up some tea."

"Not for me, thanks. I can't stay."

Esther looked back at him and said, "Okay, but Katie needs some. She is doing better though. Her voice sounds much better this morning. Still, I think she needs to stay at least another day, maybe two. On your way out of town, stop by and I'll have some food for you men to eat tonight."

"You don't have to do that. We can fend for ourselves."

"You better take it while you can. I may not offer forever," she laughed.

"I'll be back then and can't wait to see what our special is for tonight. Remember, I'll have five others, maybe six if this man shows up and I hire him. I'll also have Tad unless you want him home before supper."

"No, you feed him, and I'll come out and get him later. I want to see the ranch. I'll bring Adam with me, of course. You don't mind do you?"

"Not at all, Tad is great, and I'd love to show you the ranch. Why don't you eat with us?"

"No, that's a very busy time for us, and we are both needed here. I'll be out when things start to slow down. Thanks for the invite, though, I appreciate it."

"I'll see you later, Mrs. Schmitt."

"It's Esther to you."

"Thank you, Esther. Bye for now."

She waved and turned to go into the kitchen. Michael mounted the stairs and made his way up to Katie's room. The eyes of the elderly man never moved from watching the big man as he walked up the stairs and out of sight. He just shook his head and muttered to himself, "Never have seen anyone that big."

The knock startled Katie. She didn't know whether to answer or not. Her heart raced, and her eyes were wide, darting around the room looking for a place to hide. Should she speak? What if it was Red?

"Katie, are you in there? It's me, Michael."

She let out a puff of air, not even realizing she had been holding her breath. Her smile lit the room like the sudden brilliance of a sunbeam when the rain passes.

"Yes, Michael, come in."

"Did I wake you?" He said as he came in the room.

"No, to tell you the truth, you scared me. Esther knocks, then says 'Katie,' and comes in. So, when you knocked and didn't speak, I was afraid Red was at the door. Will I ever get over the nightmares? He scared me so. I keep reliving the whole thing in my dreams. Sometimes I wake up trying to scream, but nothing comes out."

"Your voice is a little stronger today. Are you enjoying the lemon drops?"

"Very much. What a sweet treat! Those were rare when we were growing up. Also, yes, I believe my voice is a little stronger, not quite as hoarse. Michael, you didn't answer my question."

"I'm sorry. What question?"

"Will I ever get over the nightmares?"

"I truly believe you will. I believe God will take them away and replace that bad experience with some unbelievable joy."

"Oh, I could really use some joy. I am happy to see you. What's happening out on the ranch?"

"Well, I've hired Josh, Esther and Adam's son. He's just returned from service in the cavalry. I've also hired J. R. Riley. He goes by Riley. He uses big words and complicated sentences most of the time when he speaks. He really is a very nice man. I know you will like him. Then there are the Tucker twins. I'm here, in part, to see why they weren't at the ranch this morning as arranged. I also hired a man named Wulfgang Schurtz. He has a patch over one eye and a scar running down his face through that eye. It looks like a sword or knife wound. Maybe he was in the war. I didn't ask him. I think he has been rejected and ridiculed for his wound. Who a man is inside is more important to me than what he looks like. Granted, sometimes what a man looks like helps determine what his character is like. For instance, if he doesn't bother to keep himself clean or doesn't take care of his animal, he probably isn't the kind of person I want working for me."

"Like Red?"

"Definitely like Red! Wulf is not like that. He was clean, and his horse is in really good shape. He seemed like a good choice to me, so I hired him."

"What are the men up to this morning?"

"Well, I put them to work cleaning out the tool shed and making repairs on it."

"Oh, Michael, what happens if they find the money? Do you think they'd tell us or split it and keep quiet?"

"I hadn't thought about the money. No, I don't think they would be dishonest about it. Josh knows about your parents. He certainly wouldn't keep it or let either of the others even suggest it. Riley wouldn't even think it. I can't be certain about Wulf, but with the other two there, he wouldn't do anything. No, I think the money is safe if it is in the tool shed."

"Oh, I just feel like I need to get out there as soon as I can. I'm feeling much better." Katie had to stop and clear her throat. She looked at Michael with a bit of a sheepish grin on her face. "When do you hope to start rounding up the cattle?"

Casting her a sideways glance, Michael replied, "I wanted to start that today, but with the twins not showing up we'll have to start that tomorrow, maybe. We need to do it soon. If we wait too much longer, we may be late getting the cattle to San Antonio. We don't want to take them to Ft. Worth; we can get a better price for them in San Antonio. They don't have as far to walk going there so will weigh more and generally will be in better health. If we don't get started tomorrow, we will still be busy with all that needs to be done around the ranch. We also need to get a temporary corral built up on the range as we round up the cattle. So, we will trust the Lord God's leading."

"Then I need to be home tomorrow so I can cook for you men."

"We'll have to let the doc make that decision. Don't worry about us. I know Josh knows how to cook."

They laughed at this and then discussed how she wanted her garden laid out and exactly where. With Tad coming out, he could get that project started. She could join in when she came home.

Michael took his leave with a promise to come back and let her know what had happened with the twins. As he opened the door, Esther was just carrying the tray of tea things down the hall. He took the tray and set it on the small table in the room. He left leaving the women to carry on the conversation without him.

"Too much girly-to-do for me, Lord, let me get back to the ranching and I'll be a happy man," he said as we walked down the stairs.

"Sir, are you the man hiring cowhands at the Kurtz ranch?"

Michael couldn't believe he had almost run right over the wizened old man standing in front of him. He needed to be more aware of his surroundings.

"Forgive me sir; I am sorry I almost knocked you down."

"No, no, it was all my fault. I stepped in front of you. I thought you saw me."

"What can I do for you?"

"Well, I hope you can offer me a job. I sure do need the work and there aren't many who will hire someone my age. I guess they are afraid I can't hold my own with the cattle, or I may just drop dead."

They both smiled at this statement.

"Have you been a cowboy all your life?"

"I left it for a while to work my own place when I married. I left and started working for others when some lowdown, good-for-nothin' shot my wife and our little girl. We had been married less than two years. I just couldn't stay there. I've been riding the trails ever since. Well, 'til a couple months ago, when the rancher I have been working for sold his ranch and moved out to California. The new owners didn't think they needed a seasoned cowpoke around so they let me go. You looked like you would be fair, so I decided to ask if you still needed someone to work."

"My name is Michael. What's yours?"

"Clyde Jessup. Nice to meet you, Michael."

"Well, Clyde. I appreciate your asking for work."

A shadow crossed Clyde's eyes as he anticipated a refusal from Michael.

"I sure do need someone to help with our roundup, drive to San Antonio, and general upkeep of the ranch. Do you feel up to doing all of that?"

A glint of hope sparked in those now-dark eyes.

"I sure can. I may have a little arthritis, but I can still hold my own and teach some of the younger men a thing or two."

"I'd be happy to have you on board if you think you can stand three men who are as different as night and day and two teens just beginning their manhood."

"Sounds exciting. I don't believe there will be a dull moment."

"I think I should tell you, the owner of the ranch is a young woman, Miss Katie Kurtz. She was attacked yesterday by Red Galliger. He's in jail now and Miss Kurtz is recuperating here in the hotel with Mrs. Schmitt watching over and taking care of her. Miss Kurtz, Katie'll be going with us on the trail drive to cook. How do you feel about a woman on the drive?"

"As dangerous as it is, I wish I had taken my wife with me. I might still have her if I had. That decision is up to you. I understand why you would want her close by. How old is she?"

"I'm not sure. I think she must be twenty-one or twenty-two. She can't be much older than that."

"She will have enough adventure still in her to do fine. If she were older, she would be very aware of the dangers and too afraid to go. I have no objections to having a woman on the ranch or even on the drive. You are the foreman?"

"That I am. I am about to go see about our two teens. They didn't show up this morning. I sure hope they are still going to work. Once I get them settled in at the ranch, they won't be missing work."

"You want me to take the sign down in the hotel?"

"No, better wait 'til I see what has happened to our boys."

"I'll wait right here for you."

"That'll be fine. Oh, yes, I want to see the sheriff just for a minute too. I think I'll do that now."

As Michael walked over to Brian Daniels' office, Clyde sat outside and watched the world as it passed by and analyzed everything he saw. He noticed some men leaning against the bank and looking in every now and then. They seemed very nervous. He decided he just might walk over to the sheriff's office too.

Michael and Brian were talking about Red as Clyde opened the door and stepped in. They looked up at him when he entered.

"Sheriff, I could be wrong, but something looks real funny over at the bank. Either some men are checking it out for further mischief, or something is going on inside that might mean trouble. It just doesn't look right to me."

"Thanks, I'll check it out."

"I'm going with you," Michael said. "You don't need to do this alone."

"I'll be fine, but just in case, let me deputize you. Do you swear to uphold the laws of the land and this state?"

"I do."

"I deputize you with the authority given me by the state of Texas."

"Let's go."

"I'll stay here with the prisoner," Clyde said.

Michael and Brian walked in the direction of the bank watching to see if they could pick up on what Clyde had noticed. Sure enough, there were two men, strangers, leaning against the building and looking very nervous. They kept looking inside the bank window and then out again at the street. Michael and Brian moved to the other side of the street toward the hotel to keep from being obvious about their approach. They wanted to be behind the two and take them out before anyone came out of the bank, but they needed to come from the alley to do that. The two didn't seem to be very interested in them, so they kept walking toward the livery. After they were past them, they crossed back over and went in the alley next to the saloon, around the back and up the alley next to the bank. Five horses were ground-tethered at the back of the bank.

"Just keep your hands where I can see them." Brian said.

Brian had his gun in the back of one and Michael had his in the back of the other. They removed their guns and then instructed them to move into the alley next to the bank. Brian and Michael tied and gagged the men then went back out front. Just as they moved into the same place the two had been, three men came running out of the bank and turned right into the gun barrels of the sheriff and Michael.

"Halt right there, or you're dead," Brian yelled.

The first man out raised his gun, and Brian fired his. The outlaw fell back holding his shoulder, dropping his gun and the bag he was holding. The other two took one look at Brian and the giant standing next to him with guns raised and decided this was not a good time to try to fight it out.

"Michael, help me get these 'weasels' over to the jail, then I'll get Doc to take a look at this one's shoulder. I appreciate your help today."

The banker, Mr. Tompkins, and Martin, the teller, came out and saw what had happened. They looked directly at Brian smiling worried kind of smiles.

Wringing his hands and then wiping them on his pant legs, Mr. Tompkins explained, "There was just me and Martin in there. It was two against three. They had guns, and we didn't. We decided to give them the money. It just wasn't worth our lives, what with Martin having one boy and another child on the way. I just gave them the money."

"You did the right thing, Mr. Tompkins. We'll get these five locked up. I hope the marshal comes soon. I'll be running out of room if he doesn't. Pick up the bags of cash, Mr. Tompkins, and go put it in the bank vault. I don't think you should keep the bank open today. You and Martin need to go home and see your families."

"Thanks, Sheriff, we'll do that."

With that, Mr. Tompkins picked up the money, his hands obviously shaking, and handed it to Martin. They turned to go into the bank. Once inside, Mr. Tompkins closed and locked the door so they could put the money in the vault and lock it up in there. Martin turned the closed sign out so everyone would know the bank was closed. When they completed their task, they would go out the back way and lock that door behind them.

Michael had noticed sweat beaded on Mr. Tompkin's brow as he turned to enter the bank. Martin's complexion was as gray as ash. Silently he agreed. These men did need to go home to see their families.

The sheriff got the men tied together and shuffled them off to the jail with Michael's help. When they entered, Clyde was sitting behind the desk with a shotgun in his hands.

"Whew, I sure am glad it's you. When you told me who you have in the jail, I started getting worried that those men just might be thinking about coming over here to bust him out. I thought I'd better be ready for them if they did."

"Smart thinkin'. Thanks. And thank you for tipping me off to the bank robbery. How did you know?"

"I have made it a practice to observe. I look at everything and try to analyze it. It helps when making decisions. I made a big one once and don't think I made a good one then. It cost me the love of my life, and I don't want to make any more really bad decisions. So, I analyze, and then use what I see and know to decide what to do."

"Well, I'm going to thank God for you and your discernment."

"God took my wife and child away. I don't trust him."

"I trust him with my life and thank him daily for saving my soul."

With that, Clyde got up and left. He wasn't angry, just not willing to hear it. When Michael looked out the window, there was Clyde sitting on the front porch of the hotel, watching the world again.

"I'm headed to the blacksmith shop. I need to see about the twins. They didn't show up this morning."

"They're over there. I saw them working for their pa bright and early."

"Huh. I wonder what that's all about? I guess I'll go on over and see."

"Michael." Brian said.

"Yes?"

"Thanks. It was good to have you with me today."

"You're welcome, Brian. I'm always glad to help."

Michael closed the door softly behind him as Brian locked the last cell door. The moaning coming from the one robber reminded him he needed to go and get the doc.

Michael walked directly to the blacksmith shop. There stood Mr. Tucker and the boys who were covered with sweat and dirt tending the fire and working on some wheels. Mr. Tucker looked up and squinted at Michael.

"What do *you* want?"

The smell of body odor was strong, but Michael thought he caught a whiff of alcohol as well.

"Mr. Tucker, I've come to speak with the boys about work. They didn't show up this morning as we agreed."

"Well, I decided I needed 'em more 'an you do today, so I had 'em stay with me."

"Mr. Tucker, you know I hired the boys with your permission. You know I need them. If you needed them, why did you allow me to hire them?"

"Well, I didn't know I'd need 'em today."

"Mr. Tucker, we have an agreement, and I have an agreement with the boys. I need them to come out to the ranch. I have work I need them to do. I was counting on them."

The look on the boys' faces brightened up with hope. Michael saw what looked like a bruise on the side of Wade's face.

"They cain't come."

The shadow of doubt and fear crossed their faces again. Their eyes darted from one man to the other. Michael could tell they wanted to come with him but were afraid of their father.

"Mr. Tucker, when someone agrees to pay you for your work, when they come and pick up their purchase, you expect them to pay you, don't you?"

"Course I do!"

"Do you let them keep the money they were going to give you just because they say they need it more?"

"Course not!"

"Then why would you think it was all right for you to keep the boys when you and they had agreed they would come and work for me?"

"Well, I'm 'eir pa, and I said so."

"That was not our agreement. They agreed to come to work this morning. I have spent time away from the ranch that I can't afford to come and look for them. I need them to work. Now, come on boys and let's get going. I need you to report to work. You'll be staying at the ranch, so get your belongings and meet me at the hotel in fifteen minutes."

"Yes sir." They said in unison and walked out of the shop toward home.

"Why, who do you think you are telling my boys what to do?"

"I am their employer. As long as they work for me, I can tell them what to do, just like you do to your employees."

"I don't have any employees."

"You don't pay your sons?"

"Course not! They're my kids."

"It's time those kids earned some of their own money and found out what it means to be a man who can take care of himself. I am giving them that chance."

"Who's going to help me?"

"You could hire someone."

With that, Michael turned and walked out of the shop. It was good to breathe fresh air again.

"Father, there are so many here who don't really know you. Please help me to be a blessing to them and a witness for you. Open their eyes so they can see."

"Michael!"

Michael lifted his head and looked to see who was calling his name. There on the front porch of the hotel was Esther. He walked in her direction.

"Doc McConnell was just here. He said he believed Katie could go home in a few days, but he said if she got upset and really wanted to go home, she could. He would rather keep her here a few more days. Her throat is basically healed, yet he is still worried about her mental health. He told me he really thinks she will have some mental distress over this for some time, and the longer she waits, the better she can cope with going back home where all this happened. If you want her to come home, we can bring her out about midmorning if you would like."

"I'm not at all sure she should leave. I don't want her to rush it, and I tend to go along with the doc. It will probably be better to let her stay for at least a few more days. That is, unless you need the room."

"That is *not* a problem. I love Katie and would be delighted for her to stay right here. I won't encourage her to go; in fact, I will support both you and the doc. We can see how it works out. She is anxious to be there, and she wants something to do.

I'm afraid I've waited on her too much. She was up and dressed when I left her. I think she wants to go down for supper tonight. I wasn't sure she should. What do you think?"

"She has always been afraid of what people would say and do to her in town after what her father experienced."

"I can't say that I blame her. I'll make sure Adam and I eat with her. Why don't you join her for lunch?"

Michael looked at Clyde sitting there. He knew Clyde was taking in the conversation.

"I'd like to do that, and it's time for lunch. This is Clyde, our newest hand, and the twins are to join me here in a few minutes. How about if we all eat together in the dining room? Do you think Katie will come down?"

"I can ask her."

"I hope she feels up to it. Maybe it will help her to feel more comfortable tonight."

Esther disappeared through the door and Michael looked at Clyde, who looked like he was studying the people as they walked by.

"How about it, Clyde, do you feel like eating lunch with a pretty lady?"

"Might as well. Gotta meet her sometime, might as well do it over lunch."

"How about going in and getting a table for five?"

"I can do that."

Clyde went on in and just then the twins came running around the corner and straight for Michael, each carrying a burlap sack.

"Are those your things? Where are your horses?"

They looked at him and then said in unison. "Pa said if we was gonna go out there and work for you, you'd have to let us ride your horses. He wouldn't let us brung ours."

The boys' expressions said more than they were willing. Their pa was drunk or close to it and was feeling really mean. Those boys were glad to get as far away from him as they could, even if they had to walk.

"I have the wagon at the livery with a horse to pull it. You boys can take that back with you. When we get to the ranch we'll have to see what we have for you. Not much is there as far as horse flesh goes."

"Well, if we could come back in tomarra, maybe Pa would change his min' and let us have the horses. He's jest not feeling well t'day."

"Okay, let's have some lunch and we'll see what happens when we get to the ranch."

"Lunch? Ya mean eat some food in the middle of the day?" Cade asked.

"That's right."

"Wow!" They said in unison.

"Don't you usually eat in the middle of the day?"

"No, we ain't eaten lunch in years. We's lucky if we get somtin' to drink. Ma works, Pa works, we's left on our own. We could sneak some, but we wouldn't do that to Ma. She has to really watch it when it comes to spendin'. Pa watches ev'ry penny."

"Well, let's go in and find our seats."

They entered the restaurant and looked for Clyde. He had them all set in a corner of the room with a round table just right for five. The four of them had a seat and the boys began to study what was written on the board displaying what was available for lunch.

"Looks like it's fried chicken or grilled steak, boys. What are you feeling up to?"

"Fried chicken!"

"That sounds good to me too," added Clyde.

"Well let's see here. I think I'll go with steak. They cook it over mesquite. I'd have to eat two chickens to fill me up."

The laugh behind him caused his heart to take a little leap. He turned, and there she was. All the men at the table rose. She looked so good dressed and with her hair done. She looked more rested than she had out at the ranch. She was still too skinny.

She needs to get some meat on those bones, Michael thought.

"You look refreshed and beautiful. Will you join us and try one of their steaks?" He said as he offered her a chair.

"Thank you so much. This will be delightful. I see we have some new faces in our group."

"Yes, this is Clyde Jessup, he joined us this morning. These are the Tucker twins, this is Wade, and this is Cade."

The twins elbowed each other; he had gotten them right!

"Gentlemen, this is Miss Katie Kurtz."

Each man sat after she did, murmuring their comments on how nice it was to meet her or to see her up and about. Michael could not take his eyes off her. He could not get over how different she looked now compared to when he lifted her into the wagon. She still was thin, but her color was so much better. He thanked the Lord for his watch and care over her.

After everyone had had their fill and had gotten to know each other better, they decided to head on out to the ranch. Katie reluctantly moved toward the stairs, looking back over her shoulder toward the departing men. The only one who looked back was Clyde. When he saw her, he paused, leaned over, and spoke to Michael. Michael turned and looked back, then nodded. To Katie's great surprise Clyde turned and walked back to where she stood.

"Miss Kurtz, you look like you would rather stay downstairs than go up to your room again. I'll keep you company if you would like me to."

"Thank you, Clyde. How kind of you. Yes, I would like that very much. Those four walls were beginning to close in on me."

Katie began to cough and clear her throat. She looked around to see if she could find Esther.

"Miss Kurtz, could I get you something to drink? I wouldn't mind at all."

"Clyde, you don't have to do that, but I do need some hot tea. My throat is feeling a little raspy."

"I'll see to it right away. Why don't you sit right here, and I'll bring it to you. Then, we can watch the people as they come in and go out of the hotel and restaurant. We can guess what they have been up to or where they are going." He noticed the ugly bruises on her neck where the awful hands of Red had choked her.

Coughing again, Katie smiled, "Sounds delightful. Thank you, Clyde."

He went back into the restaurant and came back shortly with one hot tea, a cup of coffee, and some lemon drops.

"I seemed to have gotten more than I asked for. This is quite the place to add lemon drops with their tea."

"Did the lady behind the counter know it was for me?"

"Yes, I did mention that to her."

"That's why. The doctor wants me to suck on these for my throat. I'm going to become so dependent on them, I'll have to buy them by the wagonload. Do you think I will tire of them?"

"It has been my experience that too much of a good thing seems to become a bad thing. If you eat them only a little here and there, I think you'll be all right with them. Just don't overdo it. Oh, look at the hat on that woman. Is that the latest fashion or is she just trying to get everyone's attention?"

Katie laughed and looked at him. She laughed again at the expression on his face. He looked like he was sucking on some bitter alum.

"Now, Clyde, don't you appreciate the finer styles straight from New York City? I must say I wouldn't be caught dead wearing something that outrageous. Those long feathers and big sunflowers make her look like she's going out in the wild and wants to blend in."

After this, the game began in their observation and analysis of the people passing. Katie felt the darkness in her soul recede just a bit more. She was beginning to feel quite human again. No one had given her an angry look or said a rude word to her. Maybe town wasn't so bad after all.

CHAPTER 14

Michael and the others moved on out of town and back to the ranch. The twins looked like they had gotten the best present they had ever received. As they rode on into the ranch, they saw the three men working up on the roof of the tool shed. Piles of belongings were scattered all over the area around the shed. Michael looked at the mess and shook his head.

"What's happened? I had not planned for this to be major job. They were supposed to organize the tool shed, not rebuild it!"

They rode into the yard and took their horses to the barn. The twins took the wagon and unhitched the horse and put her back in her stall. Michael walked up to the tool shed, shaded his eyes, and yelled up to the men.

"What are you doing?"

"The roof was a mess. Leaking would not describe what it would have done in the next rain. I think this may have been on Katie's dad's list of things to do in the winter, because he had the wood and shakes all ready for a roofing job. It looks like there will be just enough for this shed," Josh said.

"Why all the mess outside?"

When Riley opened his mouth to answer, Michael thought, *I shouldn't have asked.*

"Well, you see, it's like this. One thing leads to another. We were going to clean out the tool shed, get it organized and back in proper order, just like you petitioned. Then when we removed everything from the shed and could see the roof, it was then we realized it desperately needed to be fixed. So, we asked ourselves as well as each other, 'Why put everything back in before fixing the roof?' We started on the roof and, as you see, we're almost done. With the three of us working and with the two ladders to help us carry the wood up, it went exceedingly fast. Now that you're here, you can get the tools organized the way *you* want them and *put* them in the shed while we finish up here."

"Sounds reasonable. I'm going to send the twins out to the bunkhouse to stow their things. Their pa was not in 'good health' this morning, and they were helping him. He wouldn't let them bring any horses with them. We are going to have to do something about that."

"He must have been feeling really bad then if he didn't allow them to bring horses out on a ranch to do cattle work." Riley pointed out.

"I think he'll rethink that when he's himself again."

"We can pray to that end," Josh said as he picked up the hammer and some nails and began fitting the shakes in place.

The noise of work around the ranch rang through the hills. The ranch was alive again.

Katie would be so happy if she were here, Josh thought. He lifted his head and looked all around the ranch. It *was* a beautiful sight, again, just like its owner.

"Tad, you go over and start tilling the soil in the kitchen garden. Here, take this hoe and off you go!"

"I always help Ma with her garden. I know just what to do."

"You're a good boy, Tad. She'll be out later to get you. Let's see how much you can get done by the time she gets here."

"Okay, I'll see if she thinks I'm worth the eggs!"

Michael and Tad laughed and then Tad took off running toward the back of the house, carrying the hoe and a bucket with him.

The twins came out of the barn and walked toward Michael. Michael glanced their way and waved to the other men.

"Did you get everything put away?"

"Yes, sir," they again said in unison.

Michael wondered if they were attached at the brain.

"Well, I want you to take your things and find a bed in the bunkhouse. It's right over there behind those trees. You'll be able to tell which beds have been taken, I hope. If you can't, just put your things down and then come back here, and we will get you acquainted with your surroundings. We'll find you something to do as well."

"Yippee!" They yelled together then took off running toward the bunkhouse, the sacks of their belongings flopping against their backs like dead chickens.

It wasn't long before the boys came back, running all the way.

"If only I had that much energy!" Riley mused.

"You and me both," added Wulf. "We'd be through up here if we did."

"Mr. Michael, there's a horse in the bunkhouse stalls. He looks like he hasn't had anything to eat, and there's no water left in the bucket. You want us to feed him?"

Michael's eyebrows rose and he looked at each man in turn. He silently questioned each one. As they looked back at him, they shrugged their shoulders and shook their heads indicating they didn't know about the horse.

"Well, I guess that must be Red's horse. I hadn't even thought about him since all of the happenings of yesterday and today. From what I hear, he wasn't too good to his animals. He probably rode them until they dropped and then bought or stole another one. What's his general condition?"

"He looks pretty good, just hungry," Wade said.

"He looks good enough to ride," Cade added.

"Well, I'll check with the sheriff and see what he says about the horse. We might have one for you boys if it's okay with him."

"Can we go get him and put him in the barn with the others? He needs to have something to eat and drink."

"Why don't you boys go get him and rub him down real good? Then turn him out in the pasture and let him run. He probably needs the exercise. He can eat some grass and then we can feed him with the others later. Make sure there's water in the trough. Rub the others down and you can turn them out for a bit as well. Then make sure the goats have hay and feed."

"Yes, sir!" They yelled back over their shoulders as they ran down the lane toward the bunkhouse.

"Well, let's see what we have here. Oh, by the way, I hired a new man in town. His name is Clyde Jessup. He stayed back in town for a bit to keep Katie company."

Josh jerked his head up at these words and felt a surge of emotion fire through him he found hard to explain.

"Why did he do that?" Josh asked, trying to keep his voice under control.

"Well, she looked mighty lonely and…oh, you don't know, she came downstairs and had lunch with us. So when we left, she was going to go back up to her room. Clyde felt like she looked lonely and like she really didn't want to go back up to her room. He's good about reading people and situations. Anyway, he suggested he stay with her a while until she was ready to go back up stairs."

"How do you know his intentions were honorable?"

"I just know," Michael said, glancing at Josh and seeing the red creeping up his neck. Josh's brow wrinkled and he squinted down at Michael.

Michael smiled a crooked little smile. He then looked right in the eye at Josh and said, "She'll be just fine. You'll see. Clyde wouldn't hurt a flea."

"Well, Katie is far from being a flea! I just don't want her hurt any more, that's all. Are you sure he will take care of her and not try to get too close?"

"What do you mean, Josh?"

"Ah, you know what I mean."

"Do you really think I would leave her in his hands if I didn't trust him to be a complete gentleman with her?"

"Well, no, that's not what I mean. What I mean is…Oh, just forget it!"

With that, both men went back to work. Josh's hammer came down harder than it had all day, and he worked with a new intensity. Riley and Wulf looked at him and then each other, smiled and shrugged. The shed was clean and all organized before supper. They all pitched in to get the tools organized and put away. Riley and Wulf went up to help Josh finish nailing the shakes on the roof. They worked hard to keep up with him.

Josh prayed silently as he worked. "I don't understand how I'm feeling, Lord. Why should it bother me that Clyde stayed to visit with Katie? But, I must confess it does."

Riley looked up into the sky. "The weather is perfect! I wonder when the rains will hit? April showers bring May flowers. It's March and the wild flowers are in bloom, but I know that the rains will be coming soon. We need to get those cattle rounded up and taken to market as soon as we can."

"Riley, you are just full of wisdom." Wulf squinted against the sun as he passed him some more shakes.

"Where are those boys?" Michael asked.

"There's the horse out in the pasture, so they are finished with him. You want me to go and find them?"

"That shouldn't be too hard, Riley. If we just get real quiet, we should be able to hear them!" Wulf said making his way back down the ladder to get more shakes.

"You could be right, Wulf. We could try that."

They all stopped talking and working and just listened. At first they heard nothing, and then they could hear just a distant sound of the goats. There were some noises coming from the barn.

"I'd better go check." Michael said looking toward the barn.

"I'll do it, Michael. I've had some experience with boys." Michael looked at Riley and raised an eyebrow. "I'll tell you about it sometime when I tell you the rest of my story. Best go check on them now." With that, Riley descended the ladder and sauntered toward the barn.

"It's going to take some getting used to having teenagers around. I don't want to be a babysitter. I need to know I can trust those boys," Michael sighed and looked at the other men.

"They do seem to be very young."

"They're about sixteen, Wulf, so they *are* young, but old enough to get into trouble."

"That they are. I well remember." Wulf shook his head and climbed the ladder to take over what Riley was doing.

CHAPTER 15

"Do you feel like taking a little walk, Katie?" Clyde asked. "It might do you some good to get out and get some fresh air. If you get tired, we can sit on a chair or bench out on the boardwalk and just people watch out there. It's amazing what one sees."

"I don't know, Clyde. I'm still a little nervous about being around people."

"You'll never get over it until you expose yourself to the rest of the world. I won't let anyone bother you."

"If I begin to feel uncomfortable, you'll bring me right back here?"

"Of course I will. I don't think that will happen. From what I have seen, people are just going about their own business and not really paying you any mind, except for the occasional young man walking through. I don't blame them a bit looking your way. It's a beautiful sight to see."

"Oh, Clyde, you are too kind. I don't believe they are looking at me in the first place. Maybe they were looking at you and wondering what you were doing with the likes of me!"

"Oh no, believe me, that was not what they were thinking."

Smiling at her, he stood and offered her his hand.

"Shall we?"

"Oh, all right. I'm not going to get over this until I see if I'm strong enough to face the outside world, am I?"

"No young lady, you are not."

They walked outside without seeing Esther watching from the restaurant door. She wiped the tear that slowly traced its way down her cheek. It felt like she had just given birth again. Her precious Katie was testing her boundaries and one day would feel free to go where she pleased.

They walked toward the general store, but Katie didn't want to go in. She said she would rather just walk around town and see what she could see.

"Look at that cowboy over there. He's just gotten paid, and he is trying to decide what to do with his money. Should he spend it in the saloon and maybe lose it all in a game of chance? Should he send some back to his ma? Should he go to the general store and buy some new boots? I bet he goes to the restaurant to buy as close to a home-cooked meal as he can after being out on the range or working the cattle and eating beans and biscuits most of the time."

"Clyde, you are something else. Shall we sit and see what he does?"

"Whatever you wish, Princess."

They sat, and within just a couple of minutes the cowboy pushed himself away from the wall he had been leaning against and walked across the street to the hotel.

"Why, you are a mind reader, Clyde. I'd better watch what I think from now on."

"I've just had years of studying humans and human nature."

"Well, it's just about magic the way you do it."

With that, they got up and walked around a bit more before deciding that Katie was tired and ready to go back to the hotel to get herself a nap.

"I really appreciate you taking time to keep me company, Clyde. I didn't want to go back to my room right away. You staying with me has helped so much. Now, I understand how you knew. I appreciate Michael allowing you to stay."

"I believe Michael would lay down his life for you, Princess. He thinks a heap of you."

"He feels responsible for me. He believes God sent him to the ranch to take care of me. He has been very good about doing that."

"I don't know about God sending him. I don't hold much for God being involved with or even interested in people as individuals."

"Well, I'm not so sure. I was always so angry at God, blaming him for all the things in my life that went wrong. I was always asking why."

"Did he ever answer you?"

"No, but Michael said that since God is in control, since he is sovereign, we should just trust him. We don't see the big picture, but we can be sure that God has our best interest at heart, even though it doesn't look like it from where we are."

"I don't know that I would have that much trust in anybody. I feel better if I'm in control."

"That's the way I was feeling. Michael asked me if I knew what was in everyone's mind and heart. I said no. Then he asked me if I would trust someone with my life who knew those things and could make decisions based on what was best for everyone involved. Well, I couldn't say no to that, but I did say I would think about that."

"That's what I would have to do, think about it."

"I've been thinking about it, and I think my problem is still that I want to be in control, just like you do. Then I ask myself, is that pride?"

"Ouch! That hurt. I've always looked down on prideful people. Maybe I better take a closer look at myself."

"Me too. I look at Esther, and I see her depending on God, and she seems to have so much peace."

"Well, what, after all, does she have to be bothered with? She has a perfect husband and two perfect sons."

"Yes, and she has had very many miscarriages even though I believe she would be the perfect mother. Why would God allow her to be with child and then lose that child, not once but many times? I ask myself, do I really have to know that? It really isn't any of my business. Esther said it was to draw her closer to him. I don't understand how that can be. I need to talk more with her about it."

"Well, here we are back at the hotel. How are you feeling?"

"Much better, thank you. I am ready for a nap. I appreciate you staying with me, but I suppose you should be getting on to the ranch. I should be out there tomorrow. I'll see you again then."

"I'll look forward to it. It has been my experience to benefit from not rushing things. If the doctor thinks you should rest a little longer here, then maybe you should think about that too. Thank you for consenting to walk with me. Can you make it up the stairs without help?"

"Yes, thank you for asking. Good-bye, Clyde."

"Good-bye, Princess."

As she walked up the stairs, she turned and saw him watching her ascend. She gave him a wave and walked the rest of the way feeling lighter at heart than she had since before the attack. He waved back and turned to go but watched her until she was out of sight.

"She would be just the age of my little one. I just can't see letting anything happen to her," he mumbled to himself as he moved to get on his horse and ride out of town to the ranch.

Riley let his eyes adjust to the change in light when he entered the barn. He could hear laughter and some other noises somewhere above him. He looked up and was covered with a dusting of hay.

"What are you boys doing?" he asked.

"It's my turn!"

"No, I want to go again."

"No, it's my turn!"

"I just want to show you how to do it, again."

"I can do it; I'll show you."

Riley was just about to shout at them to get down when one boy came flying from the loft holding tight to a rope. Riley caught his breath, jerked his head to the side, and saw the pile of hay and a pitchfork prongs up in the dirt beside the pile.

"Noooo!" yelled Riley.

Before he could move, the boy dropped and landed in the hay just inches from the pitchfork. His wide eyes stared up at Riley.

"Get down the ladder right now!" Riley yelled at the identical face staring down at him.

"What do you boys think you're doing? I'm not sure what you were told to do, but I know it was not to swing on a rope from the loft in the barn and see if you can land closer than anyone else to an upturned pitchfork without being hurt or killed!" Riley was trying hard to keep his voice even and was not really succeeding.

The twins looked at him with their eyes full of regret. What Riley couldn't figure out was if that regret was for their foolishness or for getting caught. He took a deep breath, cleared his throat, and managed to calm himself.

"I know you are just 'boys,' but it is time to grow up. You've been hired to do a man's work. You said you were up to it. Now, Michael agreed to give you a chance. You need to pull your weight around here. What do you have to say for yourselves?"

Cade looked up into Riley's eyes. He looked back at Wade and then at the pitchfork.

"I don't know what got into Wade…and me. He, uh, we just got it in our heads that flying off the loft and landing in that pile of hay would be just the thing to do to have a little fun. Mr. Riley, we weren't done with our chores yet. It was wrong. There is a time to play and a time to work. Now is the time to work. We're sorry. We will try to remember and not get pulled into tomfoolery again."

"Wade?"

"Yes, sir?"

"Do you feel the same way, or are you going to let Cade be the only man here?"

"Well, sir, I wasn't the one to suggest it. Cade, he said…"

"Wade, I don't care who suggested it. That really doesn't matter at this point because both of you were doing it. You could have refused and kept working. It was your decision as well as his. Now, are you going to be a man and own up to it, or are you going to make excuses for your behavior rather than take responsibility for it?"

"I ain't never thought of it that way before. I guess when you put it that way, I don't have a choice. I did agree to it, and I did do it. I'm sorry, sir. It won't happen again."

"That's good. We don't have time for shenanigans. Now, I see only one horse out in the pasture and the goats still don't have their hay and feed. You get that done before supper, or you don't eat. The horses better be taken care of correctly or you will have to rub them all down again. Don't waste time by doing a job halfway by rushing through it. That will only cause you to spend more time on it to get it right. I'll check to see if you have done a good job. Remember, 'Whatsoever you do in word or deed, do it heartily as unto the Lord, not unto men.' Is that clear enough? You do your chores like Jesus is looking over your shoulder, not me, and you will not miss supper."

The boys looked at each other and then at the retreating back of Riley. They punched each other in the ribs with their elbows and then took off toward the other horses. They were determined to do the job right and to do it as quickly as possible. The sun was getting lower in the sky, and they really didn't want to miss supper. They knew if either one of them didn't do the job right, both of them would suffer the consequences. They agreed to check each other's work, and work they did. Every now and then one would say to the other, "Sure was fun, though, wasn't it?" They would burst out laughing and then get right back to work.

Riley left the barn shaking his head. He gave a full report to Michael who looked toward the barn, spat, then looked back at Riley.

"They are yours. I'm not sure I can put up with all that right now. I want you to be their mentor, Riley. Think you can handle that?"

"I most assuredly can. You can take my word for it and carve those words in stone if that will make your life seem easier to you. Just back me up when I need it."

"You've got it."

The men finished up just as Tad came running up. Michael looked at Riley and then at the others as much to say, "I had forgotten all about him!"

"Mr. Michael, can I keep it?"

Michael wasn't about to say yes until he knew what "it" was.

Tad was carrying the water pail in one hand. Michael looked in the pail.

"Whatcha got there, Tad, my man?"

"Oh, I brought you some water. I thought you might need it about now."

"Well, that is very thoughtful of you. You are so right. We are thirsty. Thank you, Tad. Now, what is it you want to keep?"

As Michael took the pail from the boy, Tad held out his other hand.

"This, Mr. Michael. Can, I mean, *may* I keep it?"

Held tightly in his grasp was a snake.

"I'll take real good care of it, please?"

"Well, now. That snake is not mine to give. That snake belongs to God. I'm not so sure he wants you to make a prisoner of one of his free creatures. I'm not so sure your ma would want it either."

"Oh, Ma won't care. She likes snakes."

"She is coming out later to pick you up. We can ask her, or you can just really think about what would make the snake the happiest. What would be best for the snake? Should he be free in the country where God put him? Should he be held in a glass jar or a box where he can't roam and do the things God designed him to do? Which one sounds like the right choice? Why don't you go and pray about it and then let God speak to your heart about it. Let me know what you think God is telling you."

"Ma's coming out here? You aren't taking me back?"

"That's right, your ma is coming out after supper time to see the ranch. Your pa is coming with her. When they leave, you will go with them."

"Well, I might as well let the snake go right now. I don't even have to ask God. Ma may let me have it, but Pa hates snakes! I could never get away with it if he knew. Aw shucks! I want a pet!"

"Have you asked your Pa if you could have a pet?"

"He'd say no."

"I tell you what, Tad. We really need a dog out here and some cats. When we get them, you will be able to play with them and treat them like your own without having them live at the hotel. I think that is the biggest problem for you owning a pet. There just isn't anywhere to keep one there."

"Really, you would do that for me?"

"Well, for you and for Miss Katie. I think she needs one as much as you do. Besides, we don't want mice in the house or the barn. We definitely need a couple of barn cats and a dog for protection, a sort of signal that someone is coming."

"Wow! I'm going to work even harder now. Want to see what I've done?"

"Sure, let's go have a look."

With that, Tad and Michael walked toward the kitchen garden plot. As soon as they got there, Tad ran over to the grassy area on the far side of the plot and let the little snake go on his way. He couldn't believe how good it felt inside to let the snake go. He knew he had done the right thing. Looking back over his shoulder, he smiled and waved at Michael and looked back at the snake which was already headed for a nice little quiet, dark place under the smokehouse. Tad ran back over to Michael who was inspecting Tad's work.

"Well, now, I must say, I haven't seen garden work this good in a long time, Tad. You did a mighty fine job. Won't Miss Katie be pleased when she comes home?"

Tad beamed with pleasure at the praise from Michael.

"Really, Mr. Michael? I hope she will be pleased. Is she really coming back tomorrow? I want to get more done before then. She needs to know I'm going to be a good helper."

"I think she may already know that, Tad. You have proven yourself more than once."

"I really like her. She is everything I would want in a big sister. Do you think we could adopt her?"

"Well, she's a bit old to be adopted officially. But I think it would be okay for you and your folks to treat her like she is one of the family. I know she would really love that."

"Can I call her 'sis'?"

"You will have to take that up with her. Find a good time to ask her. Don't just jump at her the first time you see her. She will need to be in the right mood. Girls are like that, Tad. Sometimes you have to take things slow and easy with them."

"Girls are gobs of trouble, aren't they?"

Michael laughed out loud. He couldn't help himself as he looked at this young boy, not more than ten years old, who had already figured that out.

"Bless his heart, he's going to have an easier time of it now that he knows that much," thought Michael.

"What's so funny?" Josh asked as he walked up.

"Girls, they are so much trouble." Tad replied.

It was Josh's turn to laugh, and Michael joined in.

Josh looked down at his little brother, "Yes, they are, Tad. Yes, they certainly are. Hey, look at this garden plot. It looks like a whole team of Trojans have been working here. Who did you get to help you out?"

"I did it all myself."

"Wow, Tad, you must have eaten a good breakfast and lunch. This is loads of work to have gotten done in the amount of time you've been working. I'm proud of you."

"Thanks, Josh!" Tad beamed under his brother's praise.

"Do you need any help with anything?"

"Yes, I need to find a dog and some cats."

Josh looked at Tad then at Michael. Michael shrugged.

"I told him we needed some barn cats here to help keep the mice down and a dog to be a warning of visitors. I told him he could play with them when he was out here."

All the meanings behind his words were not lost on Josh.

"I think that's an excellent idea. We will get on that right away, Tad. Maybe you can check around in town to see if anyone has any dogs or cats they need to find a home for."

"I can ask Mom. She knows everything!"

"Does she now? I better be careful what I reveal to her. A man needs to have some secrets!"

"Not from Mom. I think God must talk to her. She knows *everything*!"

"Okay, I'll be particularly honest around her. I don't want her to think I don't love her and don't trust her. She is our mom."

"Yeah, and it wouldn't do any good anyway to try to keep something from her. She just knows. I'm telling you, Josh, you just don't know. You've been away and don't remember how she just knows. I can't get away with anything."

"It's better not to try, then."

"You're tellin' me?"

Josh laughed, "Well, anyway, Michael, we're finished with the tool shed, and everything is back in and organized. I think you'll be pleased with the work."

"I know I will be. I'm really getting hungry. I think I'll go in and start getting supper on the table. Go tell the guys to get cleaned up and we'll eat in about thirty minutes. We just need to heat up some things that your mom sent out."

"I just love Mom's cooking. I can't wait to see what she's fixed."

"Well, actually, I think it is Miss Rose's cooking, but I sure can't complain about her cooking. It is great!"

"Oh, I forgot, Mom isn't doing everything now like she was. It's a good thing too. She'd be dead by now if she was. I can't believe how business has boomed. They're busy all the time."

"Well, I'll head in and start. You go tell the others."

"Right, I'll do just that. Get washed up, squirt, and help Michael, will you?"

"Oh, boy, will I!"

"Wash your face too. You're a mess of dirt and sweat," Josh said over his shoulder as he walked away toward the others.

CHAPTER 16

"e're going out to the ranch a little later to get Tad. Do you feel up to the ride, or would you rather stay here and rest?"

"Oh, Esther, I would love to go, but I really am tired. I am actually a bit shaky on my feet. I did so much with Clyde today. I think I should stay here. Thank you for asking, though. It's just Doc said I could go home tomorrow if I promise not to overdo. You have been so wonderful, but I really would like to get home. There is so much to do to get ready for the trail drive. I wonder if the men have even been out to get the cattle."

"That was not their plan today. They were working on the ranch, I believe. So, maybe if you get there tomorrow, they'll go out. Remember, we need to think about what the doctor said? I think it would be best to go out and see how things go. If you are too overly taxed by the trip or the emotional anxiety of seeing everything again, we can always come back. Let's talk to the doctor again, okay?"

"When will we go tomorrow?"

"Katie…"

"Please, Esther?"

"Oh, all right. About midmorning would be best, I think. It won't be too warm and the breakfast rush will be over."

"That sounds good to me. I think I will want to take the lemon drops with me. They have helped so much!"

"Absolutely. In fact, I think we should get you a good supply so you will have them whenever your throat starts feeling scratchy."

"Oh, you don't have to do that!"

"Well, I know I don't have to, but I will just the same. There are also some different types of teas I want to take out."

"Oh, now that I will *not* argue over. They have been wonderful! I am most grateful for what you have provided."

"And you *are* most welcome. I hope you'll look to me as a mother to you. I've always wanted a daughter, and God never gave me one. Now, I think he has. I so want to teach you things I wanted to pass on. Will you let me?"

"Of course. My mother was wonderful. But she was very closed-mouthed, I guess you would say. She didn't share much with us girls. We learned by watching her, but she didn't really 'teach' us. Don't get me wrong, I love my mother and father. They just never were what you would call 'close' to us girls. They were much more involved with our brother, Ben."

"Katie, I know your mother loved you and Abigail very much. I am sure your parents looked on Ben as the future of their bloodline and name, so he became very important to them. They knew you girls would marry and move from home, so they put their hope in their son to carry on for them. They wanted the best for you as well as Abigail, but they just didn't see the future for them and their name through you girls."

"I had not thought of it that way. Abigail and I did talk plenty about finding husbands and getting married. I just always thought we'd be close to them. Considering how much my father wandered, though, I could see how they didn't think we would move from them, so much as they would move from us. Pa did say this was our home. He didn't have plans to move from here. He had not said that before. Yet, I can't help but think, with all that is going on out in California, that Pa eventually would have gotten the wanderlust again and left. I just didn't want to move again. I was ready for a home, some roots, friends…"

"Oh, honey, I know you have been lonely." Esther leaned down and gave Katie a long, loving hug.

Tears began again for Katie, and then they sprung up in Esther's eyes as she prayed, "Oh, Father, give Katie your love and help her never feel alone again. Thank you. In Jesus' name, amen."

"Esther, why do you pray in Jesus' name?"

"Honey, you may not know this, but Adam is Jewish. He met me and I loved him from that first moment, but he did not share my beliefs. I was heartbroken to find he was not a Messianic Jew. His parents were very orthodox, so I began to study as much as I could about the Jewish faith. Because I was doing that for him, he decided to read the New Testament so he could converse with me. You see, he loved me so much he didn't think he could live without me. As a result of looking into both sides of the story, he came to realize that his faith was not complete."

"He studied the prophecies in the Old Testament and then compared them with the facts of what Jesus had done, and he could not deny that Jesus is the Messiah. He came to me and asked what he must do to be saved. I told him that all he needed to do is to pray and to ask God to forgive him of his sins and to ask Jesus to come into his heart and take control of his life. He did that right then. He said he had never felt so free. We read the Bible together and studied the Jewish faith at the same time. I wanted to learn as much as I could because I wanted to do all the right things around his family."

"Do you ever see his family?"

"Well, not now that we live out here. They live in New York. They were not happy with Adam, to put it mildly. They threw him out of their house, and we were married not long after that. Adam wanted to start his own restaurant, so we looked into what needed to be done and where to do it. The threats he received from friends of his family made us believe we needed to move far away. We pray for them to see the truth in the Scripture and understand that works and keeping the laws will not save them. We just know that they will not listen to us and that the best for everyone is for us to be here. We love it here and know God is using us. We pray for his family daily. We want them to have the same freedom in Christ that we do and feel his love like we do."

"So, why do you pray in Jesus' name?"

"Well, Jesus said that no man comes to the Father but through him. He also told his disciples that he was going to his Father to be a mediator between God and Man. We do it because we believe it is what Jesus would want us to do. I think God hears all prayers cried out to him from a sincere heart whether it is in Jesus' name or not. He is the loving God who loves us so much he sacrificed his own son so we could live for eternity."

"I have so much to think about. Is that why you have been so careful with my food and my drinks?"

"Yes, dear, I guessed your heritage and wanted you to feel comfortable, not anxious about anything. So, I have kept your things kosher. Most people don't even realize that we have a "kosher" kitchen back in the back. Rose has been wonderful to learn all that I know of kosher cooking. It really is very healthy. We have quite a few Jewish guests who come here over night on their way to visit friends or to do other business. The Rosenburgs from Boerne are regular customers as are the Weinburgs from further south. I think the Weinburgs will move to Houston where there is quite a community of Jews and life would be easier for them. Even the lunches served at your table today were served with our kosher dishes. They have a different pattern to keep them separate. It really isn't that hard once a routine is established. My help is very willing to accommodate and is sensitive to the needs of our customers."

"That is just amazing! Thank you so much! You mean the world to me."

"You mean the world to me as well. You have found a permanent place in my heart. Now, it looks like I need to get downstairs and help Rose and the others with the supper shift. You rest and I'll bring you a plate up, if you don't feel like coming downstairs."

"I think I'll rest for about thirty minutes and then come down. Thank you."

"I'll see you in a little bit, then."

"Where are the twins?" Michael asked, looking around.

"They weren't done with their chores yet. It shouldn't take them long to finish. They were close. I told them they could not eat until those tasks were completed to my satisfaction. They didn't even say anything, just started working harder." Riley explained.

"You're serious? You are not going to let them eat until they are finished?" asked Josh.

"That's right. If a man does not work, he does not eat. That was the bargain when I talked with them earlier. They understood the stipulations for them to redeem themselves before supper. If they don't get finished before the food is eaten or put away, then they don't get any. They have to finish, get cleaned up, and get in here before we eat it all, or they are out of luck...uh, or food in this case."

"How much did they have to finish?" Wulf inquired, beginning to shuffle his food around on his plate.

"Not much, they should make it. The point is they didn't believe I meant what I said, and they found out that I did. Now, that should make things much simpler in the future."

"Well, I don't want to dally in here either. I want to enjoy the meal Esther provided for us, but I would like to have the food put away and the dishes washed so she can take them back with her when they get here." Michael looked at each man letting them know he was serious as well.

"I sure am glad I got all that work on the garden done. I don't think I could go without food." Tad looked absolutely serious as well as worried.

"Tad, you are such a good boy, no one will ever have to threaten you with not being able to eat. You get your work done without having to be told."

"Well, I'll be sure to work harder in the future. I don't want that to ever happen with me."

"Very astute, young man. You are learning from others' mistakes, and in my mind that is very commendable and way beyond your years." Riley smiled at Tad.

"Mr. Riley, I don't have anything behind or beyond my ears."

With that, the table erupted with laughter.

"I guess he told you, Riley."

"He certainly did, Wulf."

Bang!

The door slammed behind the twins as they fell to the floor, shoving each other as they did.

"Are we too late?" they asked in unison.

Everyone broke into laughter again and got ready to pass the food—what was left of it anyway.

Supper had been wonderful. Katie loved being around others, especially at mealtime. They had been busy jumping up taking care of customers and then sitting down again to grab a bit to eat. It reminded Katie of a merry-go-round she had seen in Philadelphia when she was small. It delighted her then, but wore her out just watching the two going up and down and around and around to the tables. She had been glad to get back to her room to rest. Now, her friends were gone and it was quiet, too quiet. She lay on the bed feeling the tom-tom again. The night was black. Not a bird was calling "good-night." The dogs weren't even barking. Why was it so quiet?

"Esther, come back. Please, I can't stand to be alone," she whispered.

What if Red had gotten out of jail? He could be standing out there in the shadows watching to see which room I am in! Maybe I should light a lamp and make it look like someone is up.

"No, that would only signal to him which room I'm in," her voice sounded hollow in the quiet room.

What if he was already in the hall?

"Did I lock the door?" she asked herself, looking at the key still in the keyhole.

She had not been locking the door until later because everyone was still moving around in the hotel.

She heard something out in the hall. Quickly, she jumped up and moved to the door. She turned the key; the door was not locked. She heard the lock click in place. Her heart was pounding now; her hands shaking.

"Shhh!"

What if he was coming in the window? He had done it before. He could do it again. The curtains swayed just a bit. Was that the wind? Was it him? Dare she look out? If she went over to the curtains and he was there, he could grab her. Maybe she should go out in the hall and downstairs.

"No, what if he is out there? What was that noise I heard? I'm trapped," she whispered with her hands cupped over her face.

She could hear footsteps coming down the hall. The curtains moved again. She looked at the door, then the window. She was trapped like a raccoon in a trapper's trap. She stood frozen to the floor.

There was a knock on the door, and the doorknob moved just a little then stopped. She felt as if her heart was pounding on her ribcage like a hammer on an anvil.

"Miss Katie? Are you in there?"

Whose voice was that? Did it sound familiar? Sweat was pouring down her back and her face, her hands shaking so bad she didn't think she could even grab anything for a weapon. She felt like her legs were going to give way. Fear gripped her heart like iron shackles on a prisoner.

"Miss Katie, it's Sheriff Daniels. I'd like to talk with you for a few minutes if I can. Are you in there?"

Sheriff Daniels? Have I even talked with him before? I can't remember. How can I know if that is him?

"Miss Katie, Esther asked me to come over and check on you. I can wait for you downstairs if you would prefer. I know it is after dark, and a man should not be in a lady's room unescorted, anyway. So, if you will, could you come down to the lobby and speak with me for a few minutes? I apologize for not coming over sooner, but I've had my hands full."

I haven't talked with him...or have I? I just can't remember.

"I'll go get Doc McConnell. He can check you out. You must not be feeling well—or you're a very sound sleeper," he said under his breath.

"Please get Doc McConnell," she whispered.

"Did you say something?"

"Yes, please get Doc McConnell," she said a little louder.

"Right away, Miss. We'll be right back. Don't you worry. We'll bust the door down if we have to." With that, she heard steps leading away from the door and down the stairs.

A dog barked, then another. There were sounds of wagons and horses moving down the street. She could hear voices of people out on the front.

"Good evening, Sheriff. What's your hurry?" someone asked.

Katie gave a great sigh of relief. It seemed the world was turning again. It seemed as no time had passed when there was a knock on the door. She had not heard any steps in the hall. Fear clutched at her, again.

"Katie, it's Doc McConnell. What's wrong?"

Hearing the familiar voice energized Katie. She made it to the door, her legs barely holding her up. She took a deep breath. The shackles around her heart began to loosen.

"Are you alone?" she asked.

"No, Sheriff Daniels is with me. Katie, what's wrong?"

Katie turned the key and cracked the door. Standing in the hall was Doc McConnell and a very handsome man with blonde hair; she must assume he was the sheriff. She didn't see Red anywhere. She opened the door a bit more and collapsed on the floor.

CHAPTER 17

"Where am I?"

"You are in your room at the hotel. Now, tell me young lady, what happened? Are you sick? I can't find anything wrong with you, except your heart rate was sky high."

"No, I just, I don't know how to say this."

"Just tell me."

"Where is the sheriff?"

"I'm right here. Did someone try to break in?"

"No…just in my mind."

Doc and Brian looked at each other. Doc raised his eyebrows.

"Who did you think was trying to break in?"

"Red."

"Do you want to talk about it?" Brian asked.

"It might help," added Doc.

"I'm still shaking. I just don't know what got into me. It was so quiet. I couldn't hear anything except my heart pounding. There was no noise outside, and then I heard footsteps in the hall. My door wasn't locked, so I hurried over and locked it. I saw the curtains moving. I thought Red was coming in the window, but I couldn't go out the door because maybe that was him in the hall. I just got all worked up. I don't remember ever speaking with the sheriff so I didn't know if that was really him or not. Do you understand? I was scared stiff. I can't believe I made it to the door to unlock it."

"Katie, you have had a bad time. It will take time to get over it. I am not just talking about Red's attack on you. There is no medical treatment that can help you. Only God can do that, and over time you will begin to feel safe and secure again. Right now you feel safe and secure here with Esther and Adam. Perhaps you should take another couple of days, give it the weekend, and then go back out to the ranch. You can stay, and if you feel up to it, go to church on Sunday with Esther and Adam. Maybe even Michael and Josh will come out and any of the other hands who want to attend the service."

"Thank you, Doc. I have felt safe and secure here. But knowing Esther and Adam were away tonight...I don't know...I just fell apart. I think knowing Red is right out there in the jail just puts him too close for comfort."

"He's not there."

"What?"

"The Texas Rangers came and got him today. They made really good time and picked him up. They are on their way to Austin. You don't have to worry about him anymore."

"Thank you, Sheriff, but I don't think I will stop worrying until he is dead. If he manages to get away, he may come back."

"There were four men that came to get him. Someone will be watching him all the time. He won't get a chance to get away. I feel very confident of that."

"I wish I could have your confidence. He was trying to find Pa's hidden money. In a way I wish he had, then we would know where it is."

"Your pa didn't tell you where he kept his money?"

"No, Sheriff, I'm a female! Females don't need to worry their little heads about such matters." Her eyes flared with a fire she did not know was in her.

"That's stupid! Sorry, didn't mean to say that your pa was stupid. But that notion is stupid, especially if one is ill and not getting better."

"He just kept telling Ma, 'money…lie.' I don't know if he was saying the whole idea of the money was a lie and we didn't have any, or if he was trying to give Ma a clue to where it is."

"What do you remember about when he would need money? What would he do?"

"I don't remember anything special. He just would have the money whenever he needed it."

"I'm sure he was giving you a clue. He wouldn't leave your ma without any financial security."

"That's what we thought, but we couldn't find it anywhere. We had not looked all over the ranch. There was so much to do. With just the two of us to do all the work, we worked most of the time. We barely had time to sit and talk, much less look for hidden money. We had decided we could do that during the winter when things became a little calmer. Just as we were finishing up the canning, Ma died. I had no one. I was all alone. I could barely even function on the most basic level, much less start a treasure hunt."

"Who knows about the money?

"You, and Michael. You won't tell, will you?"

"No," they said in unison.

"Oh, I might have told Esther. I don't remember. I have told her so much."

"We will do some thinking about all of this. Maybe we can help," Brian said.

Doc gazed at Katie, concern wrinkling his brow. "Do you want me to give you something to help you sleep?"

"No, I don't want to do that. I think just some hot tea will help."

"I'll go get some. Do you have any of those lemon drops left?"

"Yes, Doc, I do. Thank you so much. They have helped. I feel like my voice is getting better. I'm glad he didn't do any permanent damage to my throat."

"Yes, that is a good thing. Once your voice is back to normal, you won't have that constant reminder of him."

"You are right about that. I just don't know if I can go upstairs again in the house. I think I'll have my things moved down to my parents' room and sleep downstairs from now on."

"I think that is a very wise decision. Not only will you not have to face that memory, you will be closer to both doors and to the kitchen where most of your work takes place."

"I will be so glad to get out on the trail. Then there will be no old memories, just new ones."

Doc pushed himself up from the chair, smiled at Katie, and started toward the door. He turned toward her again, thanking God for her positive attitude, and then said, "I'll go get the tea."

"Thank you, Doc," she replied, smiling back at him.

Turning toward her and taking the chair Doc had just vacated, Brian smiled and said, "I'll stay with you if you don't mind. I don't want you to get spooked again. Doc, leave the door open, will you? I want to see out in the hall. Thanks."

"Why do you need to see out in the hall?" Katie asked.

"It's more a matter of anyone in the hall seeing me. I don't want anyone thinking they have something to talk about."

"Oh, I see. Thank you, Sheriff, for having my reputation in mind. I had not even thought of what things could look like. I'm not very experienced in such matters. I appreciate your thoughtfulness."

"You are welcome. I'm just doing my job. I'll be coming around to see you out at the ranch from time to time. I hope that suits you. Esther pointed out to me that the townspeople have not been real neighborly to those people living out on the ranches. I'm going to start doing some rounds out and about, just so I can get to know people and they can get to know me."

"That's a wonderful idea!"

"Esther is going to organize a group of people to start visiting the ranches as well. We need to build a better sense of community around here if we are going to keep each other safe."

"Wow, what started all this? That would be wonderful!"

"Actually, you did. This all results from your run-in with Red and the ordeal you went through this winter. I can't get over the heartlessness of us not even going out to check on someone when we haven't seen them come into town in their normal manner. By going out and checking on them on a regular basis ourselves, the contact won't be broken and we will know the hurts and joys the ranchers are going through."

"I am amazed. What if you go and no one is home?"

"Unless the whole family goes to town or over visiting another family, someone should be home. If they are planning on a trip or say a cattle drive, I would know about it because sometime before they leave, I will have the opportunity to visit with them, and I'm sure they would bring that up."

"Oh, I see."

"You, for instance, will be leaving in the not-too-distant future on a drive. I won't expect to find anyone home, but I could still go out and have a look at your ranch to make sure nobody is trying to steal anything or bunk there on their way somewhere else."

"So, we can go on our drive to San Antonio and know you are looking out for our property?"

"Absolutely. I'll go out or send someone from town out there to check the place at least once a week. Who will be taking care of your stock while you are gone?"

"I don't know. I hadn't really thought of it. I don't know if Michael has or not."

"Well, if he hasn't, we can make arrangements for that as well. I want to take a leadership role here to make sure the town and the rest of the people who live near here and depend on us will be safer than ever before."

"I feel so much better knowing that. Thank you."

Brian's head jerked to the side as he heard footsteps. Seeing Doc coming down the hall, he went to help him with the tray.

"Here you are, young lady. I asked for three cups so we can have a little tea party."

"You are so kind, Doc. This looks simply delicious. Cookies too!"

"Will you pour?" he asked Katie.

"I will be happy to pour. One lump or two?"

"Three, I like mine very sweet!" Doc laughed!

"Same here! Brian added. "Actually, I don't know how people can drink hot tea all the time. I'll do it every now and then, but give me coffee when I'm stressed." Brian emphasized.

"Now, Sheriff, don't feel like you have to drink some tea just because we are. I'm sure you could go down and get some coffee and bring it back up." Katie encouraged.

"No, I'll drink the tea. I just wouldn't want it for a steady diet."

"I don't know what I would do without it, especially since my...uh...injury."

"I think it has helped tremendously, don't you?" Doc asked, wanting to get her mind off of the incident.

"Oh, yes, Doc, I think my voice is almost back to normal, and it has only been a few days. I want to thank you so much for all you have done."

"Esther did more than I did. She has been a saint." Doc smiled.

"Yes, you don't need to remind me. I thank God every day for her. I wish they would get back. I really miss her when she is not just downstairs. She is so full of life and brings it to every room she enters. I wish I could be like her."

"You can, Katie. I think you know her secret to a joyful life. She makes no bones about telling everyone about her Savior, Jesus."

"Yes, she has told me. Is that why she is like she is, truly?"

"Absolutely! She would be the first to say it was."

"I need to think on that for a while."

"Don't think too long, Katie. I think God is calling you to him. Don't put him off. You will regret it if you do."

"You sound like it is urgent."

"My dear, it is. Think about tonight and how scared you were. What if it had been Red who had come for you? Do you think a locked door or a third floor room would keep him out? Are you ready to face your creator? Do you know if he will bid you into his home to stay, or will he say, "I never knew you. Depart from me"?

"Oh, my, when you say it like that, I guess it is urgent. But Doc, I don't know anything about Jesus."

"I'll bring you a Bible for your very own. I'll help you find where to start reading. Then you will get to know Jesus. And if you want an earthly example of his nature, just look at Esther Schmitt."

"Hey, what about me, Doc?"

"Brian, how can I recommend you? You won't even make tea a 'steady diet'."

They all laughed, and with that the room seemed to brighten and the air seemed to cool. A breeze came through the windows, and the curtains no longer looked threatening. Katie no longer felt trapped but comfortable with her surroundings. Shortly after the men left, Esther came home and popped her head in to check on Katie before taking care of getting Tad settled in for the night.

Katie got ready for bed, got in bed, and fell into a sweet sleep. Her hand resting on her chest didn't even feel the beating of her heart, and her mind didn't hear the mournful song of "Lone-ly" that had become so familiar to her.

———

A lone coyote called from somewhere in the distance. All the men slept peacefully in their beds. An owl hooted. Night sounds were all that could be heard at the ranch. Everything else rested.

All too soon, it seemed, the rooster announced morning. The horses neighed. The cow mooed. The goats bleated. The day broke with a glorious sunrise. The men began to turn out of their various places of rest. Stomachs growled. "Time to get moving and to get breakfast on the table." Soon the ranch was abuzz with energy and activity. Katie was coming home today!

"Okay, men, we have time to get this place cleaned up before Katie gets here. Let's see how much we can get done and surprise her. After all, we aren't helpless." Michael began to give orders.

"Let's move her things downstairs and her folks' things upstairs like Esther suggested. Katie had mentioned that to her and she seemed to think that was a great idea."

"Which room is hers?" asked Josh.

"The first one on the backside of the house." Michael replied.

"Do we move all the furniture, or do we just move the clothes and things?" queried Riley.

"Hmm. I don't think the bigger bed will fit in that upstairs room. So, let's leave the beds but switch everything else. Be careful with anything breakable. We don't want to upset her. She has lost so much already. She doesn't need to lose anything that may mean something to her through our carelessness. Now, move!"

"Cade and Wade, you come with me. I have something else for you to do. Josh, you be in charge of the move since you have a mom and know what women think probably better than most of us." Michael began to walk away.

"You forget I've been away for several years." Josh said halfway under his breath.

"I'll help. I have a pretty good notion of what needs to be done."

The rest looked at Riley and raised their eyebrows in question. Riley looked around at them.

"Long story, I'll explain later."

Everybody shrugged and turned to begin work.

"Wulf, I could use you out here with me, if you don't mind." Michael hollered.

"Sure, whatever you want, boss."

"If you guys need any help with the heavy things or anything at all, don't think twice about asking us. We will be glad to help. We just need to get some other things done at the same time," Michael said.

"Sounds good to me. We'll let you know," Josh said as he waved for them to go.

"Great! Let's get to it."

CHAPTER 18

Excitement bubbled up in Katie. She couldn't believe she was going home! At the same time, fear lurked at the back of her mind. She didn't want to leave Esther and Adam, but particularly Esther. She had a sereneness about her that calmed the spirit. Katie had been thinking about all that Esther, Doc, and Brian had been sharing with her. Could there be something to this "Jesus is the Messiah" thing she kept hearing? She clutched the Bible Doc had brought to her that morning before he had pronounced her fit to travel. He also gave her a stern warning that seeing everything again would take an emotional toll on her. If she even thought she needed a few more days in town, she should come back.

Adam had helped the women into the wagon and Tad had jumped into the back. They traveled down the familiar road toward the Kurtz ranch.

"Oh, we are getting close now. Esther, it feels so good to be going home, but I have such mixed emotions. I'm so nervous."

"What's making you nervous, Katie?"

"Oh, I don't know. Seeing the place and wondering what has been done and what needs to be done. I'm not sure I can go upstairs yet. But how will I get my things moved downstairs and Ma and Pa's things moved upstairs? The men have so much to do, they won't have time. I have so many questions. At least my voice is mostly back to normal. Doc said that I was blessed, no permanent damage was done."

"He is so right. You are very blessed in more ways than one, Katie. God has really been looking out for you. From what you have told me about that still-smoldering log rolling out of the fireplace in January, it could have burned your house down with you in it if God hadn't prompted you to get up and go downstairs to 'wander around a bit.' Not to mention the first time Red came to the ranch. God blessed you then too."

"How? Oh, my skin gets all shivery whenever I think of him."

"It will take time, but you will be able to talk about and think about all of this without feeling that fear and anxiousness you still feel now. You see, most men with violence in their minds don't worry about 'the folks out back.' He could have just grabbed you and ridden off with you across his horse before your 'folks out back' would ever have been able to get a horse ready to ride after you and him. But God caused him to believe a lie and to have fear in his heart because of that lie. Oh, yes, I would say you are very blessed."

"Esther, whatever am I going to do without you? I don't know if I can hold on to sanity out here alone."

"Sweetheart, you are not alone. There are seven men out here working for you. I know that isn't much for a large ranch. It is enough to get the work done that needs to be done, if they work! I think they will. They seem nice enough to us, especially the one named Joshua."

They all laughed at that, and then Esther continued.

"I know he will work very hard. He believes as we do, and he loves ranching. Joshua will not let you down. If he does, you just let me know and I'll have to spank that boy!"

Tad really laughed at that. Rarely had he been spanked, and of course he had never seen his older brother spanked.

"They say 'Laughter is good for what ails you.' If that is so, I should be cured. I didn't think I would ever laugh, much less smile again, just a week ago. Goodness, I didn't even want to live. Thank you for all you have done. I don't know if I would have made it."

"Like I said, you are like a daughter to me and I wouldn't have had it any other way. You come see me anytime you need a shoulder or just some 'girl time.' Don't be surprised if you find me on your doorstep for the same reason."

"Look, there it is!" Tad yelled with the exuberance only a ten-year-old boy could come up with.

"I can't wait for you to see the garden, Katie. I hope I did it right."

"I know you did it perfectly, Tad. You are your mother and father's son after all." Katie smiled down at him and he beamed back at her, enjoying her praise.

"Now, we can't stay long, but we will make sure you get settled in and are fine with your situation out here. You are always welcome to come back to the hotel, Katie."

Thank you, Adam. I know I will have a home away from home with you always. I have never had that before. I don't even know how to thank you."

"No thanks are necessary. We love you."

Her heart skipped a few beats when the house came into view. How good it looked to her. For some reason, she did not expect for the house to look the same. Relief flooded her heart. Suddenly, a figure went running from the barn to the back of the house.

"Who was that?" Katie asked.

"That looked like one of the Tucker twins," said Adam.

"I don't think I have ever seen them."

"Their father is the blacksmith and their mother is a seamstress."

"I have so many people to learn about. I have been too isolated out here. I need to do better about being a part of the community. It is not good to be so alone."

"That's what God said about Adam when he created Eve for him. 'It is not good for man to be alone.' He was so right." With that, Adam gave Esther a quick squeeze as he pulled the horses to a stop.

Tad jumped out the back of the wagon and ran around to help his pa with tying the horses to the hitching post.

Michael seemed to appear from nowhere, "Well, look who's here! It's about time you got back from your 'vacation' and started taking care of us poor, underfed, ill-cared-for men."

"You look like you have really been suffering!" Adam said as he chuckled.

Michael reached up and helped Katie down from the wagon. She was so light he felt like he could throw her over his head and catch her like a small child.

She beamed at him, and then saw the other men coming toward them. She recognized Clyde, but which one was Josh? She could immediately tell which ones were the twins. Now, that would be a problem. How would she ever tell them apart?

"Josh, how have you been? It's so good to see you." Esther gave a huge hug to a very handsome, dark-haired young man. He looked so much like her, but then he looked like Adam as well. Katie had never noticed how much alike Esther and Adam really did look.

"Joshua, I want you to meet Katie, Miss Kurtz. Katie, this is our son, Joshua."

Josh held out his hand to shake Katie's hand. As their hands touched, Katie felt a tingle race up her arm. Her eyes, wide with surprise, shot to his.

"I'm pleased to meet you, Miss Kurtz. I trust you are feeling much better."

He gave no hint that he felt the same thing. Josh had been trained not to reveal what he was feeling, but he was not surprised he felt the same sensation in this touch as he had when he had carried her into Doc's office. He wanted to explore her eyes so deep, so mysterious. They had been closed when he saw her the first time. He realized he was staring at her and quickly looked to his mother. He let go of Katie's hand and turned to Riley.

"Miss Kurtz, this is Riley, J. R. Riley. Riley, Miss Kurtz."

"Miss Kurtz, I am excessively overjoyed to meet you and to find you are in good health. I trust you will be pleased with what we have been able to accomplish in your absence, even though we have suffered a bit of punishment in that we have not had the privilege of tasting the delights of your repasts."

"I'm sure we will have a delightful time deciphering what you just said, Mr. Riley. I am overjoyed to meet you. You will certainly provide, for me anyway, a mental challenge. I've not had that for a good long time now."

"I am at your service. Now, Miss Kurtz, I would like to introduce you to a fine man, a hard worker and one of your newest hands. This is Wulfgang Schurtz. He prefers to be called Wulf. Wulf, this is Miss Kurtz."

"Howdy ma'am, uh, Miss. Sorry. Pleased to meet you. If there is anything I can do for you, just holler."

"Thank you, Mr., oh, sorry, Wulf. I will certainly let you know if I need anything."

Wulf stood with his hat slowly being wadded into a ball of mangled felt. Silence lingered to almost an uncomfortable point when Riley jumped back in. "And these are the Tucker twins, Cade and Wade. They are here to serve you and to work as hard as they can to grow into honorable men."

The boys stood bug-eyed, staring at the beautiful woman in front of them. They were elbowing each other in the ribs, as usual.

"Boys?" Riley said sternly, his look conveying deep meaning.

"Howdy, Miss Kurtz. Pleased to meet you," they replied in unison.

"As am I to meet you." Katie almost laughed but held her emotions in check.

"I think you know everyone else."

"Yes, thank you all for your very warm welcome and for agreeing to work for me. Most of you are not accustomed to working for a woman. Just remember, I want us to be a team and to work together. I will do my best to keep you fed and well. Thank you again for looking after things in my absence. I know you have worked hard, and there is plenty of hard work before us. Together we can get it done. Michael, when will we need to be underway to round up the cattle?"

"We need to leave as soon as we can."

"Today?"

"That would be great, but I don't think it can be done. Tomorrow will have to do. Or maybe we will wait until Monday. A few can go out tomorrow and build a holding corral. There are still some things around here that need immediate attention that we haven't gotten done yet. We definitely need to provide something better for the goats. Also, I think we are going to want to add to that flock. We need to think about the future when we are making changes or repairs to the buildings on the ranch."

"Gracious, I had not given beyond today or tomorrow much thought, much less the distant future. Thinking closer to hand, how will we do this? Will we need to set up a chuck wagon for the roundup?"

"Yes, that would work best. We would waste many hours riding back and forth from the range to the house otherwise."

"Okay, then I will start getting my things together. Do we have a chuck wagon?"

"Yes, we do. Cade and Wade found one in the out building at the far end of the bunkhouse. It has a very good setup in it, and I think you will find it comfortable as well. You won't have to sleep on the ground, unless you want to do so." He looked at her with meaning in his eyes, remembering the earlier conversation.

"The wagon will do just fine. I'll get busy then. Did you have a sufficient breakfast?"

"Yes, we did. Don't worry about us. Is there anything we can do to help you get settled, before we unsettle you again?"

"I don't know." Katie's voice wavered as she looked toward the house. Esther took over the command.

"Come along with me and we will look at what is to be faced. Thank you, men. Tad, why don't you go ahead and start work as well. Adam, would you check on the chickens? I don't think they have been checked yet." Esther looked to Michael who shook his head apologetically.

Everyone headed toward their various tasks leaving a feeling of emptiness where there had been a feeling of family.

Katie looked at their retreating backs then turned to look at the house. A shudder went down her spine. Could she do this?

"Come on, it won't get done if we just stand out here." Esther gently took Katie's hand and began walking up the steps to the front door.

"Let's see what we need to do first in your parents' room. I know you said you cleaned it. Would you like to stay downstairs tonight?"

"Oh yes, I just don't think I could go up those stairs yet. I can't begin to tell you how shaky I feel just being back in the house."

They walked over to her parents' room and opened the door. Katie gasped.

"Oh, Esther! How did they know to do this? Oh, I can't believe it! I am so relieved."

She walked over to her chest of drawers and gently stroked the few items she normally placed on top. They were exactly as she would have placed them. Her mother's face stared back at her with that half smile she so often used. Katie lovingly caressed the face of her beloved mother.

"You would not believe it, Ma," she whispered.

She turned to Esther and there were Riley, Clyde, and Josh standing just behind her looking in.

"Thank you. I don't know what to say. I'm overwhelmed. It's just perfect."

"We didn't break anything," Clyde assured her. "We were very careful."

"I can tell you were."

Tears were beginning to form as she spoke. Josh stepped forward. He wanted to go to her, but he held himself back.

"We just want you to know we meant what was said. If you need anything, we are here for you."

With that, tears began in earnest. Esther took Katie in her arms and held her. She looked over Katie's shoulder. "Thank you, men. I think Katie needs some time to adjust to being home. You did a wonderful thing here. More than you know."

The men nodded and turned to leave. Josh turned back toward the women.

"Ma, I mean it now, anything at all you want to have done, just holler, okay?"

"I understand, Joshua. I'll be sure to let you know."

Rotating his hat in his hands, he nodded again and quietly left the house. As soon as he stepped outside, he blew out a breath he had been holding. He looked up at the sky, saying a prayer for the beautiful woman inside. He couldn't seem to quit thinking about her.

Michael met him halfway to the barn. He looked hard at Josh's face.

"Everything okay inside?"

"Just dandy. Katie's crying her eyes out and Ma's giving her comfort."

"Why is she crying? Did we do something wrong?"

"Naw, Michael, we did something right. You know how women are. They cry when they are happy. Look out if they get mad; it's best not to be around them. Find something urgent to do out on the range if that should happen."

"I don't believe running from 'trouble' is the best way to deal with it, Josh."

"I know, especially with a woman. It would just be easier if a man could do that. I know some men who have, though, and it was a big mistake. It just made the situation worse. I've seen my pa look at my ma when she has been mad and just simply tell her that she is right. Now, I know good and well she was *not* right. But then later when she had cooled down, she admitted she was wrong and needed to listen to Pa and not get so tied in a knot about things. He says it has to do with their tender side. God made them that way. He also says that God made man to love his woman no matter what and to nurture her. I hope I'll be able to do that someday, but I know it will be the hardest thing I've ever had to do."

"God will give you the wisdom and knowledge as well as the desire to do that. He will not just leave you on your own. With your attitude toward doing what God has ordained man to do and be for his wife, you are well on your way to having a happy home. It takes most men many years of strife living with a woman and learning about them before they realize that is how God intended man to treat his wife. He is to love her just as Christ loved the church and gave his life for her."

"Yes, but isn't the wife supposed to be submissive to her husband?"

"Yes. Josh, I don't think you understand the whole meaning of submissive. If the woman is loved so completely by her husband, she is going to want to do whatever he thinks is best. She will respect him and honor him and know that he has only her and their children's best interest at heart. She will trust him with all her heart. Let a man try to 'play' at loving her, and a woman will see through that in the beat of a heart. She may put up with it for a while, but not forever."

"I saw some pretty bad marriages in the army. Some men were just downright mean to their wives. Others idolized their wives to the point of being sickening. It seemed that it didn't matter which way the relationship went, the women weren't happy."

"Sounds like they weren't following what is written so plainly in the Bible. Josh, when that time comes for you, just follow Christ's example and love your wife with every fiber of your being."

"In the meantime, what do you want me to do?"

"Bring the chuck wagon up and park it behind the kitchen. Be careful of the work Tad is doing in the kitchen garden. Maybe we need to build a fence around it."

"I don't believe we have time for that right now. We have other more important things to do to get ready for tomorrow. I'll get the wagon and park it so Katie and Ma can start setting up what they need."

"I'll go check on the rest of the gang and see if there is something else some of them can do. I don't want anyone just standing around."

"Right!"

CHAPTER 19

 "atie? Do you want to start some bread and get some dinner started for the men? I can help. What are you thinking about fixing for them to eat?"

"Thank you, Esther. You always know just what I need."

"Remember, David was often at his wits' end or battling emotional times. He was being hounded by King Saul and seemed like he couldn't find anywhere or anyone to keep him safe. Finally, in the cave at Adullum he cried out to God and asked him if he didn't see how he had no one who cared for him. Do you know what God did for him?"

Katie simply shook her head.

"He sent David 400 of the worst kind of men in the country. They stayed in that cave, and he trained them to be his mighty men. They went on to become a very effective fighting force for David and for the Lord. God did not allow David to just sit and feel sorry for himself, he put him to work. That is one of the best cures for melancholy—good, hard work. So, let's get busy, shall we?"

"Let's start some bread. I know that will be good for me. I love kneading it. The dough feels so silky smooth in my hands and smells so yeasty and healthy. I feel like I'm truly home when I smell fresh baked bread. After we get it going and rising, we can decide about what to cook. I think we should make a list of what to take out on the range and on the trail. Will you help me make that list? Do you need to get back to the restaurant?"

"Let's see which question to answer first." Smiling as she said it, Esther cleared her throat and led Katie toward the kitchen. "Yes, I will help you make the list. And yes, I need to get back to the restaurant. Now I have no intention of going back before I'm sure you are doing just fine here. Katie, I don't want to just drop you off and leave, waving and saying, 'See ya soon; have a good life.' I want to be sure you are comfortable here and have the strength to do what you need to do. I think the restaurant will survive one day without Adam and me. If you want to go back with us, you certainly may. I couldn't live with myself if I was not sure you are fine out here."

"Oh, I'm so relieved! I was worried to the point of feeling ill. Thank you! I seem to be saying that so much lately. I truly mean it from the bottom of my heart."

"My pleasure, dear. Now, let's see…what a wonderful kitchen area you have! My, it is so big. I love the way the counter comes out here to sort of set the kitchen area with this kitchen table apart from the bigger table in that eating area. The kitchen isn't completely closed off from where the family can be. I'd love to see this full of people. Doesn't it get a little warm in here though?"

"You would think it would, but when these windows are open and those in there are open or the front door—I like opening the front door—there is a wonderful breeze that flows through here. Sometimes we would open the windows upstairs and that would really take the heat right out of the kitchen. We would always do that when we were canning."

Katie's throat tightened and her eyes misted. She glanced to a spot on the kitchen floor that seemed to hold her gaze. Esther looked to that spot but saw nothing particularly special about it.

Her heart knew there was a story there, but she didn't feel it was the right time to pursue it.

"What do you want me to do? I don't know my way around your kitchen yet, but I promise I will learn."

"Why don't you get the kneading bowl down? The flour is kept in that pie safe. You can get that too. I'll get the rest of the ingredients, and we'll get to work."

"Consider it done."

Before long, the two women were singing and laughing at the flour that seemed to stick to their noses and foreheads. At one point Josh stuck his head in and told them the chuck wagon was out back. The women just laughed and said that was just what they "needed," and laughed even more at their pun.

The men were engrossed in their work when the sounds of the dinner bell pealed through the air. Thankful for the break, dusting themselves off, they made their way to the back of the house to get cleaned up. There they found fresh water and towels.

Nice, thought Josh.

"Wow," said Clyde.

"I have a feeling we are in for a treat, men," put in Michael.

"I have really worked up a powerful hunger," asserted Wulf.

"You? My stomach thinks my throat is cut. I didn't realize I had worked myself into such hunger. I believe I could eat a whole side of beef."

"Ah, Mr. Riley, you know you would have to have help. We are volunteering! Right, Cade?" interrupted Wade. Cade punched him in the side with his elbow.

Everyone now expected this reaction and vowed if they could inspect the boys, they would find permanent bruises in that exact spot.

The enticing aromas coming from the open windows caused each one to hurry to get washed up.

As soon as the meal was finished, the men began clearing the table. Katie and Esther just looked at each other. Esther shrugged and indicated to Katie to sit while she could. When the table was cleared, Katie stood and told them to scoot.

"Esther and I can take it from here. Thank you for being the butlers. I don't know if I should expect that at every meal or what. I appreciate your help. It certainly proves the old saying, 'Many hands make light work.' Thank you again. It may be the last meal like that you have for many days. Starting tomorrow, remember, it is trail food for you."

"Beans! Beans! And more Beans! Yum! As long as you make them, we'll be happy."

"I'll remember you said that in a couple of weeks, Wulf."

"I will tell you that I don't think I have eaten any food as tasty as this today, ever, in my whole life. You are a better cook than my mother."

"Now, Wulf, I didn't do it alone. Remember, Esther is here, and she owns a restaurant."

"Well, maybe so, but this meal was truly a blessing. I don't use words like that often. I'm just telling you the truth."

Katie smiled and nodded as she mumbled a thank you. Her mind suddenly took her to her father looking at her, as they were swinging on the front porch swing not quite a year ago.

"I am telling you the truth, Katie. I have never lied to you, and I won't ever lie to you. Always remember that."

Not too many months later he was dead. As he lay dying, he kept saying, "Money...lie, money...lie." If he had told her he had never lied and would never lie, then why did he admit the money was a lie? Was he trying to tell her ma the money was lying somewhere but never got it out? Was she misunderstanding what he was saying?

"Katie? Are you okay?"

"What? Oh, I'm sorry. I was just remembering something Pa said. I guess I chased a little rabbit back in time. I'll tell you about it later, Michael."

"If you are sure you are fine, I'll go on out with the men."

"Yes, just fine. You go right ahead. There is no darkness here, just questions. I need to go out and see that garden again. I can't believe what a good job Tad did on it!"

Esther was giving her sons hugs and telling Tad how good the garden looked. Adam had been very quiet at dinner, but she would find out what was bothering him on the ride home, if not before. She could not get over how grown Josh had become. He looked right at home on the ranch more so than at the restaurant. She was proud of him. Katie headed for the garden. Tad ran after her and grabbed her hand. Esther started back in to clean up the mess.

"Tad is doing a wonderful job on that garden. I won't need to do a thing with it, except watch it grow." Katie said as she entered the kitchen.

"Yes, he is a good little farmer. As soon as we have this done, Katie, let's take inventory in the chuck wagon and see what needs to be washed, if anything is even in it."

"That sounds good to me," Katie said smiling. *Oh, how good it is to have another woman around. I was so glad to have Michael here, but another woman is just more comforting, especially one that is like another mother.* Katie's thoughts had taken her so deep into her memory of her mother that she didn't even notice when Esther left the house. She looked around to see what Esther was doing.

"I didn't even realize you had left," she said when Esther returned.

"I needed to go out to the privy for a little bit. You seemed so deep in thought I didn't want to bother you with that tidbit of information. You know, you need some more lye out there. The bucket is almost empty."

"Okay, I'll tell Michael. I think there is a bag of it in the tool shed or one of the other outbuildings. Pa always had some on hand."

"Wow, you have just about finished this up on your own. You really work hard, Katie. Do you need a rest?"

"Actually, it really feels good to work. I think I have rested enough the past few days. What I need now is fresh air and exercise."

"You will be getting that as soon as you leave tomorrow. If the men get everything finished up, they need to do around here," Esther smiled.

"Speaking of that, would you go out and just see if there are any pots and pans or any other cooking utensils that need to be washed. We might as well do that while this water is hot."

"I'll be glad to do that."

It was not long before Tad was bringing in tin plates, cups, forks and spoons. Esther followed shortly with some pots and pans and a coffeepot.

"There are a few more things out there, but not many."

"Well, this is good to get done. I'm glad we are starting on that project. I don't want to start on the trip with dirty things for the men to eat from or for me to cook with. 'Cleanliness is next to Godliness,' my mother used to always say."

"She was so right. I am proud of you for remembering your mother and all she taught you. You are a very good daughter."

By the end of the day, everyone had finished their work. The evening meal had been fixed and eaten. Esther, Tad, and Adam had traveled back home, and everything was set to start off in the morning. Michael had decided that things were well enough under control around the ranch that they could leave in the morning. Everyone fell into bed and went right to sleep, except for one.

"Dear Almighty One, I don't know exactly what to expect tomorrow or the next days. Please be with all the men. Help me to trust you. I have never had so many people around me who love me and treat me with so much respect. Help me to be what I need to be. I ask you to watch over us. Be our refuge and our fortress in times of trouble. Help me to understand the relationship these people have with you. I admire them so and see you in a very different light from the God of my father and mother. Open my eyes and ears that I can see and hear what you are doing and saying. Thank you for sending all these helpers, even the twins. Help them grow up. They need so much instruction and need to have a willingness to learn. Please keep the nightmares away. Help me to sleep soundly in order to get the rest I need for tomorrow. Thank you. Amen."

With that, Katie closed her eyes and slipped into the carefree sleep of the untroubled mind of a child.

———————◆———————

Suddenly, Katie's eyes flew open. *Where am I?* She looked around trying to find her bearings and then realized she was home. Darkness still held the morning at bay. Before long everyone would be up and busy. The chimes of the clock on the mantle indicated 5:00 a.m.

"I'd better get going. Everyone will want breakfast before we start off."

Her feet flew out of the bed and landed on the rug her parents had stepped on every morning after moving there. She felt the warmth of their memory comfort her as never before.

"I am so glad I am now settled in their room. I feel so much closer to them even though most of the things are mine. I sleep in their bed and walk on their rug. Lovely!"

She hurriedly dressed and began getting breakfast on for the men. By the time the coffee was ready, she had the biscuits in the oven and the eggs cooking. She decided to go ahead and cook some steak. She could do this for them since they would need it for the work of the day ahead. She could not expect to keep anything kosher out on the trail. She had learned that on the journey out to Texas. The chuck wagon fare would not be as fine as what she fixed in her kitchen. She would do her best out there and then it would only bother her a little that it wasn't like home. Her best was all she could do.

"Smells wonderful!"

Whirling around, Katie's eyes stared right into the same handsome face she had seen in most of her dreams her first night home. "Josh, you are early. I'm not quite ready."

"I came to help. May I set the table? Or is there something else you need done?"

"Oh, setting the table would be a big help. Do you know where…"

"Yes, I was part of the kitchen crew while you stayed in town learning how to accept help. I am glad you were willing to let Mother help you. I know it must have taken a great deal of courage to put aside your independence and become dependent, especially on someone who had been a total stranger."

"I had not looked at it that way. I see what you are saying," she said as she continued to work, but stealing glances at Josh as he efficiently set the table. *He really does know where everything is and how to set a table,* she thought. *How lovely.*

"Would you like some coffee?" she asked. "It's ready."

"Sure, thank you. I would love some. I need it to get my eyes wide open in the mornings."

"Is that why you came in to help?" she laughed.

"Partly, I had finished what I needed to do and just thought you might need some help this morning, since we will be leaving right after breakfast. Is the wagon all ready?"

"Yes, your ma and I packed everything yesterday. All I need to do is add my pillow and a couple of blankets, just in case it turns cold." She moved to the back porch to ring the dinner bell calling everyone to come eat.

"I can put those in if they are ready."

"Yes, they are on the chair next to the door in my parents'… in my room." Her neck and face warmed with slight red tint. She was not sure why.

He watched her every move, admiring the gracefulness of her steps and the beauty of her features. Yes, she had gained some weight which looked very good on her. She could still use some. He realized he was staring and quickly turned on his heel and walked toward her room. He emerged with the items in his arms and headed toward the wagon outside the door.

"Here let me get the door for you."

"Thank you. You want these just behind the seat?"

"That would be perfect. Thank you."

"My pleasure, Miss Katie."

"Please, just call me Katie. We are going to be working together over the next few weeks, and it would be best if we could feel comfortable around each other without the unnecessary formalities."

"Sometimes formalities are a good thing. But, if you wish, I will call you Katie."

"Thank you. I hope the time will come when I don't hear your silent 'Miss' every time you say it." She smiled, revealing a small dimple on the left side of her mouth.

"Are you a mind reader?"

"No, your face said it just before you said 'Katie'"

"I'll have to try to control my face a little better. I don't want to betray something at the wrong time. It could mean the difference between life and death."

He left the porch, and she returned to the kitchen thinking about his last statement. Could they face some situations where a simple facial expression could cause them serious harm? She had not thought of that.

"I'll have to watch my own expressions, then. I don't want to cause any more trouble."

"You're no trouble."

"Michael!"

"We heard the bell. Are we on time?"

"Absolutely. Do you need to wash up? I didn't put out a bowl of water. I just now thought of it. I was going to be so prepared."

"We have washed. We did that before we headed over, so your efforts would have been wasted. Katie, don't worry about things like that. We appreciate everything you do."

"Hear, hear!"

"Why, thank you, Riley."

"You are most welcome, gracious lady. The tantalizing aromas dancing about this room have my stomach crawling toward my mouth just trying to get to them."

"Thank you, I think," she said, chuckling.

"Oh, he is always like that. Just take out about every third word and you can understand what he is saying," interjected Clyde.

The twins elbowed each other and laughed. Wulf grunted, and Riley swatted Clyde with his hat. Michael just watched and smiled. Just then, Josh entered and wondered what had happened, but he decided not to ask.

"Please have a seat." Katie said to everyone as she indicated the chairs at the table.

That's all it took. When the clamor died down, Michael prayed for the blessing over the food and serious eating began.

CHAPTER 20

Dust was flying everywhere. Katie coughed and wondered if she had made a mistake. The wind had really picked up, and it looked like rain. Maybe that would not be such a bad thing, considering the dust.

Oh, Ma, Katie thought, *I remember this same feeling. I was not content then either. How could I forget? I complained and complained about the dust. Then it rained and the mud was worse than the dust ever was. Maybe I should learn to be content. I wonder what it will be like when we have cattle to contend with as well.*

Michael rode up beside the wagon.

"The Big Arroyo is not too far, and I believe we will find most of the cattle there still. How about you go over to that clump of trees and set up camp there? We will be rounding up the cattle and taking them to the temporary corral not far from those trees. Wulf, Riley, and Josh did a good job building one. I can't believe they were able to get that done yesterday afternoon. God was really with them. We have some good hands, Katie, don't worry about that. I couldn't have asked for a better crew."

"I just worry about the twins."

"Don't. Riley has a good hand on them, and they are learning. He is amazing with kids. I just wish I could keep up with what he says."

They both laughed, and Katie headed the chuck wagon on a track toward the trees. She smiled at the thought of being able to set up and have some food cooked when the men came in. They would be hungry. She knew rounding up the cattle would be hard work.

"They will be good and sore, I imagine. They will need coffee right away and something hardy to keep them going."

She could see the dust trail as they rode toward the arroyo. In the distance, she could hear the sound of thunder.

I hope they get the cattle out before the stream through there gets flooded. Rain from miles away can cause a flood where it hasn't even rained. "The Eternal, watch over the men. Thank you."

"Get those first cattle out of here and headed toward the corral, boys. Cade, you go with Riley. Wade, you stay here and help get some more headed out in that direction."

"Cade and I can take the cattle to the corral, Mr. Michael. Riley could stay here and help."

"Wade, do what you are told. I have my reasons."

"Aw, all right. We just always do everything together."

"You are almost seventeen now, Wade. Don't you think it is time you started taking on some responsibility of your own?"

"Yes, sir."

"Good. I'm glad we have that settled."

"We have thirteen-head here, Michael. Cade and I'll take these. There are a few more just up the stream near the bend. I imagine there are more around that corner."

"I'll let Clyde and Josh round those up. Wulf, I'll need your help further in. Let's go ahead and get those. C'mon, Wade, you are going with us."

Each man went to work. The sound of the thunder getting closer and closer warned the men they needed to hurry.

"Let's get these out as soon as possible. I don't want us to get caught in a flash flood in here, or a stampede."

"Gotcha, boss. I don't cotton to that myself. Let's get to it."

Riley and Cade corralled their thirteen-head without difficulty. Cade beamed with pride. He had done it. He had followed instructions and found it very rewarding. His elbow automatically went out but found no Wade to connect with. He realized this was the first time they had not been side by side in all of his memory.

"Wonder where Wade is at?"

"Doing his job, just like you. Cade, it's 'I wonder where Wade is?'"

"That's what I just said. Then you told me he was doing his job. What's wrong with you, Mr. Riley?"

"Never mind, Wade. Let's go round up some more cattle."

Katie had the cover over the back of the chuck wagon. The fire burned brightly in the darkening light. The coffee aroma wafted on the rising breeze. She worked hard to get their meal ready, knowing each man would be ready as soon as he rode up.

"Look at my hills, Ma. Aren't they something? This is a perfect place for camp. I can hear the cattle; they aren't far from here. I can see where the Big and Little Arroyos are. What an adventure we are on. Can you see us from where you are?" she spoke to the sky.

The silence didn't bother Katie. She was used to it. Her heart told her to listen to it. If she did, she would know everything she needed to know.

She looked up and saw a dust cloud rising. Was it a dirt devil? It was coming toward her. She quickly put lids on things that needed covers. She began rushing to secure anything that could fly away in a whirlwind. She looked again to see where it was. She saw the dust and a rider.

"Oh, I'll have to watch how I get excited over nothing. I'm surprised they are headed back this soon."

Josh rode up and dismounted quickly.

"What's wrong?"

"Nothing. Michael just wanted to know if you would want some fish for supper?"

"What?"

"The stream in the big arroyo has some beauties in it. Wade and Cade love to fish. We may not get this chance again for a while."

"What about the storm? That stream could turn into a roaring river in a heartbeat if there is much rain upstream."

"Yeah, that's what Michael said. The boys said it would not take them long to catch the fish, if I could bring back some bacon or something."

"Now, you know I don't have any bacon. What's wrong with worms? I guess they didn't want to dig? I don't know. Well, come with me." She grabbed a small shovel she used to tend the fire and a small bucket and started walking toward a dark shady spot under the trees.

"Yes, Mi…I…I mean Katie." In a few steps he caught up to her.

"I knew you would have trouble with that."

"What?" he asked grinning.

"You know. Now, here. You dig and I'll get the worms."

In no time they had enough worms for any fisherman. Josh grabbed the bucket and started toward his horse.

"Wait, I don't want them to lose my bucket. Here, take the worms and a little dirt in this. I'll wash the bucket out."

"Okay. I need to hurry."

"You wouldn't have needed to come at all if those boys were real fishermen. They would have dug their own worms."

"We are all just caught up in what we are doing and trying to outrun the rain. We weren't thinking."

"Uh-huh. I know. I had a pa and a brother."

"What is that supposed to mean?"

He reached for the container. His fingers touched hers. There was that tingling feeling again. He looked into her eyes and could see she had felt it too. Those eyes, he could get lost in them.

The sound of thunder caused them both to jerk back.

"Wow, that was a loud one."

"I'd better get going."

He mounted his horse and was gone in a flash. Katie watched his back as he rode away. She then looked down at her fingers.

Now, I wonder what that was all about. She rubbed her fingers together. She looked down and studied them. *Maybe there is extra electricity in the air because of the lightning, like when hair flies out when I take my bonnet off and snaps and crackles.*

As she worked getting things ready to eat, she could see Josh's dark eyes looking back at her in the coffee, stew, and even in the black bread she was making. As she kneaded the silky smooth dough in the kneading trough, all she could think about were his eyes. She smiled to herself.

It sure has gotten easier to smile and laugh since Michael arrived. Oh, how I missed the fun Abigail and I had. No offense, Ma, but you really didn't smile much. Why were you and Pa always so serious? There is so much joy to be found all around us. It's there right at your fingertips. She looked at her fingers and rubbed them together as she thought that.

The flash and boom were so sudden she jumped and almost dumped the bread out of the bowl.

"I need to get this in the Dutch oven and fast! It won't matter if it hasn't risen enough by the time it bakes. I expect those men to come in drenched."

"Worms?"

"Yes, worms."

"She didn't have no bacon?"

"No, she didn't, and don't expect her to ever have any."

"Golly, I hate putting worms on a hook. I guess a man has to do what he has to do."

"You better get busy if you want to catch anything. That storm is getting closer by the minute and the water from up above will come rushing down through this arroyo. If you are not careful, you'll get caught in it. In fact, I would suggest that wherever you decide to fish, you look around you for a good place to escape should the water start rising quickly. Don't risk your lives for some fish. You can always fish another day."

"You think we're daft er somethin'? I don't want to drown. Do you, Wade?"

"Naw, I never had a hankerin' to."

Josh rolled his eyes and tried not to laugh.

"Well, fellas, not too many people who drown set out to do so. It is usually an accident. So, please be careful."

"Okay, we'll keep one eye on the fish and another on the sky and water."

Josh doubted that, but didn't want to waste any more time with these two. There were cattle to round up, and he wanted to get to it before they were trapped as well. He rode back into the arroyo looking to see what he could find. Another flash of lightning and clap of thunder rolled through the sky. It was not even noon yet; the sky belied the time. It appeared to be late evening. Angry black clouds boiled up and formed the shape of an anvil at the top.

"We are really in for it. Not a drop of rain for weeks and now, just as we get started on the roundup, we are in for a gully washer. I'd better see what is happening at the corral. I don't see any tracks going deeper in."

He passed the boys on the way out. They already had three fish on the stringer.

"Wow, you boys sure do know how to fish. You only need a few more and we'll have supper tonight. As soon as you get enough, take them back to camp to Miss Katie and then come to the corral. We will need you there to help with the branding of the calves and strays."

"Yes, sir," they chorused.

With that, Josh rode out with the horse's tail flying behind.

"Just in time, Josh. We need a couple more hands here."

"Sorry, the boys needed bait, and I went back to get something from Katie. She dug some worms, and I took them to the boys. I know"—he held up both hands—"they could dig their own worms. They wanted bacon. If I had had my head on straight, I would have known she wouldn't have any. Sorry. When I left them, they already had three fish on the stringer. Those boys are good. Looks like we'll have fish tonight."

"There is nothing like fresh fish!" Wulf exclaimed. "I can't wait."

Michael and Josh looked at each other.

"I've not seen that much emotion in Wulf as long as I've known him. Granted it hasn't been that long, but I was beginning to wonder if he had any emotions," Josh whispered as they walked away.

Michael smiled. He looked back over his shoulder toward that man leaning over a fire, getting it ready for the branding.

"Did you get the branding irons from the wagon, Josh?"

"Bra...no, I plum forgot. I can't believe my stupidity. What is wrong with me? I can't seem to keep two thoughts in my head at one time. I'll go back and get them. The camp is just over that rise. It won't take me long. I'll be back before the fire is ready."

"Josh, are you sure you didn't forget on purpose just so you would have an excuse to go back over to the camp?"

"What are you talking about?"

"Never mind. Just be quick about it."

"I promise I'll be faster than a hawk swooping down on a rabbit."

"Yeah, I think I know where that *rabbit* is. You won't have any trouble finding her."

Josh laughed and rode away.

In a minute, Katie was thinking, *Here he comes, again. I wonder what's wrong.*

"Howdy ma'am! I seem to have left my brain somewhere. Have you seen it?"

"What?" Katie laughed.

"When I was here before, I forgot to get the branding irons out of the wagon."

"Oh, I don't think there are any in the wagon. I haven't seen any."

"I hope they're here," he said as he dropped the door to the little compartment on the front of the outside of the wagon. No, just tools there. Next, he looked inside under the bedrolls and saw a long narrow canvas. "Here they are."

"I don't think Esther knew they were there. She never even mentioned it."

"I think Mom would have known. It's just not something she would have thought to tell you. She has plenty of experience in many different places. I remember them telling about talking with some cowboys on a trail drive when Ma and Pa were on a trip once. I was young, but I remember Mom really being interested in the chuck wagon and talking with Cookie."

"Who?"

"The trail drive cook. They called him 'Cookie.' I need to get back. They are waiting for me. It's hard to brand without the irons."

"I would imagine so. Now, get! I have work to do."

Even as she said it, she didn't want him to go. She really wanted to know more about him. His eyes were filled with kindness. He held no contempt there for her. She felt perfectly safe with him. Maybe it was more like protected. She just knew when he left, she felt alone.

Well, I have time for that later. After all, he works for me. It's not like I won't see him again.

She turned to stir the stew that she had over the fire. As she lifted the lid, the aromas of the meat, potatoes, carrots, tomatoes, and spices filled her senses and brought back memories of another time on another trail. Tears began to creep to the surface and burn behind her eyes.

I don't want to think about it. Everyone is gone. Everyone! Why? Why did it have to happen to me?

Trust me, I will never leave you.

Katie put her hand to her heart. She felt its steady beat, but she knew there was more.

Ka-boom!

Katie dropped the spoon and jumped back falling to her knees and covering her eyes.

"That was too close for comfort. I'd better get out some rain gear. I think it is going to get really awful out here in no time." This time she was talking to the trees and anything else around her.

As she looked up, she could see a horse running toward her. "Where's the rider?" She couldn't see anyone on the horse. Without thinking, she ran out to intercept the horse waving her hands above her head. She hoped to at least slow it down or redirect its path toward where the men were. It was coming straight at her.

"Whoa! Whoa!" He came close enough for her to grab at the dangling rein. Surprised, she felt the rein tighten in her hand and pulled back on it. The horse raised its head, pulling her slightly off her feet. She came back down on her heels and dug in. "Whoa!"

He skirted around her, hooves dancing in a circle. His eyes were wide with terror. Katie felt her heart pound against her chest.

More softly, she said, "Calm down, boy, you'll be okay. Whoa, that's right. Just settle down now. Settle down."

She pulled him closer and lifted her hand to pat his neck.

"You're a big boy. Where'd you come from? I need to see if someone knows you."

The temporary corral was not that far away. The men weren't close enough to hear her yell. She could fire a shot.

Maybe that would bring someone. They were busy with the cattle. Maybe I shouldn't bother them. But what if someone was in trouble and needed help? The lightning could have spooked the horse and thrown the rider. He may have a broken leg, or worse. Oh! I hate not knowing what to do. She stomped her foot and led the horse over to the wagon and tied him to the wheel.

She retrieved the spoon from the ground and got some water out to wash it. She replaced the lid on the stew and checked to make sure everything was secure. She then climbed in the wagon and reemerged in a few minutes wearing her riding skirt.

"Well, this will have to do. You and I will get acquainted real fast, big fella. You just act like a gentleman, okay? We'll get along just fine if you do."

The horse snorted, causing Katie to giggle.

"As long as we understand each other, we will be a great team. Now, let's go see what can be done."

With that, Katie rode off toward the corral.

Michael turned as he sensed someone approaching. He shaded his eyes, squinting in the direction of the rider.

"Now what? Who is that?"

Josh turned to see what Michael was looking at.

"That looks like Katie. Where did she get that horse?"

As she rode up, Michael took in a breath. "What's going on, Katie? Where's Wade?"

"I don't know. Why?"

"You're riding his horse."

"Oh, no."

"What?"

"This horse came running toward camp just after that last thunder boom. I managed to get a hold of it and calm it down. I thought maybe the rider had been thrown or something and needed help. This was the only way I could get here to see if you knew anything or thought someone ought to go search for the rider."

For the first time she looked around. The corral was a temporary one made of small tree branches and young trees. It was enough to keep the cattle in if there wasn't a stampede or anything like that. The men had a fire going with branding irons sticking out of it. Two men had a calf down holding it still while another was standing above its rump with the red hot iron burning her brand into it. As soon as he pulled it back the other two men let the calf up and led him back to the corral. The cattle seemed to be nervous.

"...better check," she heard Michael say.

Josh turned his head and looked Michael in the eye. "I'll go," he said.

"I want you and Riley to go. One man may not be enough. You better take this horse back with you. They may need it. Let's hope they do. I'll be praying."

"Is it bad?" she asked.

"It is always bad when a man is left without his horse, especially in the wilderness."

"What if they are hurt? Should I go?"

"No." The two men said together.

"We need you to be at the camp and ready if we need anything for them there," Michael added.

"Do you think they are hurt?"

"We won't know until we get there. It could be that the horse was just able to pull away from where they had him tied, if they had him tied. Sometimes those boys don't stop to think."

"Josh, go get Riley and let him know what is going on."

"Yes, sir."

"I'll take you back to camp if you don't mind riding double," Michael said.

"No, I don't mind."

"I need to talk with Clyde and Wulf. I'll be right back and then we can go," he said as he walked away.

She stood watching Josh and Riley ride out, then watched Michael talking with Clyde and Wulf. They were nodding then shaking their heads. Clyde shooed Michael away with the back of his hand and then walked off toward the corral. Wulf actually laughed. Michael then turned and walked back toward her leading his horse.

"Curious. I wonder what that was all about," Katie murmured.

"Talking to yourself again?"

"For so long I had nobody to talk to, so it became a habit. It beats staying completely silent."

"I find great comfort talking with the Lord."

"Michael, do you know how foreign that idea is to me? I have never seen anyone talk to God like you, Esther, Josh, Adam, Brian, and Tad. Oh, and don't forget Doc. My goodness, I have been surrounded by you people who just talk with God. I am amazed. I have called out to the Eternal when I have been in trouble, big trouble like with Red. But that has been the extent of it. Except just lately, I have 'talked' with him. You all act like you have this special relationship with him, like he is standing right here."

"That's because he is. He has promised never to leave us or forsake us. He promised to live within us. When someone accepts

Jesus as the Messiah, they become the new temple of the Holy Spirit. He resides in their hearts."

Her mouth flew open, and she just stared at him.

"Come on, I'll give you a hand up." He mounted his horse and then helped her up behind him, easily lifting her off the ground.

They rode in silence across the hill and to the camp. He helped her down.

"If you need any kind of help, just fire one shot in the air. Someone will come riding back. That will be our signal for help."

"Okay. I can do that. Thank you, Michael. I don't know how I can express my thanks to you. I can't find the words to express my feelings. You have saved my life in more ways than one."

"That would be God's work through me. Thank him, Katie. I am privileged to be his servant."

With that, he rode back toward the corral and the work to be done.

Katie looked around her. Everything was quiet. The black clouds were moving off to the north. Perhaps, she wouldn't have to get out her rain gear after all.

Deciding to try to talk with God like he was right there, Katie began, "Thank you, the Eternal…God, for saving my life, for using Michael to keep me safe. Thank you for the many people you have sent into my life. The darkness is disappearing. Thank you for that as well. Thank you for the cattle, horses, ranch, and for the help you have sent my way. Thank you for giving me my voice back. Thank you for the healing hands of Doc and Esther. Thank you for everything. Help me to be mindful of you being close by and there when I need you. Oh, I guess I need you all the time, I just don't realize it. Help me to realize it. The Eternal… God, I want what Esther has. Show me how to have it. Amen."

Josh and Riley rode toward the Big Arroyo. As they neared the hills and the beginning of the arroyo, they could hear the roar of water. They topped the hill and could see the small stream that had been there before was now a churning muddy river.

"Wow, so much water. We haven't had a drop. I wonder where the boys are."

"There is no way we can get in the arroyo this way. Let's go up above and see what we can see."

As they rode up the hillside to the top of the crevice carved by years of rain and runoff, each man prayed for the boys.

"Please make them safe, Lord. Put your hand of protection over them."

"Keep them from all danger, Father, God. We trust them into your hands."

"Help us to find them, Lord. Guide our every step."

"Help them to see us, dear Father, so that we may see them. Open our eyes and theirs. We are believing them to be safe."

They rode their horses to the spot above where the boys had been fishing when Josh had left them. They couldn't see anything. The water of the river had risen far above where the boys had been.

"I can't see anything but water. I'm going to look over the edge. Let's tie a rope around my middle and wrap it around the saddle horn. I'll lie down and look over. If the overhang gives way, I'll be tied to the horse and you can pull me back up."

"Josh, let me look. They were my responsibility."

"How many times have you done this before, Riley?"

"None. You?"

"Six or seven. So, I'll do it. I know what I'm doing, and if the overhang gives way you just make sure that horse doesn't follow me over."

They both laughed at that. Riley walked over and helped tie the rope around Josh's middle, then secured it to the saddle horn.

"You're all set. I'll hold the bridle"

Josh looked over the ledge. The river was tearing its way through the arroyo. If there had been any cattle still in there, they were long gone by now. He just hoped the boys had found safety. The water was eating away at the sides of the arroyo. Dirt kept sliding in and disappearing. The arroyo would be much bigger once this flash flood was over.

"I don't see anything," he yelled.

He could feel dirt crumbling away under him. He was about to get back from the edge when he saw movement off to his left.

He yelled again, this time in that direction.

"Cade, Wade, do you hear me!"

There was that movement again. It looked like the dirt was moving, but sideways instead of down. Then he could see them— two heads poked themselves out of an opening in one of the ribs of the wall going down toward the torrent.

"Are you hurt?"

The heads shook no.

"We will lower a rope to you and pull you up."

The heads shook no.

"You cannot stay there. The river is tearing the dirt out from under you. You will fall into the river."

The heads disappeared into the opening. Josh felt helpless as he watched the rib of earth beneath the boys slowly churn away. What could they be doing? Poking each other in the side trying to decide what to do?

Josh turned and called Riley over.

"I want to move over closer to where the boys are. Do you think we can get a length of rope over to that 'cave,' if you can call it that? It's more like a rat hole."

"I think if I lower you some and you have the rope, you could throw it over to them. I wouldn't want to risk going out on that precipice. It's too dangerous."

"Then what would we do? They won't swing over. No, we've got to go out there and quick. Look at how the water is eating away at the side."

The men still could not see the boys. They moved back from the edge and went over to the outcropping of land that was eroding by the minute.

"Wade, Cade, come on out. We have to get you now! If we don't, you'll be dead."

"I don't know if they can hear you from here."

"I'll drop the rope down. Keep it tied to your horse and keep me tied to mine. I sure don't want to go down into that torrent."

"See anything?"

"No, the rope is hanging right in front of the opening. What could they be doing? Wait, there is a hand. It is reaching out for the rope. Thank you, Lord!"

The precipice just beyond the cave crashed into the once-peaceful stream that was now a churning, roaring, muddy force of destruction devouring everything in its path.

"Boys, hurry. The river won't wait. Riley, get ready. One of the boys is coming out. *Pull!*"

Riley backed the horse up. He didn't seem to be having any trouble pulling the teen.

"He's almost here. Keep going."

"We've got you, son, now get that rope off so we can throw it down for your brother."

The teen was covered in mud. He began shaking and his teeth began to chatter. Riley came back with the horse, took one look at the boy, and undid the bedroll behind the saddle.

"Here, you need this. Go over and sit down under that tree. You'll be safe over there."

"I...I...w-w-want   t-t-t-to   s-s-s-s-see   m-m-m-m-my b-br-brother."

"You will, you just need to get out of our way so we can get him out."

"H-h-he d-d-doesn't w-w-want t-t-to c-c-come o-o-out."

"Why, for the love of...why not?"

"Y-y-y-you'll s-s-see."

"Oh, for…get out of the way and go sit down. *Now!*"

"Riley, get ready. The other one has the rope now. C'mon, c'mon. The bank is washing away right under the cave. He has to get out!"

A big chunk of red clay fell into the tumbling mass of water. Rocks began to fall as well. As the base was eaten away, more and more of the upper rib began to slide down.

"*Get out now!*" screamed Josh.

He could see the back of the boy making his way out of the cave.

"Here he comes! Hold on."

As he got to the edge, it gave way and he lost his footing. He fell backward, swinging away from the side. They could hear screaming above the roar. Josh jumped up and ran to help Riley and to get away from the edge that had begun to crumble. Together they pulled back horse and rope. This time, the horse did not have such an easy time.

"What in the world? Is he bringing a boulder with him?"

Cade was on his feet helping to pull the rope. Josh let go and ran over to the edge. He ran back and got his horse. Undoing the rope around himself, he let it down to where the boy dangled.

"Grab onto this rope too. If you can, wrap it around you."

He turned to Riley. "There are two of them."

"Two?"

"Yes, two."

He looked back and saw that they had the rope. He began to help pull with his horse. He was pulling them away from the protruding end of the precipice and more into the wall of the arroyo. Cade now had the horse and took over for Josh. Josh lay down on his stomach and reached for the hand stretched out toward him.

"Hang on. I have you. Hang on, now. Don't let go!"

The muddy hand was small and slippery with wet mud. It tightened around Josh's hand and he pulled up with all his might. The small body almost flew over the edge landing right on Josh.

"I have you now, don't be afraid."

Josh slowly rolled the child off of him away from the edge. He reached over to help Wade up over the edge. As he pulled on the rope and caught Wade by the hand, a thundering sound caused them all to look toward the pinnacle. Gasping, they watched the cave collapse and the rest of the finger jutting out into the arroyo slide down and disappear into the roaring water.

"Let's get out of here. We need to get all of you back to camp."

Josh stood brushing the dirt and grime from his pants. He reached out to help the child up, realizing then that was no child. She was an Indian girl or young woman. It was hard to tell with so much dirt on her. He looked at Wade who shrugged and walked away. Josh looked at Cade and saw for the first time he had a string of fish around his neck and was grinning from ear to ear.

"We did it, didn't we? I knew we could."

"Do what?"

"Get outta that cave with the fish and the girl."

"Why the discussion over taking the rope, if that is what you were doing?" Riley glared at Wade and Cade.

"Well, ya see, Cade wanted to save the fish, but if we brought all of 'um, then there was'n no way we could brung up the fish and Willow. He fin'ly 'cided to brung just half of 'um."

"Bring."

"Huh?"

"*Bring*. It's 'bring up the fish,' and 'bring just half of them.'"

"That's what I said."

"Oh, never mind. Let's get going. Katie isn't going to believe this. For that matter, neither will any of the others."

Willow just stood looking as if she was in shock. Riley turned to his horse and grabbed his bedroll from the back. He wrapped the blanket around her and looked directly into her big blue eyes.

"Hmm, you are going to be just fine now. Don't worry, we will get you back to camp and Katie will take care of anything you may need. I'll let you ride with me. You'll be safe."

A single tear escaped her eye and rolled down her cheek. Her expression remained stoic.

"You boys ride this horse together. Did the other one get away as well?" Josh asked as they mounted the horses and began riding away from the arroyo.

"Yes sir, 'long with hers. We seen her horse runnin' afore we seen her.

"Saw."

"Saw, sorry. Th' horses musta been talkin' to one 'tuther, 'cause afore we could say boo-scat all of 'um was gone."

Wade took up the story as Cade stopped for a breath.

"Then she come arunnin' 'round th' bend yellin'. We thunk… uh, thought, sorry. She was a yellin' at th' horses, but she's wavin' her hands and just a yellin' to high heav'n. When she gets close, she grabbed my sleeve and started a pullin' and lookin' over her shoulder behind her. So's I looks and din't see nothin'…uh, anything, sorry. She was scaret a'rite, we could tell. She's jest a pullin' and pullin' so's we goes with her."

Cade didn't miss a beat as Wade stopped for a breath. Both boys were shuddering.

"I grabbed th' fish and runs after 'um. She's a pullin' Wade right toward the wall of that there outcropping that fell. I was thinkin' 'What now?'"

"You were? So's I."

"Well, we get to that wall and ya know what? There are steps in the clay and rock goin' up t' that cave."

"Ya know what else? That cave was w'ere she's a livin'."

"Ya know what else?"

"*Stop*! No more, 'Ya know what elses.'"

"Sorry," the boys said in unison.

"We get up th're an' she starts grabbing all her thins' and shov's 'um at me. I din't know what t'do. I jest look at her. She then pulls us toward the openin' of th' cave. But she stops dead still and collapses right th're. Would you b'leve it, we's trapped. We look out and th're's a big ugly wall of water jest a tearin' through that arroyo."

Riley could feel the girl shuddering and her grasp around his waist tightened. "Okay, boys, I think we get the picture. Let's ride!"

He took off toward the camp. Josh, close behind him, looked back at the boys. They looked stunned, as if they couldn't believe they had been left. They kicked the horse and started to gallop trying to make up the distance between them and the rest.

CHAPTER 21

This day certainly had not gone the way Katie had expected it to go. When the boys rode in with Riley and Josh, she had no idea they had been through such a bad time. Then to see the Indian girl behind Riley, she really couldn't guess what had happened. She could see immediately that the girl needed attention and fast. The boys could take care of themselves, but this poor little thing could not help herself. She was terrified and covered with mud.

"First thing, let's get you cleaned up. I know we don't have a bathtub here, but I can fix a large bucket of hot water, and here is some soap. I'll help wash your hair if you don't mind."

The girl just stood looking at Katie. Maybe she didn't understand English.

"Ma, what do I do?" Katie asked looking at the sky. "I'll just fix everything and then bathe her if I have to."

Just then the girl's stomach growled. "I need to get some food in you quick," Katie said as she looked her straight in the eyes. "Here, let's just wash your hands and face. We can bathe you later."

Just then the men came in to eat. Josh wanted so much to talk with Katie. Every time he looked at her his heart skipped a beat. Finally he asked, "How is Willow doing?"

"How do you know her name? She hasn't said a word."

"I don't know, I guess one of the boys said it. I never questioned it. Wade, Cade, how do you know her name is Willow?"

"Tole us."

"She told you?"

"Yes, sir."

"Did she say, 'My name is Willow?'"

"Som'thin' like 'at."

"So, Willow, would you like something to eat?"

She sat very still and looked down at the ground.

Katie was afraid the girl would get sick from sadness. Lonely and sad, she had been there. She knew what losing everything could mean; what that bottomless pit of darkness could make her wish and dare to plan.

"Willow, I'm going to sit right next to you and take care of you. You have nothing to be afraid of. Please eat something. It will help chase away the darkness."

Willow jerked her head up and looked directly at Katie.

So, she does understand what we say, thought Katie. *She also understands despair.*

Katie smiled, scooped up some stew onto a plate and handed it to her with some utensils. She then fixed her own plate and sat next to her to eat. The bread, hot and savory, made Katie smile. She had not tried it before, but cooking it in the Dutch oven, like her mother had done, worked. As she bit into it, she sighed with contentment. She then noticed that Willow was following her every move and being a shadow to her actions.

The men straggled into camp. Seeing everyone else eating, they helped themselves and had a seat wherever they could find one.

Katie wanted to connect with Willow. "You know what would feel really good after we eat? A nice hot bath! Oh, that would soothe those tired muscles and ease all the fear of what happened today. Would you like to take a bath?"

Willow just looked at Katie. Her eyes showed no understanding of what Katie was talking about.

"I think I'll have to rig up some kind of blanket curtain. I have a big bucket tucked under the wagon for doing some washing. I bet we could take a bath in that. It wouldn't be like a real tub, but it would do. I know you want to get all that clay off of you and out of your hair. That can't feel good."

Willow took a few more bites and then looked at Katie. She reached out her hand tentatively and barely touched the silky soft strands of hair hanging down her back. Her eyes, full of wonder, stared at Katie's clothes and her hands.

"You know, Willow, you look about the size of my sister, Abigail. I bet her clothes would fit you. Do you know how old you are? Uh, how many, uh, what should I say, seasons? How about winters? How many winters have you seen?"

Willow didn't say a word but went back to taking a few more bites. She made a humming sound Katie took for contentment.

"I hope it is good. I know what it is like eating someone else's cooking and wondering how it is going to taste. Mine may not taste like what you are used to, but it is nourishing. You may have as much as you like."

Michael looked at Katie and Willow. He decided it was a very good thing to have Willow here with Katie. Katie had taken on a new look now with Willow here. She seemed more content.

"How many more head do we have to brand?" Clyde asked.

Michael looked at Clyde then at the rest of the men. "The work is going quite well, considering all the interruptions and delays. We still haven't been to the Little Arroyo to check on cattle. I think there may be some roaming around yet as well. We can finish up these, and a couple of you guys can take them back to the pasture by the barn then come back out. I hate we lost that other horse. We really could use two now. The rest of us will ride out and see if we can round up some more cattle before dark. Clyde, you and Wulf take this part of the herd back to the ranch and get them put up then head back out here.

Clyde and Wulf nodded their assent, picked up the coffeepot and poured another cup.

"Wade an' me will clean the fish an' git 'em ready for t'night's supper. Ya know'd how ta fix fish, Miz. Katie?"

"Yes, boys, I think I can manage that. They will taste real good being so fresh."

"Katie, do you need anything from the ranch before tomorrow? We may finish up by late tomorrow depending on how many cattle we find and how many need branding. Clyde and Wulf can pick up anything you need."

Every man looked her way and she suddenly felt very shy. She just shook her head and smiled.

"Are you sure? We can get anything you need," agreed Clyde.

"Well, I'm going to look in Abigail's things for something for Willow to wear, but it can wait until we get back there, before we start out on the drive."

Everyone went back to what they had been doing except Josh. His eyes lingered on Katie. He just couldn't take his eyes off of her. Her movements were so fluid. He could picture her on a dance floor instead of out here around a camp in the hills. Her hair, which had been up in a bun earlier in the day now hung down in little ringlets which had escaped from the tidiness of their former home. She was intriguing. He watched as she cared for Willow and could picture her with children, lovingly taking care of them. A vivid image of him sitting in a chair by the fireplace watching her came to mind. *Wow! Where had that picture come from?* He had never really planned on marrying until he had his own place and had something to offer a woman. Here he was fantasizing about a life with Katie. He felt so drawn to her. *Yet, I am a believer in Jesus as Messiah and she is still looking for him. I will just have to pray harder for her and do what I can to show her Jesus.*

"Josh?"

"Uh, yes, ma'am?"

"I hate to interrupt your thoughts, but I was wondering if you could help me with setting up a curtained-off area so Willow could take a make-do bath."

"A make-do bath?"

"Why, yes, a make-do bath; one that will have to make-do until she can have the luxury of taking a real bath. I plan on that happening as soon as possible after we arrive back at the ranch tomorrow."

"Well, I will most certainly be happy to help in any way I can. Where do you want to set up this 'make-do' bath?"

"Where do you suggest? I don't want to have to haul the water too far from the fire to the tub, but I don't want her to be just out here in the open either."

"Well, I tell you what. Why don't I hang the blankets or sheets or whatever you have over here under these low branches, and I'll haul the water as well? That way she can have privacy and a hot bath."

"That's a wonderful idea. But don't you need to be helping Michael?"

"How about if I go ask him now if I can help you, and as soon as everything is to your satisfaction, I can go back and join him in what he wants or needs me to do?"

"Okay, that sounds good. I don't want Michael thinking I am taking you away from your work."

She watched Josh walk away toward Michael, and for the first time she really looked at him. She had not noticed his broad shoulders and his fine posture before. He walked with so much confidence; he exuded strength and control. She admired that. He had also inherited the finer qualities of both Esther and Adam. Willow tugged on her arm.

Katie blinked and shook her head.

"Yes, Willow, what is it?"

Willow pointed toward the horizon southeast of where they were.

"Now, I wonder who that is. Josh, Michael!"

Neither of the men seemed to hear her. She tried again a little louder.

"Josh, Michael!"

Josh seemed to turn his head slightly, so she tried again.

"Josh!"

This time he looked her way. She pointed in the direction of the rider. Josh looked over that way and pointed in the same direction saying something to Michael. Michael then turned and looked. He said something to Josh, who then nodded and moved toward his horse.

"Well, I guess we won't be getting that curtain made after all."

Katie turned to look at Willow, but she had disappeared.

"Willow! Where are you?"

No answer.

"Willow!"

The sun was moving lower in the sky and there was so much to do for the evening meal.

"Can this day get any longer?" Katie wondered. She moved toward the woods to see if she could see Willow anywhere. She was not going to distract the men from their work in order to look for Willow. She may have just had to answer the call of nature, for all Katie knew.

"I'll start the water heating, and if she doesn't want to use it, I certainly do," she said out loud to herself, yet again.

Katie got to work and didn't waste time worrying. Certainly this Indian girl could take care of herself better than Katie could out here in the wild.

"Well, it's not so wild. This is all still familiar and part of our ranch, nothing like crossing Louisiana and Texas to get here. Now, that was wild." Katie mumbled to herself as she worked.

She picked up the bucket and headed toward the spring just inside the copse of trees the wagon was parked next to. As she moved closer to the spring and its delightful pool, she heard singing and splashing. She moved more cautiously and crept up to a tree. She looked around the tree and to her surprise there was Willow swimming in that icy cold water, with her wet, but clean, buckskin dress hanging on the bushes nearby. Katie stepped from behind the tree holding the bucket.

"Willow, aren't you freezing? That's spring water."

"No, feels good."

She talks, thought Katie as she raised her eyebrows.

"Well, at least let me bring you some soap and a towel."

Willow shrugged as if to say it doesn't really matter.

Katie could not imagine taking a bath in the icy water and then not even using a towel to dry and invigorate her soon-to-be-blue skin. She turned and quickly walked off toward the wagon.

When she returned, soap in hand and towel over her shoulder, she found Willow still in the water.

"Here you go. Do you need some help washing your hair and getting all that mud out?"

"Please, do."

Katie, delighted Willow was now talking with her, took on the task with renewed vigor. She had a million questions, but she did not want to scare Willow speechless. She would take it slowly and ask very easy questions first. Katie reached between her legs and pulled her skirt from the back between her legs and up, and then tucked the hem of the skirt into the waistband making a pair of "pants." With that, she took off her boots and socks and gingerly stepped into the cold water. She winced at the cold. "Now, Willow, if you will just back up to me and dunk your head in the shallow water I can wash it. Just sit on that rock just under the water there and I should be able to wash your hair with ease."

Willow did as she was told and her long hair streamed down her back when she raised her head again. Katie lathered up the soap and began to scrub.

"Willow is a beautiful name. Did your mother name you?"

"No, Indians name, Weeping Willow. I cry all time when taken."

Katie felt a knot fill her stomach. This girl was not an Indian. As she washed the mud out of her hair she could see the strands were strawberry blonde. Now that she really looked at her, the skin that had been covered by her dress was light and creamy. Her eyes were blue.

"How old were you when you were taken?"

"Little, seven, I think."

"And you stayed with the Indians all this time?"

"No, I ran away. Hide in cave, then make home in little mud cave."

"You hid in the caves past that Big Arroyo?"

"Yes, caves."

"Aren't they dangerous? You could have gotten hurt and killed in those caves."

"Better than marry mean Indian."

"Oh, so you had not been in the caves long?"

"Only three years."

"Three years! How old are you now?"

"Seventeen, I think."

"You ran away when you were fourteen?"

"Yes."

"Why?"

"My Indian parents were going to force me to marry Bear Claw. I not marry him. I see how he treat his wife. She die. He say accident. I know it not accident. He hit her. He hit her hard.

She with child. She fall and have baby, too soon. Baby die and she die. She not want to live. I take horse, ride long time, hide in cave. I keep horse in cave most of time. Then find arroyo with little mud cave high up. Horse can stay out and eat grass, drink water. Safe, very safe, until today. Bad water. Big water. I scare horses. I get boys, climb into cave. Men take us out. Cave fall in water. All gone now. No where go. Find new cave. Need horse."

Katie gaped at all this talk and the news. She wondered about Willow's parents but didn't want to ask. Willow dunked her head under the water, rinsing the soap out of her hair. When she came up, what a beauty she was.

"You remind me of the story of the ugly duckling," Katie said, laughing.

"You tell story?"

"Yes, tonight, I'll tell you the story."

Willow slipped on her wet dress which now clung to her body.

"We definitely have to get you some other clothes. We cannot let the men see you like this."

As they walked back into camp, there was Michael, Josh, and Adam looking straight at them.

"Oh no!" Katie grabbed Willow and shoved her behind her. At the same time she yelled at the men. "Turn your backs!"

All three did turn but wondered what they had just seen. Katie quickly got Willow into the wagon.

"Willow, stay right here. Don't move. Don't come out until I tell you it is safe."

"I stay."

"Good."

Katie walked back around to the back of the wagon.

"Okay you may now turn around."

She schooled her expression so as not to reveal anything had been wrong.

"What was that all about?" asked Josh.

"Adam, it is so wonderful to see you. Is everything all right at the ranch? Is there some trouble? Would you like some coffee? I think it is still hot. It might be a little strong, though."

"Let's see, yes, no, yes, and that's all right, I like it strong."

She looked at him with a blank expression then smiled. "Oh, I get it. Okay then, coffee it is."

"What was that we just saw?" Michael asked.

"I don't know. What did you see?"

"A blonde woman with no clothes on?" Josh replied.

"Josh! How could you say such a thing?"

"You asked what we saw. I am used to answering questions with the truth. So, what was it?"

"Well, it was a blonde woman, but she was dressed. She just looked like she wasn't because her buckskin clothes were wet and kind of clinging to her. I did *not* think we would find anyone here. Last I saw of you, you were riding off. I didn't think you would come back to put up the bathing curtain for me. I understood that finding out who that was coming was more important. And now that I know it was your father, I am delighted he is here."

"So, who is it?"

"Who?"

"The woman."

"Oh…Willow."

"Willow?" All three men looked at her in disbelief.

"Yes, Willow. Who did you think it would be?"

"Well, with this day being what it has been, who knew what might happen next."

"So, Adam what brings you out here?" asked Katie, trying to divert attention away from Willow.

"Well, I was at the ranch checking on Tad and milking the cow, when two horses came galloping in. One was saddled, the other bare-backed. I thought I'd better check with ya'll and see if these had gotten away from you."

"Well, we have Wade's horse, so that one must be Cade's, and the other one has to be Willow's. This is great! I was so worried they had been killed in that flood."

"That's what Josh said. So, your little family is growing. I'm happy for you, Katie. I know you will love having another woman around. How old is she?"

"She's seventeen, she thinks. She may be a little older. I haven't gotten her whole story yet. I can tell you she does not want to go back to the Indians and that she is not Indian."

"I couldn't tell with all that mud on her, but after seeing her… well, never mind. She certainly didn't look Indian just now. She does look a bit reddish-brown, though."

"Believe me, Josh, she isn't Indian and it is the sun that has made her skin darker than it should be."

Adam, not wanting the conversation to get heated, interrupted and said, "I best be getting back. Great coffee, Katie. It's good to see you again, Michael, son, but Tad will wonder what has happened to me. I will bring Esther out tomorrow, and she will have some supper ready for ya'll when you get back. When I tell her about Willow, I won't be able to keep her away. I can just hear her now—'Another daughter! God is so good, Adam.'"

Everyone laughed at his attempted high feminine voice, and agreed that that sounded just like Esther.

"Adam, did you see Clyde and Wulf when you came out? They were driving some of the cattle back to the ranch."

"No."

"I was just wondering how they were getting along."

"If I can catch up to them, I can help them out a little. Their trail should not be too hard to follow."

Adam handed the cup back to Katie and mounted his horse. He spurred his horse and rode out much faster than he had ridden in.

"I think he likes ranching as well as cooking. Don't you, Josh?"

"Maybe that is where I get it. I could do this forever. It is demanding work, but it is so free out here. I'd hate to be in a building all day."

"Well, give me the comforts of home. I don't mind 'camping' as long as I know I can be back home in the not-too-distant future. I like sleeping in a bed!"

"A bed is good, but I like sleeping out under those big stars up there just as much. I can't wait for them to come out at night. I think of them as God's eyes watching over me all through the night. They are there during the day; I just can't see them, but he can see me at all times."

"That is a beautiful thought. Thank you for sharing that with me. I will tuck that away in this head of mine and think about that when I see the stars. I can tell Willow about it as well. She might find some comfort in it."

"Speaking of Willow, I guess we'd better get back to work so you can 'work' with her." Josh gave Katie a wink, and she laughed out loud. It was the most beautiful sound Josh had heard. Her eyes sparkled like sun on rippling water. He found himself wanting to hold her in his arms and tell her she would never have to be afraid again. He would be there to protect her so she could laugh and never be afraid.

Michael looked at Josh and then at Katie. He nudged Josh and said, "Let's go, times a wastin'."

Josh blinked and cleared his throat. "Oh, sure. Let's go. I can't wait to find some more cattle.

CHAPTER 22

"Riley, you come with Josh and me. Wade, Cade, you stay close and take care of anything Miss Katie needs you to do. First, I want you to go and get that mud off of you. Jump in with your clothes on; they need washing as well. "

"Where d'we go?"

"Ask Miss Katie to show you the swimming hole. Then you get cleaned up, ya hear?"

"Yes sir." The boys took off running toward the campsite and were soon over the hill.

"Well, men, let's head out and get us some more cattle," Michael said with enthusiasm.

The three men settled down into the saddle and started out.

"First, we will go to the Little Arroyo. We'll round up any cattle we find there. Then we can split up to look for more depending on how many we find there."

"Sounds like a good plan to me," Josh agreed.

"A most excellent plan. Perhaps the Lord will smile on us and we will find all the cattle we need in a nice little bundle, like a present, just waiting for us in the Little Arroyo."

"I hate to burst your bubble, Riley, but most times God wants us to work at something so we can learn from that. If he does everything for us and we don't have to put forth any effort, we just don't learn to lean on him."

"If we recognize that it was God's plan and admit he provided it, wouldn't that be showing our dependence on him?" replied Riley.

"Yes, but I think he prefers for us to work hard to get what he has provided. If it is too easy, we start getting prideful about how good we are and how smart we are. He hates pride so much. You see, pride is Satan's sin. Ole Lucifer thought he could take the place of God. Lucifer thought he could just throw God out of heaven. Well, after that little rebellion, Satan was the one thrown out of heaven. Now, he and his minions torment mankind. No, I don't think God would be pleased at all to just hand those cattle over to us in a nice, neat little package. I would be very surprised if I find more than a dozen together," explained Michael.

"I like being an optimist. I'm going to pray that God will make this little hunt just a bit easier than the last."

"You go right ahead, Riley. I plan on working hard the rest of the day."

"What do you think, Josh?" asked Riley.

"Oh, I'm afraid I have to agree with Michael. When I was in the army, nothing came easy. Everything was hard."

"What about all the battles the Israelites fought? God was right there with them. Sometimes, they didn't even have to fight. The Lord had the enemy kill each other or just run away. Sometimes he made it easy."

"True, maybe you are right. We could pray and ask him." Josh wondered if he had been selling God short. God could do it, if it was in his plan.

"Thanks, Josh. I really want to do that. I believe the two of you may have to ask forgiveness for a doubting spirit. Remember what James says: When a man asks God for something, he must not ask doubting. He who doubts is like a wave of the sea being tossed to and fro by the wind."

"I believe that was referring to wisdom."

"Michael, I believe God is setting a principle here. Yes, it was talking about wisdom, but if we need something, and it is not for some selfish desire, but one that will align with God's will, wouldn't he do that?"

"Certainly. My question is, why are you asking? Is it for a selfish desire? Or is there something here that having all the cattle in a nice neat package somehow aligns with God's will in this matter?"

"Uh, I really hadn't thought of it that way. Let me ponder my motives for a few minutes. Perhaps, I should ask God for the wisdom to discern my motives and his will."

"Now there is a prayer I can support!"

———

"Willow?"

Katie looked into the wagon for the girl. She had not heard a sound since the men left and was beginning to worry.

"Poor thing."

Katie moved back down from where the angelic girl lay sound asleep. As she backed off the wagon, she heard running behind her. She turned to see Wade and Cade tearing down the hill and straight toward her. They also were covered in mud. What a sight to behold. She held up her hands in a halting motion and walked briskly toward them.

"Willow's asleep. Be quiet," she said when they were close enough to hear.

"Michael tole us to go swim."

"I bet he did! You boys better 'swim' with some soap. Let me get you some. Do you know where the pool is?"

"No'm."

"Come with me. I'll show you the path."

"Looky at this string of fish! Can we have a bucket ta pit um in? We're gonna clean um up whilst we're down ther'."

"They are beautiful and big! My goodness, that will make a wonderful supper. Now, here is a bucket. Clean the fish first, and then take your bath. I think things will work out better that way. But wash your hands before you clean those fish."

"Why? We'll jest hav'ta wash 'um again on'st we's through with 'um."

"Because I said so. That's why."

"Ah, now ya soun' lack Ma."

"Well, then you best do what I tell you."

"Oh, a'rite."

Katie showed the boys where the spring pool was and let them have their fun cleaning fish and then themselves. As she walked back to the camp, she looked at the wonder of the trees, birds, and all of nature surrounding her. She felt a stirring in her heart and began to talk with God as if he was standing right there.

"This is just awesome, the Eternal. What a wonderful creation you have made. I thank you for Willow and for saving the boys today. I don't know if I could have gone on if anyone had been killed. I don't think I can take any more dying. I just don't. Please keep us all safe. Thank you for the horses and for providing all we need. I am beginning to see you as Esther does, and I really like you better this way. I remember a voice saying to find the light. Was that you? It seems that Josh, Michael, Riley, Esther, Adam, and even Tad are so full of light. Is that what you meant? Find them and do what they do? I need answers…God, I need to know you better. Help me to get to know you."

When she came out of the woods, Willow was standing in the middle of the camp looking at the sky with her arms spread out at shoulder height, appearing to drink in the sunlight. Katie just stood and watched her for a few minutes, then moved into the camp.

"Willow, are you all right?"

"Oh, yes! More. I free. I thank Great Spirit and his son."

"His son?"

"Yes, Great Spirit sent son to earth. He die. But, he die for me. I love him. He came back to life."

"Are you talking about Jesus? I didn't think the Indians knew about him. Isn't he just for the Gentile Christians?"

"I know Jesus since little girl. He keep me safe. Love him!"

"I don't know if you are saying you love him or I am to love him. Oh, I'm getting confused again."

"You need teach me English. I need talk better. I *not* go back."

"I can do that. One of the first things I noticed is you are not using the word 'to' so you are not forming the infinitive of the verbs. For instance, you said, 'You need teach me English.' You should have said, 'to teach'. You need *to teach* me English. Do you understand?"

"You need *to teach* me English."

Katie giggled. "Yes, but you don't have to emphasize it like I did. Just say, 'You need to teach me English.' Now, can you think of another thing you said that needs to have the 'to' with it?"

"You need to teach me English. I need talk...to talk better? I not to go back."

"You are catching on. Yes, you should have said, 'I need to talk better.' But the next sentence should have been, 'I will not go back' or 'I do not want to go back.' Or you could say, 'I cannot go back.' It sounds more like you mean, 'I won't go back,' which is more informal than 'I will not go back.'"

"You say much. Hard keep...to keep up with you."

"Yes, I did say too much. That is a different kind of 'too'."

"What you mean?"

"What do you mean."

"I mean what is different kind of 'to'?"

"No, I was correcting your sentence structure. You said, 'What you mean' when you should have said, 'What do you mean.'"

"You have book. Teach to read. I learn that way."

"Have patience, Willow. Rome wasn't built in a day."

"What is Rome?"

"A very large nation that lasted about 300 years and then collapsed."

"It faint?"

"No, it died."

"Died?"

"Look, I need to get the fish ready to pan fry and make something to go with it. I brought some potatoes. Maybe we can roast them on a stick."

"I get greens."

"Where?"

"In woods."

"Is it safe?"

"Yes, very safe. Mushrooms too."

"Okay, I'll leave that to you. I wonder how the boys are doing. If the fish is ready, I'll bring it back."

Katie gave Willow a small bucket in which to gather greens and mushrooms and headed off toward the spring pond.

"What in the world is going on?"

"What?" the twins asked in unison.

"Where are the fish?"

"Oh, we hain't dun um yit."

"I told you to do them first. Now, get out of the water and get those fish cleaned. I need to start cooking them soon."

The boys looked at each other, smiled, and then said in unison, "Yes'm."

The boys chugged out of the water where they had been having the best time splashing and dunking each other. As they came out of the water, Katie realized they didn't have a stitch on. She twirled around and began to blush.

"Why you rascals!"

Each boy punched the other in the ribs with his elbow and laughed.

"Get those fish cleaned and then get back in the water and use some soap. You have been more trouble than you are worth. I'll tell Michael not to pay you."

"Ah, ya cain't do that."

"And why not?"

"'Cause yous a woman."

"Well, this woman happens to be the owner of the ranch and Michael works for me. Now, do what I tell you, or else!"

The boys' jaws dropped and they looked at her back as she disappeared into the woods.

"Ya think?"

"Don't wanna find out."

"'Kay, then let's get to cleanin' fish and us'uns."

"Cade, she sounds lak Ma."

"Yup, women!"

Katie stomped back into camp. "'Cause yous a woman.' I'll give them a taste of what that really means. They do not want to get on my 'bad' side. I don't let it out very often, but when I do, look out!"

"Who you talking to?"

"Oh, Willow, myself, the trees, the wagon, the ants, the tree frogs, whatever will listen. I'm just a pot boiling over."

"Me understand."

"I'm so glad you are here...Men!"

With that, the two girls hugged each other and tears leaked out of their eyes.

Chapter 23

Michael, Josh, and Riley rode until they came to the Little Arroyo. They arrived sooner than Josh thought they would. Maybe it was the conversation which made the time go by so quickly. It just didn't seem quite right in his head, but what did it matter? They were there.

"I'll go up on top and look down. Josh, you ride into the arroyo. It doesn't look like it is flooded or even like it has been. Maybe all the water funnels down to the Big Arroyo and that's why this one is still small. I'll fire one shot if I see water coming. If you hear that, ride out as fast as you can, cut up this way and get out of the path of the water. Riley, you go look for cattle in that copse of trees over just beyond that hill."

"Right."

"If you find any cattle and need help, fire one shot. We will come."

"Right you are. One shot. What if I just need help?"

"Fire one shot if you need any kind of help."

"If we find cattle, we will round them up and drive them toward the pen.

"Sounds easy enough. Let's get started."

Riley and Michael looked at Josh and both nodded.

"Let's get to work. See ya in a bit, Riley. Remember, if you need help, just shoot."

"I've got it. I'll see you later then," he yelled as he rode off toward the trees.

"Michael, why does he always use such proper English? Can't he just talk like the rest of us?"

"I'm not sure, Josh. He did promise to tell us his story. Maybe he will if we ask him tonight."

"Maybe."

With that, they rode off toward the Little Arroyo.

———

"This family is growing, and I don't think that $100 and the egg money will provide for all of us. I wish I knew where that money was hidden, if indeed there is any money."

"What you saying?"

"It's, 'What are you saying?' Willow. But it was nothing. I was just talking to myself. I do that frequently."

Willow's eyes, so sky blue, sparkled with excitement.

"I, too! I not loco! If you talk to self and not loco, I not." She jumped up and down and clapped her hands.

"I talk to the picture of my mother and then to myself as well. It was a way of keeping from going crazy when I was overwhelmed with loneliness after my parents died and I was all alone."

"Oh, you make me happy!" Willow just beamed.

"I don't think I have ever seen anyone as pretty as you, Willow. You need to smile more. Do you want to continue the English lessons?"

"Oh, yes! Yes. I must learn right English. Sometimes I remember some things. I don't always use."

"Well, I'm sure your mother would be very proud of you wanting to learn it again. I will do what I can to help. Do you remember if you had learned your alphabet before the Indians took you?"

"Alphabet?"

Katie began, "Yes, A, B, C, D…"

Willow chimed in with, "E, F, G, H, I, J, K, L, M, N, O, P, Q, R, S, T, U, V, W, X, Y, Z. That all I remember."

"That's because that is all there is. That is so good. Did you know how to read?"

"Um, I remember looking in books. Yes, I think I read. I had one I really loved, but no have. Gone."

"When we get back to the house, I will take out the *McGuffey Primer,* and we will see if you remember anything. It has the alphabet in it, but it also has pictures and words under the pictures. I think you will like it."

"I like. I promise."

"I know you will! There isn't much you don't like. Let's get started on supper. I bet you know how to cook fish really well. I hope those boys have them cleaned."

"I go. You stay work here. I come back pronto."

They laughed, and Katie waved her to go on, watching as Willow nearly flew through the trees, not making a sound. Katie shook her head and began taking out the pans she would use for the meal and cleaning off the board so they could make bread.

"Can you believe this, Michael? You better check with Riley, he may have a direct line to God."

"I'm sure he does, Josh. He is a praying man. 'The fervent prayer of a righteous man availeth much.' When he said he would pray for the cattle to be all in one place, he meant it."

"Well, it sure did make our job easier. There was plenty of water, but nothing like the other arroyo. I'm sure you are right about the direction of the water flow up above. I've really learned something today about my faith, or how little I have. I shouldn't have doubted him, but I did."

"You weren't alone. I do know better. However, you cannot start thinking that the Christian walk is smooth and easy. Remember, 'Satan is like a roaring lion seeking whom he may devour.' He wants to destroy the testimony of Christians and, in that, Christ. He wants to destroy the Christian's faith and trust in Almighty God. He hates the human race, Josh, because they are God's creation, and through humanity Christ came and died so they could live. Satan had planned their destruction with Adam and Eve. He didn't know God had planned an escape for mankind. His plans are foiled, but Satan isn't giving up. He is still fighting that battle. He wants to take as many souls with him as he can. Those whom God has chosen will be saved, but that doesn't mean they won't go through trials and have temptations. No, we are constantly under attack."

"I'm glad I was chosen to be one of God's people, in more ways that one. I feel so privileged, yet so unworthy. Let's get these cattle to the pen and see if we can find Riley. He may need some help."

"Right!"

"Great day, look at that mess of fish! I had no idea there were that many. We will have a feast tonight. The boys were smart to put them in that cold spring water after they gutted and cleaned them. They are real beauties." Katie picked up a fish and held it up for Willow to see.

"You have crushed-up corn?"

"Do you mean cornmeal?"

"What cornmeal...I mean, what *is* cornmeal?"

"Good! It is dried corn, crushed between two stones and ground into a very fine but gritty substance, like flour, only not as fine."

"Yes, I think that it. I think that is it."

"No, I don't have any, not on the wagon anyway. I do at home."

"Well, sometime I make cornballs."

"Okay, how about we make bread?"

"You teach."

"Yes, I will teach you."

They began working, and Katie found Willow a never-tiring and very willing student in all things. It was not long before they were working in tandem like a well-oiled machine. Their movements looked like a precisely choreographed dance, full of grace and beauty.

Before long, the boys were put to work hauling water and chopping wood.

"Was that a gunshot?"

"Sound like it. I hope not trouble."

Katie wrinkled her brows, looked with troubled eyes into the distance, and whispered, "I do too." Her heart sent a silent prayer for the safety of the men to the Eternal. The face of Josh flashed across her mind causing her consciously to bring the faces of Michael and Riley to mind. A very light touch brought her attention back to see Willow looking at her with her sky-blue eyes. With slow deliberate words, she said, "Great Spirit, take care of our men. You love them, he love them too. Send protection over them. Give them wisdom to know what to do when faced with harm. We love you, Great Spirit. We love your son, Jesus. Give us protection from any harm we may face and the trouble we may face. Amen."

With tears sliding down her cheeks, Katie stared at Willow.

"That was beautiful. Thank you, Willow. Please tell me how you learned to pray like that."

"I remember my mother praying. She taught me about Jesus. I prayed to let him into my heart when I was six. I remember wanting to read the book. She taught me to read. I loved those words."

"I've never read the book. I am sure I can get you a copy."

"You get copy for you too. You need the book. You need Jesus."

"I have a copy, just never have opened it. Your English is getting very good. You do learn fast."

"I remember many things I had not thought for many years. Jesus knows I am ready, so I can see my mother's face, I can hear her voice. I can see my brothers and father and can hear them. I never could at the Indian village. I cried all the time. So, they called me Weeping Willow."

"Do you remember your real name?"

"Ruth Ann."

"I'm sorry. I will always see you as Willow. I think Ruth Ann is a wonderful name, but Willow fits you. Your form and grace are amazing. And you are very beautiful. You will have to be careful around the men."

"You are beautiful too. Are you careful?"

"I trust them with my life, but I am careful to be very modest around them. I don't want to tempt them to think or do things they should not."

"I understand." With that, Willow turned to continue working on the supper preparations.

CHAPTER 24

ichael's head whipped around.

"Was that Riley?" he asked.

"Had to be." Josh wrinkled his brow, thinking. "I'm trained in tracking, I'll go. You get the cattle back to the pen. I don't think they will give you any trouble. There must be at least fifty-head here. I'll see what is wrong and come back as soon as I can. If I need you, I'll fire one shot. Then forget the cattle and get there as soon as you can, okay?"

"I think that is a good plan. Where will you be?"

"I'm going to the trees. That's where we told him to go, and that is the direction of the sound of that shot. Come when you can, or I could be back shortly."

With that, Josh rode off as fast as he could in the direction of the woods.

"Father, God, be with him and with Riley. Keep them safe. Help me get these cattle to the pen without any problem, so I can go and help, if that is your will. I submit to you, dear Father. In Jesus' name, amen."

He began rounding up the cattle and felt a peace cover him. He smiled and looked up.

"Thanks."

Josh rode like he was being chased by a wildfire. He reached the trees and was quiet and listened. He heard some rustling. He pulled his rifle out and began creeping in the direction of the sound, being careful not to make a noise. He crept forward, always following the sound. He couldn't see anything, but the sound kept moving away ahead of him, so he followed it. He reached a small rise and crawled to the top, keeping low. He quickly ducked when he heard voices right below him.

"Tie him up good, Bill."

"I did. He's not going anywhere. He may not wake up."

Laughter erupted. Josh's blood began to boil. He wanted to just lean over the ledge and shoot, but he knew that would not be a good idea. He kept telling himself to keep his head. He needed to rein in his emotions if this was to turn out better than it would if he didn't keep his anger in check. He peeked over the top but could not see anyone. They must be right below him. He could hear them clearly. He did see that the other side of the rise was a ravine. He slowly moved up a little more. He could see the hat of one of the men. He looked further down the ravine. Now he could see that Riley had put together a makeshift pen using the ravine and some brush as the gate. The ravine could go back quite a way, but there must be a back wall. Cattle were moving around in the enclosure. He could use that. First, he had to find Riley and see what his situation was.

He heard a noise off to his left. He quickly rolled over on his back and looked. It was a steer, a young one. He could use that. Good. Rolling back over and scooting back, he stealthily moved toward the steer. He would use that one as a shield to get a better view and come into the ravine and get to the other side, then he could see what was going on over on the south side. He crept hunched over, and the steer didn't seem to know he was there or else didn't think of him as a threat. He was able to find a long stick and prod the steer in the right direction. Still, there was not a problem.

Thank you, dear Jesus. Keep being the shepherd through me. Only in this case, I guess we need to be cowboys, if you don't mind. This little guy is a bit bigger than a sheep. Protect Riley. Help him to remain calm in a bad time.

Josh and the steer made it across the ravine. Just as Josh was beside a big rock, one of the men shouted.

"Hey, there goes one. Let's get him and add him to the rest. I can't believe how easy this is."

"Yeah, you are always lookin' fer easy."

"Shut up, Rex. Like you don't like easy. If you would rather work, go ask for a job. Cattle rustling is better payin'."

"Yeah, as long as we're not invited to a necktie party. People frown on other people stealing their cattle."

"Is he still out?"

"Out cold."

"Let's both go and catch that steak on the hoof!"

Laughing, they both ran in Josh's direction. When they reached the rock they ran up the same path the steer had gone. Josh waited until he could hear their crashing through the woods get further away.

"There he is!"

"Shut up, you'll spook him."

The voices were getting further away. He knew they couldn't see him down in the ravine. He stepped out and carefully made his way down toward the pen. Right under where he had been looking when he came up on the ravine was Riley, hog tied.

I sure thought I saw some movement, he thought to himself. He whispered, "Riley, Riley, you awake?"

One eye cracked open and Josh knelt down and touched his arm. He could see blood on his face.

"Riley, wake up. We have to get out of here."

The eye cracked open again.

"Josh, that you? My head hurts."

"Can you walk?" He asked as he untied him.

"If I have too. I don't believe I am going to be too steady on my feet."

"Come on, I'll help you. Help me out here; try to stand up."

"I think I'm going to be sick. The world is spinning."

"Okay, here goes. He leaned his rifle up against the wall of the ravine, grabbed Riley and hefted him over his shoulder, grabbed his gun and walked toward the pen. He pulled some of the brush away and moved over to the side to lay Riley down. The cattle were restless and moved constantly. He pulled the brush back into place and then moved Riley further back in the ravine where he found a trunk of a fallen tree.

"I'll tuck you in out of sight back here. Just stay quiet. Take another nap."

"Right, with this headache?"

"Okay, stay awake, but be quiet. I have some work to do, but first I'm going to put a bandage around your head. They must have shot at you and just grazed your head."

"Yes, I never even heard them. I heard the shot, whipped around to see what was happening and don't remember anything else."

"Probably saved your life when you whipped around. Okay, just be quiet."

Josh moved back toward the front of the pen. The men weren't back yet. He saw Riley's saddle and decided to get it, wondering the whole time where Riley's horse was. He moved the brush again, grabbed the saddle, and made it back into the pen just when he heard a steer bawl. He was moving the brush back into place when he saw the steer coming down the path in the ledge. He took the saddle and ducked behind a cow.

"Riley, they are back. I have your saddle. Where is your horse?"

"I was letting her have a little freedom when they jumped me. She'll come when I whistle."

Suddenly, they could hear very loud swearing then what sounded like a fistfight going on.

"I guess they don't like you being gone and have to blame somebody." Josh whispered in Riley's ear. "Stay put, don't try any heroics; I have a plan."

"Rex, don't let him get away!"

"Yee hah! Go that way, you big brute! Pull that brush away, Bill, I'll deal with you later."

All the noise and fighting had really spooked the cattle. When he felt like enough time had passed that the brush was pulled far enough away for a cow to get through, he fired his rifle and began yelling.

"What the…"

"Run!"

The cattle, already jittery, began running at the sound of the gun. The ravine was a tight squeeze and worked as a funnel. Rex tripped on a root and fell. The cattle didn't even notice, they just kept running. Bill jumped up and grabbed a low-lying branch of a tree and pulled himself up, feet digging into the dirt side of the ravine to keep from falling and trying to get high enough above the cattle to avoid injury or death.

Josh ran up behind the cattle. He glanced at Rex and decided there was nothing he could do for the man except bury him, and that would have to wait.

"Okay, Bill, you want to come down now, or spend the night hanging there?"

"Who are you, and how do you know my name?"

"Name's Josh, and I work this ranch. I don't really appreciate you trying to steal our cattle and trying to kill my friend."

"That was Rex. He did that. He'll deny it, but he did it."

"He doesn't care about anything right now, and he won't be saying anything ever again."

Dropping to the ground, Bill looked in that direction. "You mean…?"

"Trampled."

"Did you check him to see if he's alive?"

"Bill, his skull is broken and so are his hip and legs. I don't think he has an unbroken bone in his body."

Bill walked toward Rex. Josh held a gun on him.

"Don't do anything stupid, or you'll be keeping him company. The law doesn't hold with cattle rustlers. At least you'll have time to make it right with God before they hang you or send you to prison."

Bill knelt beside Rex looking into his eyes and seeing the blank stare that had no life behind it. Blood soaked the ground beneath him and his legs were at odd angles. Rex's barrel chest was much flatter, crushed.

"Well, I guess that's that. He's beyond help."

"You have a couple of choices to make right now, Bill. One is to pull your gun or go for his and try to shoot me, but my rifle is loaded, cocked, and ready. I would advise you to avoid doing that. The other choice you have is to help me with my friend and with the cattle."

"They're long gone. It will take forever to find them in these woods."

"What's going on? Where is Riley?"

Both men whipped around at the sudden sound of the voice.

"Michael! We caught us a cattle rustler. One, anyway, the other one is dead. Riley is back there. He's hurt pretty bad. Do you have your horse?"

"Yes, tied to a tree right here. You want me to come down?"

"Yes, and bring your horse. Mine is at the edge of the woods."

"I know, that's how I knew where to find you. Thanks."

"I had to stampede the cattle. He had them corralled in a makeshift pen. Did a good job too. But now they are all over the place, I'm sure."

"Don't worry about it. We'll get them. First, let's get Riley to Katie for some care."

"Right" At the mention of her name, her face flashed before Josh's eyes. He could almost believe she was standing right there. Michael rode his horse down and made his way to where Riley sat leaning against a fallen tree trunk.

"Riley, can you hear me? Open your eyes."

"Michael, what are you doing here?"

"I heard one shot and came riding as fast as I could."

"Glad you did."

"Come on, let's get you up on this horse. Do you think you can ride?"

"Just get me out of this ravine and I'll whistle for Star. She'll come. No one else can ride her. Oh, my aching head!"

"We need to get you to Katie and see if she has any willow bark. That should help your headache and whatever else ails you. I need to replace that bandage. It is soaked through. Here, let me use this handkerchief. Wow, I think you might need a stitch or two as well."

"I don't think I want anyone sewing on me. We will see what Katie can do, but I don't want to look like Frankenstein."

"Who?"

"Josh…oh, never mind. I don't want to go into it now. Just get me back."

"Up you go. I'll lead. You just hold on."

"I'll bring his saddle. Where is your horse?" Michael looked at Bill.

"He's on the other side of the ravine. We had them tied to some trees up there. You want me to go get him?" He almost smirked when he said it but thought that might not be a good thing to do.

"No, I think you will be just fine right here and tied up." With that, Michael began tying Bill's hands behind him and then the rope around his body and arms as well. Pulling Bill with them, they found the two horses and brought them through the ravine and over to the other side. Josh had wrapped Rex's body in a blanket and brought him over to throw over the saddle of his horse, then tied him down.

They got up the bank, and then Riley gave a shrill whistle. Immediately he reached for his head. Within a minute Star was there. Bill was tied securely and being led by the rope.

"Will she let me saddle her?"

"Don't know, maybe since I am here. She may sense I need help."

Josh carefully approached Star with the blanket in one hand and the saddle in the other.

"Whoa, easy girl. That's right, just stand still now. Good, girl. Now, for the saddle. Are you sure this is your horse?"

"She knows I can't do it. She is very tolerant in an emergency. She also can sense the type of person who is trying to saddle her."

"I think that is a compliment. At least I hope so. I am doing the best I can and trying to be gentle with her at the same time."

Riley looked over at Michael. "You done yet? Michael, help me down. I'm feeling really dizzy. I think I need to regurgitate."

"You mean vomit? Here, let me get you down."

With very little effort, Michael had Riley on the ground. He found his feet on the ground, and immediately he dropped to his hands and knees and began to throw up. Michael watched to see if any blood was in what he was losing, but there wasn't.

"How is your head now?" Michael asked as he retrieved the canteen from his horse. He wet a bandana and gave it to Riley who was now lying back on the grass. After washing off his face, he glanced over to Michael.

"It feels like I have scorpions in my brain."

"We need to get you to Katie and Willow. They will know how to help you."

"I don't know if I can ride."

"We will try it. If it just makes you feel sicker, you can ride with me and we will lead Star."

"Okay, I think we can go faster if I just ride with you, Michael."

"If that is what you want to do. Josh is finished saddling Star. I'll help you up and then I'll get up behind you so I can hang onto you better. Up you go. Josh, just lead Star behind you. Riley's going to ride with me."

"Good idea. I was kinda worried. She's a good horse, but she can't hold you up there. I'll retie Bill's arms and hands so he can hang on. I'll lead both horses, Rex's and Bill's. Michael, you lead Star. Let's go."

Riley's voice was weak, but he wanted them to know, "Star doesn't need to be led; she'll follow me and stay with us."

Josh shrugged, "If you say so."

CHAPTER 25

"I'm worried about those shots. I wonder what that was all about? I hope nothing bad has happened. That bread smells good. I think it is time to start the rest of the meal. I could use some hot coffee. Will you fix it, Willow, and I'll start with these salad makings you collected?"

"How do you make coffee?"

"Okay, I'll make the coffee, and you make the salad. I'll teach you coffee making later."

Both the girls laughed. It felt so good to have someone to talk and to laugh with. What a joy to have Willow here. That old familiar tom-tom beat was gone for good, hopefully.

"I will always miss you, Ma and Papa, but it seems life is going on, and I need to be a part of it. I can't mourn forever."

In her heart she knew that was how it was supposed to be. Everywhere she looked there was life. She wanted to be a part of it. As she looked around at the beautiful hill country, she saw horses coming their way but couldn't make out the riders. Her heart jumped to her throat.

"Willow, look." Katie pointed in their direction.

"Oh, I'll get water heating. We will need some medicine. It not look...I mean it doesn't look good."

"What, I don't…oh, there are two men on one horse. I can see Josh." Again, her heart beat just a little faster. She felt butterflies in her stomach. "Is that Riley in front of Michael? Who's the one behind them?"

"Yes, it looks like Riley is hurt."

"I'll make a pallet for him to lie on."

Immediately the women set to work getting a "sick/hurt" area ready for whatever was coming their way.

By the time the men rode in, Katie and Willow had bedding laid out, water heating, and Katie's medicine box taken out and ready for what was needed.

"What happened? Who's that? Is someone dead?"

Josh hopped down and moved quickly over to Riley.

"I'll get him from here if you will steady him from up there."

"You've got it. Here he comes."

"He feels like lead. Riley, you awake?"

There was no answer.

"Hurry, let's get him over near the fire. Oh, I see you have a place ready." He looked at them with a question in his eye. He was met with silent questions from both women.

"Well? Who are they?" Katie's frustration was rising.

Michael was down and helping to carry Riley over to the bed. Katie dropped to the ground and carefully undid the makeshift bandage the men had put on Riley's head. Willow was there with a hot washrag ready to hand it to Katie. As the women worked in silence, the men marveled at how well they worked together. They didn't even have to say anything; they just "knew" what the other was thinking. Josh and Michael moved out of the way. The coffee was ready, so Michael took two cups from the back of the wagon and poured coffee for the two of them. They moved to a log where they could watch but not get in the way.

"Hey, what about me? You just gonna let me stay up here?" yelled Bill.

"We thought about it. I'll get you down, but you're going to have to be tied up with your hands behind you and tied to a tree," replied Josh.

"Anything is better than sittin' up here. Get me down."

Josh nodded and walked over to get him down. He heard a gun cock behind him.

Turning, he saw Michael with the rifle trained on Bill. "You do anything I think is out of line and you're going to need help, and the women are busy with Riley; you might bleed to death waiting for them to finish."

Bill nodded his understanding, and the thought of kicking Josh in the face and riding as fast as he could out of there left his mind. These men weren't as dumb as he had hoped they would be.

Katie glanced over her shoulder. "Michael, Josh, who are those men?"

The noise they heard coming toward them could only be the twins. Sure enough, two identical brothers clamored their way into camp dropping the firewood they had collected.

"I sure am glad you two are here. Get your horses and head toward the Little Arroyo. You should start seeing cattle before you get there. Round them up and head them on to the holding pen. I was driving them there when I heard the gunshot and left them to help out in the forest between the arroyo and the canyons. There are some in the forest as well, but we can get them later. We don't need those in the open wandering all over the place. Now, get!"

"Yes, sir!" Again they spoke in unison and elbowed each other and ran for their horses.

Katie laughed and shook her head. "I guess they are tired of hauling water and cutting wood. Are you going to answer me, Michael?"

Katie had just finished sewing up Riley's head where the bullet had grazed him when she heard a moan escape from him.

She nodded to Willow, who brought over the willow bark tea and raised his head just a bit, then pressed the cup to his lips. He took a sip.

"What is that?" His eyes cracked open. He looked into Katie's face then into Willow's. "It tastes bitter. Put some sugar in it."

"I'll get it." Willow took the cup and headed for the wagon.

"Was that Willow?" Riley looked at Katie now with his eyes wide open.

"Yes, that was Willow. Do you know who I am?"

"Katie."

"Yes, that's good. I think you will be much better as soon as you drink the tea and have some food and sleep. Your head will hurt for a few days, but I will keep some water hot for tea so you can have it whenever you need it."

"Why is she talking like that?"

"Who?"

"Willow. She doesn't sound the same."

"Oh, her English is coming back to her the more we talk. She is very smart. I think by the time we get back to the ranch no one will ever guess she was considered an Indian."

"She isn't?"

"No, her family was killed, and she was taken to live with the Indians who killed them. She was seven, so she remembers her English. She just had not used it in years. Now it is coming back to her."

"I should have known she wasn't Indian. Not too many have blonde hair."

Willow came back blowing on the tea.

"Here, you drink this. It help your head. I look for wild lettuce later. That better for your head. Willow bark good for pains anywhere, but wild lettuce help your head."

"Thank you."

"Drink!"

"Yes, ma'am."

Both women smiled and watched carefully as Riley drank his tea.

"Hey, how about me? I'm thirsty too."

Willow walked over to the wagon, took down a cup, and scooped up some water. She took it to Bill and held it to his mouth, tipping it ever so slightly so as not to dump it down his shirt.

"That's better."

"How about a 'thank you,' Bill. I would have let you sit there and not have a drink." Josh looked right at him. Bill's eyes narrowed. He shrugged his shoulders and turned to Willow.

"Thanks."

"Here, drink more." Willow placed the cup on his mouth and tipped it up. This time he drank it all.

"That's good and cold. I do thank you."

"You are welcome." With that, she walked away.

Bill watched her lithe movements as she moved over to the chuck wagon, where she began working on the meal. Katie stayed by Riley making sure he was comfortable and drinking his tea. Josh got up and moved toward her. He couldn't help himself. She was like a magnet and he was the iron. She was drawing him nearer and nearer. Michael got up and started toward the horses to see to them.

"More riders coming."

Josh looked at Michael, and then in the direction he was pointing.

"Looks like Clyde and Wulf. Can that be possible?"

"Adam was going to find them and help them. So, I guess it is."

"This is great. Maybe we can get something finished today."

"We will eat in about thirty minutes." Willow said in their direction. She had sent a warning, by the tone of her voice, that they should not ride off and not come back when the meal was ready. They could go again after they had eaten.

Katie hopped up, turned, and bumped right into Josh who was standing right behind her "looking at Riley" trying to keep his eyes from dwelling on her beauty. He so wanted to run his fingers through her chestnut hair. He realized he had his hands holding both her arms and was looking deep into her brown eyes. He was getting lost in them when he realized what he was doing. Regretting what he had to do, he let her go.

"I'm sorry, I shouldn't have been standing right behind you."

"No harm done." She rubbed her arms trying to understand the tingling going up and down them. The place where he had placed his hands to steady her felt cool now. She rubbed her arms and moved to the side.

"I'll just help Willow get the meal ready, if you will sit with Riley. I think he is going to be fine, but he really needs to rest. He lost some blood and needs to recuperate from that."

"Happy to help."

Michael rode toward the two men riding in.

"Did Adam find you?"

"Yes, he was a big help," Clyde said.

"I'm surprised ya'll got back so soon."

"When we got back to the ranch, Daniels was there and volunteered to help us. Then Adam told us to go on back, that the two of them could handle it. So, we came on back."

"What do you want us to do now?" Wulf was looking in the direction of Bill as they rode into camp. "Why is he here?"

"You know him?"

"Yeah, his name is Bill. He worked at a ranch where I was, but they fired him. He's trouble."

"You don't have to tell me. He and his buddy, Rex, were trying to steal our cattle. They shot Riley, didn't kill him, but I think Rex would have if it had not been for Bill keeping him from it.

Anyway, Josh surprised them and set off a stampede. Rex was trampled and Bill was 'caught up a tree'."

"Brian is going to stay at the house. He said it was 'his turn'."

"Is that right? I'll take Rex and Bill in as soon as supper is finished. You and Clyde help find the cattle that we lost rescuing Riley. I knew it was going too easy when we found them all in a bunch at the Little Arroyo. We heard a shot and Josh went to investigate. I was driving the cattle back when I heard another shot. So, I just left them and took off toward the woods."

"Sounds like you have had some excitement."

"Well, I'm ready to get Bill out of here and get back to our regular work."

Looking all around, Clyde turned to Michael, "Hey, where are the twins?"

"They are out rounding up some of the cattle."

"How long have they been gone?"

"Oh, I guess, a little over an hour, maybe a little more."

"Want us to go and help them?"

"Katie and Willow will have supper ready in about fifteen minutes. Better stay here until you've eaten. If the boys aren't back, I'll send you out to spell them and they can come eat."

"Sounds good to us. Right, Wulf?"

"I'd much rather be doing that than just sittin', especially with him in the camp. Who's Willow?"

All three looked over toward Bill, then in the direction of Willow.

"I can't believe how much has happened since you left. Remember, when I sent you with the cattle back to the ranch, we had found Wade's horse. We found them and had to rescue them from the raging river which was now running out of that arroyo. When we rescued them, Willow was with them. Seems she ran away from the Indians. She had been captured as a child. So, now Katie says she has a sister again. The way those two women work together, you'd think they were sisters and had been working side by side all their life. Beats me."

"Riley okay?"

"I think he will be all right. The girls have fixed him up, and he will rest some before getting back on a horse. He has a really bad headache."

"They shot him in the head?"

"I'm not sure where they were aiming. Riley heard something and turned just as the bullet hit him. It grazed his head, pretty deep. Katie had to take stitches. Don't say anything about Frankenstein."

"Who?"

"Doesn't matter. Riley doesn't want to look like him, so don't mention it."

"Don't see how I can when I don't know what it is."

"Good, then I won't say anymore."

Supper was delicious. Willow fed Bill. Clyde and Wulf ate quickly and rode out to spell Wade and Cade. Michael made plans to take Bill and Rex to Brian and saddled the horses. Josh offered to help the women clean up, but they insisted he stay with Riley and see if he could get the man to eat some fish.

"He's out of his mind if he doesn't. You ladies are amazing. I've never had food like this out on the trail."

Both women smiled their thanks. Katie felt a slight burn up the back of her neck. She hoped it didn't show. She was not used to blushing.

"What is it about this man that has me blushing? Ma, did you feel this way when you first met Papa?"

"What are you saying?"

"Oh, nothing, Willow, just talking to myself, again. I'll have to stop doing that now that I have you to talk to. I guess I miss my ma and papa.

"Oh."

A sadness clouded Willow's eyes. She suddenly turned, grabbed a bucket, and headed toward the woods.

"Where are you going?"

"To get more water. I'll be back."

"We don't really need more water, Willow."

"I go."

"What did I say? Why are you mad?"

"Not mad."

With that she walked into the woods.

"She's an odd one. You'd better watch yourself. She could stab you in your sleep." Bill watched Willow disappear into the woods.

"You have no right to talk like that about Willow. You don't even know her, Bill, so just be quiet. Anybody who'd shoot somebody else…why, you're the one I should be watching."

"Well, I didn't mean it that way. I just think she is maybe a little crazy, that's all."

"Why, what did she ever do to you, except give you a drink and help you eat? It seems like you should be taking up for her rather than talking bad about her behind her back."

"What's going on?"

"Michael, are you ready to take this *man* out of here? I'm sure ready for him to be gone."

Michael's brows arched up and his eyes speared Bill.

"I didn't do nothing."

"No, just talked bad about Willow. I'm more than ready for him to be gone."

"Your wish is my command, my lady. Let's get on the trail, Bill. I have a friend I want you to meet."

"I'll be happy to be gone from here. Being tied to this tree ain't no fun. Could I get a little privacy before we leave?"

"No, you can have all the 'privacy' you want or need when we get on the trail back to the house. I'm not leaving you alone for a minute especially in the woods!"

"Don't that beat all. A man can't even relieve himself before gettin' on his horse."

"That's right. Just get used to your discomfort until we are out in the open and I can keep an eye on you."

Katie had to stifle a laugh. She had never thought of that, and now it seemed comical. She didn't want to embarrass the men. She kept her back to them and pretended to be working hard on keeping the food hot for the twins.

After Michael and Bill left, she turned to see Josh staring at her.

"I must admit you showed great self-control just a minute ago."

"Why, what do you mean?"

"I could hear them all the way over here. I know you could hear them. I hope you weren't embarrassed by the crude conversation."

"Not at all. The body has natural functions it needs to have in order to keep one healthy. It just shows how Bill doesn't know how to act around a lady."

"You are so right. Riley's sleeping soundly. Do you think he should be?"

"I don't see why not. Do you think that is a bad thing? I always thought sleep was a good thing for someone who is sick."

"We had an Army doctor who was very worried when someone had a head wound and went to sleep. He was afraid they would go to sleep and not wake back up."

"Maybe we should wake him and give him some more tea. I'll fix it."

"I'll try to wake him." Josh saw some movement out of the corner of his eye and looked toward the woods. "Oh, Willow, let me take that. It's heavy and sloshing all over you."

"Thank you."

Katie hurried over to Willow and as soon as Josh had the bucket, gave her a big hug. "Willow, I'm sorry if I hurt your feelings or said something to make you mad."

"No, I just suddenly got very sad and realized I don't have anything to remind me of my mother. I had to go talk to Jesus. I'm better now."

"You must be. Your English is mostly back. Oh, here come Wade and Cade. Will you fix some more tea for Riley? I'll get their fish cooking and see if they want any salad or bread."

"Yes, that goo…uh, will be good."

Josh put the bucket of water down. "Then let me go and try to wake up Riley. We'll see if he is getting better."

"Thank you, Josh."

"For what, Katie?"

"For being here to help. I know Riley will be thankful, as I am."

"I'm happy to be of service to all of you." He said that, but he only had eyes for Katie.

Her neck began to get hot, and she could feel the warmth creep up to her cheeks. "What is wrong with me?" She asked herself as she stared at his broad, retreating back.

Lord, I believe I love that woman. I can't get her out of my mind and all I can think of is spending the rest of my life with her. Please, show me your will, he hesitated as he knelt beside Riley, *"And Lord, bring Riley healing with no permanent harm to him. In Jesus name, amen."* As he finished, he stole a look back at Katie, smiled to himself, and then got back to "business."

CHAPTER 26

"Brian, are you here?"

"Michael? Is that you? What are you doing here?"

Brian emerged from the barn with a pitchfork in hand. His eyes wandered to the other man, tied up and sitting on a horse.

"What's all this?"

"His name is Bill, and that's his friend. He and his friend, Rex, were trying to rustle some cattle and shot Riley. He is fine, sort of. He'll live anyway, thanks to Josh. Rex was trampled in a stampede, and Bill here was caught. Do you have a vacant cell for him?"

"You betcha. Let me saddle my horse. Just leave him sittin' up there and I'll be ready in just a minute. I won't be back tonight, but all the animals have been taken care of. My deputy can watch him tomorrow morning. I'll drop the other one off with Curtis at the cabinet shop so he can fit him in a pine box. He'll be glad for the business. I can come back out and see to the stock after that."

"I'll close up the house for tonight and head back out to camp. I doubt we'll be back tomorrow. If we are, it will be late. We have had a few interruptions in our work today. I'll tell you all about it when we get a chance."

"I'm about done here. Just tie the horse to that rail and I'll come back out and get Bill situated in town. Go ahead and close up the house and get back if you need to. I'll probably be gone before you're finished. I'll let Esther know. I think she was planning on bringing out food for tomorrow."

"Right. Thanks."

———

"Wulf, go find those kids and get them to help us brand these calves."

"Ah, Josh, they can't rope for nothing. All they can do is wave their arms and yell."

"We need to give them a chance to practice. Go get them. They can hold the legs or hand you the branding iron."

"Oh, all right! They are nothin' but trouble."

"Wulf, if we want to get done tonight, we need the help."

"Yea, I guess we do."

Wulf stomped toward his horse, Pferd, and headed toward the camp. They had managed to round up fifty-seven-head, about twenty of them needed branding. They were all safely in the pen.

I bet Michael will be surprised, Wulf thought to himself.

"Wulf, you're back. You want some coffee?" Katie asked.

"Nah, we need the boys to come help with branding."

"But it's nearly dark. How are you going to brand at night?"

"With their help, we may get done. If not, we'll start again tomorrow."

"Wade, Cade! Come here, you are needed to help with the branding. Hurry!"

They came running and headed straight for their horses.

"I had them washing dishes. I think they'd rather help you."

With that, Wulf laughed one of his rare laughs from deep inside.

"You need to do that more often. Your whole body changes into something joyful. Most of the time, you are too serious, Wulf. You need to laugh more."

"I reckon. But this life gives very little to laugh about. I'd best be goin' or we won't get anything done."

"I'll keep the coffee hot."

He tipped his hat and rode off.

"What a strange man. I wonder what his story is," Katie said to herself.

"Whose story?"

"Oh, Willow, you startled me. You're so quiet. I was talking out loud again. I was referring to Wulf."

"He scared me at first. I think he is afraid to let the real man out. He must have been hurt deeply by someone." Willow hung her head a bit, and looked up at Katie.

"You may be right, Willow. Perhaps that's how he got his scar. Someone betrayed him and he not only got hurt outside, but inside as well."

"I think so. He's healing now, just like me. Jesus is so good. He's always there working."

"Willow, I don't understand. How can Jesus work when he was killed?"

"Yes, he died. But he rose again from the dead. He *is* alive and cannot die again. He's with God the Father."

"Then how is he here?"

"His spirit is here. He and the Great Spirit are one. He lives in us. I feel him."

"How do you feel him?"

"I can feel his peace. Sometimes, I hear his voice in my heart. Josh knows what I'm talking about." Her eyes wandered in his direction, where he was still sitting with Riley and talking softly to him.

Katie was surprised to feel the pang of jealousy hit her. She turned her back and stared off toward the darkening hills. There wasn't much of a sunset tonight. *"I can't let myself be jealous of Josh and Willow. Michael's very special to me. But I feel something more when I'm around Josh. I love the way he looks at me. I wish..."*"Now, Katie, get back to work and quit worrying about Josh and Willow."

"Are you talking to yourself, again?"

"Yes, I'm sorry. It is a habit I can't seem to break. I missed my sister so much when she died, I started talking to her. Then when Ma died, I really started talking to myself when I wasn't talking to her picture."

"Talk to God. He will listen *and* give you answers."

"I'm so afraid to do it. I love what I see in Esther, Adam, Josh, Tad, Michael, Brian, and Doc. I just wasn't raised that way. I don't want my parents to be mad at me. I like to think they are watching me."

"I like having God watching me. He loves me forever. He never dies. He's always there. When I am alone and remember he is there, I am never really lonely."

Katie's eyes looked at Willow with an intensity that could have drilled a hole in her.

"I sometimes forget and let loneliness fill me up," Willow admitted. "I feel much better when I remember."

A tear slipped out of the corner of Katie's eye. She wanted that peace. She wanted what everyone else had.

"How do I get that?"

"You tell God you are sorry for all the wrong things you have done, even the wrong thoughts. Then ask him to send his son into your heart to live with you. Tell him you believe that he sent his son to die for you so you could live with him forever."

"Do I need to light some candles or something? Is there some special way it has to be done?"

"No, nothing like that. You just talk to God. You can look up into the sky. I like to do that. But God is everywhere all the time. You don't have to do anything special. He's always listening."

"I think I'll go for a little walk. There is a bright moon tonight, so I'll have some light if I am gone long. Willow, thank you."

"I'll pray for you. I'll keep the coffee warm. You don't worry. I'll take care of the men. You go."

Katie nodded and started walking toward the spring pond in the woods. She couldn't get the idea out of her head of never being alone again. How wonderful that was. *Jesus was like the sacrificial lamb at Passover. He even died at Passover. How could we have missed that all these years?*

She sat down on the log the boys had pulled over close to the water when they were cleaning the fish. She looked at the water and began thinking over all the things she had learned as a Jew and all she had seen in these Gentile Christians. *None of them had hurt her, except Red, and he was bad. All he wanted was her and the money. Funny how the money had been so important to me. Now, I can see how God has taken care of everything. Maybe someday I will find the money. If I do, it will be when God wants me to find it.* With that thought, she bowed her head and began her talk with God. It wasn't hard, she'd been talking with people she couldn't see for years, first her sister, and more recently her ma. As she talked, tears began to fall in earnest. Her heart was breaking with the realization of all of her sin. Suddenly, her burden was lifted and she felt the peace she had heard described so many times by her friends. She started to laugh and cry at the same time. What a joy! Now, she wanted Wulf to know true joy and just laugh. His heart had been so broken by someone. He needed to know about this wonderful love she was feeling, and Clyde too. He had shared some sorrows with her. Now, she had more than just "I'm so sorry, Clyde," to share with him.

Father, God, the Eternal, I ask you to help me to help others who are hurting. Help me to find out more about you and Jesus. Amen.

She didn't realize it had gotten really dark until she stood to leave. The moonlight streamed across the pool, shining like diamonds dancing on the water. *How beautiful! I'd better hurry back.*

"Where did she go? It's dark. She could be hurt."

"She is fine, Josh. Quit worrying. She will be back soon. She just went for a walk."

"I feel responsible for her. Somebody has to take care of her. She is fragile. You don't know what she has been through. If anything happened to her, I couldn't live with myself."

"Will you be quiet, Josh? You are hurting my head."

"Sorry, Riley. I'm just so worried."

"'Be anxious for nothing, but in everything, with prayer and thanksgiving, let your requests be made known unto God. And the peace of God which passes all understanding will keep your hearts and minds through Christ Jesus.' Now, settle down. And please be a little softer when you speak. One would think you were trying to give orders to the coyotes up on those bluffs."

"Pray with me, Riley. I need your strength."

"I'll be happy to pray with you, but you need the Lord's strength, not mine."

"You're right. Let's pray."

Just as they finished praying for Katie's safety and her soul, they heard a noise coming from the woods. Katie fairly skipped into the clearing.

"Where have you been?" nearly slipped from Josh's mouth, but when he saw her face and the look of pure joy in her eyes, he knew. He stood and walked over to her. He took her in his arms and gave her a hug. He leaned back and let his hand cup her face, rubbing his thumb along her cheek. Her eyes deep with questions looked back at him.

"I was so worried something would happen to you. I wanted to go find you, but Willow wouldn't let me. Riley wouldn't either. Thank God you are all right."

"I am more than all right, Josh. I have found Jesus! I can't believe the joy I feel right now. You must teach me all you know. I must get Riley to teach me too. I have so much to learn."

"Do you have a Gentile Bible, one with the New Testament?"

"Oh, yes, I do. I had forgotten. Doc gave it to me. I haven't read any of it, I am sorry to say."

"That would be a really good thing to do. I'll help you. We all will."

"We should pray for Wulf and Clyde. They need this. They have some deep pain too."

"Yes, they do. Father, I thank you for drawing Katie into your loving arms and showing her the love of your son, Jesus. We join together now, to ask you to do the same for Wulf and Clyde. Dear Father, you know the heartaches and emotional as well as physical pain they have experienced, and you know exactly what they need. Make us sensitive to their needs and to be loving examples to them of how you provide for us in every way. You are the answer to their needs. Open their eyes, Lord, so they can see. Protect them from all harm so they can see you before they have to stand before you. In Jesus' name, amen."

"Wow! Josh, I didn't expect you to pray immediately for them. I just thought we should pray for them, I didn't have a timeline in mind."

"You were right. We did need to pray for them. I saw no reason to put it off. I have seen many times in my parents' lives my mother say something and my dad do it immediately. I thought it was strange so I asked him about it. He explained to me that women are much more sensitive to the world around them and seem to hear God's voice more quickly than men. He has found if Mom tells him he should go visit ole Ted down the road a piece, he'd better do it. When he does it, he finds it was the right thing to do at the right time. He has never been sorry. So, when you said it, I did it. I saw no reason to put it off."

"I should be very careful what I say then."

"If God lays something on your heart, I hope you will say it to whoever needs to hear it. Don't keep it back thinking that you may be out of line."

"My pa would never have told me that. He would have said that a woman was to be seen and not heard, or something very similar."

"I truly believe God made Eve to be Adam's helper. Adam was to be Eve's protector and head, but he was also to listen to her and to love her."

"That is so beautiful! I can hardly take it in. I'm going to have to read about that. I've only been told about our first mother and father, not anything about their relationship or their roles, just that they 'were'."

"That is not the only beautiful thing I see. Has anyone ever told you how very beautiful you are? Your eyes are so deep and warm. I could get lost in them. Your hair reminds me of the mane of my horse when he is running free across the plains with the sun shining on the flying hair, making parts of it look like fire."

As Josh spoke softly to her he leaned closer. She looked up into his eyes being drawn into their depth.

"So, is the coffee hot?"

Katie let out a small yelp and jumped when she heard the gruff voice of Wulf not ten feet away.

"Why, yes, it's pretty strong by now though. If you would like me to make some fresh, I will."

"Naw, I'll just drink what you have here. It's probably fresher than you think." As he said that, he looked straight at Josh.

Josh cleared his throat and moved toward his horse. "I'll just take care of Ranger. He probably needs a rubdown. Is everyone coming back?"

"Yeah, it's kinda hard to work out there in the dark." Wulf added with a smile in his voice. "The kids did a pretty good job. They are quick learners. Their minds do tend to wander a bit, but they'll be fine if they keep their minds on their job." With that, he looked pointedly at Josh, then turned and took a seat on a log near Riley.

"You are so right, Wulf. That is true for all of us. We could all remember that." Josh said, understanding the double meaning behind Wulf's words.

"Yep!" said Wulf, nursing his cup.

"Katie?"

"Yes? Who spoke?"

"It was Riley, Miss Katie. He has his back turned," said Wulf.

Katie walked over and squatted next to Riley. As she did, Wulf got up and walked to the fire. She picked up Riley's hand in one of hers and ran her other one over the part of his brow not covered by the bandage.

"What do you need, Riley? You're not feverish. That's a blessing."

"Yes it is. So are you. I do need some water, and could you get someone to help me so I can go and relieve myself?"

Josh walked over and squatted on the other side of Riley.

"Certainly. Josh, can you help Riley? He needs to take a walk."

Understanding crossed Josh's face. "I'll be happy to help him."

"I'll get him a cup of water. He's thirsty."

She brought the water as Josh helped Riley sit up. As she handed the cup to Josh, that tingling sensation traveled up her arm. She looked at Josh and was going to ask if he felt that, but he was looking at Riley and helping him with the cup. He put it on the ground and helped him up. As they walked away toward to trees, Josh didn't even look back at her.

Maybe that tingling means rain is coming, she thought to herself.

"Katie, do you think I could use this?" Willow asked as she came from the direction of the front of the wagon holding a gun. Wulf choked and coughed on the drink of coffee he was taking.

"What on earth do you need a gun for?"

"I want to learn how to shoot better than I do. I need some practice."

"You know how to shoot?"

"All Indians learn how to shoot. We have learned that neither bullets nor swords know the difference between men and women or children. It is better for us to know how to use these weapons than to remain ignorant of them and die upon them needlessly."

"Wow, I'm learning so much. So are you! Just listen to your English."

"Yes, it's coming back to me. I thank you for your help. It's so good you did not try to talk to me in broken sentences or try to make me understand, but just kept talking in your normal way. I have learned much from it."

"I'll say. You sound more like Riley than I ever could."

"What do you mean?"

"Oh, his sentences are long and he uses out-of-the-ordinary words to express himself. Most of us just talk in plain, ordinary language."

"I remember now that my mother and father taught me to read when I was very little. I remember they were very educated. I can't remember why they moved out west. I have forgotten so much. Maybe I'll remember, someday."

"I have a feeling you are way past the McGuffey Readers. You are probably ready for the classics! I may have to turn your lessons over to Riley. He is far more educated than I."

The men began to drift in and make preparations for turning in for the night. Clyde took out his harmonica and began to play. Josh and the twins sang some of the songs. Michael took out his Bible and began reading Psalm 91.

"'He that dwelleth in the secret place of the Most High shall abide under the shadow of the Almighty. I will say of the Lord, he is my refuge and my fortress: my God; in him will I trust. Surely he shall deliver thee from the snare of the fowler, and from the noisome pestilence. He shall cover them with his feathers, and under his wings shalt thou trust: his truth shall be thy shield and buckler. Thou shalt not be afraid for the terror by night; nor for the arrow that flieth by day; nor for the pestilence that walketh in darkness; nor for the destruction that wasteth at noonday.'

"I think this is an appropriate reading for today. I have been amazed at all that has happened today and all that could have happened and didn't. We have Riley with us and the twins. We have an addition to our family now in Willow. What a delightful blessing! We may not have been aware of God's wings being over us today. Further down in the Psalm, David said about God, 'He shall give his angels charge over thee, to keep thee in all thy ways.' I know and certainly have felt the help of his angels with us over the last week and a half and even before. They are with us always to help us and protect us. I just want to reassure you, all of you, that God loves you, and his wings are covering over you to protect you from harm. Nothing can happen to you outside of the will of God."

"You don't mean to tell me that it was the will of God that Riley was shot in the head?" asked Clyde derisively.

"Yes, I do. I praise God for that. For if God had not been with Riley today, he may have been killed. As it is, the bullet only grazed his head. He will fully recover and won't really even have a bad scar from the event. We all have to suffer. Christ had to suffer, and he was sinless. How much more we should suffer, being sinful beings, but God sent Jesus in our place to pay the ultimate price for that sin—his life. I'd willingly suffer so much more than I do in exchange for that gift."

"I really hadn't thought of it from that side of the coin."

"Life on this earth is not going to be easy. Just asking Jesus into one's heart isn't going to take away all the bad things that may come into our lives in the future. We have to continue to live life following God's will no matter what may happen. He wants faithful, obedient followers. He doesn't really care about all that we may accomplish for him. I mean, does God really need us? No, not really, but we *really need him*. He is God. He is the Almighty, omnipotent, one and only. He doesn't need anything or anybody. But he loves us and sent his Son to pay the price for our sins. There is no greater love than that."

Clyde looked straight at Michael and then hung his head. "Nobody has ever explained it that way to me. My wife and little girl were killed by stray bullets in a gunfight over nothing. She had gone into town to buy some fabric for a new dress to wear to church. They never came home. I was on a cattle drive and had just gotten back. I was working out in the barn when the sheriff came out to tell me. I can't tell you how it hurt to have to hear those words. I never went back to church. If God was that mean, why should I love him? Katie looks just like how my little girl might have looked if she had been allowed to grow up. I'd do anything to protect her."

Katie, tears beginning to slide down her cheeks, smiled a Mona Lisa smile and then looked at Clyde. "Clyde, I gave my heart to Jesus today. The grief I have been carrying around for my brother, sister, father, and mother has been lifted so much by the joy and peace I now have. I want you to feel that same release. I have a feeling your wife and daughter are in heaven asking God to heal your heart. I don't know if I can say the same for my family. They didn't know Jesus. I probably won't see them again."

More tears slowly made their way down Katie's cheek. "I know you could if you just won't reject the love and free gift of salvation that comes to us from God. You have the chance to see them again. Will you take it?"

Clyde got up off the log and walked past the light of the fire. The bright moon clearly showed his silhouette as he walked a little way and then fell to his knees, his hands pressed against his face.

Michael looked deeply at Katie and then smiled. "Praise God! Thank you, Father, this child of yours has come home. One of your chosen ones has thrown off the bondage of her forefathers and has embraced the freedom you offer in Christ."

The twins kept looking at one another, and then back to the fire. Clearly, they were unsure of what they were supposed to do. Willow stood and moved to the front of the wagon. She would not return. Katie found her later, asleep, her hands clasped in prayer.

"Well, that's a fine howdy-do. I'm going to bed. Then I'll get up at midnight and go watch the herd for a spell."

With that, Wulf walked over to his bedroll and tucked himself in. The wind had picked up, and the flames of the fire began to dance and spark. It was beautiful, almost like they were rejoicing in two souls being saved from destruction in one day.

Josh stood and announced he would take the first watch. He wasn't sleepy yet and needed to think about some things. He saddled Ranger and took off toward the corral.

"I guess I'll go back to bed, but I'm telling you now, I want to work tomorrow. My head is just fine. I didn't join this team just to sleep."

"Riley, we will see just how fit you feel in the morning. I'm praying you will be better. But we will leave that in the hands of the Great Physician."

"Right. Well, he will have me fit tomorrow. There are cattle that need to be found. I think Star knows just where to find them. I'm the only one who can ride her, remember?"

"Okay, but you will not take a watch duty tonight." Michael's look let everyone know he would brook no argument on the matter.

"I can promise you that."

"Michael, can I talk with you, privately?"

"Certainly, Clyde, where to?"

"Let's just walk out here a short piece."

"How can I help you, Clyde?"

"I want to apologize for the way I talked to you. I have been so bitter for so long, I just needed to get it out, I guess. Katie sure made me think. Do you think God will have me? I'm not so young any more, and I have arthritis. I can't do much."

"I told you all he wants is for you to repent from your sins. As a result, you will be faithful to him and obedient to his will, as long as you remember what he has done for you. It is the Christians who have forgotten what God has done for them who become the 'hypocrites,' as so many call them. Read his word every day and meditate on what you have read. Hide his word in your heart and that will help keep sin away. Remember, none of us is perfect, and we will sin. We just need to remember to ask for forgiveness when that happens. We will never lose our salvation, just our fellowship."

"I want to pray now, will you help me?"

"I would be honored."

Katie looked up at the stars. Her heart was singing with joy. Michael was so right. They had been blessed that day. She had a sister. She had the twins who weren't killed by the flash flood. She had Riley who had not been killed by the rustlers. She truly felt "under his wings." In her mind, she saw the face of Josh and the look he had given her earlier. What was she feeling toward him? Love? Suddenly, she felt very tired. She looked around and saw the twins still sitting by the fire, just staring at it.

"Why don't you men go on to sleep?"

"We're 'fraid t'go ta sleep."

"Why is that, Cade?"

"I'm Wade."

"Oh, sorry. You're going to have to wear something so I can tell you apart."

There was a pause. Nothing was said. She looked at them again. They were still staring.

"So, why is that, Wade?"

"Why's what?"

"Why are you afraid to go to sleep?"

"We might die."

"God saved you from certain death today. Do you think he would just let you die in your sleep tonight?"

"What if he'ad ta save us 'n order ta save Willow?"

"Do you think the Eternal—God—is that small that he can't save whom he will save without having to save everyone around them?"

"Yep."

"You boys need to realize just how big God is. Come look at this."

They got up and followed her out far enough from the fire that they could see the sky and be sure they would not disturb anyone.

"Now, look up there. God created that, more stars than we can count. On a dark night, when the moon isn't so bright, you can see even more. And that is just a very small part of his universe. The earth is his footstool! I think if God can make everything out of nothing, then he certainly could have saved Willow and let the two of you die, if that was his plan!"

"Wow! Look et all thum stars."

"Think about all that has happened today. Yes, God has had his wings over us today just like a mother hen keeps her chicks under hers to protect them. You boys need to think about what God has planned for you. And if I were you, I'd start practicing better English. Riley will be up and about tomorrow, but he will have a headache more than likely, so don't use improper English around him, or me, if you don't want to hear about it. Now, go to sleep! And say your prayers. Thank God for all he has done for you. If you haven't already done it, ask him into your heart. Ask him to forgive your sins."

As Katie finished cleaning up the coffee cups and putting more wood on the fire, she heard the boys say just above a whisper, "Thank you, God, for all you dun fer us'ns today."

She smiled and said, "Amen."

CHAPTER 27

atie stretched and felt the pull of tight muscles. As she rolled over, she realized Willow wasn't there. She threw back the covers and jumped up to put on her clothes. She rushed out of the wagon.

"Hey, quit rocking the wagon. You'll spill it."

"Why didn't you wake me? How long have you been up? Where is everybody?"

"You were sleeping so soundly I didn't want to disturb you. I woke up before the sun rose and couldn't get back to sleep, so I got up and made coffee. When everyone smelled that, they got up. I fed them eggs, but I couldn't find any bacon so I scrambled them in butter."

"Jews don't eat pork."

"Okay. So, why don't you have bacon? Are you saying you are a Jew?"

"Yes, that is exactly what I am saying. Pigs are unclean animals and we shouldn't eat them."

"I will have to ask Michael about all that."

"About all what?"

"Clean and unclean. He knows all about the Bible. Can you believe it? I dreamed in English! By the way, the mood this morning was so good. Everyone was very cheerful. Wulf, of course, was sad faced. I think he is fighting with God."

"Well, I think you are right. What are you making?"

"Medicine."

"Medicine? What for?"

"Well, I don't know what you have back at the ranch, but you don't have anything much on the wagon. At least I couldn't find anything. I'm working on a red clover compound to fight infection."

"Oh, where did you learn how to do this?"

"The Indians know about so many roots, leaves and bark and how they help with things that are wrong with the body. I learned from them."

"You are such a wealth of information. I am so glad your English has come back to you. Do you remember Indian?"

"Yes, I will always remember it, I think. I spoke it as long as I did English."

"Do you need help?"

"No, I'm about finished here. I think we will be going back to the ranch today. Riley was feeling so much better and insisted on going back to the woods to find 'his' cattle. He said Star would show him where they are. This time he did not go alone. I think one of the twins went with him. Those boys need to be separated for a little bit so they can start thinking on their own."

"I agree with you. They do depend on each other. There are so many stories in just the lives represented here in our team. I think that is what he called us last night."

"Who?"

"Riley."

"It fits. A team of horses works together and gets the job done. Our 'team' works like that."

"Yes, it does. You know, I have fallen in love with everyone of them. They are all very special." Katie looked up into the broad sky and smiled.

"I think you may feel that one of them is more special than the others."

"What do you mean, Willow?"

"Oh, Katie, I see the way you look at him. I can even see you looking at him when he isn't here. And I've seen the way he looks at you. Don't even try to tell me you don't know who I'm talking about. There is something going on in your heart. Don't deny it."

"I'm struggling with my feelings. I am so grateful to Michael. He is so very special to me. But, I feel so much more when I look at Josh or feel his touch. Michael is warm and comfortable. He is a real comfort to me, but I feel like he is more of a father or brother than anything more. Josh's touch almost burns my skin. He is tender and so much more than a comfort. I don't want him to go anywhere that he won't be coming back."

"You know as well as I do, sometimes those we love can't come back. We can't hold them closer to our heart than we do God. He wouldn't like it and neither would we. It would cause such a struggle inside we couldn't stand it. If we truly love God, he must come first."

"You are only, what, seventeen? How did you get so wise?"

"Remember, I told you there was a book I loved to read? It was the Bible. I would read it and read it every chance I got. I think God knew I would not have one for many years. I memorized verses and when I was taken by the Indians, I kept those verses in my heart. I remembered stories from the Bible and could see examples of the same things happening in the tribe's people. Then there was an old Indian, like a grandpa to me, who would give me words of wisdom as I was growing up. He would talk to me about the Great Spirit and how he takes care of his people. I always pictured God and his people as being those who believe in him. I don't know if that is what he was talking about, but I think not. I think 'his people' in his mind were the Indians."

She had braided her hair in one long braid which hung down her back. The sun sparkled off of it as she worked on her red clover medicine. Katie reached out to touch it.

"Your hair is so beautiful. I've never seen a color quite like it."

"If I ever get captured by the Indians again, I will cut off all my hair."

"Why?"

"They would not stop touching it. Some even pulled it to see if it was real. A shaved head is a disgrace to them. Maybe they would leave me alone if I did that."

"I have never suffered like you have, and I thought I was the only one to feel such deep pain. I'm so sorry I've been so self-centered."

"You haven't. Remember, we've only had one day together and it was really full. I don't think you are self-centered at all."

"Well, to show you that I mean it, I will go and get firewood. I'll see you later."

"Be careful, with the weather warming like this, the critters will be coming out of their winter sleep."

"Don't worry. If I see a bear you will hear me scream and come running through the woods."

"I'm not worried about the bears as much as I am the snakes."

"What?"

"Oh, nothing. See you!"

With that, they waved at each other, and Katie moved into the woods. She wandered further east of where they had been going to and from the water hole. She saw a large pile of dead branches next to an outcropping of stones.

"How convenient. Thank you, the Eternal, God, for providing such a nice pile of wood."

She wasn't that far from the campsite and turned to look back to see if there was a better way back before she loaded her arms with wood. As she turned back to begin picking up small branches, she heard the sound she dreaded the most.

"There are no babies out here. That sound could only come from a rattlesnake. *Oh, Abigail, Oh, Abigail. Aaaaaaaak!*"

Willow heard the scream. She whipped around and grabbed the gun and fired once then started running in the direction of the sound. She couldn't see Katie anywhere.

"Where is she, Lord? Show me the way. Keep her safe. Keep her safe."

Briars tore at her arms and legs, but she ignored them. In the distance she could see the pile of brush and the rocks.

"Oh no! Oh no! Lord, no, not there. Keep her safe."

As she got closer, she could see Katie lying on the ground on her side but with her face toward the sky. A snake was sliding away from her. Willow took aim and fired. The snake's head went flying, its body continued to wriggle. Willow walked carefully toward Katie, aiming the gun in every direction, looking for more snakes.

"This is the perfect place for a whole nest of snakes. Why did I let her go?"

Willow couldn't see any other snakes. She didn't hear any.

"Maybe they are still sleeping. Oh, let it be so, Lord."

She dropped down on her knees beside Katie looking for any sign of a snake bite. She pulled up her dress; boots covered her legs nearly to her knees.

"Good. Good."

She carefully lifted her arms and looked for any puncture wounds, rubbing her hands gently over the skin. Next she looked at her neck. Her pulse was strong. She could see the heartbeat in her neck.

"Katie! Willow! Where are you?"

"Over here. Hurry, Josh!"

Willow stood and waved her arms over her head until she could see him coming to her through the same briars that had torn at her own flesh. He looked pale.

"Hurry. Take Katie back to the camp. I don't think she has any snake bites, but I did shoot one."

He looked at the headless snake still writhing on the ground not too far from where they stood. He quickly lifted Katie and turned to go back the way he came.

"No, go this way. I don't want her to get scratched by those briars. I won't be able to tell if there is a snake bite if she is bitten."

"Oh, right. Why don't you lead the way back."

"Yes, that good. *Ack!* I mean that is good."

They entered the camp, and he quickly had Katie in the wagon. Willow was in the wagon before he had gotten completely out of the way.

"Now go and find some firewood and start boiling water."

"Okay. Anything else I can do?"

"Pray!"

"Abigail, dear, would you go and gather some firewood? We are really low. I'll need more to make supper."

"Sure, Ma, I can see a good pile of brush over on the edge of that wood."

"Katie, you help me get things ready. It won't take long for her to get back with some wood."

Katie whispered to Abigail as she walked off. "Great! You get the fresh air and exercise while I stay here and lift heavy pots and pans out. Just how does one stay kosher on the trail? Impossible! Nothing is clean out here!"

"I'll hurry back and help."

"I love you, Abigail. You are so sweet. You never see anything wrong."

Abigail laughed and moved in the direction of the brush.

Katie and Ma worked to get things out of the wagon. They had just set a pile of pots and pans down on a quilt when they heard the scream. They looked up and saw Abigail running toward them waving her arms. Katie ran to meet her.

"Abigail, what is wrong?" she yelled as she approached her.

Abigail was crying hysterically. "Snake!"

Katie grabbed her. She could see blood coming from two small holes in Abigail's upper left arm.

"Oh, no. Don't run. Here I'll help you. Calm down. Abigail, calm down. Please calm down."

Her lips were already turning blue. Her face was swelling.

"Oh, no. Abigail, stay with me. Don't leave me. Abigail, please calm down."

———

The vision of Abigail faded away, and now all that was left was the horrible darkness again, that swirling pit of emptiness. Down and down Katie traveled. "Lone-ly, Lone-ly" filled her ears. What happened to the light?

"Katie, stay with me. Don't leave me. Katie, wake up!"

"I didn't see any kind of bite, not even a mosquito bite. There's not a bump on her head. She didn't hit it on a rock or anything." Willow's voice was quiet.

"It's okay, Willow. Just go and fix some tea. I'm going to sit here and keep talking to her. She has gone into a dark place, and I need to draw her out."

"I know I need some tea. Do you want some? I'll fix her some in case she wakes up. No…for when she wakes up. Oh, and I'll keep praying."

"Thanks. Come on, Katie girl. I need you. Please don't go where I can't follow. Stay with me. I love you…I never thought I would say that to anyone. I have never seen a woman I even considered as a woman I could love. You were so hurt the first time I saw you. I lifted you out of the wagon and carried you into Doc's office. I knew then there was something special about you. Mom sees it too. She loves you like her own daughter. Please don't leave us, Katie. Our world won't be as bright and so full of light as it has been since God brought you into our lives. Oh, my heart couldn't take it if you left me just as I've realized how much I love you."

He looked around and saw two cups of tea sitting there on the wagon seat. He picked one up and took a sip. "Ouch! Too hot. Lord, have I made an idol out of Katie? Have I allowed her to take my eyes from you? You have said it is not good for man to be alone. I believe you have brought her into my life to be my life mate. She is a double child of yours, just as I am. We have been through so much. I have not even told my parents about the horrors I saw out in the field. You allowed me to come back here so I wouldn't become as inhuman as so many of the men who are out in the wilderness, battling the 'enemy.' Lord, please send her back to me. Purge her of this darkness that takes her. Allow us to have the life of promise you have made to your children. May I have the courage to follow Christ's example and say with all purity of mind and heart, 'not my will but yours be done.' I give her to you, Lord, as a sacrifice as pure as any. If it is your will to take her from me, help me to know you have someone better for me. I trust you. You are my God, my only God."

"Josh?"

The voice was so soft he could hardly hear it. His hand had been smoothing her hair down and then rubbing her cheek. He looked down to see her eyes still closed. Maybe he hadn't heard it.

"Josh?"

There it was again, stronger this time.

"I'm right here Katie. I'm right here. Please open your eyes."

"No."

"Why not?"

"I heard the most beautiful things and I don't want to open my eyes. I might find out it was all a dream."

"If you open your eyes, I promise to say some beautiful things to you. You won't be sorry. Just don't leave me again. I couldn't stand it."

Her eyes fluttered and then opened looking right at him.

"Oh, Katie, are you really awake?"

"I am."

"I love you so much. Do you think you could love me? I would work so hard to be a good husband."

"What are you saying?"

"Beautiful things?"

She laughed. "Yes, I love you. You have brought something very precious into my life. I don't think I could stand it if I lost you. I have lost so many people close to me. I've been so afraid to love again, because they all leave me."

"I won't leave you. We belong to the King. When we leave this earth we go to heaven and will live eternally with him. We will be there together. So, even death should not scare us."

"I don't want to have death separate us before we can be together. I want to get to know you and have you tell me your burdens and let me share them. I don't think my pa ever did that. I think that is part of what killed him. He was so burdened. So was Ma. She just died of a broken heart. I wasn't enough for her."

"You are more than enough for me. I can't believe how generous God has been. I don't deserve you. I know this is not the best place or circumstances for this, but I can't wait. Will you be my wife? I can't think of anything that would make my life more perfect than to have Christ and you in my life forever. I love you more than I thought I could ever love anyone."

"Oh, Josh, I never thought I would marry. I thought no one would have a Jewish girl. I was so alone. Are you sure? Are you very sure?"

"Yes, so very sure. I know God meant for us to be together. Remember, technically, I'm a Jewish boy. Will you have me?"

"Yes, I will have you. I will be very proud to be your wife."

He leaned down and kissed her very gently. He drew back and looked at her. She sat up, turned, and threw her arms around his neck and pulled him to her, sealing their promise of forever with a kiss to remember.

The sound of clapping caused them to jerk apart. Everyone was standing around the front of the wagon watching.

"Finally, now maybe I can get some work out of that man!"

"Michael!"

"I mean it, Katie. All he has done is look toward camp. When he heard that shot, Wulf told me he was on his horse riding like the wind toward camp before the sound died away."

"I'm glad he did. I couldn't have carried her out of the woods without his help," Willow said.

"You were a very smart woman to fire off that gun."

"I knew that was your signal for help. I needed someone's help, fast!"

"Well, we have all the cattle rounded up and most of the ones that need it are branded. I think we can head home, as soon as we eat a little something. Whatever you have cooking sure smells good."

"Well, let's get to it then. Josh, do you think you can help Katie down?"

Laughter rang throughout the woods, sending squirrels scampering in every direction.

CHAPTER 28

After they ate, Wulf, Clyde and the twins said they would stay and finish branding, then follow everyone else in with the cattle. Michael, Josh, Riley, Katie, and Willow broke camp and made sure everything was cleaned up and the fire put out. Josh stacked some firewood near a tree at the edge of the woods so the next time they made a camp there, or just came out for an evening under the stars, the wood would be ready to build a fire.

It was late in the afternoon before they pulled back onto the ranch proper. Brian was there as were Adam, Esther, and Tad. As soon as the wagon stopped, Katie jumped down, not waiting for any male help. She ran to Esther and threw her arms around her.

"Oh, Esther! The most wonderful thing has happened!"

"What? Tell me."

"I gave my heart to Jesus. I can even say his name and not feel like I am saying a forbidden word. Oh, my heart is so free. The peace I have I can't begin to explain to you. Thank you! Thank you so much for all you have done and the prayers you have prayed. I would not be here today if it had not been for you."

"Oh, I think you would. I do thank God for using me. But if it had not been me, he would have used someone else."

While Esther and Katie spoke, Josh pulled his father aside and whispered in his ear. Adam slapped his son on the shoulder, grabbed his hand, and shook it vigorously, laughing all the time. They then walked off in the opposite direction talking quietly to each other.

Katie felt a tug on her skirt.

"Miss Katie?" Tad's big brown eyes stared up at her clearly pleading with her. "Please, come look at the garden."

"I would love to." Katie bent down and gave him a reassuring hug.

Her eyes wandered in the direction of the garden and almost flew out of her head. Tad and she all but ran over to the site.

"Is the whole thing planted? It looks like an army has been at work. Did you do this all by yourself?"

"Mostly, I did have a little help." He shyly looked up at his mother who had just walked up.

She laughed. "I just couldn't stay away. I do need to spend a little more time at the restaurant than I have been these past few days. Rose and Liz do a wonderful job, but there are things that come up that just are not their responsibility, and I feel bad not being there to handle those things. Adam has the hotel running smoothly and would love nothing better than to be out here more. I see now where Josh gets his love for ranching. How did he do? Was he a big help?" Her voice held a bit of anxiousness. She wanted to be very proud of her sons. She had every right to be.

"Oh, yes. He will be the best rancher you have ever seen. He seems to have a second sense about him. Yes, he was very helpful." Katie's smile was brilliant as she spoke.

Esther glanced around and spied her husband and son deep in talk and walking idly around toward the front of the house. She looked back at Katie and smiled. Her heart felt a joy she dare not acknowledge, not yet.

"Oh, I brought out a sack of lye. The last time Tad went in the privy, he told me it was completely out of lye. He couldn't find any in any of the out buildings, so I just brought out a sack. I'll get the bucket and fill it. It will be easier to bring the bucket out than to take the sack in."

"I can get it."

"No, I will. You take care of pulling the wagon over where we had it to load, and we can unload it."

Katie turned to move toward the wagon and saw Brian sitting on the seat next to Willow. He was holding the reins, but they were talking and didn't look like they were going to go anywhere.

"Hey, Brian, could you drive the wagon over here?"

Brian looked over at Katie and nodded his head. Willow looked down into her lap. The wagon moved slowly toward where Katie indicated.

"Katie! Katie! Come here!"

Katie spun around toward the privy where Esther was wildly waving. She ran to her.

"I picked up the bucket to take it over to fill it, and look."

Katie's eyes traveled down to the corner of the small structure where Esther was pointing, afraid she would see a snake. She gasped. Her hand flew out and she leaned down to pick up the mostly buried metal box.

"What is this doing here?"

"What is it?"

"It's the money box. Pa had it on the wagon when we came west. This is what I have been looking for. Now, everything makes sense. Oh, Esther, do you understand? Every time Pa went into town he would use the privy. I thought it was because of the bad experiences he'd had in the one before. But now I see. And he kept saying 'money, lie.' Ma and I thought he was saying 'L-I-E' but he was saying 'L-Y-E'."

"Let's take it inside and wait for Michael to get finished up with what he is doing. Then we can decide what to do."

The women looked over toward the house and could see the wagon, now parked where Katie had indicated, but Brian and Willow were still sitting on the bench of the wagon.

"I wonder what that is all about?"

"Katie, can you not guess? Who is she, and tell me where you 'got her'? She is just beautiful."

"Let's wait 'til supper and we can tell everyone. There is so much you don't know. Where are Adam and Josh?"

"Having a father-son talk, I imagine."

"Oh." Katie felt her cheeks turn pink and hot again. Would she ever stop blushing? Esther let out the most delightful giggle and gave Katie a hug.

Released from Esther's hug, Katie briskly walked over to the wagon. "Okay, let's get busy getting this thing unloaded and cleaned up."

Brian got down and helped Willow down. It was clear he didn't want to let go of her.

"Let me help. I don't know where anything goes, but I learn fast," Willow said enthusiastically.

"I'll say. Here, let me show you around the house and especially the kitchen. Willow, I want you to know that I am planning on you staying with me. I have plenty of room. This is your home now, as well as mine."

Tears formed on Willow's lower lid. She managed to keep them from falling, but her nose turned a bright red. Katie giggled and gave her a quick hug.

"So, tell me about Brian? What were you two talking about?"

"Oh, nothing really. He just wanted to know who I am and where I come from. He said he had not seen me before and wanted to get to know me. He's the sheriff and wants to know all the people he is to protect."

"I'm sure he will do that. Here, this is your room. There are clothes in here that were my sister Abigail's. I think they will fit you. I know that leather is comfortable and can take much of abuse, but I just want to see you in a calico dress with your hair done up. You will look like a princess. I can't get over the color of your hair."

"Funny, that's what Brian kept saying. He said there aren't many blondes around here and now he isn't the only one."

"Oh, he did, did he? Well, the other men better not hear that, or he won't hear the end of their teasing."

"What do you mean?"

"You'll see. Let's go back downstairs. We need to get you fully acquainted with the kitchen."

"I love how the downstairs isn't divided. It's all wide open, so if we are cooking we can still see what is going on in the other part of the room. I love the big, stone fireplace. This is a beautiful home, so much better than my cave."

Brian, Esther, and Tad were bringing in food items and pots and pans from the wagon.

"I'll keep the laundry out here. We can do the wash later."

"Thanks, Esther. You really have this under control. Willow, let's get started with heating the water for washing these pots and pans properly. The well is out front."

Brian quickly grabbed the bucket and started toward the door. "No, let me go get the water. That will be too heavy for you women."

"Thanks, Brian." Katie watched for just a moment and then went back to work. Willow, however, kept watching him move until he was out the front door and out of sight.

"Now, Willow, here is where we keep the flour and sugar and all those kinds of things. The root cellar has all the canned goods. Out back you'll find the meat hanging in the smokehouse that's just beyond the privy. We also have a springhouse where we can keep milk and butter cool."

Willow twirled around looking in every direction. "Wow! I didn't know you lived in a mansion."

"I don't. But this house is too big for just one person. I hope you will be glad to stay here with me."

"Where else would I go?"

"Into town. You might want to move into the hotel and find work with Esther or someone else. I don't want to force you into a decision."

"No, I love the big outdoors. I love the ranch and you. I'll stay here."

"Great! That is settled. Now, let's start putting away all this food."

Katie glanced around and then looked at Esther. She mouthed, "Where is it?"

"Under the sink." Esther mouthed back.

Brian came back in with the water. Adam and Josh were taking care of the horses and working in the barn. Tad said he had some things to do in the garden and was gone in a flash.

"Well, now we are getting things done. I wonder what time Michael and Riley will get here with the lead herd?"

"Anytime now, I suspect. If you ladies need anything done, just give a holler. I'm going out to see if I need to help get things ready for the cattle. Oh, and by the way, Katie, Bill and Rex had a price on their heads for cattle rustling. I sent off for the money. I let you decide who is to get it since I'm not sure what all happened out there."

"God is so good. Just a month ago, I didn't know where I would get the money to work my ranch. I didn't even want to live. Now, look. I have friends, some I would call family, money in the bank and at the general store, people working for me, and I can afford to pay them. Brian, what can I do for you? Surely, you need something."

"I think you have done more than you know. You are a very special lady and don't even know it. You have changed so much since I first saw you. You have really changed since the roundup. I truly pray your dark days are over."

"Yes, I don't think I will go there again. I have Jesus in my life now. When you have his light, how can darkness abide there? I feel so free. I grieve for my parents, brother, and sister. I just wish they had known the truth. I don't think I would have ever come to know the truth if they were still living. I know that sounds selfish, but I believe it is a fact. I never would have met any of you. Oh, God is so good. I will not stop praising him for all he has done. I may never understand why my family couldn't come to him. I will leave all of that up to God. It is in his hands to take care of in his almighty wisdom."

"Here come the men with the cattle. Let me run. I should have been out there. Call any of us if you ladies need anything."

With that, he ran out the door and let it slam behind him.

"Men, they are always in a hurry," said Katie with her hands on her hips.

"Or sometimes not!" replied Esther.

The three women laughed 'til they had tears running down their cheeks.

After supper, the hands moved on out to the bunkhouse. Brian had gone back to town. Katie, Josh, Adam, Esther, Michael, and Willow sat around the table with the metal box sitting there in front of Katie. Tad had fallen asleep on the couch which faced the fireplace in the living room part of the downstairs.

"Are you going to open it?"

"I'm almost afraid to. God has shown me that he provides everything we need. I don't know what is in this box. It may be one dollar, or a hundred. I just want to keep trusting in God's provision and not on what my pa had laid aside."

"I don't think that will be a problem. Maybe that is why God kept this hidden for so long. He wanted you to come to the point of depending on him to provide for you. For so long, your pa's money was all that was important to you. Greed can eat up a person, as we saw in Red. Brian told me he was shot and killed trying to escape the Rangers. You don't have to worry about him anymore, Katie."

Tears came to her eyes. "I'm so sorry. I now wish he had found out what a blessing knowing Jesus as his savior could be. Now, he will never know."

Michael pushed the box a little closer to Katie. "Go ahead, open it."

"Okay."

She lifted the lid and gasped. Inside were stacks of bills and gold coins.

"I can't handle this. Josh, you and Michael count it."

When they were finished counting, Michael looked up and said simply, "Five thousand dollars and another thousand in gold coins."

"What? I can't believe it! But how? I never thought we had that much money."

"Evidently your father was a very good businessman. He knew how to save. Look at this ranch, it is a gold mine with all its resources."

"The pot of gold. He wasn't kidding when he said that. Oh, Pa, how I wish you could be here and see all that has happened. How God has provided and shown his love to us, his chosen people. He is not all about punishment. He is about love."

"I feel funny about bringing this up, but I feel I have to do it."

"Yes, Josh, what is it?" Katie adoringly looked at him.

"Katie, I truly love you. I have since the first moment I saw you. If you feel in any way that I have asked you to be my wife because I want this ranch and all that goes with it, please tell me now. My heart may never heal, but I will walk away and try to prove to you that you are all that is important to me."

"Oh, Josh. I don't see how you could have known about the money. I didn't know until this minute how much there was. The ranch is hard work. If you thought it would be an easy get-rich scheme to marry me, you would be so wrong. No, I don't think you thought that at all. Esther, he wouldn't think that, would he? He isn't that kind of a man, is he?"

"No, dear, he is not. I am surprised he even said it. Did anyone here at the table think Josh would marry for money?"

No one spoke for a long moment. Then Willow looked straight at Katie then at Josh.

"I saw how he came to save her. How he prayed for her. How he cried over her. There is no greed in this man's heart. He loves her with a pure love and would sacrifice his life for hers. You have nothing to fear from him, Katie. He is a good man, a godly man."

Tears were running down the cheeks of all the women and the eyes of the men pooled with tears.

"I would like to ask you again, in the presence of my parents and your family of Michael and Willow, will you, Katie Kurtz, consent to be my wife? I promise I will love you with an everlasting love, provide and care for you, always."

"Oh, yes, Joshua Schmitt, I will consent to be your wife. You are everything I have ever dreamed of in a husband. I respect you and love you so much."

Esther clapped her hands. "Hallelujah! Praise God, I will have my daughter twice over. You are my joy, Katie. I am so proud to have you in my life."

"I have a sister to replace my sister. So, now you have two daughters. Willow is so much more to me than I thought my sister ever was. She sees deep into the heart and has so much discernment. She is truly a sister to me. I love you so much, Willow."

"I lost two daughters. God has replaced them fully grown and so beautiful in body and in spirit. I don't think I can take much more."

"There was a bounty on Bill and Rex. Brian has sent off for it. He told me to use it as I felt right since he didn't know exactly what happened out there. Help me decide. Tell me if you think I'm wrong. I want to give it to Riley. He is the one most hurt by those two men. Indeed, they planned to kill him. God's hand spared his life. I think he is the one who deserves it more than anyone. What do you think?" She looked into Michael's eyes.

"Yes, Katie, you are so right. Riley has another task to do, he won't be staying with the ranch. He will be near. This money will help him do the job God has for him to do."

"You are being very mysterious, Michael. I hate to lose him, but I will not stand in the way of God. I will help any way I can."

"Well, I think we can afford to pay our men tomorrow. We will need to get ready for the trail ride to San Antonio. Katie, you will have to stay here. Both you and Willow are needed here. Adam, how do you feel about being a cook on the trail?"

"Oh, I'd love it! I had no idea I would love ranching as much as I do. It will give Josh and me some really good time together as father and son. We haven't had that since he came home."

"What about the restaurant? The hotel?" asked Katie, concerned.

"My dear, I have not been needed at either place for a very long time." He looked at Esther and smiled. "Any decisions that need to be made in the next little bit, darling, I trust to you and anyone you want to help advise you."

Esther smiled, "I love you, too, my beloved."

"Oh, this is too much. I can scarcely take it in. I will have to pray about this and sleep on it. God will give me peace," sighed Katie.

"Esther, you know that Willow and I will help. I'm sure we can find someone to help with the livestock. There is little that will need to be done while the men are away."

Josh put his arm around Katie's shoulders and pulled her toward him.

"You have a wedding to plan too. I plan to marry you as soon as we can after I get back from the cattle drive. Does the preacher come through this week? We can talk with him on Sunday if he is here. What is today anyway? Please, don't keep me waiting too long?" Josh looked dead serious as he said that.

The laughter around the table helped to dispel the anxiety that had taken hold of some. Tad awoke and rubbed his eyes.

"What's so funny."

"I'll tell you on the way home. We need to get going, or make beds here! We'll see you sometime tomorrow, Katie and Willow." Esther hugged each girl as she went to get Tad ready for the ride home.

"Come back, anytime."

CHAPTER 29

he house was quiet as the two girls stood at the door and watched the wagon pull out onto the road. They turned and gave each other a hug.

"I am so glad to have you here, Willow. Please make yourself at home. It is your home too. I don't want anything to come between us."

"I will stay until the wedding. Then I think I'll go and live at the hotel for a while. I want to get to know Esther better. She's a very special lady. If I'm going to be her daughter, I want to know her very well. Besides, you and Josh will want some privacy at least for a while."

"Well, I guess you're right on that one. I can't blame you for wanting to get to know Esther. If I know her as well as I think I do, you will be seeing more of her here than you think. She will bring Tad out. I'm going to be tutoring him. There is no teacher in Crystal Springs right now, so there is no school. I promised I would teach him if he would help with the garden. Well, as you can see, he has done the garden. Now, I need to do my part."

"Will you teach me as well?"

"I can't think of what you may need to know. Your English has improved so much, one would never know you were speaking in broken English just a couple of days ago."

"I want to know more than English. I need to know numbers and history, and where the countries are. I want to know more about, well, everything!"

"I'd love for you to sit in on the lessons as well."

"I think I am going to go on up and get ready for bed. I'm very tired."

"Thank you for all your help today. I'm going to get the coffee set up for tomorrow. All I will have to do is start a fire and it will be ready sooner than anyone will expect. I think I'll have a kettle of water ready. I need some tea. I'm staying downstairs. The men moved my room down after I was attacked by Red. I was thinking about moving back upstairs, but since I'm getting married soon, I think I will stay down here."

"Good idea. You'll be able to get to the kitchen quicker!"

They both laughed and went their separate ways. Katie entered the kitchen. As she did, she heard a noise out on the porch. He heart started pounding. *Now what?* She looked around for a weapon. Maybe she wasn't quite over the attack after all.

"Katie, are you in there?"

She stepped back outside, took his hand. "Josh, what are you doing here? I thought you were going out to the bunkhouse."

He gently pulled her back out under the night sky. "I walked halfway there and stopped to look up at the stars. I just couldn't go back without coming back to get one last look at you. You put the stars to shame." She looked up at the dazzling array of stars displayed in all God's glory.

Looking intently at her, he leaned toward her and wrapped his arms around her gently holding her head as he pressed his lips against hers. His hand moved to the tender flesh of her neck sending a shiver through her. He pulled away and looked into her eyes.

"Maybe we'd better get married before I leave! I don't know how much restraint I can handle."

"What are you talking about?"

"Never mind. You'll find out. Just plan that wedding for as soon as possible."

With that, he turned on his heels and marched off toward the bunkhouse.

Give me strength, Lord. Help me to flee from sin. Keep her safe in your loving arms, under your wings, while I am away.

Katie almost skipped back into the house and then turned and locked the door. She quickly got the coffee ready for the morning, finished a cup of tea, and blew out the lantern.

"All is at peace. I am safe under your wings. Thank you, the Eternal God, dear Father, for all your many blessings. All glory to you, and may I never forget it," she whispered as she entered her room and felt his presence surround her.

EPILOGUE

The church bell was ringing. Katie and Josh came out in a shower of seeds and flower petals. Adam had been Josh's best man. Michael had given Katie away. Willow was her bridesmaid and Tad had carried the ring. Texas wild flowers were in abundance everywhere. It was the happiest day of their lives.

The reception was held at the hotel. J. R. Riley looked his best in a new suit. He had moved into the hotel and was building a modest home next to the school where he would open his academy in the fall. Crystal Springs was thrilled to have such a qualified man teaching their children.

Willow, dressed in a striking green dress, floated among the guests seeing to their needs and directing them to the food. "Mom" (as the girls had begun to call Esther), relished the sight, glowing with happiness and pride. It was a party to remember. All the hands were there, smiling from ear to ear. Wulf even laughed a time or two. Clyde had become his best friend, and they were a common sight out on the range working together like a fine clockwork machine. Clyde constantly showed Christ's love to the still-bitter man. He was making progress.

"How long do we have to stay here?" Josh whispered in Katie's ear.

"We haven't even cut the cake yet. Mom went to so much trouble. Josh, give her the time she deserves. We have a lifetime together!"

"But I want you right now!"

"I know, sweet! Anything worth having is worth waiting for."

"Do you know how miserable I was out on the trail? It's a good thing Michael kept me busy. That new hand, Todd, is really good. God is so good. His timing is perfect."

"Yes, and you will do well to remember that today! We will be able to leave when God's timing says it is time to leave."

"Are you always going to do that?"

"What?"

"Use my words to correct me?"

"Is that not what I should do? After all, you are so wise. I can't come up with anything better."

"Oh, now that is diplomacy. You should be negotiating peace with the Indians up north."

"I think I have better things to do right here." She gently tapped a finger on his broad chest.

"Oh, now you have done it. Let's go cut the cake so we can leave!"

"I think you need to go talk to Brian. He looks rather down. What could his problem be? I hope there is not some criminal here he is keeping his eye on."

"I'll go and talk with him."

"You are a darling. I love you."

Josh walked across the room to where Brian was leaning against one of the posts in the lobby of the hotel.

"What're you looking at, Brian. Is there some suspicious character who has invaded the party?"

"I think I see a skunk."

"What?"

"Just look at that." He nodded his head in the direction of Willow.

"She is no skunk. She is a vision of loveliness. Besides Katie, I have not met a more gracious lady."

"Not Willow. Look at that man she is talking with. Who is he anyway? He doesn't belong here. I think I'll need to have a talk with him."

"Now, hold on. That's Todd. He is the new hand Michael hired when Riley left. He's a good man. You don't have to worry about him."

"Oh don't I? Look at the way he is looking at her. She doesn't even see how he is leering at her. I need to wash his mind. He's thinkin' stinkin', dirty thoughts."

"Maybe you are, if you think he is. Perhaps you need to give your heart and mind a good looking at. Brian, what has come over you? Wait a minute! Maybe I know. Are you jealous? If you are, then what you feel toward Willow isn't as pure as it should be. I think we need to find someplace private and have a little prayer time."

"Later, I'm leaving."

With that, Brian stalked out of the hotel and over toward his office. Josh turned around to move back toward Katie. She had just walked over to Willow and entered the conversation. He moved that way.

"Where did Brian go?" asked Willow.

"Oh, he had something he needed to do. He hated to leave, but he felt like he had to."

"I'm sorry. I didn't even get to talk with him. I was just getting to know Todd here. I wanted him to meet Brian. He is interested in being a lawman. I told him Brian is the best!"

"If I see Brian, I'll tell him to make it a point to come and talk with you, Todd. Why didn't you say anything about that out on the trail?" Josh asked.

"Oh, I thought maybe Michael would go ahead and fire me if he knew I have other interests."

"As long as those other interests don't interfere with your work, he won't complain. Besides, being a ranch hand is good training for becoming a lawman. When we are out on the trail, we are the law. There are men out there who are trying to steal what doesn't belong to them and to harm those who may get in the way."

"Thanks, I'll remember that. I think I'll go on back to the ranch now. Thanks for the advice."

"I hope you'll remember it."

"I'll sure give it a try. Excuse me, it looks like Michael is ready to leave and he wanted me to help him with something out at the ranch. I'd better get going."

Josh and Katie looked toward the door and saw Michael standing there smiling at them. He nodded and turned in the doorway to leave, then briefly turned back and smiled. When he did, Katie gasped. The light from the lanterns seemed to engulf him and his silhouette looked just as it did the first time she saw him, the first time she had smiled in six months. He looked like he had angel wings! Just as soon as she saw it, it was gone.

"Did you see that?" she asked Josh not even looking his way.

"See what?"

"Michael," she whispered.

"Of course, I saw Michael. Why are you whispering?" Josh looked close into her eyes. There were tears gathering in them. "What's wrong?"

"It was just so beautiful. I feel overwhelmed." She simply stared at the now-empty doorway.

"It's time to cut the cake. Come on over here, Katie and Joshua," Esther called in a melodic tone that hinted at the love she shared with both of them and understanding of their desire to get on their way.

"Finally!" Josh whispered to Katie. She laughed out loud and then covered her mouth with her hand.

"Mom, your timing is impeccable. Thank you for the rescue."

"I remember your father on our wedding day. I know what you are thinking, Joshua my boy. Don't get in a hurry. Enjoy the journey. You will never regret it."

"Thanks, Mom, for everything!"

The cake was cut, served, and eaten. Then the couple left for the ranch in a buggy bedecked with white streamers and flowers. Tin cans were tied to the back of the buggy. As soon as they were out of town and nearing the ranch, Josh stopped the buggy and looked up into the starry sky, the new moon a black orb barely visible against the night sky.

"Lord, thank you for this blessed day, the day you have made us one in your sight. As we enter the ranch and our new life together as husband and wife, we ask you to guide us even as we consummate this marriage. We want you to be a part of every aspect of our lives, the good and the bad. Never leave us, Lord, and keep us under your wings even when we must be separated from one another."

He turned to Katie and gave her a long and deepening kiss. "I love you, Mrs. Joshua Schmitt. I think we'd better get into the house and finish this conversation indoors."

Ranger took them down the lane and to the house without any guidance from Joshua, who was too busy kissing his wife.

When the buggy stopped, Josh stepped out and easily lifted Katie down and scooped her into his muscular arms. He knew there was someone nearby to take care of the horse and carriage. Without looking back, he carried her up the steps and into the house, closing the door behind them with his foot, and didn't put her down until they entered their bedroom. Josh held her close as he turned down the lamp that had been lit in preparation for their return. Katie felt safe and protected in the safety of Josh's arms and secure in the knowledge that God would always be with them both, keeping them safe under his wings as he had promised.

AUTHOR'S NOTES

s I began writing, the original family immigrating to Texas was of Irish descent. The main character's name, Katie, was definitely Katie and would not change. However, as I wrote I began to realize this family was Jewish. That made me wonder, but I continued to write. In February, I told my husband I needed to go to San Antonio to pay a visit to the relatives and do some research at the "big," of course, Texas museum there. We flew out to San Antonio in March where my cousin and her husband picked us up to begin our research. We visited the Institute of Texan Cultures and found so many reassuring facts substantiating much I had already written. There was a wonderful actual chuck wagon on display and a docent filled us in on trail life, the various cattle drive trails taken, and where they went. The most striking thing I learned was that there indeed were Jews who immigrated to Texas, most of them German. I was born in San Antonio and most of my mother's family lived there or in nearby towns. I know there is a tremendous German population in the hill country, and yet it had not occurred to me until then that the people of Crystal Springs were, for the most part, German. (Talk about a blonde moment!) That started me reading much about the Jews in Texas during the 1800s. They came there, many of them, because of religious, political, and financial persecution in Germany, and then in New York, etc. There were so few who settled in the hill country; they did not have enough men for a minyan to form a synagogue. If they wanted to go to a synagogue, they would have to travel many days to Houston, Austin, or Dallas. As a result, many of them moved on to those cities. The ones who stayed either remained Jewish by descent, but ceased to practice any of the Jewish religious laws, or they converted to the protestant faith, realizing that Jesus is the Messiah. I am honored to be used to bring light to this little known group of believing Jews, who found peace in the death and resurrection of the Promised One and passed that heritage and good news on to others.